*For a decade of sharing her patience, understanding, friendship,
gentle humor, wisdom, prodding, and faith with me,
this book is dedicated to*
Beverly Lewis
Senior Editor
Bantam Books

SILENT
TREATMENT

SILENT
TREATMENT

MICHAEL PALMER

BANTAM BOOKS
NEW YORK · TORONTO · LONDON · SYDNEY · AUCKLAND

This is a work of fiction. Names, characters, places, and incidents are either the product of the author's imagination or are used fictitiously. Any resemblance to actual persons, living or dead, or locales is entirely coincidental.

ISBN 0-553-09516-1

Published simultaneously in the United States and Canada

Bantam Books are published by Bantam Books, a division of Bantam Doubleday Dell Publishing Group, Inc. Its trademark, consisting of the words "Bantam Books" and the portrayal of a rooster, is Registered in U.S. Patent and Trademark Office and in other countries. Marca Registrada. Bantam Books, 1540 Broadway, New York, New York 10036.

PRINTED IN THE UNITED STATES OF AMERICA

ACKNOWLEDGMENTS

My deepest thanks to Susan Palmer Terry, Donna Prince, David Becher, Shana Sonnenburg, and especially Paul Weiss for their contributions to this novel.

And my special appreciation to Stuart Applebaum, Bantam Senior Vice President and Director of Public Relations, for his encouragement, insights, energy, and dedication to books.

M.S.P.

SILENT
TREATMENT

"The Doctor will see you now."

The moment Ray Santana heard Orsino say the words, he knew he was going to die, and die horribly.

Ten hours or so had passed since his adhesive tape blindfold had been ripped away. Ten hours of being gagged and lashed to a high-backed chair—his head and chin taped so tightly, so expertly, that he could not move at all. Ten hours of listening to the mariachi bands and singers in the street above and knowing that for all the good they would do him, the revelers might as well be celebrating their Fiesta de Nogales on Mars. Ten hours without seeing any movement except the comings and goings of a huge roach.

The roach was an inch and a half long. Maybe two. It padded out of a crack in the mildewed basement wall and made its way, in no particular hurry, to the floor. Ray followed the insect with his eyes until it left his field of vision, and waited for its return. For a time, he wondered about roaches—how they had sex, whether they chose one mate for life. For a time, he pictured his own family—Eliza singing as she whipped together her incredible paella . . . Ray Jr. diving headfirst into third. For a time he thought about his life before Eliza—the Road Warriors, the drugs . . . his decision to leave the gang and try college . . . the irony of his ending up as an undercover agent for the DEA.

Now, after ten meticulously careful years on the job, he was about to meet The Doctor. And soon—very soon, he suspected —he would be dead.

For no reason that he could understand, things had blown completely apart. The end of nearly three years of work was at hand, and it was time to put together federal indictments and call in the troops. His cover was as deep, as airtight as it had ever been. The meeting to turn his evidence over to Sean Garvey from the home office had been set up with Priority One precautions—four hours of steady movement, half a dozen decoys and back-checkers, and a route along which it was impossible to be followed. But suddenly, Alacante's men were all over them. And in seconds, just like that, it was over. Not one shot in defense, not one punch. Just . . . over. Garvey had been hauled away to God only knew where, and Ray had been blindfolded, crammed in the trunk of a Mercedes, and driven back into town. After an hour, he was dragged to the cellar of a house and then through a long, damp tunnel to this basement.

Ray wondered if The Doctor had already been to see Garvey.

Ol' Garves might hold off for a little while in naming names, Ray figured. But underneath his slick veneer, he was a wimp. The first sight of his own blood, the first hit of real pain— the electric cattle prod or knife or vise or whatever the hell they used—and he would be spilling his guts. He would give up every fucking name he could think of, believing in his heart of hearts that if he didn't cause Alacante's people too much trouble, they might let him live. Wrong!

". . . Tijuana? . . . Oh, that would be a guy named Gonzales. He's had a little fruit stand downtown for the past three years, but he's really a U.S. Fed. . . . Vera Cruz? Yeah, I know that guy, too. . . ."

Shit, Garves, I'm sorry, Santana thought suddenly. *I understand . . . What the hell. I'm a field man. You're a suit. I can sit here like King Tut, thinking you're trash for giving in to them. But they haven't touched me yet. Besides, you don't know a tenth of what I do about the Mexican undercover organization. And I don't plan on telling that part no matter what. My goddamn initiation into the Road Warriors was worse than anything these creeps can do to me here, for chrissakes. Just do your best, Garves. Just do your best. Try not to make it too easy for them.*

Another half hour passed. Possibly longer. Santana closed his eyes and wished he could just will himself dead. Or at least asleep. The air in the basement was stagnant and heavy with mold. Sucking it in through his nostrils took so much effort that sleep was impossible. How ironic. After three years, he had amassed enough information for several dozen major indictments. His only real failure was not pinpointing the famous Alacante Pipeline—the tunnel connecting one or more houses in Nogales, Arizona, with counterparts in Nogales, Mexico. Now, unless he was sorely mistaken, he had not only found the Pipeline, he had actually been dragged through it. Eliza was right, as usual. He should have gotten out while he could—started up the landscaping business he was always talking about, and left the heroics to the crazies. Now . . .

There was a scraping noise behind him—a portion of the wall was being swung aside. Seconds later, Orsino came into view. An Alacante lieutenant and a remorseless killer, Orsino had survived a shotgun blast that had left him without half of his lower lip and jaw. What remained of his mouth was all on the right side of his face. Ray wondered if perhaps Orsino liked it that way.

"It is time," he growled, with the inflated pride of a small man thrust into the company of a legend. "Time for you to meet The Doctor."

An average-looking man in his early forties, medium height, stepped forward. His face was remarkable only for how completely *unremarkable* it was. Not handsome, but not unattractive. No unusual features. No tics. No scars. Brown hair cut short. Hairline not receding. No glasses. He was wheeling a stainless steel cart on top of which was a tattered leather valise. His back was turned to Ray as he flipped the suitcase open.

Ray's knuckles blanched as he clutched the arm of the chair.

"My name is Perchek. Dr. Anton Perchek," the man said.

Santana's stomach tightened. Bile shot up into his throat. The name was a death sentence. *The Doctor*. Everyone in the agency—everyone in Washington—knew who Perchek was. But as far as Ray knew, no one had ever seen so much as a photograph of him.

"I can tell from your expression that my name is one you recognize," Perchek said, favoring Ray with an enigmatic smile. "That's good. That's very good."

Ray's mouth had gone dry. Anton Perchek, M.D., Soviet-born and -trained, had long ago left his native country. Now, he belonged to no country and to every country. A true son of the world. For over the years, The Doctor had built a reputation for being the best in the world at what he did, which was to keep torture subjects alive, awake, and responsive. He was seldom without employment. Sri Lanka, Bosnia, Paraguay, Iraq, South Africa, Haiti—wherever there was conflict or political repression, there was a demand for his services. There were even rumors—unsubstantiated—that he did occasional jobs for the CIA. A U.S. federal grand jury had indicted Perchek in absentia for complicity in the deaths of several American undercover operatives, two of whom Ray knew well.

"So, Señor Santana," he said, his Spanish unaccented but sterile. "Would you prefer I address you in English?" He waited for a response. Then he turned and noticed the adhesive tape pulled tightly across Ray's mouth. He chuckled at his own oversight. "My apologies, Señor Santana. Señor Orsino?"

His half mouth twisted in what might have been a grin, Orsino stepped forward and viciously tore the tape off—first from across Ray's face, then from under his chin.

"So," Perchek asked again. "Spanish or English? What will it be?"

Ray flexed the tightness and spasm out of his jaw.

"Your Spanish is better than mine," he said.

"I've been led to believe your Mexican Spanish is quite good, actually—especially for someone from the Bronx. But very well. English it will be."

His English, with perhaps the slightest British tinge, was no less fluent than his Spanish. Ray suspected that the man could have conversed in any number of languages.

"I speak twelve others, actually," he said, as if reading Santana's mind. "Although my Arabic and Swahili may be getting a bit rusty."

His average face smiled down at Ray. But in that moment, Ray noticed something that wasn't the least bit average. It was the man's eyes. The irises were as pale as any he had ever seen—almost translucent. *Ice blue* was the closest he could come to labeling them. In fact, ice blue was a near perfect description, for they were as hard and as cold as a human's eyes could be.

"I don't know what this is all about." Ray forced out the words.

The ice blue eyes sparked. Otherwise, Perchek's demeanor remained unchanged.

"Then we shall help you learn," he said.

He handed Orsino a length of twine and motioned to the light fixture overhead. Once the twine was secured and dangling down, Perchek turned to his valise. He produced a plastic bottle of intravenous solution, connected it to a plastic infusion tube, and suspended it from the twine.

"Zero point nine percent sodium chloride," he said, pulling on a pair of rubber gloves. "Normal saline."

He tightened a latex tourniquet just above Santana's left elbow, waited a few seconds for the veins to distend, and then slipped in an intravenous catheter with the ease of one who had performed the maneuver hundreds of times. Next he wrapped a blood pressure cuff around the other arm and secured it in place.

"Listen to me," Ray said, struggling for a tone of calm and reason. "Orsino, you've got to listen. I was setting up that Fed, Garvey. He was about to sell me some information on the new DEA strategy against Alacante."

"You are lying," Orsino said.

"No, it's the truth."

"We shall see what is the truth and what is not," Perchek said, drawing up a slightly turbid solution into a large syringe. He inserted the long needle through a rubber port into the infusion tubing, and taped the syringe to Ray's forearm. "We shall see very soon. Mr. Orsino?"

Orsino knelt, positioning himself so that his face was just a foot or so from Ray's. Santana mentally recoiled from the man's breath, heavy with the odor of cigarettes and garlic, and stared with revulsion at the yellowed half rows of teeth.

"Names," Orsino said, a small bubble of spittle forming at the good side of his mouth. "The Mexican undercover agents. All of them."

Ray looked past the man to where Perchek stood. He wondered what awaited him within the tattered valise. Truth serum, perhaps. Reputedly, Perchek usually left the dirty work to his employers. His job was to use his drugs to keep subjects alive and awake. But it seemed hard to believe the crass, slow-witted Orsino would have the patience and skill required to do an effective job of inflicting just the right increments of pain.

"I don't know any of them, Orsino," Ray said. "You've got to believe that."

During his year of training with the agency, there were a number of classes the cadets had shared with their CIA counterparts. One of them was formally entitled Dealing with Hostile Interrogation. The trainees referred to it as Torture 101. The instructor, a former fighter pilot named Joe Dash, had spent four years in a Vietcong prison camp. He had no eyes.

"There are three things you must always believe when being hostilely interrogated," Dash stressed. He believed that there were always three points essential to any subject. Three—no more, no less. *"First, that anything you are promised in exchange for answers is bullshit. Second, that if you don't give them what they want, they may decide to hold off killing you and try again another day. And third, and most important, that as long as you are alive, there's a chance you'll be rescued."*

"We want those names," Orsino said.

"I swear, I don't know any of them. You've got to believe me."

"There are three stages you should go through in responding to hostile interrogation. Each stage should be dragged out as long as humanly possible. First, deny knowing anything. And keep denying it. Next, admit that you know some things, but give them misinformation—especially if they'll have to spend time verifying what you say. The longer it takes them to determine you're lying, the better the chance that you'll be rescued—take it from one who was. The third stage is telling them what they want to know. Whether you are forced to that stage or not depends a little on what you're made of and a lot on how good your interrogators are."

Orsino reached out a meaty hand and squeezed Ray's cheeks so tightly their insides touched.

"I'm glad you didn't tell us," he rasped.

He stepped back. Immediately, Ray was transfixed by the ice blue eyes.

"Do you know any chemistry at all, Mr. Santana?" Perchek asked. "No matter. You may be interested to know the chemical name for the contents of that syringe. It is four-chloryl, four-hydroxy, trimethyl, six-fluorodimethyl carbamate. Actually, there are two chemical side chains as well, so the name is even longer."

"I'm impressed," Ray said.

"The short chemical name is hyconidol hydrochloride. A chemist friend did the synthesis, but my own research produced the concept."

"Bravo."

"You see, Mr. Santana, at the end of every pain nerve in the human body is a chemical transmitter that connects it with the next nerve and fires it off. The impulse shoots up that nerve, and another jet of transmitter connects it with the next. Et cetera, et cetera. Eventually—quite rapidly, actually—the message is transmitted from the point of injury to the pain center of the brain and . . . ouch!"

"Nicely put."

Santana already knew where Perchek was heading. He was sure his understanding showed in his eyes.

"Hyconidol almost matches, atom for atom, the pain fiber neurotransmitter chemical. That means I can fire those nerves off all at once and at will. Every single one of them. Think of it, Mr. Santana. No injury . . . no mess . . . no blood. Just pain. Pure pain. Except in the work I do, hyconidol has absolutely no clinical value. But if we ever do market it, I thought an appropriate name for it might be Agonyl. It's incredible stuff, if I do say so myself. A small injection? A little tingle. A larger one? Well, I'm sure you get the picture."

Ray's mouth had become desert dry. The pounding within his chest was so forceful that he felt certain The Doctor could see it.

Please don't do this, he screamed silently. *Please . . .*

Perchek's thumb tightened on the plunger.

"I think we'll start with something modest," he said. "Equivalent, perhaps, to nothing more than a little cool breeze over the cavities in your teeth."

The last voice Ray heard before the injection was Joe Dash's.

There are three ways a man can choose to handle dying. . . .

6 YEARS LATER

For twelve years, the Jade Dragon on the Upper West Side of Manhattan had prided itself on exceptional food at very reasonable prices. As a result, on an average weekday its 175-seat capacity turned over twice, and on weekends as many as five times. Tonight, a warm Friday in June, the wait for a table was half an hour.

Seated in his customary spot, Ron Farrell was commenting to his wife Susan and their friends Jack and Anita Harmon on how the place had grown since he and Susan had first eaten there almost a decade ago. Now, although they had moved three times, they made a point of coming to the Jade Dragon alone or with friends every other Friday, almost like clockwork.

They were nearly done with a meal that the Harmons had proclaimed as good as any Chinese food they had ever eaten when Ron stopped in mid-sentence and began rubbing his abdomen. With no warning, severe cramps had begun knotting his gut, accompanied almost immediately by waves of nausea. He felt sweat break out beneath his arms and over his face. His vision blurred.

"Ronnie? Are you all right?" his wife asked.

Farrell took several slow, deep breaths. He had always handled pain well. But this ache seemed to be worsening.

"I don't feel well," he managed. "I've . . . I've just gotten this pain, right here."

"It couldn't be what you ate," Susan said. "We all shared the same—"

Susan's face suddenly went ashen. Beads of perspiration sprang out across her forehead. Then, without another word, she lurched sideways and vomited on the floor.

Standing by the kitchen door of the crowded restaurant, the

young assistant chef watched the commotion grow as one by one, the four customers at table 11 became violently ill. Finally, he reentered the massive kitchen and made his way nonchalantly to the pay phone installed for the use of the hired help. The number he dialed was handwritten on a three-by-five file card.

"Yes?" the man's voice at the other end said.

"Xia Wei Zen here."

"Yes?"

The chef read carefully the words printed on the card.

"There are four leaves on the clover."

"Very good. You know where to go after your shift. The man in the black car will take the empty vial from you in exchange for the rest of what you are now owed."

The man hung up without waiting for a reply.

Xia Wei Zen glanced about to ensure no one was watching, and then returned to his station. Work would not be nearly so taxing for the rest of his shift. For one thing, there was a good deal of money awaiting him. And for another, there would be many fewer orders coming in from the dining room tonight.

The call came into the emergency room of Good Samaritan Hospital at 9:47. Four Priority Two patients were being transported by rescue squad from a Chinese restaurant twenty blocks away. Preliminary diagnosis was acute food poisoning.

Priority Two. Potentially serious illness or injury, non-life-threatening at the moment.

It was a typically busy Friday night. The nurses and residents of the large teaching hospital were already three hours behind. The twenty available treatment rooms were full, as was the waiting room. The air was heavy with the odors of perspiration, antiseptic, and blood. All around were the sounds of illness, misery, and pain—moans, babies crying, uncontrollable coughing.

"Ever eat at a place called the Jade Dragon?" the nurse who took the call from the rescue squad asked.

"I think so," the charge nurse answered.

"Well, next time you might want to consider Italian. One

rescue is on the way in with two probable food poisonings. Two more will be leaving shortly. Altogether, two men, two women, all in their forties, all on IVs, all vomiting."

"Vital signs?"

"The numbers are okay for the moment. But according to the crew on the scene, none of them are looking all that good."

"Fun and games times four."

"Where do you want them?"

"What do we have?"

"Seven can be cleared if you can talk Dr. Grateful Dead, or whatever the hell his name is, into writing a few prescriptions."

"Perfect. Put whoever looks worst in there and the rest in the hall. We'll move them into rooms as we can. Might as well order routine labs and an EKG on each of them, too."

"Chop chop."

Ron Farrell grunted in pain as his litter was set on the emergency bay platform and telescoped up into transport position. He was on his side in a fetal position. The pain boring into his stomach was unremitting. Jack Harmon, who had quickly become even sicker than Susan, had been transported in the ambulance with him. Now, Ron saw him wave weakly as the two of them were wheeled through the automatic doors and into the commotion and fluorescent glare of the intake area.

The minutes that followed were a blur of questions, needles, spasms of pain, and examinations from people dressed in surgical scrubs. Ron was wheeled to a small room with open shelves of supplies and a suction bottle on the wall. The staff had addressed him courteously enough, but it was clear that everyone was harried. Ron's personal physician wasn't affiliated with Good Samaritan, as far as he knew. There was really nothing he could think of to do except wait for the medication he had been promised to take the pain away.

"You are feeling better, yes?" a man's voice said in a thick foreign accent that Ron could not identify.

Still in the fetal position that gave him the least discomfort, Ron blinked his eyes open, and looked up. The man, dressed in blue surgical scrubs like most of the ER staff, smiled down at him. The overhead light, eclipsed by his head, formed a bright halo around him and darkened his face.

"I am Dr. Kozlansky," he said. "It appears you and the others have developed food poisoning."

"Goddamn Jade Dragon. Is my wife all right?"

"Oh yes. Oh yes, I assure you, she is most fine."

"Great. Listen, Doc, my stomach's killing me. Can you give me something for this pain?"

"That is exactly why I am here," he said.

"Wonderful."

The physician produced a syringe half full of clear liquid and emptied it into the intravenous line.

"Thanks, Doc," Farrell said.

"You may wish to wait and thank me when . . . when we see how this works."

"Okay, have it your—"

Farrell was suddenly unable to speak. There was a horrible, consuming emptiness within his chest. And he knew in that moment that his heart had stopped beating.

The man continued smiling down at him benignly.

"You are feeling better, yes?" he asked.

Ron felt his arms and legs begin to shake uncontrollably. His back arched until only his heels and the back of his head touched the bed. His teeth jackhammered together. Then his consciousness began to fade. His thoughts became more disjointed. His dreadful fear lessened and then finally vanished. His body dropped lifelessly back onto the bed.

For a full minute the man stood there watching. Then he slipped the syringe into his pocket.

"I'm afraid I must leave you now," he whispered in a voice free of any accent. "Please try to get some rest."

1 YEAR LATER

CHAPTER 1

Harry Corbett was on his fifteenth lap around the indoor track when he first sensed the pain in his chest. The track, a balcony just under an eighth of a mile around, was on the top floor of the Grey Building of the Manhattan Medical Center. Ten feet below it was a modestly equipped gym with weights, the usual machines, heavy bags, and some mats. The fitness center, unique in the city, was exclusively for the hospital staff and employees. It had been created through the legacy of Dr. George Pollock, a cardiologist who had twice swum the English Channel. Pollock's death, at age ninety, had resulted from his falling off a ladder while cleaning the gutters of his country home.

At the moment of his awareness of the pain, Harry was actually thinking about Pollock and about what it would be like to live until ninety. He slowed a bit and rotated his shoulders. The pain persisted. It wasn't much—maybe two on the scale of one to ten that physicians used. But it was there. Reluctant to stop running, Harry swallowed and massaged his upper abdomen. The discomfort was impossible to localize. One moment it seemed to be beneath his breastbone, the next in the middle of his back. He slowed a bit more, down from an eight-minutes-per-mile pace to about ten-and-a-half. The ache was in his left chest now . . . no, it was gone . . . no, not gone, somewhere between his right nipple and clavicle.

He slowed still more. Then, finally, he stopped. He bent forward, his hands on his thighs. It wasn't angina, he told himself. Nothing about the character of the pain said cardiac. He understood his body, and he certainly understood pain. This pain was no big deal. And if it wasn't his heart, he really didn't give a damn where it was coming from.

Harry knew his logic was flawed—diagnostic deduction he would never, ever apply to a patient. But like most physicians with physical symptoms, his denial was more powerful than any logic.

Steve Josephson, jogging in the opposite direction, lumbered toward him.

"Hey, you okay?" he asked.

Still staring down at the banked cork track, Harry took a deep breath. The pain was gone, just like that. Gone. He waited a few seconds to be sure. Nothing. The smidgen of remaining doubt disappeared. Definitely not the ticker, he told himself again.

"Yeah. Yeah, I'm fine, Steve," he said. "You go ahead and finish."

"Hey, you're the zealot who goaded me into this jogging nonsense in the first place," Josephson said. "I'll take any excuse I can get to stop."

He was sweating more profusely than Harry, although he had probably run half as far. Like Harry, Steve Josephson was a general practitioner—"family medicine specialists," the bureaucrats had decided to name them. They were in solo practice, but shared night and weekend coverage with four other GPs. It was just after six-thirty in the morning—earlier than usual for their run. But this would be a busy and important day.

At eight, following morning rounds and an emergency meeting of the family medicine department, the entire MMC staff would be convening in the amphitheater. After months of interviews and investigation, the task force charged with determining whether or not to reduce the privileges of GPs in the hospital was ready to present its findings. From the rumors Harry had tapped into, the recommendations of the Sidonis committee would be harsh—the professional equivalent of castration.

With a portion of Harry's income and a significant chunk of

his professional respect on the line, the impending presentation was reason enough for the ulcers or muscle spasms, or whatever the hell had caused the strange ache. And even the committee report was not the foremost concern on his mind.

"We've been running together three or four times a week for almost a year," Josephson said, "and I've never seen you stop before your five miles were up."

"Well, Stephen, it just goes to show there's a first time for everything." Harry studied his friend's worried face and softened. "Listen, pal, I'd tell you if it was anything. Believe me I would. I just don't feel like running today. I've got too much on my mind."

"I understand. Is Evie going in tomorrow?"

"The day after. Ben Dunleavy's her neurosurgeon. He talks about clipping her cerebral aneurysm as if he was removing a wart or something. But I guess it's what he does."

They moved off the track as the only other runners in the gym approached.

"How's she holding up?" Josephson asked.

Harry shrugged. "All things considered, she seems pretty calm about it. But she can be pretty closed in about her feelings."

Closed in. The understatement of the week, Harry mused ruefully. He couldn't recall the last time Evie had shared feelings of any consequence with him.

"Well, tell her Cindy and I wish her well, and that I'll stop by to see her as soon as that berry is clipped."

"Thanks," Harry said. "I'm sure she'll appreciate hearing that."

In fact, he doubted that she would. As warm, bright, and caring as Steve Josephson was, Evie could never get past his obesity.

"Did you ever listen to him breathe?" she had once asked as Harry was extolling his virtues as a physician. "I felt like I was trying to converse with a bull in heat. And those white, narrow-strapped tees he wears beneath his white dress shirts—pul-leese. . . ."

"So, then," Josephson said as they entered the locker room, "before we shower, why don't you tell me what *really* happened out there."

"I already—"

"Harry, I was halfway around the track from you and I could see the color drain from your face."

"It was nothing."

"You know, I spent years learning how to ask nonleading questions. Don't make me regress."

For the purpose of insurance application forms or the occasional prescription, Harry and Josephson served as one another's physician. And although each persistently urged the other to schedule a complete physical, neither of them had. The closest they had come was an agreement made just after Harry's forty-ninth birthday. Harry, already obsessive about diet and exercise, had promised to get a checkup and a cardiac stress test. Steve, six years younger but fifty pounds heavier, had agreed to have a physical, start jogging, and join Weight Watchers. But except for Josephson's grudging sessions on the track, neither had followed through.

"I had a little indigestion," Harry conceded. "That's all. It came. It bothered me for a minute. It left."

"Indigestion, huh. By indigestion do you perhaps mean chest pain?"

"Steve, I'd tell you if I had chest pain. You know I would."

"Slight correction. I know you *wouldn't.* How many men did you lug back to that chopper?"

Although Harry rarely talked about it, over the years almost everyone at the hospital had heard some version of the events at Nha-trang, or had actually composed one themselves. In the stories, the number of wounded he had saved before being severely wounded himself had ranged from three—which was in fact the number for which he had been decorated—to twenty. He once even overheard a patient boast that his doctor had killed a hundred Vietcong while rescuing an equal number of GIs.

"Stephen, I am no hero. Far from it. If I thought the pain was anything, anything at all, I'd tell you."

Josephson was unconvinced.

"You owe me a stress test. When do you turn fifty?"

"Two weeks."

"And when's the date of that family curse?"

"Oh, come on."

"Harry, you're the one who told me about it. Now, when is it?"

"September. September first."

"You've got four weeks."

"I . . . Okay, okay. As soon as Evie's situation is straightened out I'll set one up with the exercise lab. Promise."

"I'm serious."

"You know, in spite of what everyone says about you, I always thought that."

Harry stripped and headed for the showers. He knew that Steve Josephson, in spite of himself, was staring at the patchwork of scars on his back. Thirty-one pieces of shrapnel, half a kidney, and a rib. The design left by their removal would have blended into the pages of a Rand McNally road atlas. Harry flashed on the incredible sensation of Evie's breasts gliding slowly over the healed wounds in what she used to call her patriotic duty to a war hero. *When was the last time?* That, he acknowledged sadly, he couldn't remember.

He cranked up the hot water until he was enveloped in steam. Two weeks until fifty. *Fifty!* He had never experienced any sort of midlife crisis that he could think of. But maybe the deep funk he had been in lately was it. By now the pieces of his life should have fallen into place. Instead, the choices he had made seemed to be under almost constant attack. And crumbling.

He thought about the day halfway through his convalescence when he had made the decision to withdraw from his residency in surgery and devote his professional life to general practice. Something had happened to him over his year and a half in Nam. He no longer had any desire to be center stage. Not that he minded the drama and intensity of the operating room. In fact, even now he truly enjoyed his time there. But in the end, he had realized, he simply wanted to be a family doc. *Simply*. If there was one word that was most descriptive of the life Harry had chosen for himself, *simply* might well be it. Get up in the morning, do what seems right, try to help a few people along the way, develop an interest or two outside of work, and sooner or later, things would make sense. Sooner or later, the big questions would be answered.

Well, lately things weren't making much sense at all. The big answers were just as elusive as ever. More so. His marriage was shaky. The kids he had always wanted just never happened. The financial security that he had expected would gradually develop over the years was tied to a brand of medicine he was not willing to practice. He never allowed his office to become a medical mill. He never sent a collection agency after anyone. He never refused anyone care because the patient couldn't pay. He never moved to the suburbs. He never went back for the training that would have made him a subspecialist. The result was a car that was seven years old and a retirement fund that would last indefinitely—as long as he didn't try to retire.

Now, his professional stature was being hauled up on the block, his wife was facing a neurosurgeon's scalpel, and just four weeks from the first of September in his fifty-first year, he had experienced pain in his chest.

The hastily called family medicine departmental meeting accomplished little. Each physician who spoke during the emotional forty-five-minute session seemed to have different information about what the findings of the Sidonis committee were going to be. In the end, no motions were passed, no actions of protest approved. Aside from presenting a unified front at the amphitheater, there was nothing to do until the specifics of the task force's recommendations were known.

"Harry, you didn't say a word in there," Steve Josephson said as they left.

"There was nothing to say."

"Sidonis and his vigilantes are on a witch hunt, and you know it. Everyone's scared. You could have calmed them down. You're . . . you're sort of the leader of the pack. The unofficial kahuna."

"A kind way of saying I'm older than most of the others."

"That's hardly what I mean. I deliver babies. Sandy Porter strips veins and does other stuff in the OR. The Kornetsky brothers are better in the CCU than most of the cardiologists. Almost every one of us does some procedure or activity that might be taken away today. You're about the only one who does all of them."

"So? Steve, what are we going to do? Challenge the specialists to a medical Olympics?"

"Oh, this is crazy. Harry, I don't know what's come over you lately. I just hope it's not permanent."

Harry started to respond that he didn't know what Josephson was talking about. Instead, he mumbled an apology. He had never been a fiery orator, but over the years his directness and commonsense approach to resolving conflicts had earned him respect in the hospital. And he certainly had never backed away from a fight. He could have—*should* have—said something. Members of the department, especially the younger ones, were genuinely worried about their futures.

The crisis at MMC was the direct result of the hospital being named as codefendant in three successive malpractice suits over a period of a few months. All three suits involved GPs. Harry felt the epidemic of litigation was nothing more than coincidence. In the new medical order of sue first, ask questions later, similar numbers could probably be produced to show that specialists were equally vulnerable. But the medical staff had panicked and the Committee on Non-Specialty Practice had been created. Caspar Sidonis, a charismatic, widely known cardiac surgeon, had been made its chairman.

Sidonis and Harry had never hit it off, although Harry never really understood why. Now they were on opposite sides of the table, playing a high-stakes game for a pot that was of value only to the GPs. And Sidonis held all the cards.

"Steve, I'm sorry," Harry said again as they turned down the passageway that cut through the emergency room, "I guess I *have* been down lately. And I really don't know why. Male menopause or something. I feel like maybe I need—I don't know, some sort of windmill to charge."

The corridor, a shortcut from the room where their meeting was held to the amphitheater, was closed to the public but not to hospital staff. Today, the ER was humming. The rooms to either side of them were all occupied. Major surgery, minor surgery, orthopedics, ENT, pediatrics, minor medical, major medical, cardiac.

"Each one a story," Harry said as they walked through.

"Yeah," Steve mumbled. "Well, after today we better get used to having to read the Cliffs Notes."

A nurse rushed past them from behind and into one of the two cardiac rooms.

"Give him another three of morphine," they heard a resident say as they neared the room.

"How much Lasix has he gotten?"

"Eighty, Doctor . . ."

"This is V. tach. I'm almost certain of it."

"His pressure's dropping, Doctor."

"Dammit! Someone was supposed to have called cardiology."

"I put a page in for them. They haven't answered."

The two GPs stopped at the doorway. The patient, a husky black man, probably in his early seventies, was in extremis, sitting nearly upright on the litter, gasping for breath. Loud gurgling welling up from within his chest accompanied each inhalation. His heart rate was nearly one hundred and seventy. The young resident managing the case was a decent enough doctor, but he had developed a reputation for losing his cool in difficult situations.

"What is his pressure?" he asked.

"Maybe seventy, Doctor. It's quite hard to hear."

There was undisguised urgency in the nurse's voice. Her repeated use of the resident's title was a demand that he do something.

"We can't wait for cardiology," he said. "Get ready to shock him. Someone please page cardiology again. Janice, I want three hundred joules."

Steve Josephson, his eyes wide, looked over at Harry.

"Pulmonary edema," Josephson said.

"Right you are," Harry replied.

"But that's not V. tach on the monitor."

"I agree. Plain old garden variety sinus tachycardia, I would say. Due to the stress of the situation."

"We can't let him shock that."

Harry hesitated for just a moment, then nodded. The two of them moved to the bedside.

"Sam, that's sinus tach." Harry whispered softly enough so that no one but the resident could hear. "Try to shock that and you might kill him."

The resident looked first at the monitor and then at the nurses and technicians surrounding his patient. In seconds his expression went from confusion to anger to embarrassment, and finally to relief.

"You want to take over?" he asked suddenly. "Please, go ahead."

Without answering, Harry picked up a towel and dried the perspiration that was pouring off the patient's brow. He glanced at the plastic identification bracelet.

"Mr. Miller, I'm Dr. Corbett. Squeeze my hand if you understand. Good. You're going to be okay, but you've got to try and breathe slower. I know it's hard and I know you're frightened right now, but you can do it. We're going to help you. EKG, Steve?"

"Maybe a small anterior MI," Josephson said. "He's beating too fast to tell for sure."

"Hematocrit?"

"Fifty percent. If he's not a smoker, his blood is concentrated big time."

They looked over at the resident, who shook his head.

"Lifetime nonsmoker," he said. "But what's his red blood cell concentration got to do with all this?"

Harry's exam disclosed no ankle swelling and no other signs of excessive fluid. Heart failure, from whatever cause, was producing back pressure throughout the pulmonary circulation. Serum, the noncellular part of blood, was being forced through the blood vessel walls and into the man's lungs. As a result of the serum shift, the red blood cells, too large to pass through the vessel walls, were becoming sludge. Harry checked the man's pupils for the constriction that would signal marked narcotic effect. The pupils were small, but not yet pinpoint.

"Three more of morphine," he said. "Please get me a phlebotomy bag. We're going to take some blood off him. Get ready to intubate him if we have to." He toweled the man off again. "Mr. Miller, you're doing great. Try to slow it down just a little bit more."

"Excuse me," the resident whispered, astonished, "but you're going to take *blood* off him?"

"We are."

"But . . . but nobody does that anymore."

"You're doing better and better, Mr. Miller," Harry said. He turned to the resident. "No one does this anymore, huh? Well, we do, Sam," he said. "Especially when someone's hematocrit is as elevated as this man's. Just because a method's not high-tech doesn't mean it's useless. Trying to get fluid off him with diuretics often isn't as effective as what we're about to do. And in someone whose blood is already this concentrated, diuretics are quite a bit more dangerous. Any fluid you get off with diuretics will just concentrate his red cells even more. If those red cells get thick enough, sooner or later a vessel could clot off. Pressure, please?"

"Holding at eighty. Easier to hear," the nurse said.

Harry nodded to Steve Josephson, who inserted the large phlebotomy needle into a vein with a dexterity belied by his thick fingers. Instantly, a column of blood glided down the tubing and began to fill the plastic collection bottle.

The reversal of Clayton Miller's pulmonary edema was spectacular.

"I . . . I'm breathing . . . a . . . little . . . better . . . ," he managed after just a minute or so.

"What do you think, Steve? Another hundred cc's?"

"If his pressure stays up, I would say maybe even two hundred."

Harry adjusted the needle slightly, and the flow of blood increased. For another minute, there was only silence.

"Oh my God," Miller said suddenly, filling his lungs with a long, grateful swallow. "Oh my God, I'm better . . . much better."

He was still breathless, but much less so. The cardiac pattern on the monitor had slowed to one hundred. The shape of the complexes now appeared quite normal. Two nurses exchanged looks of exuberant relief. The resident stepped between the two GPs.

"This is incredible," he said. "I don't know what to say. Mr. Miller, Dr. Corbett and Dr. Josephson really came through for you—for me, too."

The older man managed a weak thumbs up.

"Listen," the resident went on, "I heard about that committee they formed to alter your privileges. If you need me to write them about what went on here this morning, I'll be happy to."

"It may be a little late for that," Harry said, "but why don't you drop Dr. Sidonis a note just the same. He might actually read it, as long as it starts with the greeting 'Your Grace.' "

There was a soft noise behind them. The three of them looked toward the doorway just as a stony-faced Caspar Sidonis turned and stalked off toward the amphitheater.

CHAPTER 2

"Green Dolphin Street." The Wes Montgomery arrangement. The tune started up in Harry's head almost as soon as he had settled into a seat in the last row of the amphitheater. "Green Dolphin Street." Harry tapped out a riff with his fingers on the metal armrest. He loved music of all kinds, but he was a fanatic for jazz. He had played bass since junior high school and still sat in with a combo when he had the time. Over the years, he had come to appreciate that "Green Dolphin Street" tended to pop into his head when he was keyed up—tense, but ready for action. He had hummed it heading into organic chemistry exams, and later on throughout his family practice boards. And of course, during the war, it seemed he was always listening to it either on tape or in his imagination. Now, for the first time in a hell of a while, it was back.

"Full house, Harry," Doug Atwater said, gesturing toward the rapidly filling amphitheater. "You'd think they were giving away free stethoscopes."

MMC was the largest of the three hospitals contracting with the Manhattan Health Cooperative. As the vice president responsible for marketing and development of the rapidly expanding HMO, Atwater had an office at each of them. He had come to the company six or seven years before from someplace in the Midwest. There were many, including Harry, who believed that without Atwater's creative energy and business sense, the Cooperative and its hospitals might well have gone under some time ago. Instead, Manhattan Health had captured a decent share of the market and become a real force in the business. Like Harry, Atwater was a devoted jazz fan, although he didn't play himself. The two of them managed to hit a club every three or four months. And from time to time Doug would stop by C.C.'s Cellar when Harry was sitting in with the combo that regularly played there.

"Did Sidonis or anyone on his committee speak to you about all this?" Atwater asked.

"Of course. Dan Twersky, the psychiatrist, got assigned to interview me. You know him? He couldn't have been more pompous or condescending if he had tried. He wanted to know how Marv Lorello could have sewn up that guy's thumb so badly. I told him that as far as I could tell, Marv didn't sew up anything badly. Twersky asked why Lorello didn't call in a hand surgeon. I told him that all anyone could do was clean up the gash and suture it closed. The most skillful hand surgeon in the world might easily have gotten the same unfortunate result Marv did. Sometimes circulation to a wound isn't all it should be, and there is some tissue loss. He said I sounded a bit defensive of GPs. I told him that a thousand times out of a thousand I would choose to repair that cut without calling in a hand surgeon, and that nine hundred and ninety nine of those times the two halves would heal perfectly. Twersky just sat there and smiled. It was an *Anything you say, Doc, as long as you don't count on ever fixin' my thumb* kind of smile."

Atwater reached over to give him a supportive pat on the shoulder.

"Harry, you're a hell of a doctor," he said. "And nothing Sidonis or his committee can do is going to change that."

Steve Josephson maneuvered down the row, nodded a greeting to Atwater, and settled into the seat next to Harry.

"They just took Clayton Miller up to the unit," he said. "The man's doing great. A save of the highest order. After you left, once his breathing was back near normal, he started talking baseball nonstop. He was a pro—a teammate of Satchel Paige in the Negro baseball leagues. And get this: apparently his son works for the Yankees. He says that any time you or I want tickets, we've got 'em."

"My kind of patient," Harry said.

"What gives?" Atwater asked.

Harry deferred to Josephson, who detailed the event with all the drama of a fighter pilot recounting a dogfight. Atwater listened, enthralled.

"Too bad Sidonis doesn't know what you did," he said.

"He does. I don't think he's impressed enough to call off the vigilantes, though. In fact, I don't think he's impressed at all."

"Well, just the same, you guys are really something. I listen to you and I honestly wish I could be on the front lines instead of sitting up there pushing pencils. Say, Harry, what's the story with Evie?"

"She's coming in later this week. Probably the day after tomorrow."

Atwater pulled out a black memo book and wrote down Evie's name and *Flowers*.

"She's a hell of a gal," he said. "I know she'll do great."

Evie's headaches, which she had first attributed to allergies, then to stress from her job, and finally to stress from Harry, had proven to be caused by something far more structural and virulent. Harry spent several frustrating weeks trying to convince her to see a doctor and get a CT scan. Finally, she ended up on the neuro ward, with thick speech and a weak right arm. The tests revealed a large berry aneurysm on her anterior cerebral artery, which had bled and then sealed over. Evie was lucky. Rapidly, her neurologic symptoms had resolved. A period of rest coupled with serial CTs was her neurosurgeon's recommendation. Now, it was time for the bulge in the vessel wall to be repaired.

"Harry," Atwater said, "be sure and let me know if there's anything Anneke or I can do to help the two of you out."

"Anneke?"

Doug's smile was mischievous. When he and Harry went out to hear music, he invariably showed up with a date—always a different one, and each, it seemed, younger and more attractive than the last.

"She's half Swedish and half German," he explained. He thought for a moment, and then added, "I guess it's the top half that's Swedish."

"Hail, Caesar, we who are about to die salute you," Steve Josephson said, gesturing toward the small stage at the lower end of the amphitheater. Caspar Sidonis had just taken his place at the microphoned table in the center of his six-member committee.

"Could I have your attention, please," Sidonis said, tapping at his microphone. "Let's get started. We have a good deal of important material to cover. . . . Please, would you all take your seats. . . ."

"If people keep talking, I wonder if he'll start throwing things like he does in the OR," Josephson whispered to Harry. "I've heard he's had enough complaints filed by scrub nurses to fill the phone book. The hospital doesn't do anything about his tantrums because they're afraid he'll take his act somewhere else. The guy brings in millions of dollars."

"Whatever Caspar wants, Caspar gets," Harry sang to the "Lola" tune.

"I don't have very good vibes about this at all, Harry."

"I can't think of any reason you should."

Caspar Sidonis, in his early forties, had a matinee idol's good looks, which he augmented by being impeccably and expensively dressed at all times. He had been first in his class at Harvard Med and never, ever let anyone forget it. He had also won MMC's tennis and squash championships several years running, and was rumored to have been a collegiate boxing champion.

"Green Dolphin Street" intensified in Harry's head. Funk or no funk, he did not want to be told what he could and could not do as a physician—not by HMOs, not by insurance companies, and especially not by a pompous, overblown, crank-'em-through supertechnician like Sidonis. He glanced around the hall at the other GPs, thinking about all those years of study, the countless hours of continuing-ed courses, their willingness to endure the low prestige and even lower reimbursement that went with being a family practitioner. They deserved to be rewarded, not restricted.

"Harry, for chrissakes, say something. They're crucifying you."

Doug Atwater, seated to Harry's right, clenched his fist in frustration as, one by one, the Sidonis committee's recommendations were presented to the medical staff. To Harry's left, Steve Josephson was shaking his head in disbelief. He had tried arguing against the first of the committee's proposals, which required that a board-certified obstetrician be present for all deliveries. Josephson had once made headlines when, as a passenger stuck in a disabled subway car, he had successfully delivered the twins of one of the other passengers. Now, it seemed possible that deliveries in such situations would be the only ones he would be allowed to perform.

The vote, despite Josephson's emotional arguments and well-publicized heroics, was nearly unanimous. Only the three GPs who still did deliveries voted *nay*. The rest abstained, perhaps believing that the staff would conclude they were responsible enough to police themselves, and back off from supporting the other restrictive resolutions.

"There goes the new refrigerator," Harry said.

The next resolution, requiring GPs to turn over their Coronary Care Unit patients to a cardiologist or internist, passed easily. The cardiologist who had taken over Clayton Miller's care was one of the few dissenters who wasn't a GP. Then came the vote to limit surgical participation by GPs to first assisting only. Again Sidonis's committee prevailed.

"History will refer to this next one as the Marv Lorello Proviso," Harry whispered as discussion began on the last of the committee's proposals.

"It is recommended," Sidonis began, adjusting the Ben Franklin reading glasses that Harry sensed he wore more for his image than for his vision, "that all suturing done in the Manhattan Medical Center emergency ward by a non-surgical specialist be approved in advance by the senior emergency physician on duty."

The murmur around the amphitheater suggested that many were surprised by this final, and perhaps most humiliating proposal. Harry had had advance warning, but the words stung nevertheless.

"There have been," Sidonis went on, "a number of cases reported to our complaint committee, and to our liability carrier, in which improper technique was used or faulty judgment displayed by certain non-specialists. Mrs. Brenner of our risk-management office has assured me that developing some sort of internal pretreatment screening policy could significantly reduce the number of claims against our non-specialty staff members."

He glanced vaguely in Marv Lorello's direction, and several dozen pairs of eyes followed. Lorello had joined the staff just a few years before after serving three years on a reservation in the Indian Health Service. He had impressive academic credentials and a refreshing idealism about practicing medicine. The malpractice suit—his first—and the subsequent fallout from it had hurt him deeply. Harry did his best to remain externally placid. But "Green Dolphin Street" was playing on, up-tempo now and louder.

Then suddenly, the music stopped. It took several seconds before Harry realized he was on his feet, his six-one frame the center of attention of everyone in the amphitheater. He cleared his throat. The faces stared up at him, waiting.

"If it's all right with the chairman," he heard himself saying, "I . . . um . . . I guess there are a few things I need to get off my chest before we vote on this last—and for the family practitioners, most degrading—proposal of this commission." He paused for objections and half felt Sidonis was about to voice one. The silence, however, was total. "Okay. Thanks. It's not my intention to belittle anyone's specialty by implying that someone with less training might be able to do exactly what it is they do. But I do want to stress that we generalists are well trained to do *some* of those things. We are board-certified in family medicine, not half-assed medicine. We went to medical school just as you did, we had residencies just as you did, we care about our patients and continue our education just as you do, and most important, we recognize our limitations, just as I hope you do.

"Most of us can handle being treated with the sort of disdain I've heard expressed here today." He looked pointedly across the auditorium toward Sidonis. The impressive silence continued. Not a cough. Not a clearing of a throat. Not a creaking of a seat. "We can handle it because we believe in the specialty of medicine we have chosen. Now, we've become something of a convenience to the insurance companies and

HMOs. They call us primary care physicians. By that they mean medical traffic cops, screening the mundane and insignificant complaints so that the much more expensive specialists won't have to deal with them. And that's okay. Most of us have adjusted to that new order, too. Just as we'll adjust to first assisting on simple appendectomies and other operations we have performed dozens of times ourselves, or turning our coronary care patients over to someone they don't know.

"But this—" Harry gestured to the huge screen behind Sidonis, on which was displayed the last of the committee's recommendations. "This I simply cannot accept. You know, we doctors persistently lay the blame for the malpractice crisis on lawyers. There are too many lawyers. The contingency system is wrong. The way they advertise is inflammatory. Well, that may be so. But that is hardly the whole story. Patients don't know us anymore. We don't portray ourselves as partners in the business of keeping them healthy. Instead, most of us come across as just what we are—specialists, interested only in making sure that the body part we have become expert at works properly. Hey, lady, I'm sorry you have to get to Brooklyn, I never drive past Forty-second Street. Well, I know how to suture. I've sutured wounds you wouldn't believe in situations you wouldn't believe. I'm damn good at it. So is Dr. Josephson, here, and Marv Lorello, and every one of the rest of us who chooses to sew up our patients when they cut themselves. I don't need to be told what I can and cannot fix. None of us does.

"So I say, *enough*. The return to the kinder, gentler days of the rumpled, overworked family practitioner makes for great conversation around the medical cocktail party circuit. But when the chips are down, no one's ready to challenge the great god science, and to say that there's still a place for doctors who know their patients as whole people, and want to care for them regardless of what is wrong. I wish that instead of limiting this session to medical staff members you had invited some of those patients to be here. Once you understand what *having* a doctor means to them, perhaps you will remember what *being* a doctor should mean to us. These proposals are all humiliating and unnecessary. But this one is even worse than that. Don't pass it."

Harry hesitated and then sank to his seat. The heavy silence continued. Finally, Steve Josephson reached over and took his hand.

"Thank you," he said hoarsely. "Thanks for trying."

Then, from across the amphitheater, the applause began. It spread quickly around the hall until nearly everyone had joined in. Then they were standing. Several of them cheered out loud. Others rapped on the wooden seatbacks in front of them. Caspar Sidonis sat rigidly in his seat, crimson beneath his perpetual tan. The other members of the committee shifted uncomfortably.

"It appears there is a great deal of sentiment surrounding this proposal," Sidonis said after he had finally managed to reestablish his authority. "I would suggest that perhaps we should table further discussion until our committee can meet again with the risk-management people and reconsider this issue."

"No, let's vote!" someone shouted out.

"How about another vote on all those proposals," another yelled.

Suddenly the entire medical staff seemed to be talking and arguing at the same time. Sidonis, bewildered and unsure of how to handle the situation, looked about for help. He was bailed out by the chief of the medical staff, a burly orthopedic surgeon who had twice been an All-American linebacker at Penn State.

"Okay, everyone, cool it!" he barked out. "That's it. Thanks. I want to thank Dr. Sidonis and his committee for a job well done. It seems this last issue is controversial enough that we ought to sit on it for a while. I know this whole business of who does what is not easy, and would like to praise the staff for its courage and the nonspecialty practitioners for their understanding." Two physicians booed. "Come on, grow up," the chief snapped. "We gave Dr. Sidonis and his committee a mandate, and they have lived up to it. Now, I think we owe them a round of applause."

Grudgingly, the staff complied. The session ended with a word of praise for the hard work of the Sidonis committee, and a plea for understanding and unity among the staff.

"You primary care physicians are still the foundation of our medical delivery system," he said. "Never forget that."

Harry accepted the handshakes and congratulations of Doug Atwater, Steve Josephson, and a number of the other staff members. But he knew that while he had helped the GPs save face, their loss of stature was severe. The groundswell of support following his speech had not changed that. He worked his way free and headed down toward the exit by the amphitheater stage. He was nearly there when Caspar Sidonis stepped in front of him. For a moment, Harry thought the former boxer was going to take a swing at him.

"Enjoy your little show while you can, Corbett," he said. "It's not going to make a bit of difference around here. You've always been a wiseass. But this time you've picked the wrong person to fuck with."

He whirled and stalked away.

"Asking you over for tea?" Doug Atwater asked.

Harry recovered and forced a smile.

"There's something going on with that guy and me. Something beneath the surface that I don't even know about," he said.

"Forget about him," Doug replied. "Come on. Let me buy you a Coke. You're a hell of a guy, Harry. A hell of a guy."

CHAPTER 3

It was midmorning when Harry finished dictating two discharge summaries and left the hospital for the six-block walk to his office on West 116th Street. The day was cloudless and just cool enough to be invigorating. Still, despite the weather, he sensed the return of the persistent flatness that had been dogging him for months. It was a feeling unlike anything he had ever experienced before—even during his year of pain and disability. And his failure to simply will it away was becoming increasingly frustrating. Distracted, Harry stepped onto Lexington Avenue against the light and narrowly missed walking into a Federal Express truck.

"*Hola*, Doc, over here!"

The cabby, dropping off a fare, waved to him from across the street. It took a moment, but Harry recognized the husband of one of his obstetrics patients—one of his *last* obstetrics patients, he thought grimly.

"*Hola*, Mr. Romero. How's the baby?" he asked once he had made it across.

The man grinned and gave an A-okay sign.

"You need a ride anyplace?"

"No. No, I don't, Mr. Romero. Thanks anyway."

The man smiled and drove off.

The brief exchange gave Harry a boost. He started walking again, picking up his pace just a little.

The canary yellow Mercedes convertible was parked by the hydrant in front of the building where Harry had a ground-floor office. Phil Corbett was grinning at him from behind the wheel.

"Shit," Harry whispered.

It wasn't that he disliked his younger brother. Quite the contrary. It was just that Phil was harder for him to take on some days than on others. And today was one of those days.

"A mint condition vintage 220SL with sixteen thousand miles on her," Phil said, motioning him in. "I just picked her up at my midtown showroom. Do you have any idea what this baby's worth?"

Phil's formal education had ended one month into community college, when he gave up trying to compete with Harry and joined the Navy. Three years later he was back in civilian clothes, selling cars. The profession was tailor-made for his ingenuous smile, uncluttered psyche, and perpetual optimism. Five years after his first sale, he bought out the owner of the agency. After that, he began to expand. Now, six agencies later, he had two daughters and a son in private school, a lovely wife who couldn't spend what he made even if she wanted to, and a three handicap at one of the most exclusive country clubs in New Jersey. He also had no trouble dealing with life's big questions. He never asked them.

"Eight hundred and seventy-three thousand, four hundred and ninety-two dollars and seventy-three cents," Harry said. "Plus tax, destination, and dealer preparation charges. You been to see Mom?"

"Tomorrow. How do you know how much this cost?"

"I don't. That's my total lifetime gross income. I went down to the home last Tuesday. She didn't know who I was."

"I guess that's the upside of having all those strokes."

"Very funny."

Phil studied his older brother.

"Harry, you okay? You look terrible."

"Thank you."

"Well, you do. Bags under your eyes. That thumbnail chewed down again."

"I've got a lot on my mind, Phil." He glanced at his watch.

"Listen, I've only got a couple of minutes before I've got to see patients."

"So what are you so worried about? Evie? When's she going to have that operation?"

"In a few days."

"She'll do fine. She's made out of . . . um . . . ah . . . steel."

"Don't start, Phil."

"I didn't say anything bad."

"You were about to."

"Why should I have anything bad to say about my sister-in-law? She calls and asks me to help her talk my brother into accepting this pharmaceutical-house job he's been offered. I tell her that even though it's a grand-sounding title, and maybe more money, I think my brother ought to decide for himself if he wants to give up his medical practice to push pills and design magazine ads. She calls me a selfish bastard who's threatened by my brother's moving up in the world. And she says maybe a dozen words to me since. Why should I have anything bad to say about her?"

"She was right, Phil. I should have taken the position."

"Harry, you see people when they're sick and you help them get well. Do you know how wonderful that is?"

"It's not enough anymore."

"Hey, you're forty-nine. I'm forty-four. It's my turn for a midlife crisis. You're supposed to be through yours already."

"Well, I'm not. I don't know, Phil, it's like . . . I spent too much time just accepting things as they were in my life. I didn't set enough goals or something. Now it seems like I don't have anything to push against. I should have taken that job. At least there would have been some new challenges."

"You're doing fine, Harry. It's that birthday coming up that has you rattled. The big five—"

"That's okay, Phil. You don't have to say it."

Harry had discussed the Corbett curse with his brother, but only once. Phil's dismissal of the theory was as emphatic as it was predictable. On a September first their paternal grandfather, just a few months past his seventieth birthday, had dropped dead of a coronary. Twenty-five years later—*exactly* twenty-five years later —their father had had *his* first coronary. He was precisely sixty years and five weeks old on *that* September first. That he didn't die on the spot was both tragic and, to Harry, immaterial. The two years he lived as a cardiac cripple were hell for everyone.

September first. The date had been circled on Harry's mental calendar since his father's heart attack. But after one particular lecture at a cardiology review course, he had highlighted it in red.

"It may be due to societal factors or to genetics," the cardiologist had said. *"Possibly both. But we frequently see a pattern in families which I call the Law of Decades. Simply put, a son's first cardiac event seems often to occur precisely ten years earlier than did his father's. Obviously, there are exceptions to the Law. But check it out. If you have a fifty-four-year-old man with a coronary and a positive family history, there's a good chance his father will have had his first event at age sixty-four. Not sixty-three or sixty-five. Ten years on the button. . . ."*

"But physically you're feeling all right, Harry," Phil said. "Right?"

"Sure. Sure, Phil, I'm fine. It's probably just that I haven't had a two-week vacation in almost three years, my car is falling apart, and—"

"Hey, believe it or not, that's actually one of the reasons I stopped by. I have a great deal for you on a new C220. Dealer's cost. Not the dealer's cost we tell everyone we're selling to them at. The *real* dealer's cost. A new Mercedes. Just think how much Evie'll love it. Who knows, she might even—"

"Phil!"

"Okay, okay. You said you needed a challenge, that's all."

Harry opened the door of the roadster and stepped out onto the pavement.

"Give my love to Gail and the kids," he said.

"I'm worried about you, Harry. You're usually very funny. And even more important, you usually think I'm funny."

"You're not funny today, Phil."

"Give me another chance. How about lunch sometime next week?"

"Let's see what happens with Evie."

"Okay. And don't worry, Harry. If you really need it, I'm sure something will come along for you to push against."

★ ★ ★

After twenty-one admissions to Parkside Hospital, Joe Bevins could close his eyes and tell time by the sounds and smells coming from the hallway outside his room. He even knew some of the nurses and aides by their footsteps—especially on Pavilion 5. More often than not, he was able to get the admissions people to send him there. The staff on that floor was the kindest in the hospital and knew the most about caring for chronic renal failure patients who were on dialysis. He also liked the rooms on the south end of the floor best of any in the hospital—the rooms with views of the park and, in the distance, the Empire State Building.

It wasn't a great life, having to get plugged in at the dialysis center three times a week, and having to be rushed to Parkside every time his circulation broke down, or an infection developed, or his blood sugar got too far out of whack, or his heart rhythm became irregular, or his prostate gland swelled up so that he couldn't pee. But at seventy-one, with diabetes and nonfunctioning kidneys, it was a case of beggars can't be choosers.

Outside his door, two litters rattled by, returning patients from physical therapy. One of them, a lonely old gal with no family, had lost both her legs to gangrene. Now, they were just keeping her around until a nursing home bed became available. *It could be worse*, Joe reminded himself. *Much worse*. At least he had Joe Jr., and Alice, and the kids. At least he had visitors. He glanced over at the other bed in his room. The guy in that bed, twenty years younger than he was, was down having an operation on his intestines—a goddamn cancer operation.

Oh, yes, Joe thought. No matter how bad it got for him, he should never forget that it could always be worse.

He sensed the presence at his door even before he heard the man clear his throat. When he turned, a white-coated lab tech was standing there, adjusting the stoppered tubes in his square, metal basket.

"You must be new here," Joe said.

"I am. But don't worry. I've been doing this sort of work for a long time."

The man, somewhere in his forties, smiled at him. He had a

nice enough face, Joe decided—not a face he took to all that much, but not one that looked burnt-out or callous either.

"What are you here to draw?" he asked.

Joe's doctors almost always told him what tests they had ordered. They knew he liked to know. All three specialists had been by on rounds that morning, and none had said anything about blood work.

"This is an HTB-R29 antibody titer," the man said matter-of-factly, setting his basket on the bedside table. "There's an infection going around the hospital. Everyone with kidney or lung problems is being tested."

"Oh." The technician had an accent of some sort. It wasn't very marked, and it wasn't one Joe could place. But it was there. "Where're you from?" he asked.

The man smiled at him as he prepared his tubes and needle. The blue plastic name tag pinned on his coat read G. *Turner, Phlebotomist.* Trying not to be obvious, Joe looked down at his clip-on identification badge. It was twisted around so that it was impossible to read.

"You mean originally?" the man responded. "Australia originally. But I've been here in the U.S. since I was a child. You have a very astute ear, Mr. Bevins."

"I taught English before I got sick."

"Aha. I see," Turner said, glancing swiftly at the door, which he had partially closed on his way in. "Well, then, shall we get on with this?"

"Just be careful of my shunt."

Turner lifted Joe's right forearm, and gently ran his fingers over the dialysis shunt—the firm, distended vessel created by joining an artery and vein. His fingers were long and finely manicured, and Joe had the passing thought that the man played piano, and played it well.

"We'll use your other arm," Turner said. He tightened a latex tourniquet three inches above Joe's elbow, and took much less time than most technicians did to locate a suitable vein. "You seem to take all this in stride. I like that," he said as he gloved, then swabbed the skin over the vein with alcohol.

"All those doctors don't keep me alive," Joe said. "My attitude does."

"I believe you. I'm going to use a small butterfly IV needle. It's much gentler on your vein."

Before Joe could respond, the fine needle, attached to a thin, clear-plastic catheter, was in. Blood pushed into the catheter. Turner attached a syringe to the end of the catheter and injected a small amount of clear liquid.

"This is just to clear the line," he said.

He waited for perhaps fifteen seconds. Then he drew a syringeful of blood, pulled the tiny needle out, and held the small puncture site firmly.

"Perfect. Just perfect," he said. "Are you okay?"

I'm fine.

Joe was certain he had said the words, but he heard nothing. The man standing beside his bed kept smiling down at him benevolently, all the while keeping pressure on the spot where the butterfly needle had been.

I'm fine, Joe tried again.

Turner released his arm, and placed the used needle and tube in the metal basket.

"Good day, Mr. Bevins," he said. "You've been most cooperative."

With the first icy fingers of panic beginning to take hold, Joe watched as the man turned and left the room. He felt strange, detached, floating. The air in the room was becoming thick and heavy. Something was happening to him. Something horrible. He called out for help, but again there was no sound. He tried to turn his head, to find the call button. From the corner of his eye, he could see the cord, hanging down toward the floor. He was paralyzed—unable to move or even to take in a breath. The call button was no more than three feet away. He strained to move his hand toward it, but his arm was lifeless. The air grew heavier still, and Joe felt his consciousness beginning to go. He was dying, drowning in air. And there was absolutely nothing he could do about it. Nothing at all.

The pattern on the drop ceiling blurred, then darkened, then faded to black. And with the deepening darkness, Joe's panic began to fade.

From beyond the nearly closed door to his room, he heard the sound of the cart from dietary being wheeled to the kitchen at the far end of the hallway. Next he caught the aroma of food.

And after twenty-one hospitalizations at Parkside, most of them on Pavilion 5, he knew that it was exactly eleven-fifteen.

★ ★ ★

Seven of the ten chairs in Harry's waiting room were occupied, although three of them were taken by the grandchildren of Mabel Espinoza. Mabel, an octogenarian, graced him with the smile that no amount of pain or personal tragedy had ever erased for long. She had high blood pressure, vascular disease, hypothyroidism, fluid retention, a love affair with rich foods, and chronic gastritis. For years, Harry had been holding her together with the medical equivalent of spit and baling wire. Somehow, the therapeutic legerdemain continued to work. And because of it, Mabel had been able to care for the grandchildren, and her daughter had been able to keep her job.

Harry reminded himself that there were no Mabel Espinozas connected with the position of Director of Physician Relations at Hollins/McCue Pharmaceuticals.

Mary Tobin, Harry's office manager-*cum*-receptionist, oversaw the waiting room from her glass-enclosed cubicle. She was a stout black woman, a grandmother many times over, and had been with Harry since his third year of practice. She was notably outspoken regarding those subjects on which she had an opinion, and she had an opinion on most subjects.

"How did the meeting go?" she asked as he entered her small fiefdom to check the appointment book.

"Meeting?"

"That bad, huh."

"Let's just say that all these years you've been working for a baritone, and from now on you'll be working for a tenor," Harry said.

Mary Tobin grinned at the image.

"What do they know? You'll make do, Dr. C.," she said. "You've been through tough times before, and you always find the right path."

"Keep telling me that. Any calls I need to deal with?"

"Just your wife. She called a half an hour ago."

"Is she okay?"

"I think so. She'd like you to call her at the office."

Harry headed past his three examining rooms to his office. In addition to Mary Tobin, he had a young nurse practitioner named Sara Keene who had been with him for four years, and a medical aide who must have been the twentieth he had hired from the nearby vocational tech. One of that group he had fired for stealing. The rest had left to have babies, or more often, for better pay. Sara looked up from her desk and waved as he passed.

"I heard about the meeting, Dr. C.," she called out cheerily. "Don't worry."

"If one more person tells me not to worry, I'm going to start worrying," he said.

His personal office was a large space at the very back of the once elegant apartment building. In addition to an old walnut desk and chairs, it contained a Trotter treadmill which he had used for cardiac stress tests until the associated malpractice premiums made performing the tests prohibitively expensive. Now, he used the mill for exercise. The walls of the office, once paneled with what Evie called "Elks Club pine," had been Sheetrocked over at her request and painted white. They held the usual array of laminated diplomas, certifications, and testimonials, plus something only a few other physicians could put on their walls—a silver star from Vietnam. There were also three original oils Evie had picked out, all contemporary, all abstract, and none that Harry would have chosen had he been left to his own tastes. But the majority of his patients seemed to like them.

There were three pictures in frames on the desk. One was of Harry and his parents at his medical school graduation; one was of Phil, Gail, and their kids; and one was of Evie. It was a black-and-white, head-and-shoulders publicity shot, taken by one of the city's foremost photographers. There were several dozen snapshots of her in his desk that Harry would have preferred in the frame, but Evie had insisted on the portrait. Now, as he settled in his chair, Harry cradled the frame in his hands and studied her fine, high cheekbones, her sensual mouth, and the dark intensity in her eyes. The photo was taken just before their wedding nine years ago. Evie, twenty-nine at the time, was then, and remained, the most beautiful woman he had ever known.

He picked up the phone and dialed her number at *Manhattan Woman* magazine.

"Evelyn DellaRosa, please," he said, setting her likeness back in its spot. "It's her husband."

Evie had been the consumer editor for the struggling monthly for five years. Harry knew it was an unpleasant comedown for her from the network television reporting job she had once held. But he admired her tenacity and her commitment to making it back into the spotlight. In fact, he knew something good was going on in her professional life. She wouldn't tell him what, but for her even to mention that she was working on a story with big potential was unusual.

It was three minutes before she came on the line.

"Sorry to keep you waiting, Harry," she said. "I had this technician ready to blow the whistle on the dog lab in the basement of a building owned by InSkin Cosmetics, and the bastard just wimped out."

"Are you all right?"

"If you mean do I spend one minute out of every hour not thinking about this damn balloon in my head, the answer is, I'm fine."

"They had that meeting at the hospital."

"Meeting?"

"The Sidonis committee report."

"Oh . . . oh, yes. . . . How did it go?"

"Let's just say I should have taken that job with Hollins/McCue."

"Dawn breaks on Marblehead."

"Please, Evie. I admitted it. What more can I say?"

He knew there was, in fact, nothing he could say that wouldn't make matters worse. His decision a little over a year ago to turn down the offer had nearly been the final nail in the coffin of their marriage. In fact, considering that he could count on one hand the number of times they had made love since then, the fallout was probably continuing.

"I got a call from Dr. Dunleavy's office a little while ago," she said.

"And?"

"A bed on the neurosurgical floor and operating room time

have become available. He wants me to come in tomorrow after-noon and be operated on Thursday morning."

"The sooner the better."

"As long as it's not *your* head, right?"

"Evie, come on."

"Listen, I know I had promised to come hear you play at the club tonight, but I don't want to now."

"That's fine. It's no big deal. I don't have to play."

He took care to keep any hurt from his voice. Throughout their dating and the early years of their marriage she had loved his music, loved hearing him play. Now, he couldn't recall the last time. He had been looking forward to this small step back toward the life they had once shared. But he did understand.

"Harry, I need to talk to you," Evie said suddenly. "Can you come home early enough for us to go out to dinner?"

"Of course. What gives?"

"I'll . . . I'll talk to you tonight, okay?"

"Should I be worried?"

"Harry, please. Tonight?"

"All right. Evie, I love you."

There was a pause.

"I know you do, Harry," she said.

CHAPTER 4

Kevin Loomis, first vice president of the Crown Health and Casualty Insurance Company, slipped a folder of notes into his briefcase, straightened his desk, and checked his calendar for the following day. He was a meticulous worker and never left for the evening without tying up as many loose ends as possible. He buzzed his secretary and turned on a mental stopwatch. In six seconds she was in his office.

"Yes, Mr. Loomis?"

Brenda was fabulous—smart, organized, loyal, and an absolute knockout. She was a legacy to him from Burt Dreiser, now the president and CEO of the company. Kevin suspected she and Dreiser had something going outside the office. But it really didn't matter. Dreiser had bumped him up to the corner office over a number of others who had more seniority and, in some cases, more qualifications than he did. And as far as Kevin was concerned, if Dreiser was sleeping with Brenda Wallace, more power to him.

"Do we have anything else we need to take care of?" he asked. "I'm just getting set to leave for the day."

"Second and fourth Tuesdays. I know," she said, a smile in her eyes. "I wish you well."

The poker game. For years, Dreiser, who was a legendary workaholic, had uncharacteristically left the office at four o'clock on the second and fourth Tuesdays of every month. Some sort of explanation seemed called for. Brenda was far too efficient and observant not to wonder. The poker game fit the bill perfectly. Now, Kevin had taken over not only Dreiser's former title, office, and secretary, but, as far as Brenda Wallace was concerned, his seat at the high-stakes card game as well. Second and fourth Tuesdays. Four o'clock. In fact, Dreiser had made a point of corroborating the poker story to Kevin's wife, Nancy. The necessary rite of passage up the corporate ladder comfortably explained her husband's twice-monthly overnights in the city. The avowed secrecy surrounding the game's location explained the need for her to communicate with him by beeper only.

"I've won maybe once in the four months I've been playing," Kevin told Brenda dryly. "I think that might be why Burt invited me into the game in the first place. He could tell I was a greenhorn. Listen, seeing as how Oak Hills has decided to renew with us, I think we ought to do something for them. You have the names of the members of the school board and the head of the union. Send them each some champagne. Better still, make it chocolates. Godiva. About a hundred dollars worth for each should do fine. Put something nice on the cards."

"Right away, Mr. Loomis."

She left after favoring him with a smile that would have melted block ice. His successes were hers, and the Oak Hills school system renewal was a triumph. The system was huge, one of the largest on Long Island. And by and large its teachers were young and healthy. *Young and healthy*—the golden words in any group medical coverage. It was a feather in Kevin Loomis's cap, to be sure. But the victory really belonged to The Roundtable. The Oak Hills system had been apportioned by the society to Crown. Any competition for the contract would come from nonmembers. And of course, dealing with nonmember competitors was what The Roundtable was all about.

The Oak Hills coup was meaningful on another level as well. Kevin's first four months as Burt's replacement on The Roundtable had been marked by controversy. A troubling situation had developed that had resulted in the group's moving their meetings from the Camelot Hotel to the Garfield Suites, and the situation had involved Kevin. But in truth, nothing that had happened was his fault. Hopefully, the others saw it that way, too. He had no idea what would happen if they didn't.

He picked up his briefcase and overnight bag and took some time to survey the panorama of the city, the river, and the countryside beyond. Kevin Loomis, Jr., had risen from gofer to first vice president, from a gerbil-village corkboard cubicle to a corner office. His parents, had they lived, would have been proud—damn proud—of the way he had turned out. He swallowed against the fullness in his throat that memories of them always seemed to bring. Then he headed out toward the elevator bank. His transformation to Sir Tristram, Knight of The Roundtable, had begun.

The Garfield Suites was on Fulton, a block and a half from the World Trade Center. The cab ride downtown from the Crown Building took twenty minutes. Kevin rode quietly, staring out at the passing city, but seeing little. The remarkable changes in his life could not have come about much more abruptly had he won the lottery. To be sure, he was good—very good—at what he did, which for years had been to sell insurance. He had been a member of the industry's Million Dollar Roundtable for sales five years running, a branch manager, and then a successful department head at the home office. For a relatively young man from the far wrong side of Newark, those were accomplishments enough. But suddenly, Burt Dreiser had started inviting him out to lunch, and soon after that, to dinner.

What do you think of . . . ? What would you do if . . . ? Supposing you were asked to . . . ? First came the questions, phrased and rephrased, over and over again. Then, with Kevin's responses apparently acceptable, came the secrets. The sales force's well-publicized roundtable had a counterpart, Burt explained, at the high executive level. But unlike the Million Dollar Roundtable, which was an industry honor to be extolled in ads, on letterheads, and on business cards, membership in *this* Roundtable was not only very exclusive, but very secret.

By the time Kevin had agreed to become Sir Tristram, replacing Burt Dreiser as Crown's representative, he realized that he already knew too much to refuse and remain employed. His rewards for accepting the appointment were the promotion, a generous raise, and an annual bonus of one hundred thousand dollars or one percent of what The Roundtable saved or made that year for Crown, whichever was higher. The deal was, Dreiser assured him, on a par with that accorded the other knights.

Following the recent scare, a number of steps had been instituted by the knights to protect their small organization and its members. Adhering to one of them, Kevin paid off the cabby at Gold and Beekman and made a two-block detour to the Garfield Suites, cutting through a store, and doubling back once as well. Certain he was not being followed, he entered the hotel lobby. His reservation, under the name George Trist, was already paid for. Anyone trying to backtrack from that name to the source of payment would find only a dummy business account with a set of directors who had long ago died. Sir Galahad, in charge of security, did his job well. He was paranoid about details. And after the undercover reporter had been discovered, he had become, if possible, even more obsessive.

Across the lobby, Kevin saw Sir Percivale waiting for the elevator. Percivale was with Comprehensive Neighborhood Health Care, the largest managed care operation in the state. Kevin knew that much about the man, but no more. Not his name, not his title at CNHC. Burt told him not to worry about such things—it had been three years before *he* knew the names of all six of the other knights. Their eyes met for just a moment, then Percivale was gone. Kevin glanced at his watch. In three hours they would be meeting, along with the others, on the nineteenth floor.

He crossed to the registration desk. The secrecy, the code names, the nature of their projects . . . Kevin thoroughly enjoyed the intrigue and mystery that surrounded their small society. And gradually, he was learning to cope with the less appealing aspects of it as well—some of the methods employed to achieve their goals and, of course, the constant risk of discovery.

Number 2314 was a two-room suite with a decent view of the World Trade Center. Kevin stopped in the living room and twisted open a Heineken from the ample supply in the refrigerator. Then he stripped off his tie and laid his suit coat over the back of a chair. He had just kicked off his shoes when he tensed. He was not alone. Someone was in the bedroom. He was absolutely certain. He took a step toward the hallway door. There were house phones by the elevator. He could call Galahad or hotel security.

"Hello?" a feminine voice called out. "Anybody out there?"

Kevin crossed to the bedroom doorway. The woman, in her early twenties if that, stood by the edge of the king-size bed. She had obviously been sleeping, and now was brushing out her waist-length, jet-black hair. She wore a bit too much makeup for Kevin's taste, but in every other regard she was perfect. Her Asian features, her slender body, her high, full breasts, her legs. Perfect. Her emerald dress was wet-suit tight, slit up the right side to her hip.

"Who are you?" he demanded.

She set the brush down, smoothed the front of her dress, and moistened her lips before she spoke.

"My name is Kelly."

"Who sent you here?"

"I . . . I don't understand."

Kevin glared at her. After what happened with the reporter, surely this was either a joke or some sort of test.

"Where did you come from? That's a simple enough question. How did you get in here? That's another simple question."

Fear sparked in the woman's dark eyes.

"A man met me outside the door and let me in. Each of us was given a room number to wait at. I . . . I'm here to please you in any way that you want."

"Just sit down there and stay there," Kevin said, motioning to the bed. "No!" he snapped as she reached behind her back for her zipper. "Just sit."

He stalked to the living room, slamming the bedroom door behind him.

According to Burt Dreiser, the women had been part of second and fourth Tuesdays for most of The Roundtable's six-year existence. Lancelot, who had been there from the beginning, was responsible for them. And until two months ago, there had never been a problem. Those knights who wanted sex had it. Those who wanted nothing more than a massage or a lovely companion for dinner got that. The escort service Lancelot employed was one of the most upscale and discreet in the city. But somehow, they had been penetrated—not by a cop, but by a reporter.

Kevin snatched up the phone.

"Mr. Lance's room, please."

Lancelot, Pat Harper of Northeast Life and Casualty, was the only member of The Roundtable whom Kevin had met before joining. In stature and appearance, Harper was anything but a Lancelot, with an expansive gut, ruddy complexion, fat cigar, and high-pitched laugh that were far closer to Dickens than to Camelot. Kevin had once played in the same foursome with him during an industry-sponsored charity golf tournament and had been beaten by a dozen strokes. Harper had a wife and three or four grown kids. Beyond that fact, Kevin knew nothing of the man except, of course, that he liked young, beautiful women.

"Lancelot, this is Tristram," Kevin said. "I thought we decided no more women."

"Ah, Kelly . . . What do you think of her? A ten and a half, don't you agree?"

"Yes, except she's not supposed to be here."

"Oh, lighten up, my friend. Life is too short. We decided no more women from the *old* escort service. Kelly and the others are from a *new* one. Don't worry, every one of them has been checked out. There won't be any more screwups."

The name the reporter had used was Desiree. She had spent two Tuesdays with Sir Gawaine and two with Kevin. The owner of the escort service had learned of Desiree's duplicity from one of the other women, whom the reporter had tried to interview and who was certain that the impostor had recorded her sessions with her two clients. At Galahad's insistence, the escort company was terminated immediately, and Roundtable meetings were moved.

During the tense questioning that followed the discovery, Kevin learned a bit about Gawaine, the last member admitted to the group before he was. From the very beginning, Kevin had found the man's button-down composure and varsity club accent threatening. Gawaine seemed to fit right in with the others, while Kevin's hardscrabble Newark upbringing made him an instant outsider. Now Kevin knew that he and Gawaine had at least one thing in common: both were contented family men who had never wanted or received more than a massage and some conversation from their escorts.

Apparently, however, Lancelot had been given the green light to start up again with a new service. Kevin was about to tell the guy that no more women were to be sent to his room. But he remembered one of Burt Dreiser's warnings about The Round-table.

"So much is at stake," Dreiser had said, "that nobody trusts anybody. The best thing you can do is not to stand out in any way. Look and act like everyone else, and you'll do fine."

Kevin had drawn the conformity line at screwing the women Lancelot brought in. But he had never mentioned that to anyone. In fact, if he and Gawaine hadn't been asked during Galahad's investigation whether or not they were actually having sex with Desiree, no one in the group would have known.

"Listen, Lance," he said now. "Don't take it personally. Kelly's beautiful. I'm very pleased with her. I was just making sure there weren't any problems. That's all."

He set the receiver down and returned to the bedroom. Kelly, slowly stroking her thick mane of ebony hair, smiled up at him from the bed.

"Is everything okay?" she asked.

The sight of her sitting there, her right leg exposed to the hip, sent an uncontrollable surge of blood to Kevin's groin.

"Everything's fine," he said. "Listen. How about calling room service and ordering dinner. Get anything you want for yourself. I'll have a filet. Medium rare. And then maybe a massage. Are you good at that?"

"I am very good at that," she said.

★   ★   ★

Harry had lived in Manhattan for much of his adult life, but until today he had never been in Tiffany's. With Mary Tobin's help, he had freed up the last hour and a half to make earlier-than-usual rounds at the hospital and head home. The idea of doing something special for Evie had been his. The suggestion to do it at Tiffany's had been Mary's.

Now, silently humming Joe Kincaid's rendition of "Moon River," Harry tried for George Peppard's *Breakfast at Tiffany's* nonchalance as a saleswoman laid one prohibitively expensive gem after another on the black velvet display cloth.

"This tennis bracelet is quite charming," she said. "It has alternating beautifully matched rubies and diamonds, each an eighth of a carat."

"My wife doesn't play tennis too often. . . . Um . . . how much is it, though?"

"Thirty-six hundred, sir."

Well, then, perhaps I could see something in a Ping-Pong bracelet?

Eventually, he settled on a half-carat diamond pendant flanked by two small rubies. Evie loved precious stones. With the help, Harry suspected, of her ex-husband and ex-suitors, she had amassed a sizable collection by the time he started dating her.

"I want to sell every piece I have," she said, soon after they were married, "so we can buy a camper and drive across the country."

Harry knew that Evie had never been camping in her life and suspected that she would not be too enamored of black flies and blackened burgers. The declaration was part of her commitment to moving her life out of the fast lane and into whatever lane she perceived him to be traveling. Eventually, though, she stopped talking about the simple life and put her jewels into a safe-deposit box. They never did go camping.

There's nothing to worry about. . . . I hope this will mark a new beginning for us. . . . Everything's going to be all right. . . . Believe it or not, there are places I want to take you where you can actually wear this. . . . Harry considered then rejected any number of messages for the card, before writing simply "I love you."

I need to talk to you. . . . With Evie's words playing over and over in his mind, he took a cab to the co-op they had owned since shortly after the wedding. The sixth-floor apartment, five decent-sized rooms and a tiny study, was in a well-maintained building on the Upper West Side, a block from Central Park. Over Evie's eight-plus years there, the flat had changed, in her words, from "exquisite" to "adequate" to "small," and, most recently, to "depressing."

I need to talk to you. . . . Health? Money? The marriage?

Her job? Could she possibly be pregnant? It had been so long since she had *needed* to speak with him about anything. Maybe she finally wanted to clear the air and start over again.

There were two apartments on the sixth floor. The narrow hallway between them always seemed imbued with Evie—possibly some combination of her perfume, shampoo, and makeup. As usual the scent evoked powerful impressions of her. But this evening Harry was too distracted to pay much attention. He knocked once and then used his key.

"Harry?" she called out from the bedroom.

"Yes."

"I'll be right out."

From her tone, he knew she was on the phone.

Harry set the Tiffany's box on the dining-room table and paced idly. The apartment was immaculate, brightened by several vases of fresh-cut flowers—Evie's trademark. An Eric Clapton album was playing on the CD player. Clapton was one of Harry's favorites. He wondered if Evie's playing it now was significant.

"You want a drink?" he asked.

"I have a vodka and tonic on the kitchen counter. Just add a little ice for me. . . ."

She must be off the phone.

". . . I'll be out in a minute. I made reservations at the SeaGrill if that's okay."

"Fine."

Harry tried unsuccessfully to read something—anything—into her voice.

She emerged from the bedroom wearing black slacks and a red silk blouse. The colors looked smashing on her. Then again, most colors did. She kissed him on the cheek—nearly an air kiss.

"Was it hard getting away from the office?" she asked, retrieving her drink.

"Not really. Mary cleared my schedule and canceled me out with the band. She can do anything she sets her mind to."

"How's she doing?"

"Mary?"

"Yes."

Harry couldn't remember when Evie had last asked about

his office staff—or, for that matter, the guys in the band or his co-workers.

"The arthritis in her hips is pretty bad. But in general she's doing fine. Are *you* okay?"

"As well as can be expected, I guess."

She sipped her drink. Harry gave up trying to see behind the small talk and instead handed her the necklace. She seemed genuinely charmed and impressed by the gift and immediately replaced the gold chain she was wearing with it.

"This is really very sweet of you," she said, glancing again at the card.

"I just wanted to be sure you know that everything's going to be okay."

Her smile was enigmatic, but there was unmistakable sadness in her eyes.

"You always tell me that things have a habit of working out the way they're supposed to."

"That's me. Harry Corbett, mild-mannered GP by day, impenetrable philosopher by night."

"Well, I think this time you've got it right, impenetrable one. Things do have a way of working out."

She gazed out the window, absently fingering the pendant. The early evening light glowed against her pale skin and highlighted her flawless profile. She was, if anything, even more strikingly lovely than she had been when they first met.

"You . . . um . . . said you needed to speak with me."

Even as he heard his voice saying the words, Harry cursed himself for not having more restraint. If she felt ready to say something, she would have said it.

She glanced at him and then turned back to the window. "I —I just wanted to spend some time talking together tonight," she said. "After all, medical science may have broken through the envelope, but brain surgery is still brain surgery."

"I understand," Harry said. But in truth, he was not at all certain that he did. "So . . . are—are you hungry?"

"I will be by the time we get there."

"Want to walk?" The question was almost rhetorical. Evie was invariably in too great a rush to get wherever she was going to walk.

"Let's do that," she said suddenly. "Let's walk. Harry, this is a beautiful necklace. I'm really very touched."

Harry searched for the cynicism he had grown used to from her but found none. His fantasies about a return to the life they had once had began to simmer. Evie had already turned and started toward the bedroom when he realized the phone was ringing.

"I'll get it," she called out, hurrying down the hall. "I want to get my purse anyhow."

Harry shrugged and, still feeling uneasy, went to the kitchen and set his glass in the sink. Through the eight Bose speakers mounted throughout the apartment, Eric Clapton was reminding him that nobody knows you when you're down and out.

Down the hall in the bedroom, her hand cupped over the mouthpiece of the phone, Evie was holding a brief, hushed conversation.

"No . . . no, I haven't told him about us yet," she said. "But I'm going to."

She set the receiver down and held the diamond pendant up where she could see it.

"At least I *think* I'm going to," she murmured.

CHAPTER 5

Galahad . . . Gawaine . . . Merlin . . . Tristram . . . they arrived at the nineteenth-floor conference room at prescribed times, in prescribed order, and by prescribed routes. Galahad had chosen the hotel and meeting room and set up the protocol. He had also checked the room for listening devices and cameras.

Although the women from the escort service were hired to stay the night, Kevin Loomis—Sir Tristram—had sent Kelly away an hour or so before he left his room. He loved his wife and was satisfied with their sex life. But every man had his limits. Nancy did not like giving backrubs as much as she liked receiving them. Five minutes of uninspired kneading was about the best effort she could muster. But Kelly was tireless, and the sweet-smelling oils she produced from her bag would have pleased a potentate. Spending an entire night with her would have stretched his willpower beyond the breaking point.

Now, reasonably relaxed from the perks of power, Kevin checked the time, dialed Merlin's room, and allowed the phone to ring six times. Certain that Merlin had left, he took the elevator to the second floor, then a different elevator up to the eighteenth. The security measures seemed excessive to him, but they did heighten the sense of always being on the edge of danger and discovery, and from games of highway chicken in high school to several dozen jumps in his thirties with a skydiving club, Kevin had always been drawn to that feeling.

He took the stairs to the final story, checked the corridor, and slipped inside room 1902, the Stuyvesant Suite. Three other knights were already there, seated at places marked with their Roundtable names on small gold plaques. They greeted him with businesslike smiles and nods. Percivale, Lancelot, and Kay arrived next, exactly three minutes apart.

Except for Galahad's having taken absolute control over security, there was no leader of the knights. They took turns chairing the meetings, which began at seven-thirty and continued until there was no more business to transact. In Tristram's four months with the group, two sessions had already gone well past midnight. Both of them had focused on the security breach by the reporter calling herself Desiree. For an exhausting three hours, the knights had grilled Kevin and Gawaine, dissecting their recollected conversations with the woman word by word.

Did she ask you about what your business was? . . . What did you say? . . . Did you mention any of our names? . . . What did she seem the most interested in? . . . Did she ask your last name? . . . Did you tell her? . . . Did you make love with her? . . . Get undressed with her? . . . Fall asleep while she was with you? . . . Did you leave her alone in the room with your wallet? . . . Your clothes? . . . How about your briefcase? . . . Is there any way she could have drugged you? . . .

Throughout the questioning, Galahad, as prime inquisitor, had never been antagonistic. But there was a coldness about him, a professionalism, that Kevin found unnerving. Even more disconcerting was Kevin's feeling that the interrogation focused much more on him than on Gawaine, who radiated self-assuredness, entitlement, and breeding. Kevin had kept himself on red alert during the session and felt indescribable relief when it was over. Tonight, at some point, Galahad would bring them up to date on his investigation of the woman. Kevin hoped it would be the last he ever heard of the matter.

He surveyed the group as the men settled in and readied their notes. At thirty-seven, he was probably the youngest, with Gawaine a close second. Lancelot, Pat Harper, was probably the oldest—mid-to-late fifties, he guessed. Every one of the men was accustomed to power and status. Less than half a year ago, Kevin was nothing more than the employee of a Roundtable member. Now he was their comrade in arms. And he felt certain that in time, as they came to know his resourcefulness and commitment, they would come to accept him as their equal.

"Okay, campers," Merlin said. "Let's get started."

Merlin, who was leading the August meetings, was in his forties and prosperously endomorphic. He was intelligent and insightful, but his flippant sense of humor seemed to Kevin to be out of place given the seriousness of the business of The Roundtable. If anything went haywire, each of them risked disgrace, unemployment, fines, even prison. And while the CEOs of their companies certainly knew of the existence of their small society, there was no proof whatsoever of that connection.

"Any comments, anecdotes, new jokes, or bawdy stories before we begin?" Merlin continued. "Okay, then. Finances first. Lancelot?"

Lancelot put aside the unlit panatela he was chewing, cleared his throat, and distributed computer printouts around the table from the top of a small stack. Such printouts were the foundation on which The Roundtable was built.

"Our private account currently stands at just under two hundred and sixty-two thousand dollars," he began. "That means we're going to need fifty thousand dollars per member company to bring us back over the six-hundred-thousand-dollar operating capital we have agreed on. Everyone's stayed pretty much within his budget except Percivale. You'll have a report on that, yes?"

There was a silent, tense exchange between the two men, which Kevin was in a perfect spot to observe. Clearly Percivale, the man from Comprehensive Neighborhood Health Care, did not enjoy being singled out. This was Tristram's eighth Roundtable session, but he was only now getting a handle on the various knights. The one most respected, and perhaps most feared, was Galahad, an officer with a managed care company. Percivale, on the other hand, seemed to have less influence and carry less responsibility than the rest.

If there was a clique, the insiders seemed to be Galahad, Lancelot, Merlin, and possibly Kay, a wizard with numbers who was the group's actuarial expert. Tristram and Gawaine, still under microscopic scrutiny, were regarded as fraternity pledges. And Percivale, though tolerated, seemed like an outsider. Kevin had once asked his sponsor, Burt Dreiser, whether or not there was an inner circle of knights on The Roundtable. Dreiser's reply had been a reassuring pat on the back and an enigmatic reminder that total trust takes time.

"I've put the figures together from the past two months," Lancelot went on. "They are excellent, as you'll see for yourselves. Perhaps the most significant statistic, provided courtesy of Sir Kay, is that the average age of our companies' subscribers now is four point one years *below* the average for the rest of the companies doing business in the metropolitan area."

The knights acknowledged approval of the information by tapping their pens on the table. Kevin did not know the exact figure, but he did know that each of those years translated into tens of millions of dollars in payout savings annually. The trick was to avoid group subscribers who were slow to terminate their older employees, or worse, those who actually hired people over forty. Weeding out such groups was a skill The Roundtable had mastered.

One by one, the other knights made their reports. Gawaine was applauded for obtaining the names of at least 80 percent of the women in southern New York State who had had abnormal PAP tests in the past year. The tests, even those showing only minimal inflammation and no suspicious precancerous cells, would be used to label as a preexisting condition any cervical cancer occurring within the twelve months allowed by state law, or to exclude those women from coverage altogether. Other insurers, or perhaps Medicaid, might take them on, but that was their problem.

Percivale distributed a printout giving updated information on the benefits managers of the largest 250 businesses and unions in the area—not only such data as income, marital status, education, automobile make, home value, and religious affiliation, but also hobbies, alcohol consumption, cocaine and marijuana use, sexual preferences, and a grade on a one-to-ten scale of "approachability." The knights voted to court seven of the managers aggressively.

Merlin called on Sir Tristram next. Kevin, still self-conscious in the spotlight, felt he stammered far too much in his presentation. His area of responsibility, political action, had been Burt Dreiser's. The insurance industry already had strong lobbies in both Washington, D.C., and Albany, so Dreiser had concentrated his efforts on a few key state legislators, the insurance commissioner, and one of his deputies. In most cases, the only leverage needed was money. But the commissioner had been a harder nut to crack. It took Dreiser's private investigator nearly six months to get decent photos of the man—videos, actually—sharing his hunting cabin with a seventeen-year-old summer intern from Oneonta.

"The information Merlin presented at the last meeting proved correct," Kevin reported now. "The commissioner *had* spoken with some aides about retiring. I have contacted him through our channels and made it clear that this would be an unwise decision at the present time. At the moment, he is reconsidering. I think he will see things clearly."

Kevin had no idea how The Roundtable would handle matters if the commissioner decided to call their bluff. According to Burt Dreiser, such a situation had never arisen. The secret, he said, was meticulous research and preparation—that and never making a request that was too far beyond the previous one.

There were nods of approval from around the table. Kevin tried for the matter-of-fact expression with which the older knights acknowledged success. Despite the Desiree debacle, their regard for him was clearly on the rise. And he loved it. Next to Nancy's saying she'd marry him, Dreiser's offer of a seat at The Roundtable was the most significant event in Kevin's life. The fact that the group was breaking the law meant little to him. In a highly competitive industry, the strong grew stronger, and the weak were doomed. Collaboration among corporations, while technically illegal, made perfect business sense.

"Okay, brethren," Merlin said. "Any other comments on Tristram's information? Suggestions? Good enough. Excellent job, Tristram. Excellent. Now, if there's no further business, let's have an update from Galahad."

The security chief cleared his throat, set a portable tape player on the table, and took over the meeting. Kevin hoped that his expression at that moment did not reflect the anxiety he was feeling at having the subject of Desiree come up again.

"Let me bring all of you up to speed on our mysterious

escort. Lancelot has spent a good deal of time interviewing Page Proctor, the woman who runs the escort service. My own man has spoken with several of Proctor's employees. We've been trying to identify this Desiree, but so far with no luck. She never gave Proctor a phone number. Instead, she called in on certain nights to see if work was available for her. Somehow, she learned that Proctor had found out she was a reporter. She didn't call in for almost a month. Then, last week, she called to see if Proctor would grant her an exclusive interview. Unfortunately, Page lost her cool completely and cost us a chance to find out who Desiree is. The only thing she did right was to record the conversation. Here's a portion of it."

He switched on the tape player.

"*. . . I've got to know why you've done this to me.*"

"*I did nothing to you.*"

"*My clients are very upset. I've lost an account that was paying over ten thousand dollars a month. Some very angry and anxious people are still after me to find out what you have learned, and what you intend to do with the information.*"

"*Page, I told you. I'm working on a story about upscale escort services. Yours was just one of several I worked for.*"

"*What are you going to do with the story?*"

"*I can't tell you that just yet.*"

"*Those people want to know.*"

"*Then tell me who they all are, and I'll invite them to come and ask me.*"

"*You're a very selfish person.*"

"*Do you have any other questions? . . .*"

"She goes on," Galahad said, "but that's the gist of it. All the woman ever admits is that she's working on a story about escort services. She didn't mention us or the insurance industry once to Page. We've checked with people at the local TV stations, newspapers and magazines, and even a friend at *60 Minutes*. No one knows anything about an escort service story."

"I was certain you would have found out who she is by now," Percivale said nervously. "Do you think we're safe?"

"What options do we have?" Lancelot chimed in. "How can we buy her off if we can't find her?"

"First of all," Kay said, "we don't have any idea whether she even knows about us. Second, we're not going to allow anyone to blackmail us. That is inevitably a losing proposition."

Kay had aristocratic features and a gentle but persuasive voice. From the expressions around the table, it was clear his opinion carried weight.

Galahad shrugged. "Tristram and Gawaine swear she didn't ask more than a few passing questions about their line of work. But neither of them has recordings of their sessions, and you can bet this woman does. My sense is that she's probably telling the truth when she says she's working on an escort service story and nothing more. But obviously I can't be certain."

"*So?*" Percivale said.

"I don't see how she could have any hard data on us," Kay said, before Galahad could answer. "My guess is the whole thing's a coincidence."

"Even so, maybe we should hold off meeting for a while," Percivale offered. "In fact, I move we suspend operations for two months."

No one bothered commenting on the motion. Merlin handled the vote, which was initially six to zero in favor of continuing on the second and fourth Tuesdays. Percivale at first abstained and then made the decision unanimous.

"So, we're done, then," Merlin said. "Galahad, do you intend to keep trying to find out who this reporter is?"

"I do. We've come too far to allow anyone to threaten our work."

"Just don't do anything too rash," Merlin said. He smiled and added, "At least, not until you're certain none of our companies is carrying a policy on her."

CHAPTER 6

Harry had seen and experienced enough of what could go wrong in hospitals to fear ever being a patient in one. Each day, every day, thousands of patients were cared for at hospitals in and around Manhattan. Most physicians, nurses, aides, and technicians were dedicated, competent, and focused. But invariably, on any given day, some weren't. There were simply too many patients, too many illnesses, and too many caregivers with human frailties for the system ever to be perfect.

Over his twenty-five years in medicine, Harry had confronted or heard about all manner of disasters, many of them beyond anything he could have imagined. Orange juice given intravenously by a nurse who had misunderstood a physician's telephoned orders and was too intimidated to call back and question them. A lethal dose of medication administered to a child because a harried physician omitted a decimal point. B-positive blood inadvertently finding its way into the bloodstream of an A-negative patient. Then there were the countless IVs that emptied far more rapidly than they were supposed to, the bedrails carelessly left down, and the unanticipated psychoses in response to tranquilizers or sleeping medication.

Along with the preventable disasters were the so-called complications—the documented *and accepted* 1 percent, or 0.1 percent, or 0.01 percent adverse reactions to medications and invasive procedures that were enumerated in the textbooks,

PDR, and package inserts, and were only of concern if they happened to happen to you.

With such thoughts refusing relegation to the back of his mind, Harry made his way through the corridors of MMC to the neurosurgical unit on Alexander 9. It was five past eight in the evening. Visitors were streaming toward the exits. He had hoped to make it up to the floor earlier, but a long-standing patient of his had been brought to the ER vomiting blood. Now, having stabilized the man's bleeding ulcer, he had finally been able to sign out to the doc on call.

Earlier in the day, he had met Evie at the main lobby and walked with her to the admissions office. He offered to stay with her during the pre-admission ritual, but she declined. She seemed preoccupied and distracted, just as she had the night before. Certainly the surgery was on her mind. But there was something else. Harry felt certain of it.

The evening before, they had walked from their apartment to the SeaGrill in virtual silence. Although they talked some during dinner, only one topic of substance was discussed. Evie made him promise to fight any attempt to prolong her life if there was brain damage of any kind. And as they were walking back to the co-op, she apologized for not having put the energy into their marriage that she might have. There was a bittersweet finality to the way she said it. Harry acknowledged the apology, but could not read its significance.

Alexander 9, an "L" with fifteen rooms on each arm, was in transition from evening to night. The corridors were empty except for a nurse's aide wheeling a patient back from the lounge and a janitor readying his large, metal-enclosed floor buffer. The nurse's station was midway between the elevators and Evie's room. An attractive, redheaded nurse with high-gloss crimson nail polish was seated behind the counter writing notes. Harry had never seen her before.

"Hi, I'm Dr. Corbett," he said.

"I know," the woman said. "Your wife's doing fine."

"That's great. I spoke to her on the phone a while ago and she sounded okay, except she was a little distressed about her roommate."

The nurse's face wrinkled in distaste. "She's not the only one. We've all just about had it up to here with Maura Hughes. I really think there ought to be a hefty tax on alcohol to pay for the medical treatment of people like her. Don't you?"

"I don't understand."

"Alcoholics. Oh, I thought your wife told you. Her roommate, Maura's, in the DTs. Unfortunately, there are no other empty beds on the floor."

"Evie said she wasn't too bad."

"As long as the Librium is working she isn't. She came to the floor from the OR three days ago. She was on a big bender and fell down the stairs of her building and fractured her skull. The CT scan showed a collection of subdural blood, so she had to have it drained. She did great until yesterday when she suddenly began complaining about the spiders crawling along the ceiling and the ants under her sheet."

"That certainly sounds like the DTs."

"Oh, it is. Believe me. She's disrupted the whole floor. Those people are so self-centered and inconsiderate. They never stop to think of the consequences of their drinking, if you know what I mean."

Harry had heard enough. Where had this woman been for the last fifteen years?

"Sorry to get here after visitors' hours," he said, "but I had a man in the ER with a GI bleed. Is it okay if I visit with Evie for a while?"

"Sure. If Maura-the-moaner gets to be too much for you, we'll just tighten her restraints and move her into the hall. As a matter of fact, she's due to have a visitor soon, too. Her brother called a little while ago. He's a policeman, of all things. He doesn't get off duty for a while and he wanted to see her. I almost told him to bring in a whip and a chair."

"Well, Miss"—he checked her name tag—"Jilson, I appreciate your bending the rules for me."

"Anytime. Your wife is very beautiful, Dr. Corbett."

"Yes . . . yes, thank you." Harry hurried away from the woman and down the hall to room 928.

". . . so they're just mean to me. Mean and nasty. They don't like me because they think this goddamn floor is clean as a whistle and I keep pointing out the bugs that are crawling everywhere. God, I hate bugs. I hate them. Stuck-up, snobbish, know-it-alls . . ."

Several doors from the room, Harry could hear Maura Hughes's steady stream of babble. He had treated every form of alcohol withdrawal during his residency at Bellevue and over his years of private practice in one of the more indigent areas of the city. DTs—delirium tremens—while at times amusing, was potentially lethal: heart rate up, respiration up, core temperature up, nervous-system irritability marked, fluid loss through perspiration and hyperventilation intense, fluid intake minimal to none. He had seen studies showing a mortality rate from DTs as high as 25 percent. And Maura Hughes was three days post craniotomy as well. She was a medical time bomb, the last roommate he would have chosen for Evie.

Harry glanced down the hall at the janitor, placidly working his buffer from wall to wall. He had on a Walkman and was bobbing his head in time to the music, totally oblivious to the life-and-death dramas being played out all around him. Harry wondered what it must be like to have a shiny floor be the extent of one's professional responsibility.

Evie had the bed next to the windows and farthest from the door. The curtain separating the two beds was pulled. Harry glanced at Maura Hughes as he passed. She was restrained to the bed with a cloth Posy harness. Her wrists were secured to the bedrails by broad leather straps. She wasn't old. He could tell that much about her, but little more. Below her turban bandage, dense, violet bruises enveloped both of her eyes and ran down to the corners of her mouth. Her oxygen prongs had dislodged from her nose and were ventilating her left ear. Her cracked, arid lips were drawn back in a strange, twisted rictus. Harry's first impression was that she was snarling at him. Then he realized that she was smiling.

"Hi," he said. "I'm Evie's husband, Harry."

"Double, double, toil and trouble, fire burn and cauldron bubble," she replied.

Harry managed a smile of his own and stepped beyond the curtain. Evie accepted his kiss on her forehead without reaction.

"She knows Shakespeare," he whispered.

"Actually, she knows a lot of things. It's just that the insects and snakes and spiders keep getting in the way."

"The creepy crawlies. It would be sort of humorous if the

insects and such weren't so damn real to her. She should be through this in another day or so."

"Ouch! Get off my sheet, you filthy bug! Hey, will someone please come over and help me!"

"Go say something," Evie urged. "Try and calm her down."

Harry walked back around the curtain.

"You're too late, Gene," Maura said to him. "It bit me and it's gone."

"Sorry." Harry realized now that she was even younger than he had originally thought—possibly in her mid-thirties. "My name's Harry. Not Gene."

"Well, you look like Gene Hackman."

"Thanks. I like Gene Hackman."

"So do I. I thought you were an actor."

"I'm not. Why would you think that?"

"Your pin."

For a moment, Harry had no idea what the woman meant. Then he remembered the pin his niece—Phil's oldest daughter, Jennifer—had given him. It was a tiny depiction of comic and tragic faces—a prize she had won for drama at school. A year or so ago he had helped her place it on the lapel of this particular sports coat, and there it had remained. He rarely even thought about it being there. Maura Hughes had identified it from eight feet away.

"I'm impressed that you saw this," he said.

"I notice things."

Suddenly she began squirming and fighting her restraints.

"Dammit, Gene," she snapped, "do you have any Southern Comfort on you or not? You promised and— Shit, Gene, watch out! Right there on the wall by your head. What is that? A scorpion? A shrimp?"

In spite of himself, Harry glanced at the wall.

"Try and get some rest," he said.

He returned to his wife, who was lying almost flat in bed, staring up at the ceiling.

Don't shut me out, he wanted to insist. *After nine years, on this of all nights, why can't you share some of what's going on inside you?*

"There are no empty beds on the whole floor," he said

instead. "No place to move either of you. If the nurses can't medicate her anymore, perhaps they can give you something."

"I don't want anything," she said, without turning her gaze from the ceiling. "I want my brain functioning at maximum capacity right up until the last possible moment."

"I understand. You're going to do fine." It was then Harry saw the IV—a bag of 5 percent dextrose in water, hanging from a ceiling hook nestled in the dividing curtain, delivering tiny droplets through flow-control tubing. "When did that go in?"

"A few hours ago."

"I didn't even notice it. I wonder why they put it in tonight and not in the OR tomorrow. Do you know who ordered it?"

"The anesthesiologist, I think the IV nurse said."

"Hmm."

"What difference does it make?"

"None, I guess."

A prolonged, uncomfortable silence followed.

"Look, Harry," she said suddenly, "I think I need to be alone."

The words hit him like a slap. He stared at her, uncertain how to respond.

"Could you please tell me what's going on?" he said finally.

"Nothing's going on. I . . . I just have a lot on my mind." She took a deep breath. Her tension seemed to ease a bit. "Look, they said I could eat until midnight. I'll tell you what. I'm dying for an extra-thick chocolate malt from Alphano's. Pick me up one, then we'll talk. Okay?"

Alphano's Ice Cream Emporium was two blocks beyond their co-op—a fifteen-minute drive from the hospital if the traffic was reasonable. But Harry felt grateful to have something— anything—to contribute.

"Done," he said, rising. "I'll be back within the hour. And we don't have to talk. I'll be happy just to hang with you for a while."

He bent to kiss her but again there was no response. He settled for another peck on her forehead.

"Gene, Gene, lean and mean. Keep him loose and keep him clean," Maura Hughes sang as he passed.

Out in the hall, the buffer man had stopped his work and

was kneeling down, Walkman still in place, scowling at the motor of his machine when Harry walked by. Harry felt strangely pleased to see that the man's life wasn't so uncomplicated after all.

Farther down the hall, the nurse, Sue Jilson, smiled up at him as he approached.

"Leaving so soon?"

"My wife asked for a milk shake that's only made at a place on West Ninetieth. I can be back by nine-thirty, if that's okay."

"No problem."

"Would you like one?"

"Thanks, but no thanks. I made a deal with my jeans to keep fitting in them. How's the moaner?"

"Agitated and a bit disoriented. She could probably use some more medication if it's ordered."

"I'll check. There's nothing any of us like better than sedating Maura."

"Thanks. See you in an hour."

Harry drove to the West Side through a misty rain and fairly heavy traffic. The line in Alphano's was longer than usual, the service slow enough to be irritating. He ordered an extra-thick chocolate malt. Then, wondering if Maura Hughes might be lured out of orbit, he ordered a second one. If she couldn't handle it, he would make the sacrifice.

It was nine-thirty by the time he left the ice-cream parlor, and close to ten when he reentered the hospital. After visitors' hours, only the main entrance was open. Harry crossed the deserted lobby and flashed his plastic ID at the security guard, whose desk blocked the main corridor to the hospital.

"I've got to have you sign in, Doc," the man said. "After nine."

Harry scribbled his name and destination. The guard glanced at it.

"Alexander Nine," he said. "You going up there for the Code Ninety-nine?"

At that instant, the overhead page began urgently summoning Dr. Richard Cohen to Alexander 928.

Harry hurried toward the elevators. Something had happened to Maura Hughes, he was thinking. She hadn't looked that great when he left, but she certainly hadn't seemed in imminent danger. Then suddenly he remembered that Richard Cohen was a member of the same neurosurgical group as Ben Dunleavy, Evie's neurosurgeon. Cohen was undoubtedly covering for the night. Gripped by an intense foreboding, Harry kept jabbing at the elevator call button until one of the doors slid open. The ride up to Alexander 9 took an eternity.

Room 928 was halfway down the far arm of the "L." The nurse's station and near corridor were deserted. Harry set down the bag from Alphano's and sprinted down the hallway, his heart pounding in his throat. It took only a moment after he rounded the corner to have his worst fears confirmed. There were half a dozen nurses and med students standing outside room 928, craning to catch a glimpse of the action. Maura Hughes, still restrained in her bed, had been pulled to the far side of the corridor. Standing beside her, stroking her hand, was a young, uniformed policeman.

Harry raced past them all and into the room.

The scene was one he had witnessed or participated in hundreds of times over the years. The monitors, the lines, the crash cart, the defibrillator, the nurses, physicians, and technicians moving grimly from equipment to bedside and back like a platoon of army ants. Only this time, at the center of the controlled chaos, intubated through her nose and being ventilated by a rubber bag, was his wife. The cardiac monitor showed a regular rhythm. Every ten seconds or so, though, her arms extended to the maximum and rotated inward, turning her palms away from her body in an eerily unnatural position. *Decerebrate posturing.* A horrible prognostic sign. Almost certainly, her aneurysm had blown. He moved to the bedside. The nurse, Sue Jilson, was the first to realize he was there.

"When did this happen?" he asked.

The neurosurgical resident who was running the resuscitation looked up.

"This is Dr. Corbett, her husband," the nurse explained.

"Oh, sorry," the resident said. "Her aneurysm appears to have ruptured. Dr. Cohen is covering for Dr. Dunleavy. I just got word that he's on the way up."

"What happened?" Harry asked. "I left her just a little over an hour ago and she was fine."

Sue Jilson shook her head.

"About half an hour after you left I went in to medicate Maura. I heard a moan from behind the curtain. When I looked, your wife had vomited and was barely conscious. The initial blood pressure reading I got was three hundred over one-fifty. One pupil was already larger than the other."

Harry stared down at Evie, his mind unwilling to connect what he was seeing with what he knew of cerebral hemorrhaging. He reached down and gently lifted her eyelids. Both of her pupils were so wide that almost no iris color could be seen. He felt numb, dreamlike. It was already over.

Dr. Richard Cohen rushed into the room. He already knew the patient's history, he breathlessly told the resident. The resident gave him a capsule summary of the past thirty-eight minutes.

"You've done everything right," Cohen said as he examined the inside of Evie's eyes with an ophthalmoscope.

He quickly checked her reflexes and response to pain. Then he used the end of his reflex hammer to firmly stroke an arc along the soles of her feet from heel to great toe. The Babinski reflex—the great toe pulling up instead of curling down—was a grave, grave sign that her cerebral cortex, the thinking part of her brain, was no longer influencing the movements of her body. Harry watched, stunned.

"We'll get a CT scan," Cohen said grimly, "but in all honesty, I don't think we can get her to the OR. The brain swelling is enormous. Both of her optic discs are showing severe papilledema."

Papilledema—the optic nerve engorgement caused by marked, usually irreversible pressure within the skull. The finding made the evolving scene even more surreal.

"She . . . she doesn't want any heroic measures," Harry heard himself saying.

"Arterial line's in," another resident called out. "Her systolic is still two-ninety."

"That's very strange," Cohen said. "We've given her a huge amount of antihypertensives already, but her pressure hasn't budged."

"But wouldn't you expect her pressure to be up like this with a large hemorrhage?" Harry asked.

"Temporarily, maybe. Most CNS bleeds do have a period of marked rise. But they almost always respond to conventional treatment, and the residents have already gone well beyond that."

"Oh, God," Harry whispered, still feeling detached and unreal.

"We'll keep trying to get her pressure down," the neurosurgeon said. "And we'll get a CT to document what we already know. Meanwhile, Harry, difficult as it is under these circumstances, there's something you should be thinking about."

"I understand," Harry murmured.

Evie was a young, completely healthy woman, whose only organic problem was her aneurysm. At the moment, she was the sort of prize coveted by every organ transplant specialist—a source of life or sight for any number of people.

"Let's get the scan and then I'll let you know," Harry said. "Meanwhile, go ahead and begin tissue typing."

CHAPTER 7

After half an hour, the battle to control Evie's astronomical blood pressure was finally won. But everyone involved in the case knew that the war had already been lost. Harry stood helplessly by the door as the respiratory technician adjusted the controls on the ventilator that was now Evie's only link to life. There were IVs in both her arms and tubes into her stomach, bladder, and lungs. Every minute or two, in response to nothing in particular, her entire body would tighten and extend into a decerebrate posture. This nightmarish scene was one he had witnessed many times in his professional life and in Nam. But emotionally he had never become very adept at dealing with it.

There was inevitably a part of him unwilling to accept the simple truth that it was over.

Wait. Give me another five minutes. Just be patient. This woman's going to get right up and walk out of here. . . . You'll see. . . .

"No, thank you," he replied to a nurse who offered him coffee. "I . . . I've got to call Evie's folks."

He glanced at the corridor behind him. Maura Hughes seemed calmer. Her brother, a carrottop with a face too youthful for the uniform he wore, continued stroking her hand as he watched the unfolding horror in room 928. It was quarter of eleven. The CT scanner would be free in five minutes. Blood samples had been sent off to the lab for tissue typing. On the way back from the CT scan, assuming nothing had come up that would send her to the operating room, Evie would get the first of what would probably be a series of electroencephalograms. Two flat or near flat EEGs twelve hours apart were considered to be the electrophysiologic equivalent of death. Harry reached up unaware and brushed aside a tear that had worked its way to the top of one cheek.

"Corbett, what in the hell is going on here?"

Still half-dazed, Harry turned toward the voice. Caspar Sidonis stood several feet away, hands on hips, his expression pinched and angry.

"I don't know what you're talking about," Harry managed. "But right now I'm a little busy. You see, my—"

"I'm talking about Evie, dammit!" Sidonis snapped. "Oh, never mind."

He pushed past Harry and into the room. Richard Cohen, the neurosurgeon, was again checking Evie's eyes. Sue Jilson was on the other side of the bed adjusting the IV.

"Dick, what happened here?" Sidonis asked.

"Oh, hi, Caspar. This woman a patient of yours?"

"No. She's . . . she's a close friend."

"Well, her husband is right over th—"

"I don't want to hear from him, Dick. I want to hear from you. Tell me what happened."

It was a demand, not a request. Cohen, taken aback by the physician's aggressiveness, quickly regained his composure.

"You know she was pre-op for repair of a berry?"

"Yes, yes. Of course I know."

"Well, a little while ago, Sue Jilson, here, came in and found her unresponsive, with one blown pupil and a systolic pressure of over three hundred. We've thrown the whole pharmacy at her and we've still had a bitch of a time getting her pressure down to one-thirty, where it is now. Meanwhile, her other pupil's blown. She has bilateral papilledema indicative of massive intracranial pressure, and she's posturing."

"Jesus." Sidonis looked shaken.

From the doorway, Harry watched, stunned, as the cardiac surgeon reached down and took one of Evie's hands gently in his.

Then, with his other hand, he caressed her cheek. Richard Cohen looked on nonplussed. Sue Jilson was wide-eyed.

"Dick, does she have any chance at all?" Sidonis asked.

To any physician, let alone one of Sidonis's pedigree, the answer to the question was inescapable. The neurosurgeon looked at him queerly.

"I . . . um . . . I don't think so, Caspar," he said. "We're waiting to take her down for a CT and an EEG."

"Was he in here with her?" Sidonis gestured toward the doorway.

"Pardon?"

It was only now that Harry shook off his own reluctant fascination with what was transpiring and moved into the room. As far as he knew, Sidonis and Evie might have met in passing at some staff party or other. But certainly she had never spoken of the man.

"Caspar, do you know my wife?"

Sidonis whirled like a startled cat. "You know damn well I do. Were you in here with her before . . . before this happened?"

"Of course I was with her. She's my wife. Now, just what in the hell—"

"Dick, was anyone else in here after him?"

"What?"

"I said, was anyone else in here with Evie after Corbett?" Sidonis was nearly shouting.

"Caspar, calm down. Calm down," Cohen said. "Let's go out in the hall and talk."

Leaving the respiratory technician behind, the three physicians left the room, followed by Sue Jilson.

"Now, what's this all about?" Cohen whispered. "Does this have something to do with the meeting this morning?"

Sidonis's fury was barely under control. He spoke loudly, without regard for Maura Hughes, her brother, or the two residents standing nearby.

"All I asked was whether anyone else came into this room between the time Corbett—excuse me, *Dr.* Corbett—left, and the time Evie was found."

"I think I can answer that question," Sue Jilson said. "There was no one else. Dr. Corbett didn't leave until eight-forty-seven. That's in my notes. The only way onto the hall after eight is through the elevators and past the nurse's station. Officer Hughes—that's Maura's brother, the man with her over there— arrived on the floor around nine-thirty, but we were already in with Mrs. Corbett. You can check with Alice Broglio, the other nurse on the floor, but I'm sure she'll confirm what I've said."

"I knew it." Sidonis's fists were clenched.

"Caspar, will you please tell us what this is all about," Cohen demanded.

"Ask him."

"Harry?"

"I have no idea what's going on," Harry said.

"Bullshit," Sidonis snapped. "Evie was leaving you to be with me, and you know it. She told you so last night at the restaurant she took you to. The SeaGrill. See, I even know the place. Now, what did you do to her?"

"You son of a bitch—"

Harry's burst of anger and hatred was almost immediately washed away by a consuming despair. There was no reason for him to doubt what he was hearing. Evie and goddamn Caspar Sidonis. Suddenly, so much made sense. The months and months of coolness and distance. The odd hours she kept. The trips out of town. The excuses for avoiding sex. Yesterday's cryptic call. *"Harry, I need to talk to you"* . . . Sidonis!

You're lying, he wanted to shout. *You son of a bitch, you're lying!* But he knew the man wasn't. For months he had felt as if he was battling a persistent, inexplicable sadness. Now he understood what he was really responding to. Without another word, he left the group and walked back into room 928.

"Give me a minute, will you?" he said to the respiratory technician. "I'll call you if there's any problem."

He turned off the bright overhead light, pulled a chair to Evie's bedside, and sat down. Beside him, the ventilator whirred softly, then delivered a jet of oxygen-enriched air into Evie's lungs, paused, then whirred again. It had been nearly ten years since they first met. *Ten years.* They had been fixed up by a mutual friend who felt certain that each was exactly what the other needed. Harry would acquire adventure, spontaneity, and some stamps in his nearly barren passport. Evie would get some desperately needed serenity and stability. She would be the sail, he the rudder. And it had worked, too. At least for a while. In the end, though, she never was able to change in the ways she had hoped to. She just . . . just wanted more. That's all.

"Dammit, Evie," he said softly, "why couldn't you at least have talked to me? Told me what was going on? Why couldn't you have given us a *chance?*"

He reached through the bedrail and took her hand. It had been stupid and naive to believe she could become a different person—or even that she truly wanted to.

A hand settled gently on his shoulder.

"Harry, are you okay?"

Doug Atwater looked down at him with concern.

"Huh? Oh hi, Doug. Actually, no. No, I'm not okay at all."

"What's with Sidonis? He's over at the nurse's station right now, phoning the medical examiner and the police. I asked him what was going on, and he just glared at me. For a moment I thought he was going to tell me to go screw myself."

Harry shook his head. This was a nightmare. *The medical examiner . . . the police . . .*

"Doug, I don't know what's going on. Evie's aneurysm has blown. She's not going to make it."

"Oh, God."

"Sidonis just announced that he's been sleeping with her and that she was going to leave me for him. He thinks she told me so last night, but she didn't."

"Oh, Harry. I'm so sorry, pal."

"Yeah. What are you doing here at this hour anyway?"

"Anneke and I were at a film. I just stopped by to pick up some papers, and the guard downstairs told me what was going on. I left Anneke in my office and came up here. Why is Sidonis calling the police?"

Harry loosened his grasp and and moved away from the bed. The thought of Caspar Sidonis touching his wife was at once saddening and repulsive.

"I was the last one in with her. He must think . . . actually, I don't give a shit what he thinks."

He left the room with Doug Atwater close behind. Transportation had just arrived to bring Evie down for her scan. Richard Cohen looked at Harry and shrugged.

"Harry, Caspar's gone to call the ME and the police. He's sure you gave your wife something to cause her pressure to skyrocket—some sort of pressor drug. I think maybe I should call Bob Lord and Owen, let them know what's going on."

Lord was the chief of the medical staff. Owen Erdman was president of the hospital.

"Call anybody you want," Harry said. "This is ridiculous."

"I'll call Owen," Atwater offered. "Is Sidonis crazy or what, Richard?"

"I don't know about crazy," the neurosurgeon replied, "but he's definitely furious. Harry, he says he spoke to your wife just as you two were leaving the house last night, and that she swore she was going to tell you about the two of them."

"She didn't tell me anything."

"Well, listen. We've got to get going. I'll call Lord from X ray. Stick around here, will you? As soon as I've seen the CT I'll be back up to speak to you. The EEG tech is on the way in, but she lives in the Bronx."

With the respiratory technician breathing for Evie with a rubber Ambu bag, the transportation worker guided her bed toward the elevator. Cohen and Sue Jilson followed, along with the two residents who had remained nearby at Cohen's request.

Doug Atwater glanced over at Maura Hughes.

"Evie's roommate," Harry explained. "The cop's her brother. She's in the DTs."

"In the DTs right now?"

"I think they've got her pretty heavily medicated. Doug, I just don't believe this is happening."

Atwater led Harry over to a molded plastic chair and motioned him to sit.

"You going to stay here in the hospital?" he asked, lowering to one knee.

"I . . . I guess so. At least until the studies are all back. Cohen wants my permission to have Evie donate her organs. I'm probably going to have to decide before morning."

"Oh, shit."

Atwater knew them as a couple about as well as anyone at

the hospital did. He had been a dinner guest at their home twice, and had double-dated with them on at least two other occasions, although the last time was probably two or three years ago. He was charming, outgoing, and at times—especially when he had had a few drinks—extremely witty. More than once, Evie had spoken of fixing him up with one or another of her friends. However, Harry recalled now, as their marriage deteriorated she had stopped suggesting a fix-up, and instead frequently encouraged him to join Doug for a "boy's night out." *Small wonder.*

"I thought Sidonis was married," Harry said.

"Not as long as I've been here. He has a kid or two somewhere. I know that much. But mostly he's married to the OR, plus his stockbroker, his publicity agent, and of course his mirror. I had even heard rumors he was gay."

Harry laughed bitterly.

"Guess not," he said.

"Listen, Harry, I'd better go call Owen. I need to check on Anneke, too. Do you want me to say something to Sido—never mind. Here he comes."

Sidonis bore down on them.

"The medical examiner's called the lab and ordered some blood samples on Evie," he announced triumphantly. "And there's a Detective Dickinson on his way over. He'd like it if you could stay until he gets here."

"I'm not going anyplace. But I have nothing to say to him or anyone else you bring in."

"Caspar," Doug said, "why are you doing this?"

Sidonis eyed the executive suspiciously. Clearly, he had placed Atwater among the enemy.

"You really don't know?" he said finally. "Evie and I have been seeing each other for over a year. Last night she told Harry she was leaving him. Tonight she checks in here with perfectly normal blood pressure, and not one symptom of her aneurysm for a month. He goes into her room, she's fine. He leaves, and not half an hour later her blood pressure's three hundred plus and her aneurysm has blown. Wouldn't you be suspicious?"

Atwater held the surgeon's gaze.

"If I didn't know Harry Corbett I might be," he said. "But you're way off base. And if what you say is true about you and this man's wife, someone ought to kick the shit out of you for busting up their marriage. Now, if you'll excuse me, I'm going to phone Owen Erdman and let him know what you've been up to. Harry, I'll be back a little later. Be cool."

"Now just a second," Sidonis protested, hurrying after him. "If you're calling Erdman I want to talk with him. . . ."

He was still railing when he and Doug Atwater disappeared around the corner of the hallway. Suddenly, the corridor was silent.

"Um . . . excuse me."

"Huh?" Harry looked around. Maura Hughes's brother, still by her bedside, cleared his throat and self-consciously smoothed his uniform shirt. Harry noticed the three stripes on his immaculate uniform. A sergeant, then.

"I'm Tom Hughes," he said, his speech free of all but a hint of New York. "Maura's my sister."

"Hi," Harry said flatly. He felt embarrassed that the policeman had been witness to Sidonis's outburst and disclosure. But in truth, not that much.

"I . . . um . . . I'm sorry for what you've been going through."

"Thanks."

"Maura says you've been very kind to her." He looked back at where his sister lay. She was asleep and snoring somewhat unnaturally. "I guess the sedation has kicked in."

"It would seem so."

"Look, I don't mean to butt in, but standing where I've been, it was impossible for me not to hear."

"Yeah."

Harry felt suddenly awkward sitting. He also felt incapable of maintaining a conversation—even one as superficial as this. He stood up and pushed the plastic chair away with the toe of his shoe. He still hadn't called Evie's family. Maybe he should call Steve Josephson as well. In anticipation of Evie's surgery, he had already canceled his morning patients and signed out to Steve until one. Maybe he should call and make it the whole day.

"Look, I'm sorry for blabbering on like this," Hughes said. "I know you've got a lot on your mind and the weight of the world on your shoulders. But there's something I really need to tell you."

Harry hesitated, then crossed the corridor.

"That doctor," Hughes went on in a near whisper, "the dark-haired one, the one who claims—"

"Yes, yes, I know who you mean. Sidonis."

"Well, Dr. Sidonis seems to be making a big deal over the report from the nurse that you were the last one in with your wife before she got so—"

"Yes."

"Well, you weren't."

"What?"

"You weren't the last one. There was a man in with her shortly after you left. A doctor, in fact."

"Are you sure?"

Tom Hughes thought for a few seconds before he responded.

"Pretty sure," he said finally. "No, make that very sure."

"But . . . but how do you know that?"

Again the policeman hesitated, his gaze fixed on one of the bed wheels. When he looked at Harry again, his expression was sheepish.

"My sister told me so," he said.

CHAPTER 8

"I'm sure she doesn't look it to you right now, but Maura really is a very special, very talented, very *good* person."

After just a few minutes of conversation with Tom Hughes, several things had become quite clear to Harry: although young, Hughes was very intelligent and as sharp as any policeman he had ever met; and despite his older sister's obvious problems, he was absolutely devoted to her. He was also convinced that the man she claimed to have seen enter her hospital room had actually been there.

"A doctor in a white clinic coat came in shortly after you left," Hughes related to Harry. "Maura was apparently hollering at the time—she said something to me about the nurses never paying any attention to her unless she makes noise. The doctor smiled at her, stroked her forehead, leaned over, and whispered to her to just relax. Then he went around the curtain, spoke with your wife for a short while, and left. He was in his thirties or early forties, five foot eight or so, with brown hair closely cut, unusually dark brown eyes, a large diamond ring on the little finger of his left hand, and a blue and green clip-on tie."

"A clip-on? How could she know that?"

"I'm telling you, drunk or sober, or even in the DTs, my sister is a remarkable woman. She's an artist, a painter, and she has an incredible eye for detail."

Harry recalled the quickness with which she had spotted his lapel pin.

I notice things, she had said.

"Well, maybe some doctor came up the back way, or slipped past the nurses."

"Slipped past the nurses maybe," Tom said. "But not came up the back way. The door is locked and alarmed after eight. The nurse warned me about that when I called to ask if I could come in late tonight. Anyone who comes on or off any floor in this building after eight has to come by elevator and check in at the nurse's station."

"I guess I knew that," Harry said. "I mean I've only worked here for a decade or two. Why didn't you say something about this mystery doc to Sidonis or the nurses?"

"The way things were going down, there really wasn't much chance for me to say anything to anyone. Besides, they're not very fond of my sister here on Alexander Nine. I hardly think they would give much credence to anything she has to say—especially if it conflicts with what *they* say."

"I think you're probably right."

It was after eleven now. Rather than disturb the overextended staff on Alexander 9, the two of them had wheeled Maura back to her spot in room 928. Fifteen minutes later, the call Harry dreaded had come from neurosurgeon Richard Cohen. Evie was still in the CT scanner, but the initial images were as bad as they had feared. The hemorrhage was massive. The rapid swelling and pressure had forced a portion of her brain through the bony ridge at the base of her skull, totally and irreversibly cutting off circulation to her cerebral cortex—the gray matter responsible for all thought. Surgery was no longer even a long-shot possibility. All that remained was a series of EEGs . . . and a decision.

As Maura Hughes continued her stertorous, unnatural sleep, Harry sat opposite her brother in the dimly lit room. As much as he wanted to be alone to sort out what had transpired with Sidonis and to deal with the decision he would shortly be asked to make, he was grateful for the man's company.

"No one's been able to explain to me what the DTs is, or why my sister got it," Hughes said. "She definitely was on a bender when she fell, but I know a lot of people who are much heavier drinkers than she is and never seem to get into trouble."

"Most alcoholics coming off alcohol just get the shakes and some intestinal stuff," Harry explained. "There are two really frightening things they *can* get: seizures and DTs. Seizures usually happen in the first day or two. The DTs come on later—two days to a week or even more after the last drink. We have no way of predicting whether they'll happen at all."

"But Maura's pretty damn lucid about some things—even while she's seeing the bugs and such."

"All I can say is, that is not unusual. The mix of fantasy and reality is unexplainable. You know, I take care of a fairly large number of alcoholics in my practice. Many of them have been sober for years, some of them against monstrous odds. If you and she would like, I can have one or two of them stop by and speak with her."

"You mean AA?"

"Possibly."

"I've tried to get her to go to AA. But she never would go. Too much pride, I guess."

"Maybe you should take some videos or Polaroids of her right now."

Tom Hughes grinned at the suggestion.

"Maybe I should at that," he said. "Dr. Corbett, do you mind if I ask you a little about what's going on between you and that other doctor?"

"Sidonis?" Harry shrugged. "I think you've heard most of it already. He claims my wife has been having an affair with him, and that she planned to leave me for him. He thinks she told me all about it last night at the restaurant we went to. He even knew the name of the place. Now that I look back on our evening, I think Evie actually wanted to tell me. But she never did."

"So you believe him? I mean, there *is* another possibility. He could have been obsessed with your wife and followed you to that restaurant."

Harry looked down at the floor and swallowed at the fullness that had again begun building in his throat.

"No," he said finally. "I believe him."

"And he thinks that because of what you knew, you gave something to your wife to . . . to what?"

"To send her blood pressure up high enough to cause her cerebral aneurysm to rupture."

"God. Are there such drugs?"

"A number of them, actually. They're called pressors. We use them to treat shock, which essentially is dangerously *low* blood pressure."

"So this stuff—this pressor medication—is what? Injected? Or is it a pill, or a liquid of some sort?"

Harry smiled grimly.

"No, no," he said. "Not by mouth. The patients who need a medication like that are in too much trouble to take anything by—"

"What is it? . . . Dr. Corbett?"

Harry was on his feet.

"Maybe nothing," he said. "But it just occurred to me. Evie had an IV in her arm. D-five-W—five percent sugar water. It was what we call a KO infusion. Keep open. Just fast enough to keep the plastic catheter in her vein from clotting off."

"So?"

"It seemed a little unusual to me that she should have one in place the night before her surgery, especially when she had been so stable for so long. I even asked her who ordered it. She thought it was the anesthesiologist. But usually they establish their IVs in the OR." He headed out of the room. "If anyone calls, I'm at the nurse's station. I'll be back in a few minutes."

The order in Evie's chart read:

> *D5W; 1000cc; K.O. @ 50cc/hr.*
> *T.O. Dr. Baraswatti.*

T.O.—telephone order. Harry skimmed through the record. Baraswatti had seen Evie late in the afternoon for the preoperative history and physical required of every patient who was to receive general anesthesia. *Four-fifteen*, the nurse's note read. However, the order for the IV wasn't phoned in until six-thirty.

Harry dialed the hospital operator. Dr. Baraswatti was still the anesthesiologist on duty in the hospital. He made no attempt to mask the fact that Harry's call had awakened him.

"I don't know what you're talking about, Dr. Corbett," he said in a clipped Indian accent. "I always insert my IVs in the operating room. Why should I wish to do otherwise?"

"I . . . I don't know," Harry mumbled. He set the receiver down as the anesthesiologist was asking if there were any other questions he could answer.

Harry sat on the edge of the counter and carefully reviewed Evie's chart. She had arrived on Alexander 9 at one-thirty. At four-thirty the anesthesiologist had come up, examined her, and written preoperative orders. At six-thirty someone claiming to be that anesthesiologist had called the floor nurse and ordered a keep open dextrose infusion to be put in place. The nurse had notified the intravenous nurse on duty for the hospital. At six-fifty, the IV nurse's notes stated, she had placed an 18-gauge angiocath in Evie's left hand. A few hours later, at least according to Maura Hughes, a physician had entered their room. And a short time after that, Evie's aneurysm had burst—either as a result of, *or resulting in*, a systolic blood pressure of over three hundred.

Now, Caspar Sidonis was accusing Harry of the intravenous injection of some sort of pressor that had caused the catastrophe. Was it possible Harry was being set up by Sidonis? The physician described by Maura—real or figment—bore no resemblance to the arrogant cardiac surgeon, who was significantly taller than five eight and had thick, jet hair and a mustache. *Something was wrong . . . very wrong.* Bewildered and apprehensive, Harry returned to room 928.

Maura Hughes was awake and thrashing about.

"Right after you left she started moaning like she was in pain or maybe having a nightmare," Tom explained. "Then suddenly, like a shot, she woke up. She's all over the place right now, fighting the restraints and hallucinating even worse than she was before."

"Go ahead and ring for the nurse," Harry said. Noting that Maura was drenched in sweat, he toweled her face off and assured himself that her IV was open and running. She looked stressed, but not in danger. "It's probably just the sedation wearing off. None of the medicine we use actually changes what's going on in a DT patient's head. All it does is blunt their reaction to it. I'll check her over."

"Gene, Gene, don't be mean," Maura sang, thrashing against her restraints. She smiled up at him and suddenly adopted a Dixie accent that would have made Scarlett O'Hara proud. "I swear on my mother's grave, darlin', if you'd just get these fuckin' bugs off me I'd be all right. I'd be fine."

Using his own stethoscope and pocket ophthalmoscope, Harry did as good an exam as possible under the circumstances. Maura neither helped him nor fought him. Instead, she kept up a constant verbal stream as she tried to brush away the crawlies. The nurse checked in over the intercom. She was in the conference room getting the change-of-shift report. Unless there was real trouble, she would be in after they were done.

"I don't find anything to worry about," Harry said to Tom. "I think we're just seeing what her condition is like without the mask of tranquiliz—"

"Hey, I'm looking for someone named Sidonis. Dr. Cash Sidonis. Something like that."

Harry and Tom turned toward the door. A sallow, balding man in a polyester suit stood appraising them. He was holding a frayed, spiral-bound, stenographer's notepad from which he had read Sidonis's name. His small, sunken eyes were enveloped in shadow. From six feet away Harry could smell a two- or three-pack-a-day tobacco habit.

"Lieutenant Dickinson!" Tom exclaimed.

Squinting, the man bobbed his finger at Tom, trying to place him.

"The Yalie, right?"

Tom grimaced.

"Yes, I guess you could call me that. I'm Tom Hughes. This is Dr. Harry Corbett. Harry, this is Lieutenant Albert Dickinson. He's a detective in the two-eight. They have an opening for a detective there that I've interviewed for. He was on the panel."

"You and about half the force," Dickinson said, none too kindly. "I wouldn't count on nothing if I was you. The competition is fierce. *Fierce.* Some of the PR people and the image people think being a Yalie is to your credit. But a lot of us who work the streets ain't so sure. A lot of us look for the guy with the degree from the College of Hard Knocks, if you know what I mean. Good ol' Fuck U."

His hoarse laugh dissolved into a hacking cough. Tom remained outwardly unfazed. Harry wondered if the man's abominable rudeness was some sort of test.

"They call anyone they think graduated from college a Yalie," Tom explained pleasantly enough. "In my case, not that it matters, it happens to be true."

"Corbett, huh," Dickinson said. "You're the guy Sidonis's complaining about. After I talk to him, I want to talk to you. Bastard must have some clout to have them send me here on a night like this. Some fucking clout."

"Dammit, get off me!" Maura shouted. "Boogery little ants. Get off! I'm sick of this!"

Dickinson glanced over at her dispassionately. "Whozis?" he said, jerking his head toward the bed.

"She's . . . um . . . she's my sister Maura," Tom said, forcing himself to stand just a bit straighter.

Harry noticed that one of Tom's fists—the one out of Dickinson's line of sight—was clenched. Dickinson peered at Maura again. In ten seconds his assessment was complete. Maura Hughes was a hopeless drunk.

"Hey, do you two know why the Irish got the whiskey and the A-rabs got the oil?" he asked suddenly. "Give up? It's becuz the Irish got to pick first."

He was launching into another mucous laugh when Maura spat at him. From eight or so feet away she missed by only a foot.

"Bitch," Dickinson muttered, checking to be sure he hadn't been spattered.

"Pinhead," Maura shot back.

The night-shift nurse interrupted via the intercom.

"Is there a Detective Dickinson in the room? If there is, you were supposed to check in at the nurse's station before going into any patient room. Also, Dr. Sidonis is here to see you. He's in the conference room by the nurse's station."

Dickinson looked at Harry. "Don't go away, Corbett," he said. "You neither, Yalie."

He shoved his notebook in his suit-coat pocket and left the room. Tom waited until he was certain the man was out of ear-shot.

"This is not going to be fun," he said. "Dickinson is totally burnt-out. He wouldn't go an extra inch to help his own mother."

"But he's on a panel that picks who's going to make detective."

"NYPD logic all the way. I've been told I'm the leading candidate to get the promotion, but as you just heard, you never know. I really could've done without this little encounter with Albert D."

"Sorry."

"It's not your fault. Look, don't worry about him. Albert'll annoy you with a few questions from the detective's how-to manual just to have something to put on his report. Then, when he realizes there isn't any reason to suspect foul play, he'll leave and spend the next hour or two at Dunkin' Donuts."

"But there is," Harry said.

"Is what?"

"Reason to suspect foul play."

CHAPTER 9

Harry recounted in detail for Tom Hughes his call to the anesthesiologist and his review of Evie's chart. He was just finishing when Evie was wheeled back in. Shaken by the sight of her, Harry realized that he had already begun to think of her, of their life together, in the past tense. To all intents, the woman he had been married to for nine years was dead.

"The EEG showed a little activity," Richard Cohen reported as she was being reconnected to the monitoring and respiratory systems, "but not much. Certainly not enough to keep the various teams from moving forward if you give the word. As you know, time is pretty crucial here. Organs do begin to break down."

"I know," Harry said. "When do you plan to do a second EEG?"

"Ten in the morning."

Harry looked down at his wife. Over his twenty-five years as an M.D., he had shared every conceivable experience involving death and bereavement. But none of those experiences prepared him for this. A few short hours ago, she was the most important person in his life. A few short hours ago, Sidonis or not, they still had the chance to turn their marriage around, to make it work again. But suddenly, it was over. And now, he was being asked to validate Evie's death by authorizing the donation of her vital organs. He had always been supportive to families in such situations. When he needed them, the right words had come. But he had never had to make the decision himself.

"Leave the papers at the nurse's station," he heard himself say. "I'll sign them before I leave. But I want to see her in the morning before anyone moves ahead with this."

"I'll see to it."

Cohen thanked him, murmured a brief, somewhat uncomfortable condolence, and left the room. Moments later, her adjustments on the ventilator completed, the respiratory technician followed. Sue Jilson checked Evie's blood pressure and monitor pattern, and then turned to Harry.

"The CT tech took this off your wife," she said coolly, handing Harry the diamond pendant from Tiffany's. "I didn't see any sense in putting it back on her."

Harry looked at her stonily.

"I do," he said.

He hooked the necklace back in place. When he turned around again, he and Tom Hughes were alone with the two patients. Maura continued her almost nonstop prattle, pausing only to pick tormentors off the bedclothes. The ventilator connected to Evie again was whirring softly as it provided oxygen to organs that were now of value only when considered individually.

Tom turned off the overhead light, leaving only the dim over-the-bed fluorescents.

"I'm really sorry for everything you're going through," he said.

Harry glanced over at his wife.

"Thanks," Harry managed to say.

"If you want to talk some more about it, I have the time, and I'm not at all tired."

"In the hall, maybe," Harry said. "Not in here."

They dragged their chairs outside the door. The corridor was dimly lit and silent, save for the white noise of night in the hospital.

"You don't have to keep talking about your wife if it's too hard for you," Hughes said.

"It actually might help."

"Okay. Just don't be embarrassed to tell me to shut up. I confess that as a cop, what little you've told me so far has me intrigued. What do you think is going on?"

"I have no idea. There's probably a stupid, simple explanation for everything. The nurse who took the telephone order got the anesthesiologist's name wrong. . . . Some M.D. friend of ours was on the floor seeing another patient and stopped by to see Evie—"

"That's *two* simple explanations. In my experience, when you need to invoke more than one explanation for things happening coincidentally, none of them is the true story. Would you mind going back into the room with me for a minute?"

Harry considered the request, then followed him in.

Hughes began pacing deliberately around first Maura's bed, then Evie's, checking the walls, the light switches, and the beds themselves. Maura watched him curiously.

"Rather than assume the most benign explanation," Tom said, continuing his inspection, "for the moment let's assume the worst. Some doctor—or perhaps someone planning to pose as a doctor—called in an order to have an IV started in your wife's arm and gave the real anesthesiologist-on-duty's name. Later, he entered this room, unseen by the nurses, spoke to my sister, then administered a pressor drug to your wife. Then he left the floor, again managing to avoid being spotted by anyone. We need a motive for why he would have done such a thing, and an explanation as to how he could have made it on and off the floor without being spotted."

"Dickinson made it in here without being seen."

"One way, he did. The nurses were in their change of shift report when he came on the floor. But having *two* such opportunities—onto the floor, then off again—let alone planning on them, is asking a bit much."

"So what are you looking for now?"

"Places where our mystery doctor might have left a fingerprint or two. Too bad we don't have prints of every M.D. on the—"

"Okay, Dr. Corbett," Albert Dickinson cut in. "I guess it's time you and I had a little talk." The detective, leaning against the doorjamb, sighed wearily. "I'm required to tell you that you have the right to remain silent, but that anything you choose to say may and will be used against you in a court of law. You—"

"Wait a minute," Tom said. "Why are you reading him Miranda? Is he being arrested?"

"Not yet, but he will be. I just thought I'd get through the formalities."

"Lieutenant Dickinson," Hughes went on, "there are some things you don't know about what's gone on here."

"You wanna know what I *do* know, Yalie? I know that no matter how much they got—sex, money, power, drugs, or whatever—doctors always want more. That's just the way they are. Give me an unsolved crime where one of ten suspects is a doctor, and my money's on the doc every time. Now, Dr. Corbett, if you'd like to—"

"Lieutenant, another doctor came in to see Mrs. Corbett after Harry left here tonight," Tom Hughes said.

"There was no one. The next person to come on this floor after Dr. Corbett left here was you. And by that time, Mrs. Corbett was already on the chute. I checked with the nurses. They have all visitors logged."

"Well, the nurses are wrong. Someone was here. A white male in his forties wearing a white clinic coat. Five eight, brown hair, brown eyes."

"Who says?"

Tom's expression suggested that he was expecting the question but still had found no easy way around having to answer it.

"My sister," he said boldly. "The man spoke to her, then went around the curtain to Mrs. Corbett, and then left. It was soon after that her aneurysm ruptured."

Dickinson smirked. "Is that what you saw, little lady?"

"Pinhead. You know, you should fire whoever made you that toupee. I could paint a piece of lettuce with shoe polish and have it look more realistic."

Dickinson smiled blandly but it was clear he had been skewered. Harry realized only then that the man *was* wearing a hairpiece. Score one more for Maura Hughes's power of observation.

"Why don't you have another drink, little lady," Dickinson said.

"Maura," Tom pleaded, "would you please stop with the wisecracks and just tell the detective what you saw?"

Maura brushed at something on her shoulder but said nothing.

"Don't bother," Harry said. "I don't think the detective is going to pay much attention. Come on, Lieutenant. Let's get this over with."

"Lieutenant Dickinson," Tom asked, "do you think it would be worthwhile calling someone over from forensics?"

"For what?"

"Maybe the doctor who was here left some prints."

"Fingerprint a hospital room, huh. Sounds like a great idea to me, Yalie. I mean there couldn't have been more than, oh, one or two hundred people in here over the last day."

"Almost everyone who's been in this room, including the doctors, has a set of fingerprints on file with hospital security," Harry said. "It's been hospital policy for years, ever since a convicted child molester lied on his application and got a job as an orderly on the pediatric unit."

"Great. I'm sure forensics will be thrilled to come out on a night like this because a woman in the goddamn DTs claims she saw someone that not a single other person on this whole floor saw."

"I'm telling you, I know my sister, and I know that there was someone here."

"And I'm telling you, spiders and ants and giant snakes don't leave fingerprints. Now, Corbett, let's get this over. You'll feel much better when you get everything off your chest. . . ."

It was well after midnight by the time Harry finished responding to Albert Dickinson's unemotional and uninspired interrogation. The detective had clearly made up his mind that the scenario fed to him by Caspar Sidonis was the correct one. Harry, unwilling to allow his wife to run off with another man, had administered a blood-pressure-raising agent to her. Her death would appear to be due to the rupture of her aneurysm, and no questions would be asked. Now, samples of her blood were being sent to the state lab for analysis. If any unusual substances were found, especially ones related to raising blood pressure, there was a good chance that a warrant would be issued for Harry's arrest.

"Motive, method, opportunity," Dickinson said. "Right now, all we're missing is the method."

Harry saw no point in telling the hostile detective about the telephone order to start an IV on Evie. Pramod Baraswatti would undoubtedly check with the floor first thing in the morning. An incident report would be filed, and sooner or later, word would trickle back to Dickinson. His conclusion would, of course, be that Harry had made the call himself, setting up a port for his lethal injection.

Motive, method, opportunity.

He followed Harry back to the room.

"Yalie, I want a cop here as long as she's alive and he's on the floor."

"She's already been pronounced clinically dead," Hughes said.

"Look, are you gonna make me send someone else in here, or are you gonna show us that you're a fucking team player?"

"Some team," Hughes muttered.

"What did you say?"

"I said I'll stay here and protect her."

"That's what I thought. I've already told the nurses that I don't want him alone with her as long as she's alive."

"But—"

"Is that clear?"

"Sure, Lieutenant."

Harry followed Dickinson down the hall and watched until the elevator doors closed behind him.

"He gone?" Hughes asked when Harry returned.

"For now. He says that as soon as anything shows up in Evie's blood, I'll be arrested."

"Do you think something will?"

Harry rubbed at the persistent stinging in his eyes.

"I don't know what the hell to think," he said. "What an asshole that man is. I mean, the least he could have done was call someone in for the fingerprints. I agree it's a long shot, but it's a no shot at *all* if—"

"We don't need him," Tom said, leading Harry back toward the elevators.

"What?"

"We've got the Dweeb. He's on his way up right now."

At almost that moment, the elevator doors glided open and a slight, almost frail-looking black man emerged. He was wearing a Detroit Tigers jacket and a Detroit Lions cap, and was carrying a briefcase in one hand and a large fishing-tackle box in the other.

"Did he see you?" Tom asked.

"Nope. Walked right past me, too. I swear, Albert wouldn't see a corpse if it was hanging from his ceiling."

"I appreciate this. I really do," Tom said. "Harry Corbett, meet Lonnie Sims, also known as the Dweeb."

Sims set his tackle box down and shook Harry's hand with a linebacker's grip.

"He's with us," Tom said to the night-shift nurse as they hurried past her. "Another detective." They entered room 928. "Lonnie and I were classmates at NYU when I got my master's in criminology," he explained. "He's the best crime-scene man that school's ever produced. And he loves doing fingerprints."

"That's true, my man," Sims said, setting his tackle box on a chair and snapping it open. "That's true."

"One of my friends, Doug Atwater, has a lot of clout here," Harry said. "Actually, Tom, you probably saw him. He was here a while ago."

"Tall, good looking, sort of blondish hair?"

"That's him. Anyhow, I think he'll be able to get the print records from security or personnel, or wherever they're kept."

"Great," Sims said, slipping on rubber gloves and handing a pair to both Tom and Harry. "I have some people at the FBI lab in D.C. who can help us, too. Now, we're going to play a little acting game. Tom, do what you can to have your sister direct us, and try not to touch anything, especially those metal bed railings. Harry, you're going to play the mysterious stranger. Don't you touch anything either."

"Okay." Harry glanced past Maura's bed to where Evie lay. Even her decerebrate posturing had stopped now. She had led at least one secret life with Caspar Sidonis. Had there been others? Had one of them led to her death? He headed toward the doorway to begin his part in the performance. One thing seemed almost certain to him. The laboratory studies of Evie's blood, which could take days or even weeks to complete, were going to turn up something. And sometime tomorrow, Evie would be gone and her room scrubbed down. If they were going to have any chance at picking up the fingerprints of Doctor X, it had to be done now.

"Tell me," he said, "why do they call you Dweeb?"

Lonnie Sims glanced over at Tom.

"He . . . um . . . he did pretty well in grad school," Hughes explained. "In fact, pretty well doesn't really cover it. The truth is, if they had curved the grades in our class, only Dweeb, here, would have passed."

★　★　★

By the time Harry left the hospital, the first hint of dawn was washing over the city. The session with Lonnie Sims had taken over two hours. And as far as Harry could tell, the man was, as advertised, a genius.

"The thumb's the ticket," the Dweeb told him. "That sneaky, opposable thumb. Most forensic so-called experts dust on top of things. The key is to dust under them. Show me a lab man with floor dirt ground into the knees of his trousers, and I'll show you a man who knows what he's about."

With Maura's help, he guided Harry or Tom slow-motion through half a dozen possible scenarios, watching their movements closely and calling out, "Freeze!" whenever he wanted to check a spot for prints. The mystery Doc had not worn rubber gloves, Maura assured them. Sims dusted beneath the Formica tray tables and along the underside of the bedrails. He did the door handles and the light pulls, both sides of the headboards and footboards of both beds, and even the fixtures in the bathroom. He used special powders and an infrared light, magnifiers and a tiny, state-of-the-art camera. He lifted about fifty prints— some quite clear, some badly smudged.

In the end, he told them, if Doug Atwater could arrange access to the hospital's personnel fingerprint files, anything was possible. By the time Sims folded his tackle box, closed his briefcase, and accompanied Tom Hughes off of Alexander 9, it was 3 A.M. Harry called Phil and Evie's family. Then he sat by Evie's bedside in the darkened room for a time, his thoughts focused on nothing . . . and everything.

"You take care now, Gene," Maura said as he headed out of the room.

Harry had thought she was asleep. Only now did he realize she was quite awake and had been keeping quiet for him—for the time that might be his last alone with his wife. Perhaps her sedation had kicked in, he reasoned. Perhaps the horrors of her DTs were abating. Or perhaps she had just enough willpower to hold them off for a while.

"I will," he said. "You take care, too, Maura. And thanks for your help tonight."

On the way off the floor, he stopped at the nurse's station and signed permission for Evie's organs to be taken. The notion that somewhere, someone was about to receive the heart they had desperately been praying for did help ease the profound sadness he was feeling. But nothing helped lessen his confusion—or his sense of foreboding.

The streets were virtually deserted. Emotionally drained, Harry drove home peering through a film of gritty fatigue. He parked in the indoor garage a block from his apartment. As usual Rocky Martino, the co-op's night doorman, was asleep in a worn leather chair in clear view of anyone who chose to look through the glass front doors of the building. Although he would never admit it, Rocky was well past sixty. He would also not admit to drinking more than was healthy, or to drinking on the job, although most of the residents knew he did both. Firing him had been on the agenda of virtually every co-op meeting for as long as Harry had been part of the building. But since nothing of consequence had ever happened during Rocky's shift, and because he was a sweet guy, no action had ever been taken. Harry debated knocking on the glass, or even ringing the ancient doorbell. Finally, he took out his keys. With the first touch of metal on metal, Rocky was on his feet.

"Doc, you scared the crap out of me," he said, opening the inside door. "I thought everyone in the building was tucked in for the night. When did you go out?"

"What do you mean?"

"Well, I didn't see you go out after that Chinese food you ordered was delivered."

Harry felt his pulse jump.

"You sure it was me the food was for?"

"Of course I'm sure."

"Did you buzz me before you sent the delivery man up?" he asked.

"I . . . um . . . I think I did."

"And did the guy go right out?"

Rocky was clearly beginning to panic. He was also clearly about to lie.

"Sure," he said. "He went right up and came right down."

Harry headed for the elevator.

"Rocky, what time was that?"

"I don't know, Doc. Ten, maybe. Eleven. Why?"

Harry stepped into the elevator and held the door open.

"Because, Rocky," he said, more testily than he had meant, "I haven't been home all night, and I didn't order any Chinese food."

The apartment door was locked, but that meant nothing. They had a police lock, but he and Evie never bothered using it unless they were home. Once, when Evie had locked her keys inside, the super had gotten her in with a credit card. Harry thought about calling the police without going inside. But he was exhausted and the cops might take hours to get there.

He opened the door slowly, expecting darkness. Lights were on in the foyer and, it appeared, in every room as well. Even from where he stood, he could see that the place had been ransacked. He considered the possibility that the intruder was still inside. A sane person would definitely retreat to the lobby and call the police from there. But at that moment, Harry was feeling anything but sane. He stalked down the hall half hoping the man would jump out at him. He desperately needed someone to hit.

The apartment was empty, the carnage extensive. Every painting had been removed from the wall, every drawer opened and emptied. The mattresses had been moved and all the contents of all the closets thrown onto them. Even the rugs had been lifted. It was as if the intruder was searching for a safe. If so, he had to be disappointed. They kept little cash in the apartment, and Evie's most precious jewels—by far their most extravagant possessions—were in a safe-deposit box. Still, it seemed that a number of the most valuable portable items they owned had been taken. Evie's jewel box had been emptied. Her mink coat was gone, as was their silver, some crystal, and several small pieces of art, including a Picasso drawing Evie had taken from her first marriage that was worth maybe fifteen thousand dollars.

But it was in the small study that the most thorough work had been done. The desk drawers had been emptied and the contents screened and quite carefully set in a pile by one wall. The drawers themselves had been broken apart, the seat of the desk chair slashed. Every book from the floor-to-ceiling shelves had been opened, examined, and tossed aside. There was something wrong, Harry thought, pushing some of the mess aside with his foot. This was a robbery, all right, but a robbery with a purpose.

He wandered into the kitchen. That room had been ransacked as rudely and thoroughly as the rest of the place. He surveyed the wreckage for several minutes before noticing the four unopened white cartons on the table. Each contained a Chinese dish, now cold. Set atop one of them, in a stapled waxpaper holder, was a fortune cookie. Harry's first impulse was to heave it and the rest of the food against a wall. Instead he cracked it open.

The Beacon of Good Fortune Will Continue to Brighten Your Path, it read.

CHAPTER 10

It was almost eight when Harry finally left the wreckage of his apartment and took the crosstown bus back to the hospital. The two policemen who had been sent in response to his call had tried for a few fingerprints, but in the main, their crime-scene check was uninspired. A robbery in a Manhattan apartment was clearly of little more interest to them than a derelict shaking the coins in his cardboard cup at passersby on the street.

The officers' conclusion, arrived at after a half hour, was that this was a run-of-the-mill B and E by a professional thief who might or might not have known Harry would be staying late at the hospital. They brushed aside Harry's concern that the thief had another agenda, and told him that the best he could hope for was that some of the stolen items surfaced at a pawn-shop or fence known to the police. Meanwhile, Harry would be doing the smart thing to get what he could from his insurance company, replace whatever he wanted to, and bank any money left over.

Harry crossed the MMC lobby and headed down the corridor toward the Alexander Building elevators. All around him, it was business as usual. He wondered how many hundreds, even thousands of families he had passed over the years who were heading into the hospital just as he was today, to see a spouse or child or parent for the last time. His life with Evie had been strained and emotionally barren for a long time. But until last night, he had never completely stopped believing that they would somehow make it back to the way it once had been between them.

As he passed the nurse's station on Alexander 9, he was aware of the sideways glances and changes in conversation. No doubt the tale of Caspar Sidonis's accusation had already reached the outermost branches of the hospital grapevine. He had never enjoyed being the subject of gossip, negative or positive. Now, he shuddered to think of the distortions the Sidonis story had undergone from one retelling to the next; the simple truth was bad enough. He also knew that unless explanations surfaced for the telephone order that established Evie's IV and for Maura Hughes's mystery doc, there would be more tales to come. Many more.

Evie's parents, Carmine and Dorothy DellaRosa, were seated silently at Evie's bedside. A retired postman and an administrative secretary, married well over forty years, they were pillars of the Catholic church in their small New Jersey town. They were also as ordinary and reserved as their daughter was vibrant and spectacular. Evie was their only child.

Harry shook hands with Carmine and kissed Dorothy on the cheek. The couple had always been cordial enough toward him, but could not at their most open ever be considered warm. *New Jersey Gothic*, Evie sometimes called them.

"We think Evelyn moved her arms," Dorothy said.

"She might have. There are reflexes that cause muscles to contract. They don't really mean anything though, Dorothy. I can't let you think they do." Harry gestured to Maura's bed, which was empty and freshly made. "Where's the woman who was here?"

"Down the hall in a new room, poor soul," Dorothy responded. "The nurses said a bed just came open. They didn't want her disturbing these . . . these moments."

Harry knew that unless he asked Carmine DellaRosa a direct question, and then only one he was uniquely qualified to answer, Carmine would let his wife do the speaking for the two of them. Harry had decided against sharing news of the break-in. Sooner or later he might have to, but at the moment they were already upset enough by the tragedy and by Harry's decision to have Evie's organs donated.

On the bed beside them, Evie lay peacefully. Her eyes were taped shut, and she remained attached to a ventilator and IV. But the treatments to reduce brain swelling—hyperventilation to lower her carbon dioxide level and raise her blood pH, and diuretics to induce dehydration—had been stopped. A second set of required tests—cerebral blood-flow scan, EEG, and attempts at making her breathe spontaneously—had all confirmed the diagnosis of functional brain death.

Now, there was only the matter of saying good-bye and having an attending physician pronounce her officially dead. Then the people from the New York Regional Transplant Services would take over. He took Evie's hand and held it for a time, wondering if the DellaRosas had heard anything yet of Caspar Sidonis. Before long they would. With the cause of Evie's death clearly established as a ruptured aneurysm, there was no need for the medical examiner to demand an autopsy—especially with multiple organ donations at stake. But he had ordered extensive toxicology studies.

"Father Moore just left," Dorothy said.

"I'm sorry I missed him."

"He administered the Sacrament of the Sick to Evelyn."

"Good."

Evie had not considered herself a Catholic for years and had made no attempt to have her first marriage annulled. But neither of her parents would ever admit to the fact.

"I'm just not sure this organ business is the right thing to do. Evelyn was so . . . so beautiful."

"It's the right thing, Dorothy. Evie will be just as beautiful when this is all over—*more* beautiful. . . . Okay?"

"Yes. I . . . I suppose so. Um . . . about the funeral?"

Harry sensed what she wanted him to say.

"Would you like to make arrangements?" he asked.

"Thank you. I would."

"Anything you do in that regard will be okay. The funeral people you decide to use can call and make arrangements with the hospital."

"Do you know if Evelyn has an address book of some sort?"

"Oh, yes. As a matter of fact, she has it here. I'll call you later if you want and go through the names with you."

"That won't be necessary. I have friends who will call all the numbers. That way anyone who wants to come can do so. Our church isn't that large, but we don't have that much family, so there should be room. You'll speak to people here?"

"Of course."

Harry took Evie's purse from beneath her bedside table. She had left her wallet at home, but insisted on bringing in her makeup, some money, and her address book. He withdrew the small, leather-bound book and quickly flipped through it. The names were carefully done in Evie's meticulous block print. Many of them conjured up immediate, vivid memories of the happier years of their marriage. He was about to hand the book over when he noticed two small pieces of paper taped inside the back cover. On each was a name, address, and what looked like a social security number. Curious, Harry removed the slips and dropped them into his jacket pocket, taking pains to shield his movements from Dorothy. Oblivious, she took the address book and thanked him. Then she led her husband back to the bedside and out the door.

"She was such a beautiful girl," Harry heard her say.

Harry waited until he was certain the DellaRosas would not be returning for any reason. Then he opened Evie's purse again. In addition to some eye shadow, lipstick, blush, and a twenty-dollar bill, there was a gray rabbit's-foot key chain with three keys on it. Two were door keys of some sort, fairly new. Harry checked them against the co-op keys on his own ring. No match. The third was for a mailbox. He was about to examine the two slips of paper when Ben Dunleavy swept into the room.

Evie's neurosurgeon was respected throughout the hospital, but he was also feared for his volatility and intolerance. The decision to delay repair of Evie's aneurysm, although made on sound clinical grounds and decent data, had been his. Now, before he could operate on his patient, she was dead.

"Harry," he said.

His handshake and tone were cooler than they should have been given the circumstances. Sidonis had obviously gotten to him.

"You here to pronounce Evie?"

The neurosurgeon nodded and looked down at her. With no more drama than that, it was done. Harry glanced at the wall clock. Nine-twelve A.M. and thirty-five seconds. Officially, Evie was dead.

"Needless to say, I'm really sorry this has happened," Dunleavy said. "It's been years since I opted to do anything other than a delayed repair of an aneurysm like hers. Evie is my first fatality. I've only had two patients even rebleed before I could get them to the OR, and both of them did fine."

Harry could read between the lines of what the man was saying. He saw no sense in not cutting to the chase.

"Ben, Sidonis may have been having an affair with Evie. I don't know. But he's wrong about what he's accusing me of."

Dunleavy's gaze was dispassionate.

"I hope so, Harry," he said. "Let me know if there's anything else I can do."

He was gone before Harry could even respond. First the nursing staff, now Dunleavy. Even without hard evidence, there were already some unwilling to give him the benefit of the doubt. Harry felt an unpleasant tightening in his gut. There was going to be trouble.

He sat down in the bedside chair vacated by Dorothy and took the two pieces of paper from his pocket. They were scraps, one torn from the border of a magazine page, one from a sheet of stationery. Each had a man's name, address, phone number, date of birth, and Social Security number, written in Evie's hand, but hastily. The first was James Stallings, forty-two years old, with an Upper East Side address. The second, a thirty-seven-year-old from Queens, was someone named Kevin Loomis.

Harry put the slips in his wallet and the rabbit's foot and keys in his pocket. Then he checked the purse one last time and dropped it into the wastebasket. Finally, he bent over Evie's body and kissed her gently on the forehead.

"I'm sorry, kid," he whispered. "I'm sorry about everything."

He brushed her cheek with the back of his hand and left the room. He was nearing the elevators when, from somewhere down the hall behind him, he heard a familiar voice cry out,

"Hey, will someone please get in here! Get in here and get these damn bugs off of me!"

★　★　★

"He winked at me, Sherry. I swear he did."

Gowned and masked, nurse Marianne Rodriguez peered down into the radiant warmer where tiny Sherman O'Banion had spent virtually every moment of his two and a half weeks on earth. The neonatal intensive care unit at New York Children's Hospital was the finest in Manhattan, and it was currently filled to capacity—thirty newborns ranging in birth weight from just over a pound to ten. Sherman, born at twenty-five weeks, weighed one pound five ounces. His mother was a housewife, staying at home to care for two other children. His father worked the night shift on the assembly line of a factory. Considering his birth weight and other problems, Sherman was doing pretty well.

"Don't you wonder what some of these peanuts are going to grow up to be?" Sherry Hiller asked.

"I'll bet Sherm plays football. Have you seen his daddy?"

The infant, in his pod, looked like a visitor from another planet. There were tubes, wires, and auxiliary machines all around him. He was draped in Saran Wrap to conserve his body heat. A panel of phototherapy lights shone on him to lessen jaundice. Tiny eye shields protected him from the ultraviolet rays. A ventilator controlled his respiratory rate and volume. Sensors on his abdomen and legs measured temperature, heart rate, and blood oxygen concentration. An intravenous line placed in a tiny vein on his head provided fluid and antibiotics. A tube into his stomach through his nose delivered formula.

Marianne moved about the warmer, noting down the infant's temperature, heart rate, and color. His oxygen levels were running a bit low, and his dusky color, lab values, and exam had indicated a significant heart defect that would probably have to be surgically corrected before long. But Marianne wasn't all that concerned. She had been an NICU nurse for six years and had seen any number of infants worse off than Sherman O'Banion make it out of the hospital in great shape. Of course, there were others who were not so fortunate. Blindness from a number of factors, cerebral palsy, mental retardation, multiple surgical procedures, death—either sudden from cardiac arrest or prolonged from infection—and eventual learning disabilities were complications that every NICU nurse had to deal with, if not accept.

There was a tap on the glass from the formula room. Marianne looked over. The woman bringing the specially prepared formulas up from dietary waved at her cheerily with the fingers of a rubber-gloved hand. Marianne had never seen the dietary worker before—or at least felt fairly certain she hadn't. Per protocol, the woman wore a hair cover, mask, and surgical gown. Only her stout frame and her dark brown eyes were apparent. The chestnut eyes had a special spark to them, and Marianne had the sense that this was a cheerful person. She motioned for her to set out the formulas on the counter. The nurses would be in to pick them up. The woman nodded her understanding, did as was requested, and left the NICU.

Marianne returned to her duties, pausing to check each piece of equipment. To do her job right required almost as much mechanical aptitude as medical. But each type of apparatus was backed by a team of specially trained technicians and, in some instances, an entire department. The cost, short-term and long-range, of neonatal intensive care was astounding. Someone had once told Marianne the actual numbers, which were something like nine thousand dollars a day for difficult cases. One infant, whose mother had abandoned her in a Dumpster, had remained in the New York Children's NICU for almost nine months before succumbing to infection. There was a memorial service for the child. Only her nurses and a few M.D.s attended. The cost of keeping her alive for those months had been over a million and a half dollars.

"Okay, Sherm," Marianne said, "it's chow time."

"Bring Jessica's gruel in when you come, will you?" Sherry Hiller asked.

"Sure thing. Does anything need to be added?"

"Nope."

The formulas were in labeled bottles called Grad-u-feeders —a one-day supply for each of the infants. Some of the feeders contained supplemented mother's milk. Others were prepared from scratch. Each was sealed with a tamper-resistant seal that was essentially extrasticky cellophane tape. Marianne gloved before handling the bottles. Then, breaking the seals, she unscrewed the cover of Sherman's bottles and inserted the glucose supplement that had been ordered by the neonatologist. Next she resealed all but one bottle, using a roll of the tamper-resistant sealer that she picked up from the counter. As usual, she wondered why the department bothered with the tape when it was so easily accessible to so many people. She checked and double-checked the labels and placed all but one of Jessica Saunders's and Sherman O'Banion's formula bottles in the refrigerator. Then she returned to the warmers.

"How do you handle a hungry man?" she sang as she administered the newborn's feeding down his tube. "The *Manhandler*."

She held the formula over the infant until it had drained in completely.

"Marianne, could you do Jessica for me?" Sherry asked. "Little Moonface Logan's monitor alarm keeps going off. I think the leads are loose. I want to replace them all."

"Sure thing," Marianne said again.

Marianne was focused on delivering formula to the tiny girl when she heard the alarm from one of the nearby cardiac monitors. For half a minute, she ignored it, certain that it was coming from the loose leads on the infant they called Moonface. The alarm persisted.

"Sher, that's Moonface, isn't it?" she said, without looking up.

For a moment, there was only the continuing drone of the alarm.

"Holy shit!" Sherry cried suddenly. "Marianne, it's Sherman."

Sherman's cardiac monitor was showing an absolutely flat line. Marianne detached the feeding bottle and hurried back to his warmer. The two-week-old's chest rose and fell in response to his mechanical ventilation. He looked as he always did, except that his dusky color had deepened considerably. Now the oxygen saturation alarm was sounding as well. Marianne checked the leads. None loose. She slipped her stethoscope onto the infant's chest. Nothing. Not a beat. Quickly, she sped up the ventilatory rate and began cardiac compression.

"He's coded, Sher," she said with controlled urgency. "Call it for me and get Laura over here. Damn it all."

In less than a minute, the resuscitation of Sherman O'Banion was manned by neonatologist Laura Pressman, two pediatric residents, and two nurses. Marianne delivered meds as they were called for, but she had a sinking, ominous feeling from the very beginning. Sherman's heart rate had gone from an acceptable 130 straight down to zero. No slowing, no irregular beats. It was the equivalent of a car decelerating from sixty to zero by hitting a brick wall. Clearly, something within the infant's defective heart had blown—possibly a muscle band, or one of the fragile dividing walls. Continuing the external cardiac compressions, the NICU team began administering medications. Epinephrine . . . atropine . . . more epi . . . bicarbonate. They worked on the baby for more than half an hour. But with each passing minute, Marianne became more convinced of the hopelessness of the situation. Finally, Laura Pressman stopped her cardiac compressions. She stepped back from the radiant warmer, looked about at the staff, and shook her head.

"I'm sorry," she said. "You all did a great job."

Marianne Rodriguez accepted a consoling hug and a few words from Sherry Hiller. Then, battling back the tears she knew would come sooner or later, she set about disconnecting Sherman O'Banion's tubes and wires. The radiant warmer would be wheeled away and replaced with a freshly cleaned one. And before long, another newborn would be brought in.

Six stories below the NICU, in the subbasement, the stout dietary worker, her mask, gown, and hair cover still in place, knocked on the door of a little-used staff men's room, waited, then slipped inside, locked the door, and turned on the light.

The cardiac toxin she had used was so powerful that only a microscopic amount had been needed. Even if Sherman O'Banion's formula was analyzed, which it almost certainly would not be, no one would know what to look for, and nothing would be found.

The canvas gym bag was concealed beneath a mound of used paper towels in the tall trash basket. Ten minutes later, a man emerged from the restroom carrying the gym bag. In it were the surgical gown, hair cover, and surgical mask, as well as a pillow, a woman's wig, and a contact lens case. The man had close-cropped brown hair and was dressed in jeans, a loose sweat-shirt, and well-worn Nikes. His height, weight, and general appearance were quite unremarkable.

CHAPTER 11

St. Anne's was filled to overflowing for Evie's funeral. Outside, the day was as gray and somber as the mood within the chapel. Evelyn DellaRosa, vibrant, beauty-queen lovely, gifted as a writer and reporter, suddenly dead at age thirty-eight. There were few in attendance who weren't reflecting on the the transience of life and the vagaries of illness and chance.

The hundred-and-fifty-year-old white-shingled church fronted on the picturesque village green of Sharpston, the northern New Jersey town where Evie was raised and where her parents still lived. Today, Harry observed, it held a remarkable collection of people—really quite a tribute to Evie. But with each arrival, Harry felt as though he knew his wife less. In addition to relatives, a number of Harry's friends from the hospital, and neighbors from the co-op, there were co-workers from the magazine and various artists and patrons of the arts. There were folks from the station and network where Evie had not worked in over ten years, and a number of people whom Harry did not know at all. Shortly before the service, Evie's first husband, John Cox, now a network VP, walked in with a gorgeous young woman. As far as Harry knew, Evie hadn't spoken to her ex since shortly after their extremely hostile divorce was finalized. Yet here he was.

The days of mourning following Evie's death had been marred by visits from Albert Dickinson to Harry's neighbors in the co-op, to his co-workers at the hospital, and to Carmine and Dorothy DellaRosa. Dorothy had called Harry as soon as the policeman left, and had asked about Caspar Sidonis.

"Dorothy, I don't know if this man Sidonis is telling the truth or not," Harry had said. "And frankly, I don't care. I loved Evie, and I'm sure she loved me. Even if she was involved with this other man, which I strongly doubt, I'm sure we would have worked things out in time."

"Oh, my," was all Dorothy could think of to say.

As the service was about to commence, Harry glanced back and spotted Caspar Sidonis slipping into the last row. The sight of the man brought a strange mixture of anger and embarrassment. *Cuckold* was a repulsive word and an even more disgusting concept.

"Sidonis just walked in," he whispered to Julia Ransome, the literary agent who was Evie's closest friend in the city.

"Do you really care?" she asked without bothering to look back.

Harry thought about it. Perhaps it was her nature as a literary agent, but Julia always had a way of slicing to the essence of any situation.

"No," he said finally. "To tell you the truth, I guess I really don't."

From the moment he turned away from Evie's body and walked out of her hospital room, Harry had been trying to sort out his feelings. He thought about moving, about just leaving his practice and taking off, perhaps starting over again in one of those eternally warm, low-crime Edens the medical classifieds were always extolling. But just as he ultimately could not trade in his patients for the Hollins/McCue pharmaceutical job, he knew he would not leave them now. Not that Albert Dickinson would let him leave anyway.

Evie's casket rested on a draped stand surrounded by flowers. At the center of a wreath of white roses was a blowup of the same flawless, sterile, professionally done portrait that she had allowed on Harry's desk. There would be no burial. The day her obituary appeared in the *Times*, a Manhattan attorney had contacted Harry. Three weeks earlier, Evie had made out a new will amending a previous one. In it, she requested cremation and changed the beneficiary of her jewels and artwork from Harry to her parents—another sign that she anticipated the demise of their marriage. Harry was left as beneficiary on a $250,000 insurance policy they had taken out jointly some years before, but that was all. Nowhere in the will was there a mention of Caspar Sidonis.

Harry sat in the first row, between Julia and Evie's parents. His brother Phil, Gail, and their three children were just to Julia's right. Doug Atwater sat directly behind him. Harry felt grateful that none of them could read his thoughts, which, at that moment, were dominated by the wish that this whole thing would just be over so that he could return home. With the help of his associate Steve Josephson, Steve's wife, and a cleaning service, the apartment was pretty much back to normal, minus a few shattered drawers and the missing valuables. Now, all he wanted was to spend a night or two sitting in on bass with the combo at C.C.'s Cellar, and then lose himself in his practice and patients.

The mass was dignified and reasonably brief. Harry had been offered the option of speaking, but had declined. The priest, who had known Evie since childhood, did his best to make sense of her death, but Harry heard only snatches of what he said. He was preoccupied with trying to make sense out of her *life*. His thoughts kept drifting to Evie's IV line and to the doctor or doctor-impostor who had somehow marched onto and off of the neurosurgical unit totally unseen by any of the staff. Now, further complicating the conundrum was another riddle: three keys on a rabbit's foot chain.

"You okay?" Julia whispered as the priest was concluding his eulogy.

"Not really," he responded. "Listen, Julia, are you free for a drink tonight? There're some things going on I'd like to talk to you about."

Although he and Evie had occasionally spent a social evening with Julia and her husband, he had never been alone with her. She was several years older than Evie, slim, attractive, and sharply intelligent. Her agency was one of the more successful in Manhattan. She was working on her third marriage.

Julia considered his request. Some minutes later, during

Holy Communion, she leaned over and whispered, "Nine o'clock at Ambrosia's."

He nodded. "Thank you."

Although Phil, Julia, and Doug Atwater each offered to stay with him, Harry remained alone in the sanctuary until it had emptied.

"Is there anything I can do?"

Father Francis Moore spoke softly, but Harry was startled nonetheless.

"No. No thanks, Father. I was just thinking."

"I understand."

Harry turned and headed out. The old priest walked alongside him, a Bible cradled in one hand.

"You will be going over to the DellaRosas?" he asked.

"Yes. For a while anyhow. I'm pretty worn-out."

There was no way he could avoid going to his in-laws, but he was determined to head back to the city as soon as possible.

"I understand," Father Moore said again. "Although we haven't met before today, Dorothy and Carmine speak very highly of you. They say you're a very gentle, kind man."

"Thank you," Harry said.

They left the church with Harry a few feet ahead of the priest. Several pockets of people were standing around some distance away, talking or waiting for their rides. Harry had just reached the bottom of the stairs when Caspar Sidonis stalked over and confronted him.

"You killed her, you bastard," he rasped, his whisper harsh and menacing. "You know it and I know it. And pretty soon everyone's going to know it. You couldn't stand to lose her so you killed her."

It had been thirty-three years since Harry had last thrown a punch at someone's face. That time he had barely grazed the cheek of the bully who had been baiting him. The larger boy's retribution had been swift and memorable. This time, Harry's punch, thrown from a much better angle and with much more anger and authority behind it, was more effective. It connected solidly with the side of Sidonis's nose, sending the surgeon spinning onto his back in some low, rain-soaked shrubbery. Blood instantly spurted from both his nostrils.

Shocked, Father Francis Moore dropped his Bible. Harry calmly picked it up, wiped it on his trousers, and handed it back.

"I guess I'm not so gentle after all, Father," he said.

★ ★ ★

Ambrosia's was an eternally packed, upscale bistro on Lexington near Seventy-ninth. Harry spent an hour at the office reviewing patient lab reports and catching up on paperwork before taking a cab to the club. The drizzle that had dominated most of the day was gone, and the dense overcast had begun to dissolve. The city seemed scrubbed and renewed. It was before nine, but Julia Ransome was already there, nursing a drink at one of the tall, black acrylic tables opposite the bar. It was relatively early by Manhattan standards, even for a Thursday, but the bar was already three deep.

Julia exchanged pecks on the cheek with him. She was wearing a black silk blouse and an Indian print vest, and looked very much at home among the beautiful people.

"Who'd you have to pay off to get this table?" Harry asked, sliding onto the stool opposite hers.

"Donny, the bartender over there, has been writing a novel for the last ten years or so," she said, smiling. "I promised to read it when he finishes. In the meantime, I call ahead and he puts one or two of his pals on these stools until I get here. It's one of the perks of being a book agent. My seamstress has a first novel in progress, too. So does the plumber I can get at ten minutes' notice anytime, day or night. The trick is being able to tell which people haven't got a snowball's chance in hell of ever finishing their book. Once in a while I'm wrong. When that happens I just have to read it and then set about finding a new mechanic or dentist or whatever."

"Well, I appreciate your meeting me like this."

"If you think for one moment that I wouldn't have, I obviously haven't done a good job of letting you know you're one of my favorite people."

"Thanks."

"I mean it, Harry." Julia finished her drink and motioned the waitress over with a minute shake of her head. "You drinking tonight?"

"Bourbon neat. Might as well make it a double."

"Whoa. Double bourbon neat. Now there's a side of you I've never known."

"Don't worry. If I actually finish it they'll have to haul me out of here in a wheelbarrow." He waited until the waitress had returned with their drinks and left. "Julia," he said then, "please tell me about Evie."

The agent studied her glass. "What do you want to know?"

"At this point, almost anything you choose to share would probably be news to me. The surgeon I pointed out to you today at the church—the one who claims Evie was in love with him—is convinced I gave her something, a drug, that caused her aneurysm to rupture. He's wrong about it being me, but I'm not sure he's wrong about the rest of his theory. . . ." Harry reviewed the nightmarish evening on Alexander 9, his conversation with the anesthesiologist, and his conclusions. "Julia," he said, "I had no idea Evie was involved with another man, even though for a year or so she wasn't particularly involved with me. I just thought she might have shared some other things with you that . . . that I didn't know about."

In the silence that followed, Harry felt certain Julia was going to deny any knowledge of what he was talking about. Suddenly, though, the woman looked up at him and nodded.

"You were outmatched from the beginning, Harry," she said. "You may have been able to handle the Vietcong"—she gave him a quick, ironic smile—"but you didn't have a chance against Evie DellaRosa. She and I have known each other since she lived with me one summer during college. That's almost twenty years. She was an exciting, intriguing person in many ways, and God knows I'll miss her. But over all those years, I've never known her to be content. Whatever she had—*whoever* she had—she always wanted more. And she didn't particularly care what it took or, unfortunately, who got hurt in the process. That's the part of her—that seductive charisma—that always frightened me. It kept us from getting closer than we were. John Cox was at the funeral today. Did you see him?"

"Yes, I did."

"What did Evie tell you about their breakup?"

"That she caught him having affairs, and that when she

confronted him, he got her fired from the news staff and black-balled throughout the industry."

"Does that jibe with his showing up at her funeral today?"

"No. I have to say I was surprised to see him."

"John Cox was crazy about Evie. *She* had the affair, Harry—with John's boss. I only know what John told me and that's not much, but it was the boss, not John, who gave her the boot. *And* blackballed her. I think John would even have given her another chance. But she wasn't interested."

"Was she at all happy with me?"

"For a time—maybe a year or two. Harry, Evie needed to be in the spotlight. She needed to be at the center of the action. Part of her fought that need—that's why she married you, I think. Stability. But the stronger pull was clearly winning out."

"Did you know about Sidonis?"

"Nope. Not about him or any other men during your marriage—if there were any. I'm not sure that sort of thing was ever important enough for Evie to talk about. Or maybe she didn't trust me that much."

"I know she was dissatisfied with her job on the magazine, but—"

"*Hated it.* She was born to be in front of the camera, Harry. You know that. At least you should. From the moment she started at *Manhattan Woman* she was searching for a ticket back into the limelight."

"I've had the impression lately that she was working on something special."

"I think you're right."

"Do you know what it was?"

Julia shook her head.

"I tried to get her to tell me about it the last time we were together. All she would say was that it was big stuff, and that the producers of *A Current Affair* and some other tabloid shows were already offering her big bucks and on-air guarantees just to see what she had."

Harry stared off at a wall across the club. On it, artfully done, was a six-foot-high neon sculpture of a woman's profile and hand. She had a twenties look and was smoking a glowing cigarette in a foot-long holder. Although Evie smoked only rarely, something about the rendering reminded him of her. He suspected it would be a long time before things didn't.

"No further questions, Your Honor," he said, finishing his bourbon. "I really appreciate your coming to meet with me like this, Julia."

"Nonsense. You're a terrific guy. And whether she appreciated it or not, Evie was lucky to have you. Harry, do you really think someone purposely killed her?"

"I don't know what to think. The chemical analysis of her blood should be completed within a few weeks—sooner if the police detective who wants to mount my scalp on his lodge pole has his way. I'm concerned about what might happen if one of the tests is positive, but I'm also wondering whether I'll trust the results if they're negative."

"So you believe that woman, Evie's roommate?"

Harry studied the neon smoker as he considered the question. Two days after Evie's death he had gone back up to Alexander 9, but Maura Hughes had been sent home. "Shaky as hell, but not chasing any spiders," was the way one of the nurses described how Maura had looked upon discharge. Harry was sure that the real reason for the rapid discharge was the refusal of her insurance carrier to cover any more days. A typical scenario. Companies were shortening stays and refusing coverage with almost as much vigor as they were denying any responsibility for the consequences of their policies.

"Harry?" Julia was looking at him curiously. "I asked you a question about Evie's roommate in the hospital. You seemed like you were about to answer, and then you sort of drifted off."

Harry glanced down at his empty glass. Years of virtual abstinence had reduced him to amateur status as a drinker. He knew that being easily distracted was the first clue that if he wasn't tight yet, he soon would be.

So what, he thought. *The tighter the better.*

"Yes, I believe her," he said. "A doctor, or someone posing as a doctor, came into that room after I left. A short time after his visit Evie's aneurysm burst. I think he injected something into that IV. You know, maybe that story Evie was working on has something to do with what happened. I wish to hell I knew what it was all about."

"Did you check her office?"

"At the magazine?"

"No, the one in the Village."

"What?"

"She was renting an office—you know, workspace—some-place in Greenwich Village. Didn't you know that?"

"I . . . um . . . no. No, I didn't know that either. Do you know where it was?"

"No idea."

Harry brushed his hand over the pocket where he was carry-ing Evie's rabbit's foot and keys.

"Julia, I need to find that place," he said.

She looked at him with concern.

"You need to go home and get some sleep, Harry. That place'll be there tomorrow. Besides, if you don't know where it is, finding it may not be so easy. She doesn't have a phone there. That's as much as I remember of what she said about it."

"Thanks," Harry said. "Julia, who in the hell was she?"

The book agent set a twenty and a ten beneath her glass and guided him out of the bar into the cool night air.

"Harry, if you asked ten different people in Evie's life that question, you'd get ten completely different answers. It would be like the proverbial blind men trying to describe an elephant by whatever part they happen to be feeling. *Snake, tree, wall, stone, leaf.* They're all correct . . . but only up to a point. Want to share a cab home?"

Harry knew that she lived in almost precisely the opposite direction from his apartment.

"Hey, listen," he said. "Don't worry about me. I need to walk for a bit to clear some of this Old Grand-Dad out of my head. I'll get some rest. I promise."

They waited until he had flagged down a taxi for her, then embraced.

"Call if you need me," Julia said. "And don't drive yourself too crazy trying to see any more than the rest of the blind men."

Harry watched as the cab disappeared around the corner, then headed slowly downtown.

CHAPTER 12

Harry ambled down Lexington to Fifty-eighth and then across toward Central Park South. He loved walking the city at any hour, but especially at night. That he was in no particular hurry was just as well. The double bourbon was definitely slowing him down. For a time, he considered simply writing the whole night off by stopping in another bar or two. But he wanted to think through what Julia Ransome had told him, and he had never been much of a thinker when he was tight.

During his eighteen months in Nam, he had become something of a functional alcoholic, often drinking to excess as a means of coping with the horrors of his job. In that regard he was not much different from many of the other officers. Fortunately, he had been able to practically stop drinking after the war; and even more fortunately, he had never given in to the urge to numb his feelings with narcotics. For many of those docs and medics who did, the war was still raging, and would be until they died.

He was crossing by the fountain in front of the Plaza when he glanced down Fifth Avenue. The offices of *Manhattan Woman* magazine were on Forty-seventh Street. It was almost eleven o'clock. Unless some of the staff was preparing for production, there was no chance of his actually making it up to her office. But he couldn't face going home yet, and C.C.'s Cellar would be uncomfortably crowded. The group performing there right now wasn't one of his favorites anyway—a popular progressive quartet whose music he found pretentious. Before he had a chance to rethink the one-night bender option, he turned downtown toward the magazine office, buying a pack of mints along the way to cover the alcohol on his breath. He chewed all of them during the ten-block walk to Forty-seventh.

The guard at the desk in the lobby of the tastefully refurbished building put aside his *National Enquirer* and eyed him suspiciously. Harry explained about Evie's death and his desire to go through her things before they were tossed into a carton by someone and put into storage. He took her picture from his wallet and extracted a twenty at the same time. The guard studied the spectacular woman in the photo for a long moment, then slipped the bill into his shirt pocket and made a call. Three minutes later, Harry stepped out of the elevator and into the twenty-third-floor offices of *Manhattan Woman* magazine.

"Dr. DellaRosa, we're all so sorry about Evie. I'm Chuck Gerhardt, layout."

The man, in his early thirties with thinning, closely cut hair, had on tight black jeans and a black turtleneck. The abstract metal-and-glass sculpture suspended from his neck by a heavy chain reminded Harry of a tuba. His tepid handshake could not have cost him more than a calorie.

"Pleased to meet you," Harry said. "And thanks for your condolences. I can't believe she's gone."

Dr. DellaRosa. Harry felt rapport with Evie and those other women who chose not to trade in their surname for their husband's. There was no point in correcting the man, though. Harry had not been invited up to the office in years, and he had no intention of setting foot in the place again after tonight. He was searching for a clue—any clue as to what Evie's secret project was, or where her Greenwich Village hideaway was located. Of course, he thought, any other tidbits offering insight into the life of the stranger to whom he had been married for nine years would be gratefully accepted.

"You're lucky I was here," Gerhardt said. "First thing next week we put the rag to bed, and I have a ton of work to do. We call it *panic mode*. That's why I wasn't at the funeral today. All the bosses went, but the peons who actually do the work around here got chained to our desks."

"I'm sorry you couldn't make it. It was a beautiful service. And I apologize for disturbing you this way."

"Hey, no problem. I just can't believe Evie's gone. She was the best, Dr. DellaRosa. She'd give you the shirt off her back."

"I know," Harry said. The irony of the man's metaphor was not lost on him. "Look, I haven't been able to sit still since the funeral. I was just walking around the city and I decided to come in, see if I could get Evie's things."

Chuck Gerhardt looked at him strangely.

"Dr. DellaRosa, I'm certain the man you sent did that already. Yesterday. No, no, the day before. I remember because—"

"Did you see this man?" Harry felt every muscle in his body tense.

"Only for a moment. I happened to be by the front desk when he came. Kathy—the receptionist—took him down to Evie's office. What's wrong?"

"Oh, nothing," Harry said, feigning sudden understanding. "I know what happened. It was my partner at work. His gym's just a few blocks from here. He volunteered to come by for me a few days ago. With everything that's been going on I just forgot. Okay if I just go down there anyhow?"

"Sure."

"The end of that hall, right?"

"No . . . um . . . her office is down that corridor there. It has been for a couple of years."

"Yes, yes, of course. I haven't been here for a while."

Evie's name was still on the blond oak door. Harry went inside knowing the gesture was fruitless. He was right. The office had been picked clean. Nothing on or in the desk, nothing in the file cabinet, nothing on the walls. The books that had been in her small bookcase were neatly stacked in one corner. Harry had no doubt that every single volume had been checked for papers or hollowed-out compartments. What little doubt he had about the break-in at the apartment vanished. The robbery there was nothing more than a smoke screen to cover a thorough search. *But for what?*

Just in case, he checked the underside of each shelf, as well as the bottom of all three desk drawers. Nothing. The wastebasket was empty. Harry tried to imagine how anyone could have simply walked into the office and stripped it so thoroughly. The story presented to the receptionist had to have been convincing and smoothly told. The man, himself, must have been iceberg cool. This was no amateur.

Were the thefts from the co-op and Evie's office connected with her death? How could they not be? On impulse, Harry settled into the desk chair and switched on Evie's computer. The hard disk prompt came on. Harry responded to it and waited. But nothing else happened. There were no files. Not one. Not a piece of correspondence or an article or even a word processing program. The data in the computer had been extracted like coins from a piggy bank.

"Anything I can do to help?"

Chuck Gerhardt stood by the doorway, smiling understandingly.

Harry's weak, bewildered smile was totally genuine.

"No. Thanks, though. Thanks for everything."

Gerhardt set three ten-dollar bills on the desk.

"I owed this to Evie," he said. "Now I guess I owe it to you."

"Nonsense. Please keep it. If she thought enough of you to lend it, I'm sure she'd be happy to have it end at that."

"Oh, it wasn't a loan. She had a friend in the Village who works on unusual jewelry. This chain came undone and the medallion fell on the marble in the foyer downstairs. It broke into several pieces. I got it in Germany on a very special holiday with a very special friend. I thought it was a total loss, but Evie's jeweler saved the day."

The Village. Evie never shopped farther downtown than Saks Fifth Avenue. Even C.C.'s seemed Bohemian to her. The first time Harry had heard of any connection between her and Greenwich Village was when Julia had told him about the secret office. Now this.

"Chuck, do you by any chance know who this jeweler is?"

"Well, Evie never really told me, but his card was taped inside the box that the medallion came back in. I'm almost certain I kept it. Come on down to my office."

Harry followed Gerhardt to a large studio that was cluttered with the tools and products of his trade. The layout designer rummaged through his desk for a time, then triumphantly surfaced with a business card. *Paladin Thorvald, Fine Jewels, Antiques and Collectibles*. Harry copied the information down.

"Now you can feel perfectly comfortable about keeping the money, Chuck," he said, patting the man on the back. "You've earned it."

Harry stopped by a money machine for some cash, and then took a cab down to the Village. The jewelry and antiques shop of Paladin Thorvald was just off Bleecker Street, a couple of blocks from the Bowery. It was nearly one in the morning, but here as in many areas of Manhattan there were still a fair number of people about—some, of course, the ubiquitous shadow people, waiting for their portion of the night to begin.

Harry had no clear plan other than to show Evie's picture to anyone who would look. If he had no luck, he would go home for a few hours of sleep, and then begin again first thing in the morning. Speed mattered. Whoever had searched the apartment and Evie's office was resourceful and desperate enough to commit murder. And to make matters much worse, Albert Dickinson was out there just waiting for a positive coroner's report before pouncing on his only suspect, one H. Corbett.

Thorvald's was a small shop on the first floor of a dingy, yellow brick building. There were iron bars in front of the single plate glass window, and a small sign announcing that business hours were nine A.M. to seven P.M. Harry peered inside. A single shaded bulb illuminated a collection that seemed largely to have crossed the line separating antiques from junk. Hardly Evie's kind of stuff. There was no chance she would have gone out of her way to visit this particular shop, Harry felt certain of that. Her office had to be someplace nearby.

He tried her photo three times on customers leaving a nearby convenience store, and then on the clerk. The clerk, Pakistani or Indian, recognized Evie as a frequent customer, but had no idea where she lived. He only worked the shift from eleven on. Harry couldn't imagine his wife walking these streets alone at night. At least before today he couldn't. As he made his way from one block to the next, he sensed the shadow people getting a bead on him and moving closer. He was either a john or a mark—possibly both. Before long someone was going to make a move on him. He glanced at his watch. It was stupid to have come down here at such an hour. Now, checking over his shoulder several times each block, he looped back toward Thorvald's. Two passersby had never seen Evie, and two more hurried away when he approached. He decided to catch a cab and head on home. As he passed the antique store, he looked in again through the bars. A large, bearded man in a loose shirt or caftan was moving about at the rear of the shop.

Harry rapped on the window. The man glanced up, then pointed to his watch and waved him off. Harry knocked again. This time he held up Evie's photo and two twenties. The man hesitated, then shuffled over. In his ornately embroidered caftan, with a full beard, thick ponytail, and single, heavy, gold earring, he looked like a cross between Eric the Red and Ivan the Terrible. But his face, while it might have frightened a young child, was kind and reassuring. He peered through the window at the photo. Harry could see the recognition in his expression and quickly pointed to his wedding ring, the photo, himself, and finally to the bills. Paladin Thorvald hesitated, then shrugged, deactivated some sort of alarm system, and opened the door.

"You're Desiree's husband?" he asked after Harry had introduced himself. "I never had any idea she was married, let alone to a doctor."

Harry flashed on the many hours he and Evie had spent choosing her engagement diamond, and then their wedding bands. The news that she was wandering about the Village late at night using the name Desiree and wearing no ring would recently have surprised him much more than it did now.

"I assure you, Mr. Thorvald. I *am* her husband. At least I was until a few days ago. Could I please come in and talk to you for a minute?"

Although Thorvald did step back a few paces to allow him in, Harry could tell that the man had misgivings. He decided that there was no reason to hold back anything except that Evie's death was being investigated as a possible homicide. He handed over the two twenties.

"Here, keep these no matter what," he said.

Thorvald did not have to hear that offer twice. He shoved the bills into the deep pocket of his caftan and listened impassively to Harry's story.

"So, exactly what is it you want to know?" he asked when Harry finished. He still sounded wary.

"If you can tell me where she lived, that would be wonderful."

"Lots of different kinds of people live in the Village for lots of different reasons. One of 'em's a respect for privacy we have around here that doesn't exist in a lot of places. Live and let live, if you know what I mean. If Desiree was your wife, and if she didn't tell you about her place here, she must have had her reasons."

Harry did not have to try very hard to produce the urgency in his voice.

"Mr. Thorvald, please. Evie's dead. She was thirty-eight years old and she's dead. We had a home, friends, plans for the future. I need to know who Desiree was. Regardless of what she called herself, she was my wife. I'm certain I have the keys to her place. Please. Just point me to the right building and I'm out of here. I won't ask any more of you. Just that."

Thorvald stroked his beard and stared down at his sandaled feet.

"Two doors down," he said finally. "Newly painted red enamel door. Second floor, I think she once said. I'm not sure. I've never been in the building myself."

"Thanks. I know you didn't really want to tell me," Harry said. "I won't bother you again."

Paladin Thorvald studied Harry's face.

"I'm sorry your wife's dead," he said.

Two small panes of glass were set high in the red enamel door. Harry stood on his tiptoes and peered inside. The front entryway was deserted. He glanced about to ensure that the shadow people were still at bay, and then withdrew the rabbit's foot and keys. Within him the sliver of a notion remained that somehow he had started from a misconception and built a secret

life for Evie around it. That last bit of hope vanished as the first
of her keys turned in the lock.

He slipped inside and closed the red door behind him. The
small, poorly lit foyer, while not fetid, would certainly have benefited from a cleaning. There was a small, scarred table for magazines, two rows of mailboxes servicing about twenty-five units,
and two columns of buzzers. Harry scanned the names on the
boxes, each a first initial/last name done on a black plastic strip
with a labeler. A few names were added with taped-on pieces of
paper. None of the initials were D., and none of the names were
familiar. But apartment 2F had no name at all. The mailbox key
on Evie's ring fit that lock. The box was empty. Suddenly, there
was a soft scraping against the outside door behind him. Harry
whirled. His pulse, already on alert, was jackhammering. No one
was peering through the window, but almost certainly someone
had been.

Harry briefly considered checking the street, but thought
better of it. Whoever had been outside the door was probably no
one he wanted to deal with. All that mattered was getting up to
apartment 2F.

The first floor consisted of a dim, stucco-walled corridor
lined by several apartment doors. An uncarpeted staircase was off
to one side, narrow enough to make Harry wonder how people
on the floors above could get a couch or refrigerator into their
places. There was, as far as he could tell, no elevator. Still un-
nerved by the notion that someone had been watching him, he
ascended the staircase quietly and cautiously.

Apartment 2F was at the rear of the building. Harry approached, trying to picture Evie walking down the same hall.
Standing by the door, he listened. There was only silence. He
knocked softly. Then knocked again. Nothing. Finally, his pulse
once more making itself known, Harry inserted the second key
into the lock, turned it, and stepped inside the world of the
woman who called herself Desiree.

CHAPTER 13

The apartment was totally dark. Harry used the glow from the corridor lights to locate a lamp, turned it on and quickly closed the hallway door behind him.

The small, sparsely furnished living room was a stark contrast to their immaculate, impeccably decorated co-op uptown. It was clearly a busy writer's retreat. Cardboard folders and small stacks of manuscript pages were set out on the threadbare carpet. Each was labeled, the titles suggesting to Harry that more than one project was going on. There was an electric typewriter on a folding table, and next to it a discount-house computer desk with a PC and laser printer. Off to one side, on the floor, were a TV, a VCR and seven or eight videos, a half-filled wine rack, a cassette player and two dozen tapes. There was also a telephone. Harry listened to the dial tone for a moment and then set the receiver back down. There was no number on it. It seemed likely that some people had access to the line. But that group clearly did not include Evie's best friend, Julia.

Harry checked the front closet, which was empty, and then the kitchen. There was a supply of diet soda, a Braun coffee maker, and a microwave. The cupboards were stocked with snack foods and canned goods, and the freezer had a supply of frozen dinners and half a dozen different flavors of Ben & Jerry's ice cream, Evie's favorite.

Next to the kitchen was a small bathroom with a shower stall, but no tub. The shampoo was Evie's brand, and the mixed scent of powders and soaps reminded him of her. There was a mirrored medicine cabinet over the sink. Harry watched himself reach for it. He looked like hell—tired, drawn, and in need of a shave. He wondered if Gene Hackman ever looked this bad. Inside the cabinet were a number of unmarked bottles of pills. Harry recognized Valium, Seconol, and some type of amphetamine. He suspected the others contained various sorts of painkillers. The prescription labels had been torn off all of them. There was also a small bottle of white powder. Harry took some on a moistened finger and rubbed it over a spot on his gums. The immediate numbness it produced meant it almost certainly was cocaine. Evie had never shown even the slightest interest in drugs, and Harry could not remember her accepting so much as a hit of marijuana if it was offered to her at a party.

Desiree's drug use had to have been recreational, or at most intermittent. Double identity or not, if she was strung out on drugs, Harry would have noticed.

He opened the single drawer in the vanity and stared down in utter dismay at its contents. There was nothing in the small drawer but condoms—perhaps fifteen different styles and brands in boxes and individual packets—some common and store-bought, some from exotic specialty houses. Harry picked up one of the packets. It was labeled *Thai Tickler* on one side, and had a lewd drawing printed on the other beneath the promise *Guaranteed Pleasure for Him and Her*. Harry threw it back angrily and slammed the drawer shut. Part of him wanted to leave—simply to get out of there and forget the whole goddamn thing. He had already learned more about his wife and her alter ego than he ever would have wanted to know. And he dreaded having to face the revelations awaiting him in the pages and computer files in the living room. But he knew he couldn't back off. He had been dropped into the middle of a nightmare and the only way out for him was through it.

There was barely space in the single bedroom for a narrow dresser and a neatly made queen-size bed. Double, louvered closets filled all of one wall. Harry checked beneath the bed and then pulled apart one set of the closet doors. The evening dresses

—fourteen of them—were elegant, sexy, and far from inexpensive. On the floor beneath them were a number of pairs of dress shoes, all from the upscale shops Evie frequented. Behind the other set of doors was a collection of nightgowns, peignoirs, teddies, and other extremely provocative bedroom apparel. The hardly subtle collection was not very appealing to Harry. He was much more aroused by the feel of Evie's body beneath a flannel nightshirt, or even a plain cotton T. Perhaps his taste was the reason she rarely wore the few lacy garments she had at home. Or perhaps Evie's ways were simply different from Desiree's. Bewildered and more saddened now than angry, Harry returned to the living room and the writings that had very likely cost Evie her life.

He picked up a thin folder labeled simply *Introduction*, and opened to the first of several pages.

<u>Between the Sheets</u>
The Power and Extraordinary Influence of the Sexual Underground in America

Men call me beautiful. Women, too, for that matter. For as long as I have been aware of that reaction, I have been able to use it to my advantage. I am intelligent, well-educated, and interested in many things. But what I am most interested in is sex. Sex and power. Throughout the pages of this book you will learn how I—and the many, many women with whom I have worked and whom I have interviewed—use their looks and sex appeal to attract and control others, both men and women. You will learn of business decisions that earned or lost millions, which were made for no other reason than to please one of us. You will learn of major political appointees who were fired and others who were hired simply because one of us demanded it. Sometimes there is money paid to us to exert our influence —vast sums of money. Sometimes we exercise our control over judges, politicians, businessmen and the like simply to prove that we can.

Are we worth it? Read this book, and then decide for yourself. . . .

Harry set the folder down and opened another marked *Correspondence*. It contained letters from senior editors at several of the big-name publishing houses expressing great interest in the sample chapters of *Between the Sheets*, by Desiree. The correspondence was sent to the post office box of an agent in Manhattan named Norman Quimby. Harry had never heard Evie mention the man and wondered if he existed at all. A number of the other letters were from the producers of syndicated television tabloid shows. Those letters were written to Evie in care of a different post office box. They suggested that if she could deliver Desiree and all the material she claimed to have on tape and film, there could be serious discussion of a long-term, on-camera deal. The producers also promised to investigate how to implement a number of high-tech safeguards Evie had insisted upon to protect Desiree's identity and enhance the mystique surrounding her. One producer wrote:

> I think it's a marvelous idea to make Desiree's identity the best-kept secret since Pearl Harbor. By the time the series airs, the book will be out, and the hype we'll generate should create a phenomenon—Madame X, Sydney Barrows, Christine Keeler, and Heidi Fleiss all rolled into one, with a dash of Marilyn and the Kennedys thrown in for good measure. I can't give you hard figures yet, but let me just say here and now that if you can deliver what you claim you can, we will be able to do business.

Harry picked up one of the videos. It was labeled simply *#1*. He scanned the folders on the floor. One was marked *Vids*. Inside were six narratives, each two or more pages long, and each titled by a single number. He kept the one headed *#1* and set the rest down. Then he slipped the video into the VCR.

This tape features a woman who calls herself Briana, he read.

> She is thirty-one and a former homecoming queen at a large Southern university. By day she is a physical therapist at a clinic just outside of Washington, D.C. At night she works for an escort service. The fee for her services is $2000 a night. She has only a few clients, and she works only when

she wants to. The split with her agency is fifty-fifty. Re-
cently, she became pregnant by her boyfriend and decided
to retire from the escort service. The video—something of a
retirement present from Briana to herself—was made by a
camera hidden behind a mirror in her apartment. The
owner of her escort service knew nothing about it. Briana
was operating on her own. But she had already contracted
her services out to a powerful tobacco lobby. Her pay for
influencing the vote of the senator shown with her in this
video was $50,000. And for the video itself, another
$50,000. Her face and voice, as well as the senator's, have
been electronically obscured. . . .

Harry watched in morbid fascination as a woman with large, youthful breasts and the perfect, muscled body of a teenager allowed herself to be undressed by a man whose body was not nearly so well maintained. Calling him "Senator," she teased, rubbed, dared, cajoled, and finally loved him into the promise to drop his support of another stiff tax on tobacco products. The woman was incredibly sexy, alluring, and skilled—so much so that the senator did not last more than two minutes once their actual lovemaking commenced.

The electronic blurring of faces and voices made it impossible to identify the man, and Harry wondered if, in fact, the tape was the genuine article or something Desiree had staged. *Was Desiree herself in one or more of the videos?* Unfortunately, the likelihood of that seemed quite high. Harry decided to put off viewing the rest of them until he had gone through all the other material.

He checked the time. It was nearly two. Silently, he thanked his profession for providing him with the hour-to-hour or even minute-to-minute self-control necessary to make it through an all-nighter followed by a full day of work. He would stay here until dawn, then stop by the apartment to shower and change before heading to the hospital for rounds. As soon as he could clear out his office schedule, he would return.

He scanned the folders and loose papers, trying to decide how best to get organized. One small pile caught his eye. It was, perhaps, five or ten pages, bound by a single rubber band. The label tucked beneath the the elastic was written in Evie's hand on a yellow Post-it. It read *Business Execs. (preliminary notes) See also Desiree's Diary.*

> *They meet every two weeks at the Camelot Hotel. Young, handsome, and powerful. I was chosen by Page to join six other women—each among the most beautiful and desirable in the city. The payoff for one evening's work: a thousand in cash. One of us was assigned to each of them. My first night, a Tuesday, I was sent to the room of—*

Harry froze. There was a sound in the hallway outside the door. He was certain of it. Someone was pressed up against the door, listening. He set the papers down where they had been, tiptoed to one of the windows, and carefully raised the shade. There was a fire escape, and below that an alley. But the window and the one next to it were protected by a grate of iron bars secured with a padlock. Harry returned to the table where he had set down Evie's keys and was soundlessly picking through them when there were two gentle taps on the door. He moved a few steps forward, then stopped. There was a second pair of raps, this time more insistent. He looked about him at Desiree's papers. There was no way he could hide everything.

"Who is it?" he heard himself rasp. He moved closer to hear the reply.

"It's Thorvald. Paladin Thorvald," the man said in a forced whisper. "I got to speak to you."

"How did you get in here?"

"Please, it's very important."

Harry glanced about him again. Then, with a shrug, he undid the dead bolt. As soon as he turned the knob, two men in dark windbreakers barged in. One was tall and built like a professional wrestler. The other was much shorter but cinder-block chunky. Both had nylon stockings pulled over their faces.

"I lied," the taller one growled, shoving Harry back into the apartment.

Harry's reaction was pure reflex. He slammed his fist into the center of the taller man's face, sending him reeling back heavily against the wall by the door. Then he lashed out with his foot at the other one, connecting solidly with the side of his knee. The man dropped onto his side, cursing. Harry charged past him toward the open doorway, but the taller man whipped his leg across, sending him sprawling into the hall.

"Help!" Harry cried, scrambling to his feet.

Before he could push off, the huge man tackled him by the ankles. Harry cried out again as he struggled to free himself. He was a hundred and eighty pounds, but the gargantuan man handled him like a puppet. His face, beneath the stocking mask, was smeared with blood.

"Get the stuff out, for chrissakes!" he snapped, dragging Harry back into the apartment. "This guy's fucking crazy!"

Harry freed one foot and snapped it up against the man's jaw. His grip loosened just enough for Harry to break free once again. The stockier man, unsteady but on his feet, tried pinning Harry's arms to his sides. But Harry was possessed. He drove his elbow viciously into the man's throat, following through in a dervishlike three-sixty turn that would have made Baryshnikov proud. Once again the blocky man went down.

Harry stumbled as he headed toward the door. The hesitation was just enough for the giant to get hold of him again. But Harry's arms were still free. As he braced himself and twisted to take a roundhouse swing, excruciating pain shot through his chest and around to his back. It was the same electroshock sensation he had experienced on the track at the hospital, but magnitudes more severe. He felt his knees buckle. His vision blurred. And in an instant, both men were on him, pinning him to the carpet.

"The stuff," one snapped.

"Okay, okay, I've got it. I've got it."

Through the sweaty, dull haze of intolerable pain, Harry smelled the sickly sweet aroma of chloroform. A moment later, a cloth soaked with the rapidly acting anesthetic was pressed tightly over his nose and mouth. The dreadful ache in his chest kept him from all but token resistance. And in fact, as his consciousness began to fade, he sensed some relief that the pain was fading as well. He fought for a time the only way he could, by refusing to inhale. But with several hundred pounds pressing down on him, his tenacity was short lived.

I wonder what it feels like to be dead, was the last thing he thought before he took a single, deep breath.

> *"What are the names of the files you read?* . . .
> *"What names do you remember?* . . .
> *"Did you listen to any of the cassettes?* . . .
> *"What did they say?"* . . .

The questions floated through the pitch blackness like feathers, brushing against Harry's consciousness, then drifting away.

> *"Has your wife ever spoken to you of her work?* . . .
> *"How did you learn of this apartment?* . . .
> *"Have you known about it for long?* . . .
> *"Who else knows?"* . . .

The voice, a man's, was soft, patient, and not at all demanding. But Harry felt powerless to resist answering. The questions, droning over and over, were interspersed with slow, thick answers in a voice that was his, and yet was not a human voice at all.

> *"Let us begin again, Harry. Tell me everything you read here tonight.* . . .
> *"Tell me every name you remember.* . .
> *every name* . . .
> *every name.* . . ."

Harry was flat on his back, somehow tied to a bed. Cotton batting had been taped tightly over each eye. He could move his hands, but not his arms; his feet, but not his legs; his head, but not his shoulders.

"Let me up," he heard himself growl.

"When I am convinced you have told me everything that you have to tell me, you will be freed. May I please have some more Pentothal?"

Harry's brain had begun to clear. The horrible pain in his chest was gone, and he hadn't died—at least he didn't think so.

"Just hold still, Harry. Stop trying to move your arm. You'll feel much better in a moment."

The voice of his inquisitor was cultured and intelligent—not that of either of the men who had assaulted him. The other two were there, though. Harry could hear them breathing. He tried to picture the three of them standing by the bed, staring down at him.

"I'll need even more than that," the cultured voice said, "and fill half of that syringe with that ketamine over there. I don't believe he has anything more to tell us, but we shall see."

Harry sensed the movement by his left arm, and suddenly knew there was an intravenous line there. *You're him, aren't you,* his mind screamed. *You're the doctor on Alexander 9!*

A pleasant warmth washed over the darkness. Harry felt himself beginning to drift. And once again, the questions and his own answers began to float past him.

"What else do you remember? . . .
"What names? . . .
"What places? . . .
"What tapes? . . .
"What else? . . .
"What else? . . .
"What else?" . . .

★   ★   ★

From the depths of a warm, impenetrably dark sea, Harry sensed himself rise. His head felt swollen, his chest was a balloon. Bubbles swirled about him as bit by bit, word by word, his encounter with the two thugs and subsequent inquisition by the man with the soft voice drew into focus in his mind. He was tied to a bed and . . . *Wait!* Gingerly, he lifted first one arm, then the other. The bonds were gone. His legs, too, were free. He reached up and touched the adhesive tape over his eyes. Slowly, uncomfortably, he pulled the thick patches off. The room was pitch-black. Fighting a sudden wave of nausea, he pushed off the side of the bed and raised the window shade. Midmorning sun exploded into his eyes. He buried his face in his arm and waited.

Finally, he was able to look around. He was in Desiree's bedroom. He was fully clothed, although his shoes were on the floor by the bed. His watch was gone. There was a small, closed puncture wound on the skin inside his left elbow—almost certainly an intravenous site. Except for the furniture, the room was empty. No clothes in the closet. No perfume on the bureau. Nothing. The bathroom and living room had been similarly swept of Evie's belongings. The computer was gone, the bathroom vanity drawer emptied of its depressing contents. The medicine cabinet was bare. Evie's keys had been taken, although his own keys and wallet were on the table.

Harry sank onto the couch, aware now of a pounding headache that he suspected would not be gone soon. He picked up the telephone and called his office. Mary Tobin was immensely relieved to hear from him.

"Dr. Corbett, I've called everywhere," she said. "Even the police."

"What time is it?"

"Pardon?"

"The time, Mary."

"Noon. Almost noon. Where on earth are you?"

"I'll explain when I see you. I need to go home. I won't be in until three. Can you juggle people? I'll make up the time Saturday."

"Are you okay?"

"Let's just say I've been better. I'll speak to you later."

Harry retrieved his shoes, made one final, fruitless check of the apartment, and headed home. The answers had been right there in his hands. By not being more careful, he had blown the chance to save himself. But he did have much more insight into just who Evie DellaRosa really was. And he also had a voice . . . a gentle, cultured voice with just the hint of a British accent.

CHAPTER 14

Although it was only five in the morning, Kevin Loomis was already dressed for work. He made his way quietly to the kitchen and eased the door closed. Just because he couldn't sleep was no reason to wake Nancy or the kids. He had crawled into bed after midnight and had not drifted off for at least another hour. That made a total of about ten hours of real sleep in the days since he had first noticed the picture of Evelyn DellaRosa in the *Times* obituary section. One moment he was certain the woman in the photo was Desiree. The next moment he was certain she wasn't. There were undeniable similarities, but the woman in the photo looked younger and yet not as attractive as Desiree.

He nuked a cup of yesterday's coffee in the microwave and took it down to his basement office, a tiny space he had set up amid the boxes, out-of-season sporting equipment, heating ducts, and cinder blocks. He hadn't spent much time there since his promotion but it was still a good place to hide out and think. Besides, he thought now, it wouldn't be too much longer before the makeshift study that had served him so well was a thing of his past. Their house, a small three-bedroom on a tree-lined street in Queens, had a *Sale Pending* sign on the front lawn. It was under offer to a plumber and his wife. As soon as that sale went through, the offer Nancy and he had made on a fabulous place in Port Chester would become final. Twelve rooms, three fireplaces, and four baths on an acre and a half. It was the dream house they had thought would never be more than a dream.

New job, new car, new house, new associates, new secrets . . . it was all happening so fast. Maybe that was what was bothering him. Not the business with Desiree or Kelly or The Roundtable, but the business with Kevin Loomis. No matter how hard he tried to feel otherwise, he couldn't shake the sensation that somehow he was in over his head.

"Most of the knights have been in executive positions for years," Burt Dreiser had said on the day he finally made the offer that had so changed Kevin's life. "And they've forged a unique bond as members of The Roundtable. At first you're going to feel intimidated by them. But you needn't be. I've been watching you work around here for a long time now, and I would never have tapped you to take my place if I didn't have complete confidence in you. As long as you believe in what The Roundtable stands for—as long as you believe that our cause justifies our approach to solving problems—that's all that matters."

Kevin couldn't recall his precise response, but it had obviously been the right one. It had also been the truth. Throughout his life he had often cut corners—legal, moral, and otherwise—for things he wanted or causes he believed in. There was nothing about The Roundtable or its various programs that he couldn't accept, especially with so much at stake for his company and himself. Everything would be perfect, absolutely perfect, if only he just felt a little more at ease with the whole thing.

He smoothed Evelyn DellaRosa's obituary on his desk and reread it. Consumer editor for *Manhattan Woman* magazine fit well enough with what they knew of Desiree, but certainly not the part about her being a doctor's wife. Although she hadn't actually had sex with Kevin, she certainly had seemed ready and willing to. Gawaine had also admitted to some pretty intimate contact. He denied having intercourse with her, but Kevin always had the notion he was lying about that. Things like doctors' wives becoming call girls happened, for sure. Who hadn't read articles about suburban sex rings or watched the reports on *Hard Copy*? But Kevin certainly never thought he would find himself in the middle of such a thing. He read on.

. . . *died suddenly in a Manhattan hospital* . . .

Died suddenly. *What did that mean?*

He wondered if he should say anything to Galahad and the others. Perhaps. At the next meeting, he decided. Perhaps he should.

"What difference does it make?" he asked himself out loud.

Even if Desiree *was* Evelyn DellaRosa, what of it? There was nothing to suggest that her death had anything to do with The Roundtable. Nothing at all. Kevin's efforts to convince himself of that had almost succeeded when he fixed on the final exchange of the last meeting—the one between Galahad and Merlin.

We've come too far to let anyone threaten our work.

Wasn't that what Galahad said? It was definitely something like that, he thought. And what had Merlin responded?

Don't do anything rash. . . . At least not until you're certain she's not a policyholder with one of our companies.

Not an exact quote, perhaps, but close enough. Even at the time, Kevin had felt there was something creepy about Merlin's comment. Not the words, but the inflection, maybe . . . and the expression on his face. It was as if he and Galahad were enjoying an inside joke.

And now a woman who might be Desiree was dead . . . suddenly . . . in a hospital. . . .

Kevin was badly startled when the phone began ringing. He snatched up the receiver.

"Kevin, Burt here. Hope I didn't wake you. Listen, something's come up that I think we should talk about. Nothing serious, and nothing for you to worry about. But I wonder if you could meet me at my boat at, say, seven-thirty?"

The boat. The only place Dreiser felt truly safe and secure. It had to be Roundtable business.

"Of course," Kevin said. He cleared some tension from his throat. "I'll leave in just a few minutes."

He put the DellaRosa obituary in an envelope and pushed it into the recesses of his desk drawer. Then he went upstairs, left a note on the kitchen table for Nancy and the kids, and headed for the garage.

"Hey, hotshot, did you forget something?"

Nancy called to him from the doorway. She was holding his

briefcase in one hand and a bag of pistachios—his most enduring vice—in the other. She was dressed in the beige silk robe he had given her for Christmas. Early morning sunlight, dappled by the maples across the street, shone on her in a most appealing way. They had met in ninth grade at a church picnic and had fallen for one another immediately. Nancy Sealy was beautiful then; and now, twenty-four years and three kids later, Nancy Sealy Loomis was beautiful still. Suddenly, the vision of her was intruded upon by the image of Kelly, naked astride his thighs, stroking him patiently, expertly. For a moment, just as it had that night, his entire world consisted of her glistening, coal-black pubic hair. He had let her lick him some and even take him inside her mouth for a while—there was no red-blooded man on earth who could have said no to that. But just as with Desiree, he had drawn the line at intercourse. And for that restraint he remained grateful.

Accepting the briefcase and nuts, he kissed his wife on the cheek, then on the lips, then on the lips again—this time more passionately.

"Hey, is this an invitation?" she asked, nibbling at his ear. "Because if it is, I can call the office and tell Marty that—"

"Honey, I can't. I've got a meeting with Burt. I'll try to get home early, though. Better yet, I'll call. Maybe we can meet at the Starlight Motel."

Nancy brightened immediately at the idea.

"You mean that?"

Meeting Kevin at a motel for sex had been her oft-expressed fantasy since the one time in college when they had actually done it.

"I'll call early this afternoon," he said. "If it's possible, we'll do it."

He kissed her once more and trotted to his Lexus. That was the last time with Kelly or any other escort, he vowed. He was faithful, but he wasn't goddamn Saint Francis. Sooner or later, if he kept playing with fire, he was going to get burned. He would discuss his decision with Burt—that was just a courtesy, given all the man had done for him. But he had made up his mind. Lancelot would have to invite one less girl to the party or else do two himself. Sir Tristram was out of *that* loop.

He cut through the neighborhood and headed toward the Midtown Tunnel. Dreiser's boat, a magnificent forty-foot Bertram, was moored at a yacht club near the Seventy-ninth Street Boat Basin on the Hudson River side. Forty-second Street all the way across, then up the West Side Highway, he decided. At the last minute, he changed his mind and took the FDR. He could cross over at Seventy-second through Central Park. If he got lucky and made it there with a lot of time to spare, his laptop was on the back seat, and he had a ton of paperwork to catch up on. The portable computer had cost Crown $4500—more than he had made in six months when he was just starting out.

He slipped a Sinatra disc into the CD player and closed the windows. The custom-made sound system had twelve speakers and a twelve-band equalizer. *What a gas,* Kevin thought. *The dream machine. The dream job. The dream house.* His life was moving along like a well-oiled machine. And here he was, trying to mess it all up in his mind. He always was one to look for the catch in any situation—the cloud at the end of the silver lining. The business with Evelyn DellaRosa was probably nothing more than two women with a strong physical resemblance, and his overripe imagination at work.

Traffic in town was lighter than usual. Kevin made the dock with almost half an hour to spare. Still, Burt was already on his boat, having breakfast on the stern deck. He was a handsome fifty-one, with graying dark hair and patrician features.

"I stayed in town last night," he explained, motioning Kevin to help himself to coffee and juice.

In town meant *on the boat.* And Kevin strongly suspected that *on the boat* meant *with Brenda Wallace.* Maybe she was what this meeting was about—Burt needed an alibi.

"If you have to stay in town," Kevin said, motioning across the Hudson, "this is the way to do it."

"Your house go through yet?"

"Today or tomorrow, I think."

"Port Chester, right?"

"Yes."

"Port Chester's got some nice sections. Very nice sections."

"The house is beautiful. Nancy'll be crushed if the deal falls through."

"Let me know if any problems do come up. I'm pretty good at finding ways to solve problems."

"Thank you."

Dreiser flipped what was left of his English muffin over the stern. A seagull snagged it in midair.

"So, what's going on with you and The Roundtable?" he asked suddenly.

Kevin felt the color drain from his face.

"I don't know what you mean."

"Kevin, I was brought into The Roundtable five years ago, shortly after it was formed. After I accepted the chairmanship of Crown it became necessary for me to distance myself from the group. Our agreed-upon understanding is that should The Roundtable ever be investigated, the company CEOs would have to deny any knowledge of it. The knights wanted simply to eliminate my seat. Maybe look into bringing in someone from another company. I can't tell you how strongly I had to argue for them to allow me to choose a replacement from within Crown."

"I'm glad you succeeded."

"You should be. Let me give you an idea of what belonging to The Roundtable means to us. A year or so ago one of the knights got real bad food poisoning at some damn Chinese restaurant and then had a coronary at the hospital and died. His company CEO wasn't allowed to recommend a replacement. There had been some problems with the man. The knights, myself included, felt he lacked commitment to what we were trying to accomplish. Nobody trusted him. If he hadn't died, he probably would have gotten kicked off The Roundtable before too long. That would have been a first. But unless he changed his ways and his attitude, it would have happened. As a result of losing their representation, his company, Mutual Cooperative Health, lost something like nineteen million this past year. Nineteen million is a hit I don't want Crown ever to have to take."

"So?"

"Kevin, as I have told you many times, these men are very careful and very suspicious. This thing with that magazine reporter—what's her name?"

"She called herself Desiree, but I believe her real name might be DellaRosa. She—"

"Yes, well, that thing with the reporter upset some people. They worried about what you might have said to her."

"I didn't say—"

Dreiser raised a hand.

"Kevin, please. Let me finish."

"Sorry," Kevin mumbled.

"It was no big deal, but you were the new kid on the block. They didn't know you, so of course, they didn't completely trust you. That's understandable, yes?"

"Yes."

"Okay. The operative word here is trust. Kevin, if these men don't feel comfortable with you, they don't trust you. And if they don't trust you, you're out. And for all I know, Crown may be out, too. That would hurt us, Kevin. Nineteen or twenty million a year, and God only knows how much more in the years to come, would hurt us badly."

"I understand."

"Then why in the hell did you call Lancelot to complain about the girl he sent you?" Dreiser's voice raised just a bit.

Kevin was stunned that such a full report had been given to his CEO. He stopped himself at the last instant from making some sort of excuse or explanation. There was one thing and one thing only that Burt Dreiser wanted to hear at this point.

"It was a misunderstanding," he said. "It won't happen again."

"Excellent. Excellent." Dreiser clenched his fist for emphasis and pumped it in the air. "Kevin, I don't care what in the hell you do with those girls once they're in your room. But the more the other knights feel you're one of the gang, the quicker you actually will be. It may seem trivial to you. But believe me, when it comes to this group, nothing that goes on is trivial. There is just too much at stake."

"I understand."

"Good. You'll be fine, just fine, as long as you never forget what's on the line."

CHAPTER 15

Six days after Evie's funeral, and exactly one day before his fiftieth birthday, Harry Corbett realized he was no longer a potential suspect in a probable murder case. He was the only suspect in a definite one.

The morning had begun like all of the others since Evie's death, with Harry trying to appear focused and businesslike while his thoughts were swirling like a tornado. Although he felt almost certain that the man who had drugged and then interrogated him that night was responsible for Evie's death, there seemed to be absolutely nothing he could do about it. After leaving the apartment, he had stopped by Paladin Thorvald's shop. The two thugs who had attacked him had used Thorvald's name. But the jeweler knew nothing about them and his manner suggested that he was becoming increasingly suspicious of Harry's sanity. Harry sensed that before long, Thorvald would have company in that boat.

From Thorvald's shop he had gone to the local police station. He made it inside the front door. Then, knowing what lay ahead, he left and started for home. A block away, he screwed up his courage, prepared for yet another onslaught on his self-esteem, and went back to the station. With no keys to Desiree's apartment, all he could do was file a report and wait an hour and a half for the officer to locate the building manager. Apartment

2F had been leased to one Crystal Glass, with six months rent paid in advance in cash. Harry wondered if Crystal Glass was another of Evie's personalities or merely a display of her wit. He hoped against hope that something in the apartment might have been overlooked that would at least raise the possibility that he might not be a head case. But there was nothing. Absolutely nothing.

"Be sure to check with us if you get any further information, Dr. Corbett," the investigating officer said, earning a 9.5 on the 10-point patronization scale.

"Sure thing," Harry responded.

The two intruders at the apartment had to have been following him, he reasoned. *But for how long?* Harry worried that he might have inadvertently placed Julia Ransome in jeopardy and called to warn her. But over the intervening days, nothing had happened.

When Albert Dickinson arrived at his office to announce the new evidence that elevated his status to sole suspect, Harry was just completing a cardiac treadmill test on a seventy-six-year-old retired printer named Daniel Gerstein. Gerstein, a cantankerous survivor of the Nazi camps, adamantly refused to see any other doctor for the stress test to evaluate his persistent chest pain, so Harry had temporarily abandoned his policy of not doing them. His patient had sailed through the protocol with no symptoms and no changes on his cardiogram. Degenerative arthritis of the rib cage and shoulders, Harry told him. Gerstein demanded a more impressive diagnosis and the feel-good medicine his friends all got from *their* doctors. He settled for "advanced noncardiac thoracic arthralgia" and some Motrin.

As he watched the elderly man's heart rate climb without any abnormality on the monitor screen, Harry wondered if his own stress test would look nearly so good. The chest pain he had experienced in Evie's apartment *had* prompted him to call a cardiologist. But when he was informed the man was out of town at a meeting, he had made no attempt to contact another. Instead, he ran especially hard during his next few workouts on the track. There was no recurrence of the discomfort. And each symptom-free day dulled the memories of the numbing sensation and produced any number of plausible explanations for it.

What was really happening, he decided, was that his family history—the Corbett curse he had created—had given him an abnormally high cardiac awareness. The minor aches and pains most people would simply ignore were gaining heightened significance in his mind. His brother had to have had some chest discomfort from time to time. There wasn't a soul who didn't. Yet Phil wasn't running around checking calendars and calling cardiologists. It was because he didn't believe for one second that his genetics had doomed him to an early coronary.

Sometime soon, Harry was thinking as he wrote out renewals for Daniel Gerstein's blood-pressure pills. Sometime soon he really would call someone and set up a stress test. But at the moment, curse or no curse, there were other, more pressing concerns in his life.

That was when Mary Tobin's voice crackled through his intercom announcing that he had two visitors, an Officer Graham and a Detective Dickinson.

Dickinson directed Officer Graham, who was in uniform, to one of the chairs Harry offered, but remained standing himself, pacing as he talked. He still reeked of cigarettes and was dressed in what looked to Harry to be the same ill-fitting polyester suit he had had on at the hospital.

"So, Doc," Dickinson began, surveying the diplomas and artwork, "I told you that night in the hospital I'd be back. And here I am."

"Here you are," Harry echoed sardonically.

"That's a pretty full waiting room you have out there. You always that busy?"

"Lieutenant, do you think you could come back after five? A lot of those people out there have gone to a good deal of inconvenience to make it in for their appointments. I try to be on time."

"I wish my doctor cared so much about being on time. Dr. McNally on Central Park West. You know him?"

"I don't. Lieutenant, how long is this going to take?"

"That depends."

"On what?"

"On you, Doc. Does the name"—he pulled out his spiral-bound pad and read the word a syllable at a time—"me-tar-am-i-nol mean anything to you?"

Harry felt his heart sink. The faint glimmer of hope that Evie's blood analysis might be negative had just vanished.

"It's met*aram*inol," he said, correcting the pronunciation. "The brand name we doctors know it by is Aramine."

"And you know what it does?"

"Yes, I know what it does. Lieutenant, get to the point."

"You keep any of this me-tar-am-i-nol around?"

"It's almost never used by anyone anymore. I don't keep it around. I never have. Now would you say what you have to say and leave? I have patients to—"

Dickinson whirled on him.

"I'll say what I have to say when I am fucking good and ready," he snapped, his fists clenched. "If you can't do what my fucking doctor does, which is to keep everyone sitting around until he feels like seeing them, then call your receptionist out there and have her send them all home."

"Get out of here," Harry said. "Now."

"Or what? Or you'll call the cops?" Dickinson sighed, ostensibly to calm himself. "Look, Doc. Let's try to work together on this thing. It will be better for everyone that way."

Harry snatched up the phone to call the precinct house. Then he hesitated, set the receiver back down, and sank back in his chair.

"What do you want?" he asked.

"I want you to own up to what you did to your wife."

"What?"

"Doc, I know you did it, you know you did it, anyone who knows anything about this case knows you did it. Now all you have to do is admit it."

"I didn't do anything. Did Evie have Aramine in her blood?"

Dickinson smiled condescendingly.

"Only enough to blow the tops off the heads of the whole New York Giants football team. The ME says no one but an M.D. or someone in the pharmaceutical business would have known about this stuff. Now come on, Doc. How about it?"

"I didn't kill her." This time it was Harry's turn to sigh. As unsubstantiated as his information was, at this point there was no sense in keeping it from Dickinson. "She was killed by a man I believe is a doctor. Probably the man Maura Hughes saw come into the room. Evie was working on a story that was making someone very worried. All I know is that it had to do with high-priced call girls and very important people. She was killed to keep her from finishing it. The night after her funeral I found the stuff she had been working on in an apartment in the Village."

"And?"

"And this doctor and two of his thugs broke in on me before I could read much of it." Sooner or later he would have to disclose the nature of Evie's alter ego and her writing. But he wasn't ready yet.

"How do you know he's a doctor?"

"I don't know for sure. I just think he is because he knows his way around hospitals and drugs. He put an IV in my arm in the apartment, then he drugged me with some pretty sophisticated stuff and questioned me for several hours. Finally, he cleaned out the apartment completely and left."

"Leaving you alive after you had seen his face?"

"I . . . I never did see his face. Or the other two for that matter." He noted the cynicism in Dickinson's expression turn to incredulity. "The two thugs wore stocking masks," he explained. "By the time the doctor or whatever he is came on the scene my eyes were taped over. Maura Hughes is the only one I know of who saw his face."

It had not taken long for Harry to appreciate why the mysterious physician had let him live. Under the influence of the potent hypnotic chemicals he had told everything he knew, which was essentially nothing. The man knew he had been interrupted before he got more than a glance at Evie's material. And there was nothing in what he had read or seen that would incriminate anyone. No names, no dates, no places. If the M.D. had faith in his methods—and there was every reason to believe he was expert at such interrogations—he knew Harry posed no threat to him.

But now Harry understood that there was another, more logical reason he had been left alive. If Caspar Sidonis had not stormed in with his anger and suspicion, no one would have questioned that Evie's death was due to natural causes. Hemorrhage at any stage of the game was a well-accepted complication of berry aneurysms. The medical examiner would have signed her off without a second thought. Instead, at Sidonis's insistence, a thorough analysis of her blood was being performed. The Aramine was bound to be identified, and Harry would be available to take the blame. His murder or disappearance now would only ensure an intensified investigation of Evie's case. He had been spared death at the hands of the gladiators in favor of a more protracted demise from the lions.

"So tell me, Doc," Dickinson asked, "how do you know this guy from the apartment is the same man who killed your wife?"

"I don't—at least not for certain. Now, would you please go?"

"I have a warrant to search this office for that drug, Doc. Your condo, too."

"Oh, this is ridiculous! If I had done what you say, I certainly wouldn't be stupid enough to keep a batch of Aramine around."

"Doc, you were stupid enough to kill your wife and think you could get away with it. That's more than stupid enough to keep a batch of Aramine around. See, Graham? I told you. These M.D.s never give anyone credit for having any brains. That's why they always fuck up, and that's why they always get caught."

The young officer shifted uncomfortably in his seat and looked away.

"You're going to search this office while I'm seeing patients?"

"We don't have to if you just tell us the truth. Look, I know about your wife's affair with Super Doc. I know she was planning on leaving you. I know about the tidy little insurance policy you stand to cash in. I know about the drug you used. And I know you were the last one to see her alive. Now how about it, Doc. Maybe it was just a spur of the moment thing. She was a beautiful woman. You couldn't stand the thought of losing her. Suddenly you pass by the medication room. You think about that aneurysm of hers. Next thing you know the drug is in your hand. . . . Second degree. That's what you'd get. Nothing more. Second degree's not that big a deal, Doc. You could be out in five years. Maybe even get off entirely, you find yourself a good lawyer."

Dickinson studied the citation framed alongside the silver star. *Killed three of the enemy.* Harry knew the words were not going unnoticed. Suddenly, a thought occurred to him—a question, complete with its answer.

"Lieutenant, tell me something," he said. "If you know all this about me, and you're so certain I murdered my wife, why haven't you come here with a warrant for my arrest?"

"Pardon?"

"A warrant. Some judge or magistrate or whatever has refused to issue a warrant for you to arrest me for murder unless you find I've got a secret stash of Aramine. Isn't that true?"

Dickinson's expression—the tightness around his mouth—said that he had been nicked.

"What if it is?" he said. "In two weeks the grand jury sits. And I guarantee you that with the evidence I have to present them, they won't have any problem handing down an indictment. Graham, let's get started."

"Wait a minute, Officer." On the offensive at last, Harry had no intention of letting up. "Lieutenant, there's more, isn't there? Is it Maura Hughes? Your magistrate believed her claim about someone else being in the room after me. That's it, isn't it?"

"You killed that woman, Corbett."

"They believed her, didn't they?"

"Not her," Dickinson said, barely able to temper his frustration and anger. "Her goddamn Yalie brother. That asshole went over my head. Filed a report. Cooked his own friggin' goose is what he did. Believe me, Charles Manson will get that goddamn detective slot before he does. And don't think for a moment they bought his story, neither. He just made them decide to wait until a few things could be checked out, that's all. And as for your drunken sot witness, her brother won't be able to take the stand in her place. And as soon as anyone gets a look at her and hears what she's like, there's not a soul who'll believe she saw anything except spiders and flies. Now, are you going to let us do our work?"

"Do I have a choice?"

"No, Corbett. You don't have a fucking choice. You're a smug bastard. I hate smug bastards. And you killed your wife. I hate people who do that, too. It's just begun between us, Doc. Mark my words. I'm going to put the screws to you like you were a dime-store Erector set. And sooner or later you're going to fuck up. Count on it. Come on, Graham. Let's get started."

It took two hours for Dickinson and Graham to finish their room-by-room search of the office. Harry waited a few minutes until he was certain the detective wasn't going to return. Then he took a cup of tepid coffee and a bagel back to his office, fished out the slip of paper from his wallet, and called Maura Hughes. She answered on the sixth ring.

"Miss Hughes, it's Harry Corbett, Evie's husband. Remember?"

"I remember."

Though her words weren't slurred, her voice was husky, and her speech seemed a bit thick. Harry wasn't sure whether she was drinking again.

"How are you feeling?" he tried.

"I've been better."

"Sorry."

"But I've been worse."

He waited for more unsolicited conversation, but quickly realized there would be none. "Have the police been to see you?"

"Nope."

"Well, they just left my office, and I think they might be contacting you soon. They found a drug in Evie's blood. She was murdered." There was silence on the other end. "That Lieutenant Dickinson is certain I did it. I think it must have been the doctor you saw." Still silence. "Miss Hughes, are you still there?"

"It's Maura. I'm still here."

"Are you okay?"

"You mean am I drinking?"

Harry pictured the woman in her robe at the kitchen table of a small, dingy apartment, staring at a half-filled glass and a half-empty bottle of Southern Comfort. The image brought a heavy sadness to his throat.

"Yes, I guess I did mean that," he said. "Sorry. It's none of my business. Listen, I want to get together with you. It's very important to me."

"Why?"

"That cop, Dickinson, is on a mission to nail me for Evie's murder. He just left here after searching my office for hours while all my patients watched. In fact, there were moments when the only thing that kept me from hitting him over the head with a chair was remembering what you called him. Pinhead."

"I remember."

"Well, the only reason they haven't arrested me so far is that someone—a judge or DA, or maybe one of Dickinson's superiors—is worried that the man your brother reported you saw was actually there."

"He was."

"I know. That's why I need to see you. Somehow, I've got to find out who he is, and you're the only one who's seen him."

There was a prolonged silence.

"When did you want to see me?" she said finally.

"I don't know. Tonight?"

"Can't."

"Tomorrow, then." He considered adding that it would be his birthday—his fiftieth birthday—but decided against it. "Maura, listen," he said, "if you're embarrassed about drinking, please don't be."

"Seven-thirty," she replied. "You have my number, so I assume you know where I live."

"I do. Thanks, Maura."

"And Dr. Corbett?"

"Yes?"

"I can't remember the last time I cared enough about what I did to be embarrassed about it. But since you keep asking, the truth is that if it sounds like I've been drinking it's because I just got up from a nap. I haven't had a drink since the day I was operated on."

"Hey, that's great."

"But I was about to."

"Please—don't!" Harry did not have to force desperation into the words. Again there was prolonged silence.

"I suppose I can keep it together at least until tomorrow night. I think maybe I really don't want to drink. Maybe I'm just bored."

"Your brother said you were a painter. Have you been able to paint any since you've been home?"

"Not really. I haven't done much of anything except hang around here, take naps, feel sorry for myself, and think about drinking."

"Well, listen, maybe tomorrow night we could go out for dinner. You're the main reason I'm still a free man. I could pick your brain, and you could get away from your place for a while."

If she was as depressed as she sounded, he knew there was no possibility she would agree. He could feel her choosing the way to tell him so.

"Do I have to get dressed up?" she asked suddenly.

"Not unless you want to. When I'm not at work, jeans is as dressy as I ever get."

"In that case, sure," Maura said. "I'd like that."

CHAPTER 16

At midnight, when he officially turned fifty, Harry celebrated with a glass of champagne and a bag of Famous Amos chocolate chip cookies. He hadn't gotten cancer or been run over by a bus during the past three hundred and sixty-five days, but all things considered, his fiftieth year had been a pretty lousy one. And his fifty-first was not beginning with a great deal of promise. He indulged his self-pity for a time by flipping through his and Evie's wedding album, and then read himself to sleep with half a page of his most dependable soporific, *Moby-Dick*. Ahab wasn't having such a great year either.

At 5:45, when his clock radio kicked in, he had already been awake for nearly an hour and was finishing the set of Marine Corps calisthenics he did on the days when he didn't run. He had always been an athlete of sorts—Little League baseball, cross-country, and some organized basketball in college. He lacked the natural ability to be a star in any sport, but his competitive fire had made him a fairly consistent winner. For the past decade, though, what intensity he still possessed was focused on holding his ground against the passing years. Now, as he grunted past sixty bent-knee sit-ups on the way to seventy-five, he found he was drawing strength from his consuming dislike for Albert Dickinson.

The previous evening, Harry had arrived at home to find

the detective there, along with a new uniformed policeman. He was questioning Armand Rojas, the day-shift doorman, but stopped as soon as Harry appeared at the door, and produced a warrant to search the apartment. Following the Chinese-food deliveryman fiasco with Ročky, Harry had tipped both doormen handsomely and implored them to be on their toes. Still, he wondered, as the two policemen followed him into the apartment to begin their search, if the mystery physician had somehow gotten in there again to plant a few vials of Aramine. His other concern was that Dickinson himself might find a way to do it.

To Harry's profound relief, the one-and-a-half-hour inspection unearthed nothing. But with each fruitless minute, Dickinson became more annoyed—and more determined. By the time he and the other cop had left, he had reiterated in a variety of colorful and profane ways his threat to put the screws to Harry.

There was a small, enclosed terrace off the master bedroom. It had a view of the midsection of another apartment building, and might have been considered a solarium if it ever received anything more than token sunlight. Evie had had many plans for the room when they first moved into the apartment, but soon lost interest in them. There were similar terraces all the way up the building. Those on the upper floors had expansive views and hours of direct sunlight. Over time, the room came to symbolize those things she felt were second-rate in their life, and she absolutely never went out there.

Eventually, Harry had replaced the table, chairs, and small sofa with his exercise mat, stationary bicycle, weights, and a twelve-inch TV. Now, he turned on the early morning news and began a sequence of lifts with ten-pound barbells, aimed at maintaining strength in the muscles in his back—muscles that had been surgically repaired after being shredded at Nha-trang. The lead story this morning was about the cascading rumors of sexual impropriety that continued to plague the president and undermine his effectiveness. The second story dealt with the Republican filibuster that had all but damned the strict caps on health-insurance premiums demanded by the administration's health-care package. The third story was about Evie's murder.

"Evelyn DellaRosa, consumer editor at *Manhattan Woman*

magazine and wife of prominent Manhattan physician Dr. Harry Corbett, died of a brain hemorrhage last week at the Manhattan Medical Center." Evie's stock photo appeared behind the anchorwoman with the word MURDERED scrolled across it in crimson. "Now, according to reliable police sources, the death of the former beauty queen and television reporter is being treated as a homicide. . . ."

Harry set the weights aside and sank to one knee as the details of the medical examiner's findings were presented in TV shorthand. Behind the reporter flashed first a photo of MMC, then a close-up of a vial labeled *Aramine* with a syringe protruding from the top, and finally, one of Harry himself—a twenty-year-old shot of him in dress uniform that someone had resurrected from the photo morgue at the *Times*.

"According to police sources, the only suspect currently under investigation in DellaRosa's murder is her husband, a general practitioner on the staff of the hospital in which she was slain. Reportedly, Dr. Corbett, who was awarded the silver star for bravery in Vietnam, was his wife's last visitor before her fatal hemorrhage. Police claim the couple was having marital difficulties. No other details are available at this time. . . ."

Harry buried his face in his hands. Weariness and perspiration burned in his eyes. As promised, Dickinson was off and running. And aside from remaining as composed as possible before the eruption that was about to occur, there wasn't a goddamn thing Harry could do about it. At that moment, the phone began ringing. It was Rocky Martino, the night doorman. A film crew from Channel 11 had just shown up in the lobby, and the reporter was demanding to see Harry about the murder of his wife.

Tell them to go fuck themselves, Harry thought.

"Tell them there will be no interviews," he said, "and don't say anything to them yourself. Nothing at all. Can I get out of the building through that metal door in the furnace room? . . . Great. Rocky, believe me, I didn't do anything to hurt Evie. . . . Thank you. Thank you for saying that. Now remember, no matter how much you want to help me, don't say anything at all to anyone."

Seconds after he had hung up, the phone was ringing again.

This time it was his brother. Before Evie's funeral, Harry had shared with Phil a good deal of what had transpired at the hospital with Sidonis and Dickinson. Phil had offered then to put him in touch with a top-notch attorney, but Harry had decided to wait.

"You been watching TV?" Phil asked.

"Yeah."

"You okay?"

"Would you be?"

"When did you know for sure about that drug being in Evie?"

"Yesterday afternoon. They came and searched the office for it. Then last night they searched my apartment."

"I take it they didn't find anything. Harry, you should have called me when the cops showed up at your office. You have rights. You should have let me call my friend Mel. He's an animal. Most obnoxious son of a bitch I've ever known. I mean that as a compliment, of course. You want me to call him now?"

"How do you know him, Phil?"

"How do you think? He's bought a new Mercedes from me every year since I went into the business. This year it's a 600 SEL —the big one. Black. That's the first thing you gotta check when you get a lawyer. Not his law school or his bar exam score. The car he drives. Course, he'd cost you. You're probably looking at a twenty- or twenty-five-thousand-dollar retainer."

Harry was shocked. "Let me think about it, okay?"

"Don't take too long. Oh, and Harry—"

"Yes?"

"Happy birthday."

Mary Tobin was the next to call. Harry had made the front page of two papers. He assured her he'd be in for a full day at the office and told her not to argue with anyone who wanted to cancel an appointment or even change doctors. Rocky, then Phil, now Mary—and it was just half past six. He said a silent thanks to Evie for insisting their number be unlisted.

He stripped out of his sweats and was waiting for the shower water to heat up when the phone again began ringing. This time, he decided, the machine could answer it. He hovered close enough to hear the caller.

"Hello, you have reached the phone of Evie and Harry. . . ."

The voice was Evie's. It was both bittersweet and somewhat ghoulish to hear her speaking this way. Before he left for work, he told himself, he had to remember to record a new greeting.

"Dr. Corbett, Samuel Rennick speaking. I'm chief counsel for the hospital. If you're screening calls, could you please pick up . . ."

Harry leaned against the bathroom door frame. Steam from the shower had begun to fill the small room. *Goddamn Dickinson,* he was thinking.

". . . Okay, then. I guess I'll leave a message and then try to reach you at the hospital. . . ." The lawyer paused again. It was as if he knew Harry was listening. ". . . Dr. Erdman would like to meet with you about the developments this morning. His office, ten o'clock. If there's a problem with that time, please call his secretary. Dr. Erdman has asked that I be there, as well as Dr. Lord from the medical staff, Dr. Josephson, who is acting chief of your department, and Mr. Atwater from Manhattan Health. I'll be at Dr. Erdman's office beginning at eight. You can reach me there if need be. Thank you."

Owen Erdman, a highly political, Harvard-educated and -trained endocrinologist, had been president of MMC for nearly a decade, during which time he had overseen the physical transformation of a shabby institution and a turnaround of its shaky reputation. The jewel in the crown of his reformation had been the affiliation with Manhattan Health. But Harry knew that with the new federal health policies, alliances between caregivers were as fragile as spring ice, and an allegiance meant something only so long as it was profitable. Any piece of negative publicity for MMC had to be worrisome to the CEO.

Harry had heard via the hospital grapevine that his minor victory against the edicts of the Sidonis committee did not sit well with Erdman. Now he was responsible for more soot falling on the man's house. Harry showered quickly and then called his brother.

"Phil, I've decided to take you up on your offer about that lawyer," he said.

"Smart move, bro."

"If so, it will be the first one I've made in a while."

. . .

Attorney Mel Wetstone's retainer, "marked down twenty-five percent because Phil's such a good friend," was indeed $20,000 against an hourly rate of $350. And here the President was, Harry thought, knocking himself out and pitting brother against brother across the country to effect *health care* reform. Perhaps a bit of attention was due the legal system as well.

Harry decided to borrow the $20,000 against his pension plan, rather than wipe out a large portion of his savings. He met with his new lawyer in the family medicine conference room on the seventh floor of the Alexander Building at MMC. Wetstone was a prosperous fortyish, a dozen or so pounds overweight, with thinning dark hair that looked as if it had been surgically augmented. There was a slight wheeze to his breathing. Hard-pressed at times to forget that the meter was running at $350 an hour, Harry reviewed his complete story in detail for the first time, including the encounter in the Village with his apparent nemesis. Wetstone was a sympathetic listener and only rarely interrupted the narrative with a question.

"So," Wetstone said after Harry had finished, "what it boils down to is that you didn't do anything wrong, and people think you did. In my business that's the norm. My job will be to keep anyone from hurting you. Now, what do you think this meeting at ten is all about?"

"I don't know for certain. I've taken some stands on issues lately that haven't been too popular with the administration. Now I'm publicly giving them a black eye. I don't think they'd just boot me off the staff at this point, although I guess they could. More likely they'll want to ask me to take a voluntary leave from the hospital until the situation is ironed out."

"You want to do that?"

"No. Of course not."

"Then that'll be our goal. You told me who this Erdman is, and I know Sam Rennick. Who are the other guys?"

"Bob Lord is the chief of staff. He's an orthopedic surgeon. He resents that I led the fight to continue to allow GPs to put simple, nondisplaced fractures in casts without referring our patients to a specialist. He's very much into who's got the power and who doesn't, and I think he's pretty tight with the surgeon Evie was involved with. I can't imagine him siding with me on anything. Josephson and Atwater are a different story. They're about the best friends I have around here. Steve—that's Josephson—is the acting head of the family medicine department until Grace Segal gets back from a maternity leave. Atwater and I are both jazz nuts. We go to clubs together once in a while, and sometimes he comes to hear me play."

Harry expected the usual questions, like *"Oh, what instrument do you play?"* or *"You play professionally? Where?"* Instead, Wetstone straightened his notes and stood up.

"I want to see if I can speak with Sam Rennick before we go in there," he said. "I left a message for him to call my pager, but he hasn't."

"You said you knew him. Perhaps he's afraid of you."

Wetstone grinned, but his small, dark eyes were cold—all business.

"I don't know," he said, "but he should be."

There were fifteen floors in the Alexander Building. The elevator down was nearly full when it reached the seventh floor. By the time it reached the lobby, it was packed. A sign on the wall of the car warned passengers to guard their valuables against pickpockets. After thousands of trips, Harry had already reflexively shifted his wallet from his hip pocket to the front. He thought about what it would be like to work in a scrubbed little rural hospital with no crushes of people and no pickpocket warnings. He doubted that there was a single scrubbed little rural hospital this side of Bora Bora that would take him, should he be removed from the MMC staff.

The conference room adjacent to Owen Erdman's office featured a long, highly polished cherrywood table with rounded corners and an inlay of the MMC crest at the center. The twelve matching, high-backed chairs each had an identical crest in miniature inlaid at the top. Harry had been in the room once some years before, but was certain the remarkable set had not been there. He tried briefly to guess its value, then gave up when he realized he had absolutely no reference point. *Evie would have known*, he thought. *Possibly to the dollar.*

Steve Josephson, Doug Atwater, and the orthopedist Bob Lord were there when Harry and Wetstone arrived.

"How're you doing?" Steve asked.

Harry answered with a *How do you think?* shrug.

"Do you have any idea who could have been responsible for doing this to Evie?" Doug asked.

"Not really," Harry said, careful to stop there.

Wetstone had cautioned him against sharing his theory with anyone, even his allies.

"Remember that party game of Telephone we used to play as kids?" the attorney had asked. "Well, take it from the voice of experience. No matter how well-meaning people are, the moment words are out of your mouth and into their ears, the original version begins to change."

Despite Wetstone's caveat, Harry would not have hesitated to share the details of Evie's secret life with either Josephson or Atwater had Bob Lord not been there. Instead, there was an uncomfortable minute and a half of silence before Erdman and the hospital counsel entered the room. With them was a trim, businesslike woman introduced as Ms. Hinkle, the hospital's head of public relations. Harry shook her hand and felt as if he had grasped a Popsicle.

"Dr. Corbett," Sam Rennick began, "we wondered if you might start by reviewing the events—as you see them—from the night of your wife's death."

"Now just a minute, Sam," Wetstone rejoined immediately. "I thought we decided on what the ground rules were going to be here. . . ."

Feeling strangely distant and distracted, Harry listened as two attorneys whom he had not even known before today debated his situation. From time to time, one of the others at the table spoke up. He even heard himself once or twice. But the voices seemed distorted, the meaning of their words often lost. The whole situation was just too surreal. Instead of being keen and focused, Harry's thoughts were drifting. He tried to imagine how many hours—hundreds of hours, perhaps—he was now destined to spend in one type of legal proceeding or another. He had been thrust through the looking glass into a world where anything—however illogical or bizarre—was possible.

Inexplicably, with the discussion of his professional future raging about him, he found himself thinking about a patient of his, a teenager named Melinda Olivera, whose severe mononucleosis he had recently diagnosed and treated so aggressively that within a day, she was able to attend her junior prom. Doctoring had always seemed so straightforward to him. A patient shows up sick and you do the best you can to fix them up. Now, suddenly, there were lawyers and administrators and public-relations directors.

"I absolutely disagree." Doug Atwater's sharp words pierced Harry's mental fog. Harry had no idea what was being discussed. "I have already reviewed matters with the CEO at Manhattan Health, and he has spoken with the medical director and several other key personnel. There has never been even one complaint about Dr. Corbett—his manner of practice, his fees, or his conduct. We see no reason why he shouldn't continue to be on Manhattan Health's role of providers."

"But what will the public think if—"

Doug cut Ms. Hinkle short.

"Please, I don't mean to be rude, Barbara, but what we need is some sort of strong statement from the hospital that Dr. Corbett has been formally charged with nothing as yet, and we at this hospital . . ."

Harry heard little of what followed, but not because his mind was wandering. He had reached inside the right-hand pocket of his sports jacket for a pen. There was none. What he felt instead were two objects he knew had not been there when he put the jacket on that morning. In fact, he knew they had not even been in his possession. Slowly, he clenched his fist around them and brought them out onto his lap.

"It's agreed, then," Mel Wetstone was saying. "The hospital's posture will be one of support for a respected staff member who has not been convicted of or even charged with a crime. For his part, Dr. Corbett will refrain from any public statements without clearing them with Ms. Hinkle. And his admitting and treatment privileges at this hospital will remain intact. Does that sound okay with you, Dr. Corbett? . . . Dr. Corbett?"

"Huh? Oh, yes. Thank you all. That's excellent."

He barely managed to pull his attention from his hand, now open on his lap. On his palm lay his watch and Evie's rabbit's-foot key chain and keys, gone when he awoke in Desiree's apartment. At some point that morning, perhaps in the crowded elevator, Evie's murderer had been standing behind him, or maybe even right next to him. The keys were meant as a reminder of how vulnerable he was—a warning to be very careful what he said and to whom. But there was also another possibility, he acknowledged, even more disturbing and chilling—the possibility that he was nothing more to his wife's murderer than sport, a pawn in some macabre game.

"Pardon?" Wetstone asked.

"Excuse me?" Harry replied, again realizing he had drifted.

"Harry, you just said something like, 'I'm not going to be that easy.' What did that mean?"

"Oh, nothing," Harry said, slipping the watch and keys back into his pocket. "Nothing important."

★ ★ ★

Coroner Rules Manhattan
Reporter's Death a Homicide

Kevin Loomis stared at the headline in the *Times*. The photo of Evelyn DellaRosa was the same as the one in her obituary. He tried, as he had for the past week, to convince himself that her resemblance to Desiree was coincidental. But deep inside, he knew the truth. A month and a half ago, wearing nothing but a bra and panties, she had knelt astride him, kneading the tightness from his back as she asked in a most flattering, disarming way about him and his life.

Kevin read through the article. His hands were shaking so hard he had to keep the paper pressed to the table. At the last meeting, Desiree had been more or less dismissed as not a serious threat to The Roundtable. Then, just a few days later, she had been murdered in her hospital bed. Her doctor husband was a suspect, but no arrest had been made. *Maybe that was because he hadn't killed her.*

Kevin felt squeamish. Throughout the ride to the city, he tried to convince himself that he was reacting this way because of the intimacy, however artificial, that he had shared with the woman not so long ago. The newspapers—and by now he had read the account in all of them—told of marital problems. The *Daily News* alluded to a lover. Evelyn DellaRosa or Desiree or whoever the hell she was had been murdered by her husband, and that was that.

Kevin did not remember making even one of the turns that took him from his driveway to the Crown Building in midtown Manhattan. He parked in the underground space with his name stenciled in blue on the wall and took the elevator up to his office on the thirty-first floor. Brenda Wallace was waiting for him, barely able to contain her enthusiasm as she told him the news.

"Your wife called a few minutes ago, Mr. Loomis," she said, breathless with excitement. "She said the people buying your house have gotten their mortgage and the bank has approved the deal for your new house in Port Chester."

Standing in the doorway behind her, Burt Dreiser gave Kevin a wink and a thumbs up. His expression left no doubt that he had played a role in expediting the sale.

"I'm pretty good at finding ways to solve problems," he had said that day on his boat.

"The closing's scheduled for Wednesday," Brenda gushed on. "Mrs. Loomis says you can call her at the office if you want. She'll be there until five. She also said to tell you that the house is really no big deal, and you don't have to go through with it, but that next to the day you two got married, this is the happiest day of her life."

CHAPTER 17

Maura Hughes's apartment was on the Upper West Side, half a block from Morningside Park. Harry walked there from the office, hoping that Maura had been able to honor her promise to stay sober. Practicing in a fairly indigent area, he had encountered the disease of alcoholism in its most virulent, lethal form, as well as in its many other guises. It would be no exaggeration to say that he had seen even more tragedy caused by the bottle than he had seen in eighteen months in Nam. And it was hardly reassuring to have his future bound to a woman who had almost lost her life to drinking. Even sober, her credibility was thin. If she started drinking again, it was nonexistent.

With Maura's claims of a mystery doctor and no physical evidence connecting Harry to the Aramine injection, Dickinson had been denied an arrest warrant. But Mel Wetstone supported the detective's assertion that based on the impressive circumstantial evidence, a grand jury would produce an indictment. The attorney seemed aroused by the prospect of defending Harry in what might well become a trial of Von Bülow proportions. Sex, adultery, insurance money, a beautiful reporter's secret life, prostitution, arcane poisons, physicians. *Ringmaster of a media circus at an hourly rate of $350.* Harry tried to recall if he had ever considered attending law school.

He passed a florist, debated picking up an assortment, then

quickly rejected the notion. Flowers were too reminiscent of the hospital and too open to misinterpretation. Not that Maura Hughes had seemed the least bit interested in him as anything other than a source of Southern Comfort. But he had, over the years, endured unpleasant experiences with patients of both sexes who had misread the meaning of his commitment. In one case it was a concerned after-hours telephone call to a woman whose infatuation with him he had completely missed. Another was an extended late-night conversation at a young man's hospital bedside.

Harry finally settled on a box of chocolate-covered mints. If Maura was typical of someone newly sober, her desire for alcohol had been sublimated at least in part by a craving for sweets.

The homes improved measurably as he approached Maura's block. The apartment buildings had doormen, and a number of the brownstones were well maintained. It was nearing seven-thirty, but the evening was warm, cloudless, and quite light. Harry paused by a playground where a group of kids—black and white—were playing pickup basketball on a scarred blacktop court. They were mostly in their early teens and had no concept of teamwork, but their skills made them a joy to watch. He breathed in the energy of the city and felt some of the tension begin to ease from what had been an absolutely horrible day. The only bright spots were Doug Atwater's successful efforts to keep him, at least for the time being, on the active staff at the hospital, and the almost continuous calls and gestures of support from his patients.

Although he had no idea what to expect from Maura Hughes, he realized that he was looking forward to her company. He had played bass with the guys at C.C.'s once since Evie's death, but most of his evenings had been spent alone.

Her house was a neat four-story brownstone with six broad cement stairs rising from the sidewalk to an ornate mahogany door. There was a floor at street level, with no outside entryway and windows protected by heavy wrought-iron grates. Harry suspected this basement apartment was Maura's. He was surprised to find that of the three bells, the topmost one was hers. He identified himself through an intercom, and she buzzed him in.

"Head of the stairs," she said.

Her voice sounded sharp and animated—a hopeful sign. Harry mounted the stairs feeling some relief. As much as he needed company, having to babysit an actively drinking alcoholic was not the way he wanted to spend his free time. Maura was standing in the doorway to her apartment. His image of her from the hospital was of someone quite short. Actually, she was tall, five-nine or -ten, with a regal bearing and a willowy body that looked perfect in sneakers, worn jeans, and an oversized cotton shirt. She wore a white turban and no jewelry other than a pair of large hanging earrings—colorful chips of enamel delicately wired to one another so that they changed like a kaleidoscope with every movement of her head. She looked somewhat drawn and ill at ease. Her hand, thin and smooth, was cool. Except for the headdress, there was no way Harry could connect the lithe, unaffectedly elegant woman with the restless, wild-eyed patient he had known.

He handed her the mints. She thanked him with a thin smile that had more sadness than mirth.

"Come in. Come in, please," she said.

"Those earrings are really beautiful."

"Thanks. I made them."

Harry followed her into an expansive living room—a bright and airy square, perhaps thirty feet on a side. The narrow oak flooring was urethaned to a high gloss and scattered with Oriental area rugs. The ceilings were high, with recessed, indirect lighting that had to have been designed by a specialist in the craft. This was hardly the dingy, depressing two-room walk-up he had envisioned.

"Surprised?" Maura said, reading his expression.

Harry gestured to the walls, which were filled with wonderful paintings. The canvases were generally large and mostly oils or some kind of acrylic. But there were also watercolors and a few collages. Some, primarily portraits, were sad and starkly realistic. But the rest were abstract—dynamic worlds of color and shape, of meticulous organization and absolute chaos. Harry had never been a student of art, but he had always been affected by it. What he was sensing now was a remarkable vibrancy and an intense, overwhelming anger.

"These are incredible," he said, walking slowly about the room.

"I don't paint like that anymore. Not that I don't want to."

"These are all yours?"

"Even drunks can do things," she said coolly.

"Hey, I'm sorry if it sounded like that's what I meant. It's not. These paintings are really striking."

"Thanks. You want something? A Coke? Some wine?"

"Coke would be great."

Harry stopped himself at the last moment from commenting on the danger of keeping alcohol in the house. He followed her to the kitchen, which was small, but designed for someone who cared about cooking. To the left of it, he could see another huge room—a studio with several easels, stacks of canvases, and a large skylight. In the far corner, beneath a packed floor-to-ceiling bookcase and surrounded by ferns and various palms, was Maura's bed.

"Look, I—I'm sorry if I seem tense or nervous," she said, her back to him as she filled two glasses. "It's just that I am. I probably should have called and canceled."

She handed him his glass, led him back into the living room, and motioned him to a sofa opposite her chair. On the glass-top end table to her left was the *Times*, open to the article about Evie. Harry gestured toward the paper.

"I guess if I was having a murder suspect over for a Coke, I'd be a little nervous, too," he said.

"I hope you know that isn't it. You and I both know you didn't give that drug to your wife."

"What then?"

"Dr. Corbett, just why are you here?"

"Look, please. My name's Harry. Once I leave the office, I stop being Dr. Corbett."

"And have you?"

"Have I what?"

"Left the office. Dr. Corbett . . . Harry . . . my brother told me what you said to him about your being some sort of expert on alcoholism, and about how you have people who will help me and take me to AA meetings and all. If you're here to save my soul, I think I can save both of us a long, uncomfortable evening. My soul is in the mood to be pickled, not saved."

"Hey, I don't know exactly what I said to your brother, but I'm not an expert on anything, except maybe taking care of sick people."

"Then that's not why you're here? You're not here to ensure that I don't drink?"

"I didn't say that either. Tell me something. If you believed I was coming over to save your soul, as you put it, why did you say yes?"

"Because yesterday, deep down inside, I really didn't want to drink. Today, I do."

Harry could feel walls going up. Either he had somehow gotten off on the wrong foot or she was determined to put him there. If he tried to lie to her now about his motives, she would know. If he told her the truth or tried to lecture her in any way, he would probably be back at the playground watching basketball before his Coke was warm.

"Maura, I'm here because I'm in trouble," he said finally. "There's a cop out to crucify me, my hospital's looking for a way to drop me from the staff, and you're the only one who knows anything that might help me. I don't have any idea who you saw walk past you to Evie's bedside, or why he killed her. But the other night he could have killed me as well, and he didn't. I think he didn't because he's certain that sooner or later the police are going to arrest me. He let me go because he doesn't believe I have any cards to play. But I do—two of them, actually. I've heard his voice and you've seen his face."

"And you think that if I'm drinking I'll be of no use to you."

"I think that the last time you drank you almost died. I don't want you to die."

She studied his face.

"I really want to drink," she said.

"I know you do," he replied with genuine empathy. "I really want to run away from all this. Someplace unbearably warm where they use shells for currency and haven't heard of malpractice suits or HMOs or grand juries. But I'm not going to."

Maura opened the box of chocolate-covered mints, slid one onto her tongue, and closed her eyes as it dissolved in her mouth.

"You knew about the sweets thing, didn't you," she said.

Harry sensed a letup in the wall construction.

"That doesn't make me an expert."

She savored another mint.

"Ten or eleven thousand calories a day in bonbons and Life Savers and Kit Kats, and I haven't gained an ounce. Go figure."

"You're lucky. I just look at that stuff and my belt lets itself out a notch—go figure."

Maura said the words in unison with him and then almost laughed. *Almost.* Harry waited. She picked at the edge of the mint box, then closed it and set it on the table. He knew this was the moment. She was considering asking him to abandon his crusade to keep her sober and just leave. And if she did, he would have to go, and she would be drunk within an hour or two.

"Harry, I'm sorry for giving you such a hard time," she said finally. "I suppose you know that right now you're the only thing standing between me and the bottle of Southern Comfort I have in the kitchen."

"The only thing standing between you and that bottle is you, Maura. If knowing that makes me an expert, then maybe I am one after all."

In the silence that followed, Harry felt the topmost bricks come off the wall. *Just shut up!* he pleaded with himself. He had said what he could. Anything more might just turn her off. *Not a word. Not one goddamn—*

"What do you think of this turban?" she asked suddenly. "I'm very self-conscious about having so little hair. I tried a wig, but it looked ridiculous."

"Like Dickinson."

"Pardon?"

"Albert Dickinson. You cut him to shreds by telling him that his toupee looked like a piece of lettuce. Remember?"

Harry could tell from her expression that she did not.

"Oh, yes," she said with no conviction. "You think the turban's ugly. I can tell. Do you think I should take it off?"

"I think you should do whatever you want to."

"You still want to go out for dinner?"

"Of course."

"Even with a flaky, bald chick who keeps popping Peanut M&M's and Raisinets?"

"Try me."

She swept the turban off and tossed it across the room. Her reddish-blond hair had grown back a bit, although the scar from her operation still showed.

"You're staring," she said.

Harry knew he was, though not for the reason she was thinking. With the headdress gone, it was as if he was seeing her face for the first time. The swelling and bruises that had so disfigured her were gone. Her skin was smooth and beautifully pale, with a faint, natural blush and a few freckles highlighting her high, sculpted cheeks. Her eyes, a rich ocean green, seemed possessed of their own intrinsic light. And her mouth was wide and sensual. Harry felt his own mouth go dry.

"I . . . um . . . I don't think you need the turban," he managed.

"Okay, the turban's history. If you're still up for dinner, I'm a nut for Indian food."

"I'm up for it and I know a place."

He glanced around the room and realized that two and possibly three of the stark portraits were of Maura herself. They were skillfully done. No one could dispute that. And there was certainly a constancy in her vision of herself. But as far as he was concerned, none of them captured even a trace of the allure and gentle mystery of the woman sitting across from him.

"You know," she said, "you really are a nice guy. I'd like to help you if I can."

She took a tan windbreaker from the back of a chair and slipped it on. "Harry, did anyone ever tell you that you look like —wait a minute, I'll think of who. . . . Oh, I know, Gene Hackman. I think you look a little like Gene Hackman."

Harry looked at her curiously, uncertain of how to respond. Her expression was too matter-of-fact. *She didn't remember!*

"I . . . um . . . yes. One person did tell me I looked like him."

"Your wife?"

"No. No, it was someone else. Maura, I meant to wait until after dinner to discuss the mystery doc, but could you tell me a bit of what he looked like—how you described him to your brother?"

She seemed about to respond. Then her eyes narrowed. Harry could feel as much as see her confusion.

"You know," she said. "I remember someone coming into the room. At least I think I do. But that's all."

"You mean you can't picture his face?"

She looked at him sadly and then shook her head.

"Harry, I didn't realize it until right now, but no. I can't picture a thing from that night. Not a goddamn thing."

CHAPTER 18

"Watch that kid shoot," Harry said, as they stood by the high chain-link fence that surrounded the basketball court. "The little one with the Knicks shirt."

The teenager, smaller and quicker than anyone else in the game, obliged by sinking an off-balance jump shot from twenty feet.

"Nice call," Maura said.

They watched for a few more minutes and then headed down Manhattan Avenue toward Central Park.

"You sure you want to walk all the way to the restaurant?" Harry asked.

"I know it's hard to believe, but before I did my half gainer with a full twist down those stairs, I was a fairly decent runner."

"We walk."

Harry shared details of his own ongoing struggle to stay in shape.

"You know, you're being very patient not grilling me about that doctor from the hospital," she said.

"We can talk about it later."

"I feel terrible, but I really can't remember what he looked like. I haven't thought about the hospital much, mostly because I didn't want to. Now I want to, but it's like . . . like my brain is

Swiss cheese. Some things, some conversations are crystal clear. Others . . . ?"

"Just out of curiosity, do you remember your brother's friend, Lonnie? He was in the room that night. His nickname is the Dweeb."

"He's black, right?"

"Exactly," Harry said excitedly. "Do you remember what he was wearing? What he did that night?"

"He had a hat on. A cap . . ."

"Good. That's right. What else?"

She gazed up at a building, then shook her head sadly.

"Nothing. I'm sorry, Harry, I really am. It's like trying to remember who sat next to me in the third grade. I know I was there, and I can pull up some hazy pictures, even the dress my teacher used to wear. But no real detail."

Harry recalled how quickly she had noticed Jennifer's pin and Dickinson's hairpiece, how rapidly she had reacted during the Dweeb's role-playing scenarios. The specialized area of her cerebral cortex responsible for awareness had been functioning well that night—perhaps even more sharply than usual. But her ability to file information, or at least to retrieve it, had clearly been damaged—badly damaged, it appeared.

"It's not surprising, I suppose," he said, hoping his concern and disappointment weren't too obvious. "The concussion, the surgery, the alcohol, the withdrawal, the medications—considering all that, I think you've done pretty damn well."

"I'm sorry," she said again. "I'll keep trying. If something comes back to me, you'll be the first to know."

"Thanks. Hey, enough. I call for a change in the subject. Let's talk about art."

"And war heroes."

Over the years, in most social situations, Harry seldom carried the conversation. *Thoughtful* was the way he explained that trait; *boring* was Evie's frequent retort. But Maura Hughes was extremely easy to talk to. He rambled on as they walked and suddenly, he found himself talking quite candidly about the Corbett curse and his episodes of unusual chest pain—things he hadn't shared with anyone.

"So," she said when he had finished, "who's *your* doctor?"

"I'm getting one," he said too quickly.

She stopped, took his arms, and turned him toward her. Concern shadowed her face.

"Promise?"

Harry had no idea how long he stared into her emerald eyes before he responded.

"With all that's going on, I won't say when. But I promise."

The light changed. They crossed Columbus and were half a block from Central Park when she said, "I think you should know that my performance this evening notwithstanding, I have a steel-trap memory for things that people promise me. And I can be an incredible nag when I want to be."

"I have a feeling you can be an incredible anything when you want to be."

Harry was totally surprised to hear the words spoken in his voice. *Was he actually flirting?*

"That's a nice thing to say, Harry," she responded. "Especially considering that at this point, you've known me longer in the DTs than out."

"Tell me, what tipped you over the edge?"

"You mean drinking?"

"Yes."

She laughed.

"You think there has to be some tragedy, some horrid, dark event in my past that sent me reeling into the bottle?"

"I . . . um . . . I guess that's what I assumed, yes."

"Well, I'm sorry to disappoint you. There's certainly a lot in my past that I wish had never happened. But no single cataclysmic tragedy. In fact, if anything, alcohol was a godsend—at least for a while."

Maura talked of her upbringing by well-to-do parents—her summers at riding camps, her years in boarding school, and finally her abbreviated enrollment at Sarah Lawrence. By then, rebellion against her parents' lifestyle and hypocrisy had opened a gap between them that would never be bridged.

"Eventually, my . . . my father suffered some big financial reverses and my mother left him. He died in a car crash . . . somewhere outside of Los Angeles—far from sober, in case you were wondering. . . . A woman in the car with him was also killed."

When she spoke of her father, Harry noticed a striking

change in her expression and her voice. The muscles around her jaw tightened. Her speech became strained and halting. An opaque shade seemed to descend over her eyes—a protective membrane, shielding her feelings.

"What about your mother?" he asked, anxious to help her off the subject.

"Mother's still alive. But neither Tom nor I ever hear from her except every other Christmas or so. I doubt she's sober very often either. Probably because my parents never even spoke of such matters, for as long as I can remember I've been acutely sensitive to things in the world that were tragic or unjust."

She told of spending several years trying to write the great American novel, including two years on a Navajo reservation in Arizona. But her writing lacked fire, and her experiences with the Navajos and others who were poor and oppressed only seemed to heighten her sense of impotence. It was as if the harder she struggled to have her life make sense, the less it did.

"One day, not so much for answers as for therapy, I dusted off my paint box and stretched a few canvases. I had taken some lessons in high school, but never got into it. This time, from the very beginning, painting felt right to me. I wasn't bad either, but nobody seemed to notice my work. Then a wonderful thing happened to me—Southern Comfort. I discovered that drinking freed something up inside me—or maybe smoothed the rough edges off. I don't know. But I do know that the more I drank, the better I painted."

"Or at least *thought* you painted," Harry corrected.

"No. You may not want to believe it, but I really *was* better. The galleries saw it, and so did the people who buy art. For a time, my work was in great demand. I actually bought that building my apartment's in. Then, without my realizing it at first, I began spending more and more time either drinking or sleeping off hangovers, and less and less time painting. It's been about three years since I did anything anyone was interested in. I don't remember my last sale."

"You never got treatment from an alcohol counselor or tried AA?"

"For what? There were always reasons I drank—relationships that were in the dumper, injustices, bad reviews, professional snubs. I saw a therapist for a while. She said I just had an artist's temperament and passion. And besides, I always sincerely believed I could quit whenever I wanted to. Now, after what's happened to me, I'm not so sure."

"That's a start."

"What?"

"Realizing that you may not be able to quit any time you want to. . . ."

The restaurant Harry had recommended was on Ninety-third near Lexington. They entered Central Park at Ninety-seventh. It was eight-forty-five, but there was a fair amount of lingering daylight. They took a paved footpath down to the reservoir. The air was warm and still, the water mirror-smooth.

"I really love this city," Harry said. "Especially the park."

"Do you often walk through here at night?"

The walkway around the reservoir, as far as they could see through the gathering dusk, was deserted.

"This isn't what I would consider night yet, but the answer is yes. I don't tempt fate by bushwhacking, but the roads are safe enough here." He skimmed a small stone across the water. "Ta da. Thirteen skips. A new world record."

"How come I only counted eight?"

"I can see I'm going to have trouble with you."

Enjoying the quiet comfort they were feeling with one another, they headed up a wooded path toward the road. The last vestiges of daylight had given way to evening.

"Listen, Harry," she said. "I've been thinking, and I want to propose a deal. You think I should be going to an alcohol counselor or AA. I think you should be seeing a heart specialist to have that pain of yours checked out. The deal is this: you agree to face up to your problem, and I'll agree to face up to mine."

"I already promised you I'd do it."

"I'm talking about soon. If you want, I'll go to one of those meetings tomorrow."

"Believe me, it's not angina I've been having. I *know* angina. It's just that I'm overly aware of chest discomfort because of my family history and—"

"Deal or not?"

They stopped and looked at one another. Harry swallowed at the dryness that had recurred in his throat.

"Deal," he said. "Provided you agree not to take a drink of

any sort of booze without calling me first and giving me a chance to dissuade you."

"Deal." Her smile was warm and hopeful. Then suddenly, her expression changed. Her eyes widened. "Harry!" she cried, staring over his shoulder.

"Not a word, neither of you!" the man behind Harry growled.

Harry recognized the voice immediately. It belonged to the larger of the two men from Desiree's apartment. Harry started to turn, but the thug, several inches taller, locked an arm under his neck and thrust a gun into his ribs. Maura instinctively whirled to run and collided with the man's partner, who had come charging down the path from the road, cutting off any attempt to escape in that direction. The spot they had chosen was totally hidden from the road above and from the reservoir below. Maura cried out as the shorter, stocky one grabbed her wrist and twisted her arm high behind her back. Then he forced her off the path and up the hillside into the dense woods. Harry's captor shoved him rudely after her.

"No sucker punches this time, asshole," he snarled.

Harry tripped on a thick tree root, but the giant's grip across his neck kept him from falling. After twenty yards, the underbrush and steepness of the hill made it impossible to continue. It was much darker than it had been on the path.

"Okay, down on your knees, both of you," the taller man ordered.

He dropped Harry with a sharp kick to the back of the knee. Maura, her hand bent up nearly to the back of her neck, was powerless to resist.

"Nice body," the thug said as he forced her, face down, onto the ground. "Real nice." He kneeled on the small of her back.

"Shut up and just do what you have to do," the other rasped.

"Leave her alone," Harry pleaded. "She's no threat to anyone. She doesn't remember a thing. Nothing. You've got to believe me."

"Shut up, dammit!"

Something solid—the man's fist or the revolver butt, padded somehow—slammed down on a spot just behind Harry's right ear. Pain and a searing white light burst through his head. He pitched forward and landed heavily, air exploding from his lungs.

"No! Please don—!"

Through a semiconscious haze, Harry heard Maura cry out. Then suddenly her words were cut off, replaced by a dreadful gurgling. He could feel her kicking, her feet flailing desperately against the ground beside his face. He lifted his head. His vision was blurred, but through the darkness he could see the man with the cinder-block build straddling Maura from behind, his beefy hands tight around her throat, pulling her head up as he strangled her, bowing her back.

"No!" Harry cried, his voice only a harsh, impotent whisper. "No, don't!"

He struggled to push himself up, but the behemoth standing beside him drove him back down with a foot between his shoulder blades.

Suddenly, the man on top of Maura grunted, pitched forward and to one side, then toppled like a stuffed toy down the hill toward the reservoir. At virtually the same instant, the taller man cried out in pain and spun to the ground clutching his right arm. Instinctively, he rolled over twice and scrambled for cover behind a large oak. Harry's head was clearing rapidly, but he still could not figure out what was going on. Then he saw the man's gun lying six feet away. He crawled unsteadily toward it, expecting the giant to beat him there. Instead, the man, still holding his arm, lurched to his feet and stumbled off through the brush.

Harry snatched up the revolver and then crawled to where Maura lay. She was facedown and very still, but she was breathing. He turned her over gently and cradled her head in his free hand.

"Maura, it's okay," he whispered into her ear. "It's Harry. You're all right."

His senses keyed, his finger tight on the trigger of the revolver, he peered into the darkness, straining to see movement or a silhouette. The noise of his assailant's escape faded, replaced by a silence as dense as the darkness in the grove.

Harry checked the carotid pulses on both sides of Maura's neck. They were bounding and sharp. His own pulse was bludgeoning the inside of his head. Maura's eyes were open now, and she was sobbing softly. Harry continued scanning the woods. He set the gun on his leg and caressed the side of her face.

"He was strangling me," she said, trying to clear the hoarseness from her throat. "I couldn't breathe."

"I know. Easy does it. You're okay now."

"Wh-what happened?"

"I'm not sure. I think both men were shot, but I didn't hear any gunfire. Are you all right?"

"As soon as I stop shaking I will be. It happened so fast."

"They work for that doctor you saw. I think they wanted to kill you and leave me alive, trying to convince the police that I didn't do it."

He helped her sit up, but continued to support her with an arm around her shoulder.

"Is someone out there?" she whispered, gesturing toward the darkness.

Again they listened. Again there was only silence. Holding the revolver loosely, he helped her to her feet. The throbbing in his head persisted, along with some dizziness. A mild concussion, he decided. Nothing more. He touched the bruise behind his ear and winced from the pain. But there was virtually no swelling—no support for his story that they had been mugged. The two thugs knew what they were doing. Professionals. But someone out there had beaten them both.

He and Maura helped one another down the steep slope. The path, dark but still somewhat lighter than the woods, was empty. Harry again rested his finger on the trigger of the revolver as they searched slowly along the treeline.

"I was certain the bastard fell this way," Harry said.

"Maybe he was just wounded, like the other one."

"He didn't roll that way, but maybe."

"I'm not sure I like it here in the park anymore," she said.

"I think leaving may not be such a bad idea myself."

At that moment, she pointed at the base of a tree several feet up the slope. An arm protruded from behind it, the limp hand dangling palm up. They swung a wide arc and then approached the tree from above. The man who had so nearly strangled Maura to death was wedged against the trunk. He wore dark jeans and a black turtleneck. The side of his face was pressed into the damp soil. His visible eye was wide open, staring sightlessly up the hill.

"Here," Harry said, pointing to a spot in the upper middle of the man's back. "Look."

Maura bent down and could just discern the dime-sized hole and expanding disc of blood.

"What should we do?" she asked.

Harry felt the man's jeans for a wallet, but knew there would be none.

"I didn't hear any gunshot," he said again. "Did you?"

"No, but I was busy listening to the pearly gates creaking open."

"I think whoever shot these guys had a silencer."

"So?"

"Professional killers use silencers. Maura, I think we should get the hell out of here."

Maura rubbed at her neck.

"I'm with you," she said.

CHAPTER 19

The discovery of a man shot to death in Central Park made the late-night news and the morning papers. Police located the body at ten P.M. following an anonymous phone tip from a male caller. The victim carried no wallet and as yet had not been identified. Preliminary impression was robbery, but police were not ruling out the possibility that the shooting was an execution.

Harry entered the hospital for morning rounds, his thoughts in their now-usual state of disarray. The mystery surrounding Evie's death remained as murky as ever. And now other unanswered questions had darkened the picture even more. Who had been down there on the path in Central Park, silenced revolver in hand, ready and quite able to kill? Could the arrival of their savior have possibly been a coincidence? Was he some anticrime vigilante? No explanation made much sense.

A few things, very few, seemed apparent. Harry remained convinced that his life was not in jeopardy—he was being kept around to deflect responsibility for Evie's murder. Maura's continued survival was not nearly so assured, though. Maybe Albert Dickinson gave her eyewitness account no credence whatsoever, but clearly the murderer did.

Throughout the night she had said little of her ordeal. But Harry shuddered at the thought of what it must have been like for her, a killer's hands tightening around her throat, her spine bowed near the breaking point.

After leaving the park, the two of them had gone to Harry's apartment. Maura's place, they decided, was simply too vulnerable. And although Rocky, the night doorman, was hardly the sort of protection that would put one's mind at ease, he was better than nothing. Maura was certain that by filing a formal report supporting her story, her brother had already put his future in the department in jeopardy. This time around she insisted that he not be involved—at least not in any official capacity. Harry did not completely agree, but with all she had endured, there was no way he was going to try and change her mind. He reported the Central Park body to 911 from a pay phone. For the time being, Tom Hughes would be left out of it.

Once in the apartment they settled onto the sofa in the small, oak-paneled den and turned on the television. Maura, physically drained, said little. She sipped herbal tea, nibbled some shortbread cookies, and stared at the screen. In just over an hour, the first news report appeared on Channel 2, announcing the homicide near the reservoir in Central Park.

"Okay, Harry," she said when the brief report was complete, "I think I'm ready. Could you please tell me what's going on?"

"I wish I knew," he responded.

He told her about the bewildering, depressing discoveries he had made in Evie's Greenwich Village apartment. He told her what he remembered of the doctor with the cultured accent, and of the two men with him who had then assaulted them in the park. Maura listened without interruption.

"So, it's all about sex," she said when he had finished.

"In a way, I guess you could say that, yes. Somewhere in her —what would you call it? research?—Evie apparently crossed the wrong person. Whoever it was murdered her—or more likely *had* her murdered—in a way that should not have aroused any suspicion whatsoever. Aneurysms like hers rupture all the time. I'm certain there wasn't supposed to be any flap about it or any autopsy. But Caspar Sidonis's claim that I had reason to kill her changed all that. Now, whoever *really* did it is committed to proving Sidonis is right."

"And to eliminating the only eyewitness as well," Maura added. "Harry . . . Evie sounds like such a sad, mixed-up soul."

"Believe me when I tell you she didn't come across that way."

"What about children? Didn't you want them when you got married?"

"Oh, very much."

"But she didn't?"

"She used to say she did, but—not really. Look, I know it sounds like I should have gotten out of the marriage years ago, or never gotten into it in the first place. But believe it or not, taken on a day-to-day basis, it really wasn't that bad. We were like a lot of couples. We got up, went to work, had a reasonable amount of money, had friends, went on an occasional vacation, bought some nice things, made love—at least in the beginning. I took care of my patients, played my music, did my workouts, jogged through the park. I guess I just didn't look at it all too closely."

"I understand. I think everyone who's in a bad marriage is guilty of wearing blinders—sometimes for a long while." She leaned back and closed her eyes. "There's still plenty of time, Harry."

"For what?"

She yawned and stretched. "For whatever . . ."

Hours later, damp with sweat, Harry awoke from a dream he had experienced many times before. It was a Nha-trang dream, viewed along the barrel of Harry's gun. Beyond the end of the barrel, a young Vietcong soldier is raising his weapon. His face and expression are indelible in Harry's mind. Eyes widening in fear, he tries to level his semiautomatic. Harry's gun discharges. The youth's chest bursts open like a ripe melon. He is hurled backward into oblivion. Moments later another soldier, even younger than the first, steps into view at the end of the barrel. He spots Harry and the wounded man on the ground beside him. He raises his weapon. Harry's gun discharges once again. . . .

The television flickered across the darkened room, its volume barely audible. Maura Hughes, covered with a woolen throw, lay sleeping beside him, her head resting on his lap. Harry clicked off the set and sat in the near blackness, gently stroking her face and her downlike new hair. Not once during the entire evening had she made excuses for herself or her life, or tried to rationalize her drinking. Not once had she whined about the deadly situation into which she had been thrust. She might not have medals as proof, but in her own way, Maura Hughes was pretty damn heroic. And Harry felt drawn to her in a most powerful way. He shifted his legs. She moaned softly, then rolled onto her back and looked up at him.

"Mmmm. Am I keeping you up?" she asked dreamily.

"No. Lately I've spent more nights on this sofa than in bed. Why don't you go on into the guest room and get some real sleep?"

"Is staying out here like this an alternative?"

"If you want."

Heavy-lidded, she smiled up at him, then rolled back onto her side.

"I want," she murmured. . . .

Harry had three patients in the hospital. The first, a four-year-old girl with asthma, was ready for discharge. Harry wrote out detailed instructions for the mother, who was scarcely more than a child herself. But no amount of information or reassurance seemed to be enough to calm her. Finally, Harry took a business card from his wallet.

"Here, Naomi," he said, writing on the back of the card. "This is my home phone number. If there's any problem with Keesha, you don't even have to call the answering service unless I'm not home. But she's going to do fine."

The teen slipped the card into the pocket of her jeans, then finally accepted the discharge and Harry's efforts by giving him a hug.

The second patient, an elderly man, had been transferred back to Harry from a cardiologist following an uneventful three-day stay in the CCU. He was a toothless old gent who had been pleasantly confused for as long as Harry had been his doctor, now fifteen or so years. With social services and the visiting nurses teaming up on his case, there was a good chance he'd be back in his own place within the week. He patted Harry on the back, called him Dr. Carson, and told him to keep trying and he would be a very good doctor some day.

Harry smiled sadly at the thought of how typical, how utterly humdrum normal, rounds like today's once were. Now, as he moved through the hospital, he was aware of the stares, and the pointed fingers, and the whispers.

That's the man. The doctor who killed his wife. I can't believe they let him just walk around the hospital like this. . . .

He took the elevator to the fifth floor of the Alexander Building. The car was the very same one in which he had ridden down with Mel Wetstone. That time, Evie's killer had been one of the crowd packed in with them. This time, he was alone.

The final patient he had to see was in Alexander 505—a thirty-three-year-old architect named Andy Barlow. Barlow had been HIV-positive for two years and was now battling *Pneumocystis carinii* pneumonia, the first indication that he had developed full-blown AIDS. During those two symptom-free years, Barlow had continued work at his job with a midtown firm, volunteered countless hours at a hospice for the homeless and disenfranchised, and led the campaign for expanded needle exchange and improved local services for AIDS patients.

Another legitimate hero, Harry thought as he entered the room.

Andy Barlow, oxygen prongs in place, did not look as good as Harry would have wished. His color was sallow and somewhat dusky, his lips more purplish than they should have been. He sat propped up at an eighty-degree angle, quietly working to get air into his lungs. Still, he managed a smile.

"Hey, Doc," he said, the words punctuated with coughs.

"Hi, yourself."

Harry pulled up a chair and sat, flipping through the pages in Barlow's chart. The reports—blood count, oxygen levels, chemistries, chest film—actually looked better than the patient did. They were reason to be at least a little encouraged.

"What's the news?" Barlow asked.

"Well, the returns from these key upstate precincts say we're winning," Harry said.

"Tell that to my lungs."

"That bad?"

"Actually not," Andy said, and paused for breath. "My breathing's a bit easier and I'm not coughing nearly as much." He coughed again several times and then laughed at himself. "As usual, the man speaketh too soon."

Harry examined his throat, chest, heart, and abdomen.

"Not bad," he said, now genuinely encouraged. "How's your head?"

Andy shrugged. "I think being HIV-positive for a couple of years has helped a bit in getting ready for this, but I'm still pissed and . . . and a little frightened."

"Me, too," Harry said.

"I know. And I appreciate your saying it."

Andy Barlow wasn't the first patient with AIDS Harry had cared for, or even the tenth. Healthy habits, exercise, preventive medications, and aggressive treatment of infections had made a significant contribution to the quality and quantity of each of their lives. But a number of them had already died. This lung infection marked Barlow's first step on a new road. The questions of whether and when he would develop the full-blown disease had been answered. Now, physician and patient had to reorder their priorities and their expectations. Harry feigned another chest exam until he was fairly certain his own emotions were under control.

"You know," Andy said, "don't take this personally, but I don't think I fear dying as much as I fear being sick all the time. I've spent so much time in hospitals with my friends, I just dread becoming one of them."

"I understand. Well, I promise you I'm going to do everything I can to get you out of here pronto and to keep you out. And as far as getting sick over and over goes, I know nothing I say can take away that worry. Just try to focus on the truth that today is what you have—it's all that any of us have. The only thing you can do is try to live it to the fullest."

"Keep reminding me."

"I will if you want me to. Now listen. I really do think the IV Bactrim has turned the tide. Your film's a little better, and so's your blood count."

"Good, because I'm one of the principle designers of the renovations on the Claridge Performing Arts Center, and I want to be at the opening production on the twenty-first."

"Ten days? Hey, no problem, mon. With my stethoscope tied behind my back, even."

"Guaranteed?"

"You have my word."

Andy, an IV in his right hand, reached out and grasped Harry's right hand with his left.

Harry squeezed his hand, then turned quickly and left the room. This was a situation he would never get used to or inured to. And in truth, he never wanted to be.

He returned to the nurse's station and wrote some orders for intensified respiratory therapy on Andy Barlow. Nearby, two nurses were chatting with the unit secretary. He had known each of them cordially for some time, in one case many years. Now, none of the three broke from their conversation to acknowledge him. He flagged the new orders and set the three-ring notebook chart on the secretary's desk.

"Just a few new orders," he said.

"Thank you, Doctor," the woman replied without looking over. "I'll take care of it."

Harry gave momentary thought to forcing a confrontation with the group—a plea against being judged prematurely. He decided against it. Constitutional guarantees notwithstanding, he knew that in many minds he was guilty until proven otherwise. As long as his situation remained unresolved, there would be coolness and distance and silence. And there wasn't a damn thing he could do about it.

He trotted down to the first floor and out of the hospital. The morning was cloudless and warm, and with twenty minutes before his first office patient he could actually walk slowly enough to appreciate it. He wondered how Maura was doing. By the time he had left for work, the reality of her situation had begun to sink in for her. She seemed irritable—deflated and distracted. And although she didn't say so, Harry sensed she was thinking about how much easier everything would be with a drink. They had decided that she would return to her apartment with a friend of hers, pack some things, and move into Harry's place for a few days. Meanwhile, she could decide about calling her brother. When she did move back to her own place, Harry offered to hire a security guard.

"Until when?" she asked.

Harry didn't try arguing with her on that point. Especially since she was right. If someone, particularly a professional, wanted badly enough to kill her, she would have to go into the deepest hiding, or else sooner or later she would be dead. It was that simple.

There was one person seated in the waiting room of Harry's office when he arrived, a man he had never seen before. His face, hollow-eyed and gaunt, spoke of hard times. His black, graying hair was close-cut, and there was nervous tension about him that Harry could almost feel. He had on faded jeans, worn sneakers, and a navy blue windbreaker with a Yankees logo on one breast. Harry nodded a greeting before heading into Mary Tobin's cubicle. The man responded with a thin smile.

"Who's our friend?" Harry whispered, studying the appointment book, which showed a number of cancellations and no name written in this time slot.

"His name is Walter Concepcion. He's unemployed and has no insurance."

"What else is new."

"He's been having headaches."

"Who referred him?"

"Believe it or not, he says he read about you in the papers."

"Doctor suspected of murdering his wife—what better recommendation could any patient want?"

"Well," Mary said, "you've never turned any patient away that I could remember, so I took the liberty of having him fill out a registration sheet and questionnaire."

"Fine. It doesn't exactly look like we're going to get buried in an avalanche of appointments."

"Oh, we'll be all right. Tell me, though. How're you doing?"

Aside from almost getting Maura killed last night, witnessing a murder, and having almost no idea what in the hell is going on, not bad. Not bad at all.

"I go to bed confused, I wake up confused," he said instead.

"That doesn't make you any different from the rest of us," Mary said, smiling. "You just hang in there an' the answers will come."

She looked as strained and tired as he had ever seen her. Yet here she was with anxious callers to assuage, cancellations to accept without comment, reporters to fend off, and she was concerned with how *he* was doing. Harry added her to his list of heroes.

He picked up the clipboard with the health questionnaire

his new patient had filled out. Walter Concepcion was forty-five, with no phone, a next-of-kin—his brother in Los Angeles, and an address in Spanish Harlem. As Mary had warned, he had no health insurance. But he did list an occupation—*private investigator*. Harry introduced himself and motioned the man to follow him to his office.

"I was a licensed PI," Concepcion explained in response to Harry's question. "But I got in a little trouble a few years back and they pulled my ticket." His New York accent, without a hint of Latino, suggested he was U.S. born. "Next March I'm eligible to get it back. I still do some jobs for people, but under the table, if you know what I mean."

The tension Harry had sensed in the waiting room was physically apparent in an intermittent tic of the muscles on the right side of Concepcion's face, and in his fingers, which seemed to be in almost constant motion.

"The trouble you got into," Harry said. "Drugs?"

Without hesitation, Concepcion nodded. "Cocaine. Crack, actually. I thought I could handle it."

"No one can."

"You got that right. I been clean for almost three years now, though. No drugs, no booze, no wine. Nothing. Not that I deserve a medal or anything, but I've gotten my act back together."

"That *is* a big accomplishment," Harry said. "There's no need to put it down." He liked the man's directness. Concepcion's eyes, though deeply sunken, were bright and intelligent, and made steady, level contact with Harry's.

"Well, Mr. Concepcion, I have about twenty minutes before my next patient is due," Harry said. "Headaches are among the hardest symptoms to diagnose correctly, but I'll do my best. You may have to come back another time or two."

"That's okay with me, Doc, as long as I can stretch out my payments. I'm not broke, but I do have to balance who gets what, if you know what I mean."

"No problem," Harry said. "Why don't you go on down to room two on the left. I'll take a brief history and examine you there."

Concepcion rose and left the room just as Harry's private line began ringing.

The private line, direct to the back office, enabled Harry to make calls without tying up an office line. It also ensured that emergency calls from the hospital wouldn't encounter a busy signal.

"Dr. Corbett," he said, flipping through a small stack of mail, mostly junk, that Mary had left on his desk.

"I am very upset with you, Doctor," the familiar, slightly accented voice said. "Very upset."

Harry tensed. Even if he could somehow alert Mary, there was no extension to this line at the front desk.

"Who are you?" he demanded.

"The man you trapped and killed so mercilessly last night meant a great deal to me."

The words were spoken without emotion.

"Listen, I didn't trap anyone. Your goons tried to kill us. I'm not sorry someone saved our lives. But I have no idea who did it."

"I think you're lying, Dr. Corbett. I blame myself for not considering that you might have arranged to have yourself followed. But I think you'll see that it was an unfortunate, foolish thing for you to do. Very unfortunate and very foolish."

"Who are you? Why are you doing this? Why did you kill Evie?"

"You have become a great inconvenience to me, Dr. Corbett," the soft voice went on. "And I intend to do something about it. It would make things much easier for any number of people if you would just find some clever, painless way to take your own life."

"Go to hell."

"Dead or in prison for life. I am afraid those are now the only options available to you. If you don't wish to kill yourself now, I promise you will before I am through. The man you arranged to have gunned down last night was a close associate of mine. He will be avenged."

Harry wanted to slam the receiver down. Instead, he sat transfixed, trying desperately to find words that would make a difference.

"Why can't you just leave us alone? I have no idea who you are, and neither does Maura Hughes. She doesn't remember one thing from her time in the hospital. Nothing."

"Ah, would that I could believe that. Now, then, we come

back to the dual issue of your punishment and your suicide—both of which I consider essential. To show you how serious I am about this, I have chosen that young gentleman you were speaking to not so long ago. Barlow is it?"

"You bastard! Don't you touch him!"

"A nice enough fellow, it seems, but most unfortunate in having you for his physician."

"No!"

"Consider your options, Dr. Corbett. IV morphine is totally painless. Any number of sleeping pills would do the trick for you as well. So would carbon monoxide. Falling from a great height would provide a wonderful rush I would think, and would only hurt for a moment. A bullet upward through the palate would probably hurt even less."

"Please," Harry begged. "Please give me time. Give me time to decide."

"Oh, you have all the time you want."

"Thank you. Thank you very much."

"But I'm afraid Mr. Barlow has no time at all. Good day, Doctor."

"Nooo!" Harry bellowed as the dial tone intervened. "Damn you, no!"

Harry looked up at that moment and realized that Walter Concepcion was standing just outside his door.

"I . . . I just wanted to know if I should get changed," he said, embarrassed.

Mary Tobin, responding to Harry's shout, came rushing past him and into the office.

"Call Alexander Five," he ordered. "Tell them to get someone into room five-oh-five now. Andrew Barlow. Room five-oh-five. I'm on my way over."

"Yes, Doctor," Mary Tobin said.

"Mr. Concepcion, you'll have to come back another time."

Without waiting for a response, Harry bolted past the bewildered man, out of the office, and across the sunlit street. It was six blocks to the Manhattan Medical Center.

CHAPTER 20

In this part of the city, people were not that surprised to see a man dressed in loafers and a suit sprinting along the sidewalk, dodging pedestrians. Harry felt as if he was running through molasses. The morning was already nearing eighty and quite humid. Passersby moved aside and a few turned to watch. But most of them were looking past Harry to see who was chasing him. Harry knew he had a faster gear, but with the chest pain still unresolved, he was reluctant to use it. As it was, he felt some sharp jabs inside his left chest. And he wondered, with each block, when the debilitating, bandlike discomfort was going to take hold.

By the time he reached the hospital, he was carrying his suit coat and using one sleeve to mop sweat off his face. He dashed through the main doors, anticipating that the overhead page would be calling out a Code 99 on Alexander 5. There was no such announcement, nor had the pager hooked to his belt gone off. The lobby was crowded as usual. Out of deference to the hospital and the patients, Harry slowed to a rapid walk down the main corridor to the Alexander Building cutoff. At certain times of the day, taking the elevator might have been faster than the stairs. But Harry never gave it a thought. Grateful for his regular workouts on the track, he took the stairs two at a time. Again, there was some discomfort in his chest, but nothing major, nothing that definitely said cardiac. Muscular or gastrointestinal, Harry decided, filing the conclusion away.

The Code 99 cart was parked outside the doorway to room 505. Harry cursed out loud as he hurried toward it. He was just a few feet away when he realized that the cover had not been removed from the cart. The two nurses who had so blatantly snubbed him just an hour ago were standing nearby, chatting. They looked over at him, and he could feel as much as see their disdain.

"What's going on?" he asked.

"*We* don't know," one of the women said pointedly. "You tell us."

Harry stepped past them and into the room. Steve Josephson, stethoscope in place, was standing on the far side of the bed, hunched over Andy Barlow, examining his chest and back. The young architect, with his oxygen running almost wide open at six liters a minute, looked about the same to Harry as he had on rounds—sick but in no mortal distress.

"Stuff at both lung bases," Josephson muttered to himself. He glanced up and noticed Harry. "Hey, there you are," he said. "I was on the floor finishing rounds when the nurses grabbed me. Apparently your office nurse called and said there was an emergency with Mr. Barlow, here."

Harry approached the bed, aware that a cluster of people—nurses, the ward secretary, and a couple of residents—were now filling the doorway. He knew that no matter what he said, his credibility, already greatly diminished around the hospital, would soon be extinct. He had been set up by a maniac, and quite masterfully at that.

"I got a call on the private line in my office," Harry said, in a near whisper that he hoped would not be audible to the gallery. "The man on the phone implied that"—he looked at his patient and measured his words carefully—"that he might be planning to harm Andrew, here, in some way."

"But why?" Barlow asked, the question nearly lost in a spasm of coughing.

Harry turned to the crowd.

"Look, could someone please close the door?" he asked.

No one in the group moved. Harry stalked over to do it himself. The head nurse, Corinne Donnelly, stepped inside.

·"I'll allow you to close the door," she said. "But I intend to stay and hear exactly what explanation you have to offer for this."

Donnelly, about Harry's age, had once sent a close friend to him for medical care. Now, she eyed him challengingly, almost begging for a confrontation.

"Come on in," Harry said wearily.

The nurse nodded people away from the door and then closed it behind her. Steve Josephson rested his considerable bulk against the wall. Harry turned to his patient.

"Andy, we haven't spoken about this, but I assume you know about my wife's death and some of the newspaper and TV reports about me."

"I do. I didn't believe them."

The two sentences again sent Barlow into a racking cough. Harry wondered what this scene was costing him in stamina.

"You're right not to believe the papers," Harry said. "I didn't do anything to harm my wife. But whoever did administer that lethal injection is very angry with me—I . . . I'm not sure I know why. Apparently he's decided to hurt me by threatening my patients."

Steve Josephson said, "You mean that because this guy has some sort of grudge against you, he's killed Evie, and now wants to hurt your patients?"

"I think there are other reasons he killed Evie. I think he was threatened by some research she was doing. But as far as Andy goes, the answer is yes. I know it sounds crazy, Steve, but—"

"It doesn't *sound* crazy," Corinne Donnelly cut in. "It *is* crazy. Dr. Corbett, I think we should talk in my office."

Harry looked down at his patient.

"Whatever you have to say, you can say right here."

"Okay, have it your way, Doctor. I intend to call the nursing director right now and ask her to speak with both Dr. Erdman and Dr. Lord immediately. I don't believe your story one bit—about your wife or about this mystery caller. I don't know what's going on, what's wrong with you, but I do know that recently you've changed drastically. Maybe it's some sort of post-traumatic stress syndrome—something to do with the war. Or maybe it has to do with your wife and Dr. Sidonis. Whatever it is, you need to get help before anyone else gets hurt. And for everyone's sake, you should voluntarily take yourself off the admitting staff of this hospital until the truth comes out. This young man has enough problems without being put in jeopardy by his own physician."

Harry looked over at his longtime friend. Josephson shifted uncomfortably and stared down at the floor. In the prolonged silence, they could hear some scraping from the other side of the door. The staff was still there, undoubtedly pressing in to hear what was going on. Corinne Donnelly moved to put a stop to the eavesdropping, but Harry motioned for her to stay put.

"That's okay," he said. "Mrs. Donnelly, you're right. I need to do whatever I can to keep my patients from being endangered by this . . . this sadistic lunatic. But there's no reason to believe that taking myself off the staff will accomplish that. Closing my practice would be like admitting that I've done something wrong, and I haven't. I'm sorry, but I intend to stay on and see this thing through."

"Not if I have anything to say about it," the nurse snapped.

She turned and stalked from the room, nearly colliding with the assembly pressed against the door.

"Harry, I'm behind you one hundred percent," Josephson said. "Just let me know if there's anything I can do. I'll see you later, Mr. Barlow. I hope you know that you couldn't have a better doc."

"I *do* know."

Josephson shook hands with Andy, then patted Harry on the arm and left, closing the door behind him.

"Looks like we've both got some tough times ahead of us," Barlow said.

His breathing was more labored than it had been. Harry could see that he was exhausted and desperately in need of rest. Stress was dangerous for a man in Andy's condition. Harry felt at once angry and impotent. He was being manipulated like a puppet by a madman who thrived on inflicting pain.

"Andy, I'm sorry," he said.

"Hey, what can you do?"

"I'll call here later on to check on things if it's okay with you."

"Thanks. . . . Hey, Doc?"

"Yes?"

The young man with newly diagnosed AIDS reached out for the second time that morning and took Harry's hand.

"Everything's going to be all right," he said.

"Yeah, I know it will."

Harry turned and hurried from the room, nearly colliding in the hall with a bronze-skinned man dressed in surgical scrubs, carrying the metal basket of the intravenous service.

"Oh, excuse me, please," the man said, in a dense Indian accent.

Harry muttered that it was no problem. Aware that backs had turned and all activity had gone freeze-frame as soon as he neared the nurse's station, he left the floor as quickly as possible. Once back at his office, he would call Doug Atwater at Manhattan Health to begin drumming up support should Corinne Donnelly or anyone else try to have him removed from the staff. A call to Mel Wetstone might be in order as well.

As he headed back down the stairs, Harry found himself wondering what might have happened if, instead of shooting the two men in Central Park, the unseen gunman had captured them and turned them over to the police. Maybe the whole nightmare would have been over by now. Instead, Evie's killer had decided that Harry would pay for that shooting.

He entered the main corridor, again sensing the stares and whispers. *Could it possibly get any worse than this?*

Five floors above, the male nurse from the intravenous service strolled unnoticed into room 505 and readied his equipment by the bedside. He wore the headdress and beard of a Sikh. Andrew Barlow glanced up at him sleepily.

"Everything okay?" Andy asked.

"Oh, yes, everything is fine, just fine," the man said in staccato English. He peered down at Andrew's IV site through tortoiseshell glasses. "Just a routine check. No needles. No new IV."

"Oh, good."

Andrew smiled weakly and drifted off.

The nurse, whose MMC name tag identified him as Sanjay Samar, R.N., checked the bag of glucose and the plastic infusion tubing. Then he injected a small amount of liquid through the rubber port.

"Just to clear line," he said softly.

"Mm-hm," Andrew murmured without opening his eyes.

Sanjay was putting his metal basket back in order when he noticed a patch of white skin just inside his elbow. In the future, he thought, when he used that particular skin dye, he would have to be more careful. He left the room and walked purposefully to the stairway that was farthest from the nurse's station. His expression was all business, but beneath his spectacles and his dark brown contact lenses, his pale blue eyes were sparkling.

CHAPTER 21

"All right, Doc, let's start all over again."

"From where?"

"From the fucking beginning, that's from where."

Albert Dickinson, his rumpled suit in desperate need of dry cleaning, stubbed out one Pall Mall as he prepared to light another. The ashtray was full-to-overflowing. The small interrogation room reeked of years of tobacco, stale coffee, and body odor. Harry shifted uncomfortably in the slat-back wooden chair and wondered if he should back off on saying anything else without calling Mel Wetstone. But the truth was he had done nothing wrong. And aside from his intimate involvement in last night's Central Park murder, he had nothing to hide. Still, his troubles were piling up rapidly. And now a young man he cared very much for was dead.

Approximately twenty minutes after Harry left room 505, a nurse's aide found Andrew Barlow lying peacefully in bed without any pulse or respirations. A brief attempt at resuscitation by the nurses and residents was called off because of fixed, dilated pupils and an absolutely straight-line EKG. Although morning was the busiest, most hectic time of day in the hospital, with any number of technicians, physicians, students, maintenance people, aides, transportation workers, and nurses coming and going, none of the staff on Alexander 5 recalled seeing anyone enter or leave Barlow's room after Harry.

After receiving the news, Harry canceled what few patients he had left to see and returned, numb and dreamlike, to the hospital. Andy Barlow lay on his back in the semidarkness, a sheet drawn up to his chin. His face already reflected the early mottling of death. Harry wanted to scream, to bellow like the wounded animal he was. He wanted to destroy the room, to rip attachments from the wall, to snatch up a chair and hurl it through the plate glass window. Instead, he sat alone by the bedside, Andy Barlow's hand in his, and wept.

Before he left the floor, he placed three phone calls. The first was to inform Owen Erdman that he would be calling back later that day to set up an appointment as soon as possible. The second call was to Andy's family, and the third was to Albert Dickinson.

"If you think being the one to notify me takes you off my list," Dickinson said now, "you're crazy." He thought for a moment and then added, "But that's just the point, isn't it."

"What?"

"That you're crazy."

Dickinson could not charge him with any crime until an autopsy proved that Andy had died of something other than natural causes. But even a negative autopsy would leave unanswered questions. After all, the young architect was officially listed by the hospital as being in guarded condition, and the nurses to whom Dickinson had spoken testified that Harry's false alarm had doubtless added immeasurable stress to an already difficult situation.

"It wasn't a false alarm," Harry said, with exaggerated patience. "My office manager heard the call."

"Correction, sir. She heard the phone *ring*. Even a dumb cop like me knows the difference between hearing a phone ring and overhearing a conversation."

"Well, there was a patient of mine there, too. Standing in the hall right outside my door. He heard some of the conversation. Some of my half of it, anyway."

"Well, I guess that convinces me."

"Don't be snide."

"Then don't keep throwing ridiculous stories at me like I'm some sort of a fucking re-tard."

"The man's name was Concepcion. Walter Concepcion."

Harry reviewed the little he had learned about his new patient—former private detective, now unemployed, recovering crack cocaine addict, chronic headaches, nervous tic. Just the sort of corroborating witness Dickinson would expect him to come up with—one that would fit in nicely alongside DT-ing alcoholic Maura Hughes. Bookends.

"Get me this Walter whatsizname's address and I'll speak to him," Dickinson said.

"Listen," Harry responded, "just tell me one thing. What would I have to gain by faking such a phone call? Why would I do it?"

"Let me think. . . . Why would you fake a phone call from the man you say killed your wife, announcing that now he has decided for no particular reason to knock off some poor faggot who was going to die anyway? Gee, beats me."

"I didn't kill my wife. I didn't make up the phone call. Are you done with me?"

"You know, it could be this guy just died of heart failure or something," Dickinson went on, loosening his tie. "I mean, if I was lying there in guarded condition with AIDS and pneumonia and my doctor came bursting into my room screaming that someone was trying to kill me, I might just croak, too."

Harry sighed.

"Look, Lieutenant. I called you and told you about Andy's death. I waited around while you and your man questioned everyone on the floor. I came down here to the station without calling a lawyer. I've sat here for an hour and a half answering questions that I've answered two or three times already. I've listened to your insults and your innuendos and your accusations, and I haven't given you a hard time in any way. Right at this moment, I'm feeling incredibly bad about what happened to Andy Barlow. I really liked him, and I was working like hell to get him through his pneumonia. I think he was murdered by the same man who murdered Evie. But that man wasn't me. If you have any questions I haven't heard before, ask them. Otherwise, I want to go home."

"If that autopsy's positive, you're my man," Dickinson said.

"Fine."

"And if it's negative, you're still my man."

"That's your problem."

Dickinson moved to stub out a half-finished Pall Mall, real-ized what he was doing, and instead flicked the ash in Harry's general direction before taking another drag. Harry took his suit coat from the back of his chair and headed for the door.

"You haven't arrested me for Evie's murder because you couldn't find a DA who thought you had a good enough case. And they're right. I didn't do it."

"Tell that to the grand jury, Doc. I've got a week's pay says they're about to come down on you like a ton of bricks."

"You know how to find me," Harry said.

It was after three when Harry returned to his office. The waiting room was empty. Behind the glass of the reception area, Mary Tobin looked forlorn.

"We had already canceled and rescheduled Mrs. Gonsalves and the Silverman kids once before today," she said. "Dora Gon-salves was okay about it, but Mrs. Silverman was upset. She called just a few minutes ago to ask that her family's records be sent over to Dr. Lorello."

"Marv's a good guy. He'll take good care of them."

"You're not upset?"

"Of course I'm upset, Mary. But what am I supposed to do?"

"I don't know. Oh, Lord, I'm sorry, Dr. C. I guess this is all starting to get to me."

"Me, too."

"It's terrible about Andy Barlow."

Harry crumpled a blank intake form and clenched his fist around it.

"The bastard who killed him is going to pay," he said. "I swear he is." He threw the balled paper at the wastebasket and missed by two feet. "I had to call Andy's folks in Delaware and tell them. I hate that part of this job anytime, but I hate having to do it over the phone the most."

Mary stood up and embraced her boss. Her family had seen

more than its share of tragedy over the years, and she knew how to comfort and console. There was a special warmth in her wide girth that reminded Harry of his own mother before her recurrent strokes and weight loss of seventy or eighty pounds. He prolonged the hug for a few extra seconds.

"I'm afraid I have another piece of bad news," she said as he drew away. "Sara quit."

Harry felt himself sink. His nurse practitioner had been part of the office for over four years. She was bright, anxious to learn, and quite willing to handle most medical problems the way he would have. His patients loved her, and she actually generated a bit more money for the office than her salary. He glanced down the hall, but could tell that her office was dark.

"What happened?" he asked.

"All this stuff has been really getting to her. I think her husband's been putting pressure on her, too. She went home sick today, but she said she'll finish the week—two if you really want."

"One will be okay," Harry said, distracted. "I'll talk to her tomorrow." *Another casualty.* "Mary, did you reschedule that man Walter Concepcion?"

"Next week. Wednesday, I think. He tried explaining to me what he overheard from your end of that call from . . . from that man. I think he was embarrassed and upset about not just turning around and walking away."

"I'm actually glad he didn't. Do we have any phone number for him?"

"We do. He didn't put one on his questionnaire, but he left one later. I think the phone's in the hallway of a rooming house of some kind."

"Copy it and his address for me, will you please? I might try and get in touch with him."

At that moment, the private line in the back office began ringing. Harry tensed.

"Quick, Mary," he said, whispering although there was no one around to hear, "follow me in case it's him."

They hurried down the hall to the office. He motioned her to a spot where they could share the receiver. The phone was in its fourth ring when he snatched it up.

"Dr. Corbett," he said.

"Harry, hey, I'm glad I found you. It's Doug."

Harry covered the mouthpiece.

"It's Doug Atwater," he said, obviously disappointed. "The killer hasn't made any mistakes yet. I guess it was wishful thinking, expecting him to make one now." He waited until Mary had left, then took his hand off the mouthpiece. "Hi, Doug," he said.

Atwater was just about the only person affiliated with the hospital that he could deal with hearing from at this point.

"Harry, I just got a call from Owen wanting to know if I had heard from you. He told me about that poor guy on Alexander Five. It's terrible. Just terrible. And I know you aren't responsible in any way."

"Doug, there's a madman loose in the hospital. He killed Evie, and now he's trying to hurt me any way he can."

"Owen told me that's what you believe is going on."

"That *is* what's going on."

"Hey, there's no need to bite my head off. This is the first time you've said a thing to me about any madman in the hospital."

"Sorry."

"Harry, the nursing service has been bugging Owen that you were supposed to have called and taken yourself off the staff. Is that so?"

"No, it's not. Doug, I've spent twenty years establishing myself as a doctor. I'm not going to just chuck it now. Besides, if I don't hang in there and fight, they're never going to find the guy who's doing this. As things stand, finding him is my only chance."

Hang in there and fight. Harry thought back to the morning just a few weeks ago when he complained to Phil that he didn't have any challenges in life.

"You coming in to talk with Owen about this?" Atwater asked.

"Yes. I was going to do it a couple of hours ago, but I've been tied up with one of the detectives. Oh, you know the guy— Dickinson, that same one from when Evie died."

"Oh, no. That guy's an idiot. Does he think you're responsible for this man's death, too?"

"Of course."

"Oh, shit, Harry. I'm sorry. Listen, is there anything I can do?"

"I wish there were."

"You don't have any idea who's doing this to you?"

"Not a clue."

There was an uncomfortable silence.

"You know, Harry," Atwater said finally, "maybe you *should* consider taking a little time off from the hospital. At least until this business cools down—until the dust settles. I've been behind you one hundred percent in this thing, you know I have. But with the nurses on the warpath, and Owen having a meltdown, it's getting hot, damn hot."

"You don't believe me either, do you. I can tell from your tone of voice."

"Harry, you've got to be reasonable. There are other sides to this thing."

"Thanks for calling, Doug. Every single one of you might vote to throw me out, but I'm not quitting."

Harry set the receiver down without waiting for a reply and sank into his chair. His long-standing friend and possibly his last ally at the hospital had just bailed out. Atwater lacked the authority to get him lifted from the staff at the hospital, but he could suspend him as a provider for the Manhattan Health HMO. Manhattan Health patients probably represented 40 or 50 percent of his practice. Without them, it was doubtful he could stay in business for long.

Mary Tobin returned to his office doorway and announced that she had done as much as she could and was leaving for the day to run some errands. Harry thanked her, told her with too little conviction not to worry, and watched as she left the office. Tomorrow he would share the news of the body blow that Atwater seemed poised to deliver. He had no desire to heap more worry on her today than he had already.

He scanned his desk and the floor around it for any charts that needed dictating. There were none. He dialed Maura's apartment number and then his own, but got answering machines in both places.

Harry told each machine that he would be home by four.

Then he called Owen Erdman and set up yet another appointment to discuss his future at Manhattan Medical Center. Finally, he straightened his desk, set his feet up on one corner, closed his eyes, and tried desperately to think of something, anything, he could do to cut through the insanity that was smothering him. The ringing phone nearly startled him out of the chair. Once again, it was his private line. He lifted the receiver, but said nothing. In the brief silence that followed, Harry knew. *The killer was back. Back to gloat.*

"The autopsy on your patient will be negative," the unmistakable voice said.

"How do you know?"

"I have access to a neurotoxin so powerful and so short-lived that by the time it kills, it has already begun disappearing from the body. The final metabolism of the poison actually occurs after death. And here we have the temerity to call the Indians in the Amazon basin *savages*. I tell you, when it comes to killing, they are virtuosos."

Harry could feel the killer's arrogance and enormous ego. Having witnessed the unspeakable consequences of angering him, he chose his words carefully.

"What do you want from me?"

"Closure. That's all. Same as before. I'd prefer you did it with a note—ideally with a note admitting to the ill-advised administration of—what was it you used?—oh, yes, Aramine. The ill-advised administration of Aramine to your wife. You will at last be at peace. And I will have my closure."

"I'm no threat to you at all," Harry countered. "No one is. I can't even get anyone to believe that you exist."

Can't even get anyone to believe that you exist . . .

Harry's thoughts were suddenly racing. The man was insane, true, but he was also smart. Why was he taking a chance like this, calling Harry in the office when anyone might overhear his confession? All Harry needed was one reliable ally with first-hand knowledge, just one. He knew about the private line, and apparently, he also knew there was no way Harry could signal one of his office staff to pick up an extension. But how could he know that someone wasn't standing by, listening as Mary Tobin had when Doug Atwater called? He was bold and arrogant, but he was certainly not careless. *Why would he chance it?* Harry struggled to understand. Then suddenly he knew. *The bastard was watching the office! Right now, somewhere nearby, watching!* No other explanation made sense.

"Listen, a delivery man just came down from one of the upstairs offices," Harry said. "I just have to give him a package. If you have anything further to say to me, stay on. I'll be right back."

He set the receiver on his desk and sprinted down the hall to the front door. There was a pay phone on the other side of the street, two buildings down. *His tormentor had to be there!*

Harry charged from the building into the late afternoon glare, narrowly avoiding a yellow cab as he raced across the street. The half kiosk housing the pay phone was deserted. But it hadn't been. The receiver dangled down, swinging to and fro like a pendulum. The white handkerchief resting on the small metal counter promised that there would be no fingerprints. Harry raced to Fifth Avenue, the nearest corner. Pedestrian traffic was heavy. He scanned the street, searching for someone who looked out of place or interested in him. Nothing. Carla DeJesus, the elderly proprietor of a small variety store, stopped sweeping the sidewalk by her shop and waved. Harry waved back, walked over, and asked if she had seen anyone unusual or anyone running down the street. She had seen no one.

He wanted to scream—to lash out and hit something, anything. But his sanity was already in doubt in too many quarters.

"I'm going to find you, you bastard," he murmured as he continued straining to see anything out of the ordinary. "Whatever it takes, I'm going to find you."

He returned to lock up the office. On impulse, he tried calling his apartment again. Maura answered on the first ring. It wasn't until he heard her voice that he fully realized how worried he had been about her.

"Maura, hi, it's Harry," he said.

"How're you doing, Mr. Doctor?"

Her speech was too fluid, too singsong. His spirits, already low, sunk even further.

"Maura, are you drinking?" he asked

The ensuing pause was answer enough.

"Not enough to matter," she said flatly.

"Maura, please," he said, battling to keep both his fear for her and his anger in check. "Please stop. Stop now. I need you. Evie's killer thinks I paid to have someone follow us last night. He thinks I'm responsible for the death of his man. To pay me back, a few hours ago he killed one of my patients—a thirty-three-year-old guy. He just waltzed into his room and killed him. Then he called here to boast about it. He . . ." Harry had to stop speaking to compose himself. Maura said nothing. "Listen," he finally managed. "You're . . . you're the only friend I have right now. I don't even know what to do. The bastard said he wasn't going to stop hurting me or my patients until I . . . until I kill myself."

For another ten seconds the line was quiet.

"Harry, why don't you come on home," she said.

"What are you going to do?"

"Well, for starters, I'm going to take a shower."

Harry gave a silent prayer of thanks.

"Heavy on the cold," he said.

CHAPTER 22

Harry had dealt with enough actively drinking alcoholics to know that no promise—especially the one not to drink anymore —meant much. He took a cab across town expecting the worst. As far as he was concerned, Maura had to bear some responsibility for starting up again. But he also believed that she had been discharged prematurely following her operation at MMC—not necessarily prematurely for her surgery, or even for the DTs, but certainly for her alcoholism. She needed more time in the hospital—someone to develop a workable treatment plan. She would have benefited from social services intervention, some psychotherapy, perhaps a visit or two from people from AA, and quite possibly an inpatient stay at an alcoholism unit as well. Once upon a time, that was the way it had been done. But now, even if her physician knew this approach would give her the best shot at recovery, her insurance carrier dictated otherwise.

There were codes in the company's database for each and every disease, injury, and condition that anyone might be likely to have, everything from leprosy to blackwater fever. There were codes that set limits for hospital stays, procedures, and allowable payments. But there was no code that took into account the complexity of any individual or his or her reaction to illness—no code named "Maura Hughes," or "Harry Corbett." *Brave new medical world.*

Harry paid off the cabby, thought about picking up another box of candy—she might crave the sugar—then simply shrugged and crossed the street to his building. He felt beaten and sore. What fight remained within him was fueled by rage and frustration. Andy Barlow hadn't wanted to die. In the time he had left, he had wanted to design buildings and go to concerts and be with his friends. If Maura Hughes wanted to self-destruct, to drink until her liver or her stomach or her brain gave out, there really wasn't a damn thing Harry Corbett—or anyone else, for that matter—could do about it. *No candy.*

Maura was waiting just inside the door to the apartment. There was an overnight bag at her feet.

"I've decided to go home," she said.

Harry felt a spark of anger.

"Why?" he asked. "Because you drank? Or because you want to drink some more?"

"Both, probably. Harry, let's not debate it, okay? I'm just not any good to either of us, and I don't see where a few more drinks is going to make a bit of difference."

"Well, it will."

Harry wanted to shout at her. To remind her in the harshest terms that she had control of things Andy Barlow did not. Instead, he took a calming breath and held her by the arms. Her eyes were still clear and focused. She had almost certainly not had any more to drink since they spoke on the phone. There was still a slim chance to stop it right there.

"Let's go in and talk," he said. "Just for a while."

"Harry, please. I'm not playing any head games with you, I'm not wallowing in self-pity, and I'm not trying to get you to beg me not to drink."

"I didn't think you were. Listen, we're just having a lousy time of it—both of us. I know you feel bad about not remembering what that bastard looked like. I wish you could remember, too. But if you can't, you can't. It really isn't that important. What is important is that you're the only one who absolutely knows the truth about me and Evie. I'm counting on you to help keep me from coming unglued. And I think I can do the same for you. Now please, just come on back inside."

For a few silent seconds, she stared up at him.

"Anybody ever tell you that you look like Gene Hackman?" she said finally.

Harry was shaken. Then he noticed the mischief in her eyes.

"Well," he said, "now that you mention it . . ."

They sat on the sofa in the den, drinking coffee and trying to make sense of the events that were battering their lives. They had made very little when, an hour later, Harry's pager summoned him to call his answering service. Maura had agreed that she was not handling her alcoholism very effectively, but did not agree that she needed a couple of weeks or more as an inpatient at a rehab—especially not with Harry footing the bill, as he had offered to do.

"Anything else," she said. "Anything but the lockup."

Harry suggested she might speak with Murphy Oates, the piano player in the house band at C.C.'s Cellar. Oates, once a serious drunk and heroin addict, had been clean and sober for over a decade, though he rarely spoke about it.

"I'll be happy to speak with your friend," Maura bargained. "And whatever he tells me to do, I'll do . . . except get put away in some nut ward."

"He's probably at the club," Harry said.

"Now?"

"It doesn't open for another couple of hours, but there'll be some musicians there, playing or just hanging out. This is actually the time I like it there the most. It's dark and quiet and . . . well, sort of like a womb. You know, I just remembered that Andy Barlow once came in there to hear me play. . . ."

Harry's thoughts again entered the darkened hospital room on Alexander 5 and locked on the thin face staring lifelessly at the ceiling. From the moment he had heard Maura's thick speech on the phone, he had been holding on by the thinnest of threads. Now, he felt that thread snap, and himself begin to slide down a sheer glass wall.

". . . The lunatic admitted it, Maura," he said, pacing across the room and back. "He just called up and admitted killing Andy like . . . like he was admitting he stole the morning paper off my front stoop. And there wasn't a damn thing I could do about it. Not one goddamn thing. What am I supposed to do? I'm like a toy for him. Jump, Harry. Roll over. Play dead. How am I ever going to stop this? Who's next?"

"Harry, let's go," Maura said suddenly, taking his hand. "Let's get out of here right now. The club might do you some good, too."

"I don't know," he said. "Listen, let me find out what this page is all about. Then we can decide what we want to do."

Harry dialed his answering service. He wasn't on for his coverage group, so the call had to be something they couldn't deal with. The answering service operator, usually chatty and ebullient, sounded formal and cool. Apparently, she had joined the ranks of those certain that Harry was guilty of murdering his wife. It seemed as if word about him was spreading like a toxic fog.

"Dr. Corbett, you got a call from a Mr. Walter Concepcion," she said, making no effort to pronounce the name the Spanish way. "He said that he's a patient of yours, but that this isn't a medical problem. He said that no one else but you can help."

Harry scratched down the number, checked that it was the same as the one Mary had given him at the office, and dialed. A woman answered on the fifth ring.

"*¿Diga?*"

"*Buenas tardes,*" Harry said. "*¿Está Walter Concepcion, por favor?*"

Over his two decades of medical practice on the fringe of Spanish Harlem, he had evolved about a second grader's fluency in the language, although his accent was closer to preschool.

"*Un momento.*"

He heard her set the phone down and envisioned a woman in a print house dress walking to the foot of a flight of well-worn oak stairs.

"*¡Oye, Walter!*" she called out as if on cue. "*¡Walter Concepcion! ¡Teléfono!*" Harry's image this time was of his gaunt, twitchy new patient, slipping his feet into a pair of threadbare slippers, opening one of several doors on the second floor of the dingy boarding house, and padding down the stairs.

"*Hola,*" he said, at almost the moment Harry expected him to.

"Mr. Concepcion, it's Dr. Corbett."

"Oh, hey, thanks for calling back so quickly, Doc," he said. "Your office gal told me about what happened after that call came in. I'm sorry you're having so much trouble. I . . . I was calling to see if there might be a time for me to speak with you about it."

"Actually, I was going to call you."

He glanced over at Maura and motioned that he wouldn't be long. He wanted to get to know Walter Concepcion better before turning his phone number over to Albert Dickinson. He also wanted to prepare the man for the sort of degrading grilling he could expect from the detective. But another thought had occurred to him as well. Concepcion spoke proudly of having kicked a drug and alcohol habit. On external appearances alone he wasn't exactly a ringing endorsement for abstinence. But he was intelligent in a streetwise sort of way, and did seem to take his recovery seriously. If Murphy Oates wasn't at the club, Concepcion might be another voice of hope for Maura.

"Would you be free in, say, an hour?" Harry asked, guessing that the one-time detective would probably be free almost any hour.

"Just say where, Doc, and I'll get there."

Harry hesitated a moment and then gave him the address of the club.

C.C's Cellar was a 120-seat hole-in-the-wall on Fifty-sixth Street west of Ninth Avenue. The scarred brick walls were covered with signed, black-framed photos of jazz greats, many of whom had spent their entire lives in obscurity, enmeshed in a vicious cycle of poverty, addiction, and pain. C.C., Carl Cataldo, had died years before, and had left the club to his niece, Jackie. As far as Harry could tell, except for a few more photos on the walls and a state-of-the-art speaker system, not much had changed in the place since Carl opened it decades ago.

There were four people in the dimly lit main room when he and Maura arrived. Jackie, expansive in a stained white apron, was getting ready behind the bar. A gnarled old janitor who had been with the place since day one was sweeping out the small private-party room. Two musicians, both guitarists, were trading licks on the stage. One of them called to Harry.

"Hey, Doc, how about comin' up an' knockin' out a little bass line for us."

"Later, maybe, Billy."

"Hey, whenever, my man."

"Any idea where Murphy is?"

The man shook his head and then ran off several incredibly melodic bars of "I Remember You." Except for expressing grief about Harry's loss, no one at the club had even hinted by word or manner that they were upset by the publicity surrounding him. They trusted his music, they trusted him. It was that simple. And in a city of eight million or so, this was the only spot where he felt truly safe and accepted.

"Go ahead and play if you want to," Maura said, sipping soda water. "I'll be fine."

"Thanks, but I don't think so. I thought I might want to when we left the apartment, but right now I just want to sit with you and . . . Maura, he simply walked past everyone on Alexander Five, into Andy's room, and then out again. How could he have done that without a single person noticing? Not one."

"How did he just walk into our room the night he killed Evie? He knows how to move around hospitals. That's all there is to it. If you were evil enough and set your mind to it, you could do it just as well. There's so much stress and tension in hospitals that I'll bet most people who work there are totally focused on not making mistakes. There are probably times when you could march an elephant through the halls and no one would notice. The guy just knows how to do it."

"I guess."

"Harry, I wish I could say something to help. I really do."

"You can, dammit. You can say you won't pick up a drink again."

Her eyes sparked at his curtness. It was the first time he had spoken to her that sharply.

"I'll try my best," she said. "How's that?"

"It'll do for now."

She stared into her glass.

"So," she said, brightly, "tell me about this guy who's meeting us here. You said he's a private detective?"

"Was. He got into trouble with booze and cocaine. I don't know what he did to lose his license, but now he's trying to get it back."

"Well, I think that may be him over there."

Walter Concepcion was getting a soda water from Jackie, who nodded toward where they were sitting. He was wearing a lightweight plaid sports jacket and looked more businesslike than he had in Harry's office. Harry studied him as he approached the table, wondering what sort of impression he might make on Albert Dickinson. He moved well enough, and carried himself like someone who had once had some athletic ability. But even dressed up, he still looked wasted and chronically ill. Dickinson would never believe his claim that he had been off crack for years. Harry introduced him to Maura.

"Three soda waters on the perfect pitcher-of-beer day," Concepcion said, motioning to their three drinks. "Could it be that I'm not the only one on the wagon?"

Harry was impressed.

"I didn't say a thing," he said to Maura. "You heard the whole conversation."

"Harry's just patronizing us," she explained. "I'm the lush."

"In that case, here's to us lushes."

"I like this guy," Maura said, joining in the toast.

After five minutes of conversation, Harry knew that his office assessment of the man had been way off. Despite his sallow complexion and the persistent tic at the corner of his mouth, Concepcion was engaging and intelligent. He was born and raised in New York, but had traveled extensively in the service, and then on his own.

He spoke easily and even humorously of his drinking days and his virulent addiction to crack cocaine. But the intensity in his eyes left no doubt that this was serious business to him. At the height of his career, he was commanding thousand-dollar-a-day fees and was in continuous demand. His professional downfall came when he traded his gun to an undercover cop for some crack. At the time, it didn't matter to him—nothing mattered except his next fix. But recovery had changed all that.

"I go mostly to NA," Concepcion told Maura, when bringing up the subject seemed right. "You know, Narcotics Anonymous. But I'll be happy to go with you to an AA meeting if you want. NA, AA, Hershey Bars Anonymous—they're all the same as far as I'm concerned."

"The sooner the better, I guess," Maura said.

Jackie brought over some pretzels and another round of sodas. The two guitars had been joined by Hal Jewell, a full-time drummer who reminded Harry of Buddy Rich, and a sax player named Brisby, who was a partner in one of the most successful black law firms in the city. They were working through a classy ballad in D that Harry had never heard before. Three quarters of an hour had gone by, and between the music and the pleasant surprise that was Walter Concepcion, he had managed to smooth off a bit of the ragged pain he was feeling.

The ballad was captivating, especially with the acoustics of the near-empty room. They listened in silence until Brisby's last, melancholy note had faded away. Then Concepcion cleared his throat and turned to Harry.

"Dr. Corbett, I . . . um . . . there's something I need to tell you. I do have headaches like I told you in the office—bad ones that no one's been able to help me with. But that was only one of the reasons I came to see you."

"Oh?"

"I hope you're not angry about this. If you are, I guess I'd understand."

"Go on."

"I was going to tell you at the office, but you got that phone call and ran out before I could. Doc, I read about you in the papers. In fact, I've read absolutely everything I could get my hands on about what happened to you and your wife at the hospital. I've been fascinated by it. I even talked to a friend's sister who's a nurse there. She . . . ah . . . she told me about the argument you had with that surgeon, what's his name?"

Harry momentarily debated ending the conversation right there. But over the past hour Concepcion had come across as anything but a head case. And there was nothing threatening or obsessive in his tone or expression now.

"Sidonis," he said. "Caspar Sidonis."

"Yeah, him. I—" He looked down at his hands. "I even know about you, Maura, assuming you're the Maura from Mrs.

Corbett's room. Not that much, really. But enough to know that not too many people at the hospital believe you."

"Walter, maybe you'd better get to the point," Harry said.

"The point is, I need work. I know I don't look it, but I'm good at what I used to do. Damn good. You claim you didn't kill your wife. Maura claims someone else was in the room after you. I want to help figure out who that person was. If I help, you pay me. If I don't, you're only out expense money."

Harry stared across at him. He hadn't once thought about trying to hire someone to help him out. The idea certainly had merit, he acknowledged now. But Walter Concepcion hardly seemed the ideal choice. He felt a sympathetic pang as he pictured the man in his rooming house, rummaging through his small closet for his best clothes in hopes of landing a job.

"I don't know," he said.

"Walter, tell me something," Maura said. "From what you've read, what do you think about all this?"

Concepcion rubbed thoughtfully at the stubble on his chin.

"Well, we're not talking about a jealous husband or even an amateur here," he said. "That's for sure. We're dealing with a psychopathic, sociopathic professional killer—a man without a conscience. So I guess the most important thing I could say is that I don't believe Dr. Corbett fits that profile at all. And therefore I don't believe he did it."

"You're right there," Harry said.

"I also don't believe you hired the man who did."

"Right again. Walter, I just don't know."

Harry was drawn to a connection with Concepcion's experience and street smarts, to say nothing of the value of having another hand on board who was committed to proving he wasn't a murderer. But he was reluctant to strike a deal with a man about whom he knew so little. Maura saved him the trouble.

"It's a deal," she said.

"What?"

"Harry, you want to say yes and you know it. We're dead in the water. We don't have even the glimmer of an idea of what to do next. Walter can help us. I feel it in my bones."

"I really think I can, Dr. Corbett."

Harry took another fifteen seconds, purely for appearances.

"If you're going to be working for me, you might as well call me Harry," he said.

"You won't regret this," Concepcion said. "I promise."

He reached over and shook Harry's hand. His fingers were bony and gnarled, but his grip was surprisingly firm.

For the next half hour, Harry went over the case in detail. Concepcion listened intently and interrupted from time to time to clarify a point.

"This technician who took the fingerprints, has he heard anything at all?" . . . "Did you suspect your wife was having an affair at any time?" . . . "The two names you found in her address book, have you learned anything about them?" . . . "Do you have any idea who your wife worked for?" . . .

By the time Harry finished, they had been at the club for over two hours. The first few customers had started to straggle in.

"Well, what do you think?" he asked.

Concepcion twisted the small gold band he wore on the middle finger of his right hand.

"I think we've got to do what we can to find out who this Desiree was working for. That's where I'm going to start."

"Good luck," Harry said, genuinely impressed with the logic of the idea. "What can we do in the meantime?"

"We need to get at that face Maura has locked away somewhere in her brain."

"You mean by hypnosis?"

"It's a thought."

Harry rubbed at his eyes.

"Maura, I feel really stupid for not suggesting that."

"You've had a few things on your mind," she said. "Listen, Harry. I'll try anything. Maybe we can throw in a few extra bucks and whoever hypnotizes me can convince my subconscious that Southern Comfort tastes like borscht or Diet Dr Pepper or something. Do you know anyone who might do it?"

"Actually, I do," Harry said. "I know someone quite well. His name's Pavel Nemec. You may have heard of him as The Hungarian."

"The court of last resort for smokers," Maura exclaimed. "I've heard there's a waiting time of six months to see him."

"I took care of his son once. I have his home number back at the apartment. If it's humanly possible, he'll see us tomorrow."

Concepcion whistled.

"You must have done something pretty special for his kid."

"Not really," Harry murmured. "But Pavel thinks I did." He turned to Concepcion. "Okay then, Walter, we're in business."

"Um, almost." Concepcion looked at him warily. "I'm going to need some money for my expenses, and some more to buy information when I need to. Don't worry, I'll keep an accounting and receipts."

"Just how much are we talking about here?"

"For expenses, maybe five hundred."

"And for the other, the information?"

"I dunno. Maybe a thousand."

"Fifteen hundred dollars!" Harry exclaimed. "I thought you said no results, no pay."

"I told you, Harry, I'm a professional. I know what it takes to get information. How much do you think that guy got paid to kill your wife?"

"Okay, okay. Point made. Stop by my office tomorrow morning and I'll have the cash for you."

"Great. You won't regret this."

"You said that fifteen hundred dollars ago."

Concepcion stood and shook hands with each of them.

"Maura, we'll hit a meeting tomorrow or the next day. I promise."

"Great. I'm ready for it."

He turned to go, and then turned back.

"Oh, Harry?"

"What now?"

"If you've got it, I could really use a small advance on that expense money."

Harry handed over a twenty, then another.

"Why do I feel like I just swam into a whirlpool?" he said.

Concepcion just grinned in his engaging way and headed off.

"Have I been had?" Harry asked.

Maura shook her head.

"Hardly. You've been leading too sheltered a life," she said. "Everybody's got to eat. I trust him. Besides, he's already come up with two good ideas we didn't."

"I would have thought of the hypnotist," Harry grumbled.

CHAPTER 23

Impatient for The Roundtable to convene, Kevin Loomis lay facedown on the king-size bed in his room at the Garfield Suites. It had been a week since he learned that Evelyn DellaRosa had been murdered. Any number of times over those days, he had considered trying to track down Sir Gawaine to see if the man agreed she was Desiree. But if he was discovered by anyone in the group probing into the identity of a fellow knight, it would probably be over for him. For the moment, his plan was to keep his mouth shut on the matter and hope that Gawaine brought it up.

The young beauty who called herself Kelly knelt astride Kevin's buttocks, kneading the tension from the muscles in his lower back. Her silk Oriental dress—red this night and adorned with gold lamé—lay over the chair, alongside her black lace panties. Kevin watched her reflection in the mirror across the room, her high, firm breasts, her small, dark nipples, the perfect curves of her hips and ass. *Kelly. Another meaningless name,* he thought. Like Lancelot and Merlin and Desiree and the rest—shadow names of no substance, created only to cloak secrets. Names that vanished in the light of day.

"Is Kelly your real name?" he asked.

He saw her smile in the mirror and felt foolish knowing he was hardly the first to ask that question.

"If you wish it to be, it is," she replied softly, patiently.

Kevin closed his eyes and found himself feeling vaguely queasy. Massaging him was this most gorgeous woman, ready, if he should wish it, to take him inside her in the most intimate ways imaginable, yet forbidden to share even her first name with him. Was *she* a reporter? Or perhaps a student in nuclear physics at Columbia? Or was she just an up-and-coming whore? Kelly, Tristram, Desiree, Galahad, Gawaine. *Shadow names.*

What would Nancy say if she knew? he wondered. Would she believe he was part of it all? Did he even believe it, himself?

"I'm going to take a shower," he said, rolling over.

Kelly bent down and kissed his cock, which immediately started to harden.

"You want me to come with you?"

"No," he said, too sharply. *I want you to tell me what in the hell I'm doing here.* "Just get dressed and order something for dinner. . . . I don't care what it is as long as it's the most expensive thing on the menu."

"Filet medium rare," she said. "I remember."

As soon as Kevin entered the Stuyvesant Suite, he made eye contact with Gawaine. From the man's dress and manner, Loomis had always believed he had a prep school and possibly even Ivy League background. Tonight, his smooth manner seemed frayed, his smile a little tense.

The seven high-backed chairs circling the table were set about four feet apart. Tristram's brass nameplate had been placed in its customary spot between Kay and Lancelot. Gawaine moved toward his seat, which was almost opposite Kevin's.

Kevin caught his eye, nodded a greeting, then approached.

"How're you doing?" he asked.

"Can't complain," Gawaine said.

"Lancelot's sent me a Chinese girl this time. Eleven on a scale of ten, he calls her. He might be right. I think he's trying to make up for that Desiree fiasco."

"Yeah, probably."

Gawaine smiled uncomfortably and pulled out his chair.

Before Kevin could test him again, the meeting was convened by Merlin.

Maybe he doesn't know anything at all about Evelyn DellaRosa, Kevin thought. *Maybe he hasn't even seen any of the pictures of her.*

Galahad's financial report showed that the group's contributions had put their operating capital back over the agreed-upon $600,000. Kevin had no idea how that baseline figure was arrived at, or, for that matter, how any of their rules had been adopted. No minutes were ever kept, no record of votes, no paperwork of any kind. But everyone seemed to know exactly where projects stood and what was expected of each of them.

Kay spoke first, reporting on one of three major new programs that would be discussed tonight. He sounded quite eager to report that the votes were now in place to pass legislation permitting companies to run genetic panels on all prospective employees. First formal psychological exams and profiles, then AIDS screening, and now, finally, genetic testing. They all knew that the total package might not do one truly positive thing for the companies involved. But it would save those companies' health insurance carriers tens if not hundreds of millions.

"There'll be the usual court challenges," Kay explained. "But I think we have control of this one. I would guess it'll be a year before it's enacted, challenged, and upheld—maybe a bit longer if the labor unions latch onto any half-decent lawyers. But we *are* going to win."

"The quicker the better," Lancelot said. "As far as I'm concerned, we ought to make genetic screening a requirement for entering *kindergarten.* Goddamn mutants are everywhere."

There was laughter from around the table. Loomis faked his and noted that Gawaine's smile looked perfunctory.

Kay received a round of appreciative pen taps for his work. Percivale clapped out loud. *Tens of millions in increased profits for the industry—possibly more.* Tristram thought about the figure Burt Dreiser had quoted him the morning when they met on his boat. *Nineteen million dollars.* That was what the former knight's company had lost in one year by not being allowed to replace him on The Roundtable. *Nineteen million dollars.* Assuming Crown Health benefited similarly from his work, Tristram's bonus would be one percent of that—$190,000 on top of his base salary.

If nobody else mentioned Desiree, he decided, he was not going to be the one to break the ice.

Gawaine was called upon next to give the group an update on their newest endeavor—legislation that would enable the health insurers to decide what treatment was appropriate and not appropriate for patients with terminal illnesses. Kevin continued to watch him closely, noting how he shuffled papers and fidgeted with a pencil as he spoke. Sir Buttondown was uncharacteristically nervous. No doubt about it.

"Please note," Gawaine said, "that I refer to patients with terminal illnesses rather than terminally ill patients. Once we are allowed to define what illnesses can be considered terminal, we plan to turn our attention to determining when the treatment for those conditions is no longer cost effective. We need the right to cut off coverage for those patients who are taking up costly hospital beds and specialist care when there is ultimately no hope for them. Of course, the sooner in that process we can step in, the better. The legislative climate is excellent right now. Tristram has brought the commissioner back into the fold, so he won't be a problem. We've been nibbling at this thing for years, convincing the legislators and the public that since we're footing the bills, we should make the treatment decisions. Now it appears that we are ready to take a much bigger bite. Lancelot, do you want to go on to your part?"

Lancelot set his half-smoked cigar aside and cleared his throat. He never actually lit up a cigar during a Roundtable session, but he was rarely without his prop. He gave Gawaine a puckish grin and an A-okay sign. Tristram noted that Gawaine barely responded.

"The neat part of this program," Lancelot explained, "is a network of facilities we are calling palliative centers—PCs. These are the places where patients we determine to be terminally ill can be sent for inexpensive, bare-bones care. The ultimate hospice—something on the continuum after a hospital and a nursing home, but much less expensive to run than either. No treatments, no IVs, no therapy of any kind. Pain medication only, administered around the clock in a totally humane way.

And the best part is that we are moving ahead with designing these PCs and even setting up the corporations that will eventually run them. In some cases, we're actually purchasing the facilities that will one day house them."

There was half an hour of discussion on the palliative centers, and then Merlin took over.

"This has been a hell of a meeting," he cheered. "A hell of a meeting. Well, I'm pleased to say that the news from my front is good, too. We've implemented the employment modification program on a limited basis, and tonight I'm prepared to present the results and projected numbers on the first ten cases. The policyholder in each of these cases has been terminated from employment. Some have found new employment with companies doing business with insurers other than Roundtable members. Others continue as allowed by law to pay their premiums themselves for eighteen months. Still others now qualify for Medicaid. But in most of these cases, we're already out of the loop as their insurers. Off the hook, so to speak."

Loomis could not remember anything called the employment modification program. Apparently, Merlin was using The Roundtable's money and influence to arrange the firing of costly policyholders. If so, it was the first time that specific individuals had been targeted by the group. He scanned his copy of the printout Merlin had passed around. At the top was the heading "Qualifications"—the factors used by the computer to select cases. Below that were ten names, and beside each of them was an insurance carrier, a diagnosis, and a dollar amount. The smallest amount was $200,000, the largest $1.7 million. The fourth of the ten names was a Crown Health and Casualty subscriber.

Subscriber	Patient	Carrier	Diagnosis	Amount
4. DeSenza, Elizabeth	Ryan	Crown	Head Injury	$1,300,000

Kevin stared at the name, struggling to keep his expression bland. Beth DeSenza was a production line worker at a large garment factory just outside the city. Her son, Ryan, had suffered a freak cardiac arrest and subsequent brain damage after being hit in the chest with a baseball. Thanks to her company's comprehensive insurance coverage, Ryan was a patient in the most highly regarded—and most expensive—brain injury rehabilitation hospital in the area. Kevin had engineered the coverage agreement with her union. Beth was the only policyholder in all his years with Crown who had taken the trouble to find out his name and to write and thank him for his role in providing care for her child. She included a picture of Ryan before the accident, bat poised, smiling self-consciously from beneath a baseball cap that seemed two sizes too big.

Thank you, Mr. Loomis, she wrote. *Thank you and Crown for making Ryan's treatment possible.*

Nancy had taken the note and had it matted and framed. Now, Beth's coverage for her son, at least at the level provided by Crown, was over. The individual-policy premium was extremely expensive—almost certainly too expensive for her to continue the coverage even for the period allowed by state law. Tristram felt ill.

". . . From early indications," Merlin was saying, "provided the program is not overutilized, once we get up to speed our companies can realize a comfortable ongoing savings of three to six million dollars a month. Not exactly a bonanza, but hardly chicken feed."

There were appreciative pen taps from around the table.

"I was just wondering why the companies holding the policies weren't consulted about these individuals before they were terminated."

There was a deathly silence in the room.

"Tristram, I don't believe I understand what you mean," Merlin said finally.

His tone and expression were nonjudgmental, yet Kevin felt his pulse pounding in his ears. Everything seemed to be happening in freeze-frame. The six faces fixed on him were like those in a wax museum—imbued with expression, but not with life.

Then suddenly, his gaze was drawn to movement. Gawaine, sitting across from him, was shaking his head ever so slightly. His eyes, locked on Kevin's, blazed. Loomis watched his lips move and heard the unspoken word as if it had been shouted into his ear.

No!

With the others focused on him, Loomis felt certain he was the only one who had picked up on the warning.

"I . . . um . . . I'm sorry," he said. "What I meant to ask was why you hadn't checked with each of us for more names."

"Ah, I see," Merlin responded. "Thank you for clarifying that. I did misunderstand."

"Perhaps I can answer your question, Tristram," Kay said, "since I designed the program to select the clients. The decisions, purely business, are made by computer to keep them as rational and dispassionate as possible. As you can see from the list of factors considered, a great deal of data is evaluated before a selection is made. Each time, thousands upon thousands of policyholders are screened. This process would be virtually impossible for any of us to do on a regular basis, and certainly not with the accuracy of a computer."

The knights' attention had shifted to Kay, except for Gawaine, whose gaze remained fixed on Kevin. His face was tight and waxen. The unspoken warning continued flashing from his eyes.

"I understand," Tristram said, forcing a smile. "I understand completely."

The Roundtable meeting concluded without further incident. The knights left the Stuyvesant Suite in the inverse order of their arrival. Kevin considered trying to waylay Gawaine and demand an explanation. But he did not know the man's room number, and the danger of discovery in hanging too close to the meeting room was too great. Instead, he returned to his own room, his feelings roiling.

Kelly, wearing only her panties, lay on the bed watching a movie, eating grapes left over from dinner. She seemed completely at ease.

Kevin tossed her dress across her lap.

"Go," he said.

"But you have me until morning."

He took a fifty from his wallet and set it in her hand.

"I won't tell anyone and I don't want you to. Just be careful leaving. I'll see you next time."

Kelly tossed the dress aside, stood on her tiptoes and kissed him hungrily. He cupped her breast in his hand. Her nipple instantly swelled to his touch. Her smooth, lean body melted into his.

"I want you," she whispered.

For a frozen minute his thoughts were only of her. He had not yet given in and made love with her. But he knew he was drawing closer with every moment they were together. Perhaps that was what he really needed, he began thinking. Not to face the demons that were suddenly tormenting him, but to escape them.

"I want you," she moaned again. Still on her tiptoes, she took his swollen cock and worked it between her thighs. "I want you inside me so much."

He took her by the shoulders and forced her to arm's length. She was part of them—an extension of The Roundtable. One of the shadow names. The piece she was about to take from him would bind him even more tightly to the society. Perhaps she was even to be rewarded for getting him to fuck her.

See, Tristram, you can do it, The Roundtable would be saying to him. *You can do anything!*

"Get out," he snapped. "Right now."

The hurt on her face seemed genuine. Kevin almost laughed out loud at her skill. She dropped her dress on over her head and turned to allow him to zip it up.

"Next time?" she asked.

"We'll see. Now please, go."

Kevin waited several seconds after the door had locked behind her and then splashed an inch of bourbon into a tumbler and gulped it down. Until he had read Beth DeSenza's name on Merlin's printout, none of The Roundtable's programs had ever presented even the slightest moral dilemma for him. But they were programs that largely involved laws and the people who made them. The insurance commissioner was a pompous, politically motivated bastard—fair game in Kevin's view. The corporate sabotage made perfect sense given the dog-eat-dog climate of the insurance business. But this was different. This was a flesh and blood person. He could handle standing back behind the lines, lobbing shells down on the enemy. But this was hand-to-hand combat. And suddenly, the enemy had eyes.

Kevin was in over his head. He knew it now. And there

wasn't a damn thing he could do about it—except to adjust. The price of a ticket on this ride was a twelve-room house and a secure future for himself and his family. He had paid the fare. Now he had no choice but to hang on and make the best of it. The next time Kelly asked, he would be ready for . . . whatever.

He had poured another two fingers when the phone began ringing.

"Tristram," he said.

"It's Gawaine," the knight whispered. "Can you talk?"

"Yes, I'm alone."

"You sent your girl home?"

"Yes."

"Jesus. You are asking for trouble. Mine's in the other room."

"What's going on? Why did you stop me at the meeting?"

"I know your name. Do you know mine?"

"No."

"It's Stallings. Jim Stallings. I'm a vice president with the Manhattan offices of Interstate Health Care."

Kevin knew the gargantuan managed care company well. He had once interviewed for a sales job with them.

"Go on," he said.

"Loomis, we've got to talk. Tomorrow, noon sharp. Can you make it?"

"I can, but—"

"Battery Park. The benches on the Hudson side. Just be damn sure you're not followed."

"But—"

"Please, Loomis. Wait until tomorrow at noon, and be careful."

"One thing," Kevin said quickly. "Did you see the picture of that woman DellaRosa?"

"Of course I did."

"And do you think it's Desiree?"

"I never had any doubt about it. It was *you* I had doubts about. I wasn't sure if you were one of them or not. But after tonight I'm willing to take the chance that you're still an outsider like me. In fact, I'm betting my life on it."

Kevin listened to the dial tone for several seconds. Then he set the receiver down and walked to the window. Fourteen stories below, scant early-morning traffic flowed in slow motion along largely deserted streets. A cab pulled up and stopped directly beneath his window. A woman wearing a tight, iridescent red dress hurried out and climbed inside. The lady without a name.

The cab rolled to the corner and then turned uptown. Kevin sensed that he had seen the girl, stroked her magnificent, taut body, for the last time. He glanced at his watch. Eleven hours. Eleven hours until Battery Park.

CHAPTER 24

At three-thirty in the morning, Maura gave up trying to sleep and tiptoed from the small guest room to the den. Through his partially open door, she could see Harry asleep in the master bedroom. For a time after they returned from C.C.'s Cellar, she had thought he might ask her to join him there. He liked her. That seemed clear. But there were reasons—plenty of them— why he would want to keep some distance between them. Key among them was that she had given in to her frustration and her demons and had been drinking that afternoon.

It was just as well, she thought. She wasn't ready for an emotional entanglement any more than he was. Still, she couldn't remember the last time a man's looks had turned her on so. And more important, he was one of the kindest, most decent men she had ever met. It would have been nice just to curl up in his arms for a night and let the chips fall where they may.

She turned on the den light and ran her finger over the volumes in the bookcase, searching for something light—very light. Then again, she thought, perhaps heavy would be better. She pulled out a thin paperback of poems by Lord Byron. *Evelyn DellaRosa* was written in perfect script inside the cover. Evie was, of course, another valid reason for Harry's maintaining distance between them. Maura closed the book and slid it back. She and Harry had been through so much since his wife's death that it was difficult to remember it had only been a few weeks.

She scanned the shelves once more and finally settled on a coffee-table book on Ireland. In six hours she and Harry were scheduled to meet with Pavel Nemec. Maura desperately wanted the session to work out. Connecting with the face that was locked in her subconscious would just about balance her humiliation at having fallen off the wagon. She had never been hypnotized before and had no idea whether being sleepless for the entire preceding night would be a plus or a minus. On the other hand, if the legendary Hungarian was as incredible as his reputation, it probably didn't matter.

As Harry had predicted, the moment Nemec heard his request, a time slot had been cleared out for them.

"Exactly what *did* you do for his son?" Maura asked after Harry told her about the appointment.

"Ricard? Nothing, really. I just did a routine physical for music camp," he said. "He plays the French horn."

"And?"

"And I found a little lump that I didn't like beneath one arm."

"Cancer?"

"Hodgkin's disease, actually. Thank God it was in an early stage. It's been about six years now, so he's considered a cure."

He said it all so matter-of-factly, like she might talk about mixing paints. But Maura knew about school physicals and camp physicals and such. She had had enough of them to know that most doctors did nothing but listen to your heart. But Harry hadn't dealt with Pavel Nemec's son in such a cursory way. Harry had been . . . Harry.

Maura reflected on what he had told her of the drama swirling around him at the hospital—the call from his friend Atwater asking him to remove himself from the staff; the hearing that was being arranged to decide whether or not he would be allowed to continue to practice there.

Harry Corbett didn't deserve that sort of treatment, she thought angrily. She brushed her fingers across her feathery new hair and along the still-sensitive margins of her craniotomy scar. He also didn't deserve the treatment *she* had given him. Drinking again had been petulant, immature, and stupid. She was lucky he hadn't just handed her a bottle and booted her out.

"No more," she muttered, knowing that she had failed to

honor the same pledge many times before. "That's it, lady. Not one more drop."

She flipped through a few pages of Irish countryside and felt her eyelids grow heavy. She wondered what it would feel like to be hypnotized—if it would feel like anything at all. O'Brien's Tower atop the Cliffs of Moher in County Clare blurred, then faded.

No more. The words echoed in her mind. *Not one more drop . . .*

The aroma of brewing coffee worked its way into her consciousness. She opened her eyes a slit.

Pale morning light filtered into the den from between buildings. Harry sat on the easy chair beside the sofa. He was dressed in gray sweats with a towel draped around his neck, and had obviously just finished a workout. His dark hair glistened with sweat, and the color in his cheeks made his rugged good looks just that much more appealing.

Maura reached over dreamily and squeezed his hand.

"What time is it?" she said.

"After seven. We still have a while if you want to doze off again. I'm just being selfish by waking you up like this."

"Then I'll be even more selfish and stay awake."

"How do you feel?"

"Sober."

She knew it was the only word he really wanted to hear.

"You ready to have your brain probed by The Hungarian?"

"I am. He had just better be set to boldly go where no man has gone before."

"He's a wizard—at least that's what I've been told. Hey, listen. Evie's three-hundred-dollar coffeemaker is hard at work in the kitchen. The first thing she did after the wedding was to give away my Mr. Coffee. Hers goes to the gourmet shop by itself, mixes the perfect blend, then grinds, brews, and samples it."

"With that buildup, I'm all taste buds."

"How do you take it?"

"After yesterday you have to ask?"

Harry smiled.

"Black it is," he said.

·   ·   ·

Maura had never paid a great deal of attention to her looks. One ex-lover had said that was because she had never had to. Today, though, she took a bit more time than usual getting ready —a little makeup, the enamel earrings Harry liked, and a cotton dress instead of her trademark jeans.

She felt keyed up at the prospect of what lay ahead—frightened that the session would be a bust, but almost equally apprehensive about other possibilities. Over the two and a half years of her downward spiral she had been a blackout drinker, with little regard for the places she went or the company she kept. Now she wondered just how selective Pavel Nemec could be in unlocking her memory. Most of what was hidden away in her subconscious might just as well stay right where it was.

Nemec lived and worked at an address on the Upper East Side. Before going there, she and Harry took a cab to his office, stopping at her place to pick up an artist's sketch pad, some pencils, and some pastels, and at his bank to withdraw fifteen hundred dollars.

"I've canceled another half day at the office and gotten someone to make rounds on my patients in the hospital," he told her. "Most of my practice is pretty loyal, I think. But I'm really beginning to put some of them to the test."

She nodded sympathetically. "This is the day," she said. "This is the day it all begins to turn around. Trust me. Hey, speaking of turning around, turn this way a bit. I want to try something."

He did as she asked, and in less than two blocks she had sketched a passable likeness of him. By the time they reached the office, the drawing was quite good.

"That's amazing," he said.

"I can do better. But at least this tells me I can do it at all. It's been a while. I actually once spent a summer in Italy doing sketches and caricatures for the tourists on the Piazza Navona."

Walter Concepcion was already in the waiting room, chatting with the woman behind the reception desk, whom Maura learned was Mary Tobin. Maura was glad to see him again. Today he wore a black T-shirt, and she noticed that his arms were sinewy and more muscular than she would have expected. He had a tattoo over his left deltoid, artfully done, of a skull with a serpent slithering out of one eye.

"They called from Dr. Erdman's office at the hospital," Mary said. "The meeting is scheduled for ten tomorrow morning in the conference room next to his office."

Harry sighed.

"I guess you'll have to call my morning appointments and cancel them again."

"I already did."

"This is getting ridiculous. You know, maybe we should just close up shop for a while."

The older woman's eyes flashed.

"You do," she said, "and I'm gonna find me one of those bamboo canes. You know, the ones that take flesh off with the second stroke . . ."

"Okay, okay. We'll see what happens tomorrow."

"Fine. I called your attorney to tell him the time. He wants you to call him later today, but he said he'll be there."

"At three hundred fifty an hour, why shouldn't he be?"

"Pardon?"

"Nothing, Mary. Nothing. I'm just in my irritable idiot mode is all. It never lasts long."

"Thank goodness," she said.

Harry handed Concepcion the money in an envelope. It was clear to Maura that Harry still had doubts about the man. But she had absolutely none. Walter had already given them a place to start—the first steps of a counterattack.

"Okay, we're in business," Concepcion said, pocketing the envelope. "And don't worry, Harry. Every dollar of this will be accounted for on paper—receipts and all. I actually think we got off to a running start last night. After I got home I called about forty escort services. My line to them was that a woman named Desiree had given me the night of my life when I was last in town six months ago. Unfortunately for me, a friend had made the arrangements, and I had no way of getting hold of him for the name of the escort service. Money was no problem, but only if it was for Desiree. Three of the services made it sound as if they knew her. They said they'd try to get in touch with her and I should call back. A fourth one, Elegance, said she wasn't working for them anymore. That's the one I'm homing in on."

"Why that one?" Maura asked.

"Because the woman I spoke to initially gave me vague answers about Desiree. She took my number and said I'd be called. About an hour later, a different woman called. She said her name was Page. I think she runs the business. We played cat and mouse for a time. I mentioned money as often as I could. She denied knowing anyone named Desiree as often as she could. Finally I told her that I knew Desiree was dead, and I just wanted some information about her. I offered her five hundred dollars just to talk with me in person for half an hour. Not one minute more. And she didn't have to answer any questions about Desiree that she didn't want to. I was sure she was going to say no. But when she said again that she didn't know Desiree, I knew I had her. We're meeting tomorrow morning."

"That sounds promising," Maura said.

"It sounds like we're about to be taken for five hundred bucks," Harry muttered.

"You just hang in there with me, boss," Walter replied, the tic at the corner of his mouth firing off several times. "You don't seem to know it yet, but what you got here is the detective bargain of the century. Just keep in touch. Maybe we can get together tomorrow night and compare notes. By the way, Maura, I'll check on an AA meeting for us to go to then if you still want to."

"I'm ready."

"You have my number at home," Harry said. "Call anytime if you learn something." He hesitated and then added, "Walter, I'm sorry to be giving you a hard time. I'll try not to."

Concepcion pinched his own forearm.

"Hey, skin as thick as rhino hide, man," he said. "Besides, I haven't done anything yet except cost you money. When I do produce, and I will, I expect you to get off my case."

He shook hands with them both, waved to Mary Tobin, and headed out.

"Come on," Harry said. "We can catch a cab on Fifth."

"Okay," Maura said, battling a sudden, inexplicable case of nerves, "let's do it." She started toward the door and then turned back. "Cross your fingers, Mary," she said. "We're off to see the wizard."

.   .   .

The discreet brass placard above the bell read:

P. Nemec
Behavior Modification

Pavel Nemec greeted them warmly and served them tea and cakes in the oak-paneled Victorian waiting room of his office. He and Harry spent some time catching up on Nemec's family and on Harry's life over the years since they had last spoken. He was in his early sixties, Maura guessed, graying and very slight, but fit. She found him charming and unpretentious.

Even so, the free-floating anxiety that had begun to take hold of her in Harry's office intensified. Maura had tried so hard to reconnect with the face of the man in the white clinic coat. But the harder she tried, the flimsier the memories became. Now, she wondered whether the DTs, and the surgery, and the drugs had distorted reality so much for her that the man, in fact, never did exist.

Her hands were shaking ever so slightly. She abandoned trying to hold her teacup and instead sat quietly as Harry explained their situation. Nemec also listened intently. But midway through Harry's account, he stood and began pacing slowly behind her chair, pausing twice to rest his hands gently on her shoulders. Then suddenly he bent down, his lips close to her ear.

"There's nothing to be frightened about, Maurie," he whispered. "Nothing."

Maura was startled. *Maurie,* not *Maura.* He had definitely said that. No one except her father had ever called her Maurie. And then only until she was ten or so.

Harry stopped talking. Maura became acutely aware of the traffic noises from the street. It was happening, she realized. No couch, no watch-on-a-chain, no New Age music, no gimmicks at all. Pavel Nemec was at work—right here, right now.

He moved around to face her and placed his fingertips on her temples. Her eyes had closed now, but her mind was racing. Images and faces cascaded through her thoughts like a video on rapid search. Faces from her childhood—teachers, playmates, Tom, Mother . . . houses and rooms, rural scenes and city streets. She connected easily with some of the pictures, not at all with others. . . . Then suddenly, one scene began repeating itself over and over. It was her father, a drink sloshing in his hand, turning towards her. His rheumy eyes were cold with contempt. His words were thick and slurred. Spittle sprayed from his mouth as he railed at her.

You're worthless, Maurie . . . hopeless and worthless. . . .

You can't do a damn thing right except give me headaches. Just like your mother . . .

Except for marrying her, you're about the worst mistake I've ever made. . . . In fact, if it weren't for you, I'd never have had to marry her in the first place. . . .

"Easy, Maurie," Nemec said with gentle firmness. "He will never, ever speak to you like that again. . . . He was sick. That's all. . . . You never deserved to be spoken to like that. He just couldn't help it." Nemec cupped his calming hands behind her ears. "You did your best to please him. . . . He hated himself too much to show love for anyone. . . . He never thought about what he was doing to you. . . . You can let it go now, Maura. . . . You can let it go forever. . . ."

The swirling images began to recede. Maura knew her eyes were closed, but she could see the mystic in his gray cardigan, pacing in front of her. Her apprehension was gone now—the shroud of self-loathing that had blanketed her life for so long had lifted, leaving her with an incredible sense of peace. All those times her father had crushed her pride, belittled her. Even news of his death couldn't kill the terrible seeds he had sown. Throughout her life, each time success was in her grasp, her pathological self-doubt would lead her to find some way to sabotage and destroy it.

Worthless . . . How old could she have been when he began calling her that—seven? Eight?

Now, finally, she knew that it had never been her. Not once. She never deserved what Arthur Hughes had done to her. And, like Pavel said, he could never hurt her again.

Her eyes still closed, she saw Nemec move to the table and retrieve her sketch pad and charcoal. Then she felt him set it on her lap.

We have work to do. She heard his voice, but knew he had not spoken. *You're free now, Maura—free to see what needs to be seen. . . .*

Harry would later tell her that she had never opened her

eyes until the detailed sketch was complete. He would describe the eerie way the charcoal in her hand darted over the paper, the disjointed but absolutely unified process by which the man's face took shape. He would tell her about the moment, as she was still shading and shadowing with her charcoal stick and finger, when he recognized him.

Maura stretched her arms and worked her neck around. She felt relaxed and refreshed, as if she had just stepped from a warm spa. She knew that she had produced a drawing of the man who had murdered Evie DellaRosa. She also knew that Pavel Nemec had helped her in ways no therapist or counselor ever had. There were flaws in her perception of herself—gaping flaws for which she had never been responsible, flaws that kept driving her self-destructive behavior, flaws that had made her time and again break the promises she made to herself.

No more . . . Not one more drop . . .

She opened her eyes and looked down at the rendering. Then she drew in the man's clip-on tie and shaded it green with gold accents. Pavel Nemec was back in his chair, casually sipping tea.

"How'd you do that?" she asked.

He smiled at her kindly and shrugged.

"My encounters with clients are not always this successful. Some days it is like walking through a dense fog for me. Some days, like today, I can see with incredible clarity. I believe you have been waiting for me for some time, Maura. Possibly years."

"You did something about my drinking, didn't you?"

"No, but you did. And most forcefully, I might add."

She held up the drawing for Harry. Tears glistened in her eyes.

"I did it," she said.

"I guess you did. It's amazingly accurate."

"How do you know?"

"Because I saw him. The exact man you drew. He was right outside your room the whole time I was there, just waiting for the chance to finish what he had started when he ordered Evie's IV."

"Outside the room?"

"Buffing the floors, listening to a Walkman—the sort of

person you look at over and over without actually seeing him. The nurses never saw him come on the floor after I left because he didn't. He was already there. He left before I returned."

"Are you sure?" Maura asked.

Harry studied the drawing for just a few seconds.

"I've never been more certain of anything in my life," he said. "You two make a hell of a team."

Maura crossed to the unassuming little man and kissed him on the cheek.

"You don't know the half of it," she said.

CHAPTER 25

The day was New York City hot. By late morning, waves of steamy air were rising off the pavement and children were opening hydrants. Kevin Loomis left his air-conditioned midtown office at ten-thirty for a circuitous trip to Battery Park, a waterfront oasis on the southernmost tip of the island at the convergence of the Hudson and East Rivers. In response to James Stallings's warning against being followed, he had carefully planned every step of the journey.

Earlier that morning, Kevin had endured a forty-five-minute meeting of Burt Dreiser's eight-member executive planning staff. And although nothing unusual happened during the session, he felt constantly conspicuous and read double meanings into almost everything Dreiser said or did. By the time he checked out with Brenda Wallace and left for what he said was a long-scheduled meeting and lunch, he was perspiring for reasons that had nothing to do with the weather.

Evelyn DellaRosa had been murdered, and James Stallings, the other knight who had been with her, was terrified.

I wasn't sure if you were one of them or not. . . . What in the hell had Stallings meant by that?

Loomis crossed the street against the light, dodging a succession of infuriated cabbies. He then entered a small custom haberdashery. There were seldom more than one or two customers in the shop at a time, and at this moment, only the proprietor was there. Since joining The Roundtable, Kevin had become a regular in the place. The fitting area was in back, next to an alley door. Kevin ordered a $150 shirt, allowed himself to be measured, and then made an excuse for leaving through the rear exit. Next he took a cab ride to the East Side and walked several blocks to an IRT station, ducking frequently into doorways to check the street behind him. The Battery Park stop was at the end of the line. He arrived there with ten minutes to spare.

Still anxious about the possibility of being followed or watched, he strolled casually past a tarmac playground, pausing for a minute against the high, chain-link fence. There were twenty or so children on the swings, climbing bars, riding seesaws, laughing and shrieking with delight. Kevin thought about his own kids and about the life they were about to enter— a fabulous home with a bedroom for each of them and land enough for a huge swing set and possibly even a pool someday, a clean suburban community with top-notch schools, and a limit-less future.

Sunlight glared off the water. To the south, the Statue of Liberty stood tall against the sweltering heat. Kevin glanced about again and headed north onto the grassy mall. It was exactly noon. Carrying his suit coat now, he passed half a dozen benches, each one occupied. Office workers eating take-out lunches; a bag lady asleep on a newspaper pillow; two young mothers lolling their sleeping infants in strollers; teen lovers nestled together, oblivious to all but one another. *So normal.*

"Loomis. Over here."

Stallings, also holding his suit coat in his hand, beckoned to him from the shadow of a century-old maple. His briefcase was on the ground between his feet. The tension Kevin had picked up in the man at the Roundtable meeting was even more evident today. He glanced about nervously and constantly moistened his lips with his tongue.

"You sure you weren't followed?" he asked.

"I'm sure. Who are you worried about?"

"Any of them—Lancelot, Kay, Galahad, Merlin. Or someone they hired. Shit, Loomis, I don't know what to do. I just can't believe this is happening."

The man's apprehension was contagious. Without even knowing what was going on, Loomis felt his pulse begin to race.

"Hey, you've got to calm down," he said. "You want to walk?"

"No. No, this is a good spot. Let's sit down right here. Keep your back against the tree and a sharp eye out for anyone who might be paying too much attention to us."

Dark circles enveloped Stallings's eyes, and his pale skin was covered with a sheen of sweat. He had the look of a hunted animal.

"Lancelot came to see me a couple of days ago," he began when they had settled on the grass at the base of the tree. "His name's Pat Harper. Do you know him outside The Roundtable?"

"Northeast Life. I played golf with him once."

"Well, he picked me up after work and took me for a ride up into Connecticut. He drives a Rolls."

"That fits. I really don't know anything about him, except that his cigars make me queasy and he's a much better golfer than I am. For that matter, I don't know anything about any of the knights."

"Neither do I. The secrecy's on purpose. They really don't care if we find out who they are, but they want it to seem like a big deal. They're really into this mystique thing."

"You keep saying 'they.' Who do you mean?"

"All of them, even Percivale, I think. They're on one side of the fence. You and I are on the other. For a while I thought it was only me—that even though you joined after I did, you were one of them. You always seemed so confident, so tuned into everything that was going on. But listening to the way they grilled you about Desiree, I started to have the feeling that you were an outsider, too. Then, hearing you last night, I felt almost certain of it."

"All I can tell you," Kevin said, "is that the only contact I've had with The Roundtable or the knights has been at our meetings. I speak to my boss, of course. He's the one who picked me to succeed him. But that's all. And we never talk about The Roundtable at work—only on his boat."

Stallings gazed out at the river and took a deep, slow breath. It was as if he was getting set to dive from a cliff.

"Did your boss ever tell you they were killing people?" he asked suddenly.

Kevin pushed back and stared at the man, half expecting to see a *gotcha there, just kidding* smile.

"Hey, easy does it, Jim," Kevin said, forcing calm into his voice. "I'm sure it's not what you think."

Stallings laughed mirthlessly.

"It's exactly what I think. Lancelot started by telling me how pleased everyone was with the work I was doing—especially the legislation I drafted on the terminal-care project. He said that because The Roundtable's business was so unorthodox— that was the word he used, *unorthodox*—that each new member had to go through a probationary period. Now mine was over, and I was in a position to do my company and myself a great deal of good."

Stallings again glanced furtively about. Then he snapped open his briefcase, withdrew a computer printout, and passed it to Kevin. It was a list of "qualifications" very similar to the ones Merlin had presented at the meeting—the factors that had led to Beth DeSenza's being selected by microchip to lose her job. Only *this* list of criteria began with *Currently Hospitalized*.

"You know about the future-cost analyses, right?" Stallings asked.

"That's what Merlin was talking about—the estimate of what any illness will cost the industry over its entire course."

"Exactly. Well, this program here has a future-cost mini- mum of five hundred thousand dollars. Lancelot wants me to run it through our data banks each week and come up with two or three names. AIDS, cancer, chronic heart problems, mental ill- ness, multiple trauma, blood diseases, cystic fibrosis, even babies born under a certain weight."

"There's certainly no shortage of conditions that'll cost half a million over time."

"Much more than that, actually. A million, even two. Things like bone marrow replacements and liver transplants. A twenty-five-year-old mental patient who can't make it outside of a hospital will be in seven figures before he's thirty-five. And his life expectancy isn't much different than normal."

"What happens to the names you come up with?"

Stallings bit at his lower lip.

"I am to hand-deliver them to each of the other knights—not including you, apparently. I guess you're still on probation. Then I am to transfer into a Swiss bank account an amount equaling twenty-five percent of the total that person's care would cost my company. Lancelot explained that the funds I transfer will come from payouts to a set of nonexistent patients. He seemed very proud of the system, which he says is tried and true, and foolproof. Those were his exact words: *tried and true, and foolproof.*"

"Then what happens to the patients?"

Sir Gawaine shrugged helplessly.

"They die," he said.

"You mean they're murdered in the hospital?"

"Lancelot never used that word. My company would achieve a net savings—that's just how he put it, 'net savings'—of around a million and a half to two million a month."

"Oh, I just don't believe that. Surely there must be some other explanation."

"Go ahead and try to come up with one. I did. How else is that kind of money going to be saved?"

"And all the rest of them are doing this, too?"

"As far as I know."

"This is crazy. How can they do it? How could they keep getting away with it over and over again?"

Stallings dropped the printout back into his briefcase, snapped it shut, and adjusted each of the combination wheels.

"I don't know. But I kept thinking about that DellaRosa woman. I think whoever injected her with that stuff must be the one who . . ."

His voice trailed away. He stared off at a distant freighter. Not far from where they were sitting, a teenage girl in tight shorts and a tank top Rollerbladed past, hand-in-hand with a tall, gangly boy. *So normal.*

"Did you ask Lancelot about DellaRosa?"

"I mentioned her. But he claimed that if she and Desiree were the same person, he surely would have known it. I asked who handled matters in the hospital, and how they did it. All he said was, that wasn't his department."

"There's got to be something you misunderstood."

"Kevin, did they promise you an additional bonus of one percent of everything your company saves through your work with The Roundtable?"

"Yes."

"Me, too. Well, Lancelot took special pains to point out what one percent of a million five to two million a month comes to. He also pointed out things we all know—that the cost of caring for critically ill and terminally ill patients has spiraled out of control, that all our companies are being battered as never before, and that health care reform, what with premium caps and all, is only making matters worse. He said that the money being saved by our efforts meant more jobs and better services throughout the industry. At one point, he listed a bunch of conditions like AIDS, metastatic cancer, and muscular dystrophy. 'Truthfully, now,' he said, 'to all intents and purposes, considering that doctors have absolutely no treatments available to cure any of these diseases, when the diagnosis is made, these people are as good as dead. Right?'

"And you want to know the worst part, Loomis? The worst part is that as he talked on, I found myself buying into the whole thing! Dollars and cents, profit and loss, *cost containment*, for chrissake. I stopped thinking of the quality of these people's lives. I began agreeing with everything he said. Diagnosis, prognosis. That was it. That was all that mattered. I even started thinking about all the ways an additional fifteen thousand dollars a month would change our lifestyle. Then, at the last moment, just before I signed on, I began remembering that he was talking about *people*. That's what I believe you were thinking about when you started questioning Merlin's program last night."

"I knew one of the women on that list of his."

Stallings nodded. "That's why I kept signaling you to stop. Kevin, these people mean business. We were on our way back to the city when I asked Lancelot what would happen if I decided not to participate in this program. He said that he really didn't believe anything would happen. He explained that only one knight had ever refused to participate—Sir Lionel. That was about a year ago. But before The Roundtable could decide whether or not he'd be allowed to continue with them, he got some sort of food poisoning and died."

"Oh, God," Kevin groaned. "I know all about that guy.

When he died, his company lost its seat on The Roundtable completely. In fact, it was probably given to you. My boss used him to illustrate what I would cost our company and myself if I was ever removed and not replaced. But Jim, Lionel didn't die from food poisoning. It was from a coronary *after* the food poisoning. He died in the hospital, just like . . ."

"Go ahead, say it. Just like Evelyn DellaRosa and heaven only knows how many other patients with expensive diseases."

Kevin felt ill.

"Did Lancelot make it sound like Lionel's death was something they engineered? I mean, did he say it like a threat?"

"I don't know for sure. He's got this smile that's impossible to read."

Kevin nodded. He'd had the same response to Pat Harper.

"Well, he just kept smiling through the whole Lionel story. I wasn't sure what to make of it, but it gave me the creeps. I didn't know what to say to him."

"So how was it left?"

Stallings looked away again.

"I have until tomorrow night to come up with the first set of names and transfer the funds."

"Oh, no. And who gets the money? The knights? The guy who . . . who does it?"

"I don't know. But if you multiply my two or three clients by two or three for each of the others, that's a hell of a lot of money."

"And every one of those people just . . . dies?"

"They're all pretty sick. And there are so many hospitals and patients in the city that apparently no one really thinks about there being anything out of the ordinary going on. . . . Loomis, what are we going to do?"

"Listen, maybe the whole thing is just some sort of loyalty test," Kevin offered desperately.

"You know you don't believe that."

"Jim, I don't know anything. Why couldn't you just blow the whistle?"

"On what? On who? I have no proof of anything. Not even the name of a single patient. Besides, if The Roundtable does get exposed, I go down along with the rest of you. What about my family, my kids?"

"Well, what then? Show up at the meeting and just beg them to stop?"

"It's a possibility."

"What about Sir Lionel and his food poisoning?"

"That's why I decided to chance sharing all this with you. If there are two of us, I think as long as we stick together, we might be able to convince the rest of them to stop."

"I need to think about this."

"Just don't take too long. I only have until tomorrow to give them the names and . . . and I don't think I can do it." He checked the time. "Listen, I'm due back at the office in a few minutes. Please, Loomis, please. Don't say a word to anyone until we talk again. Okay?"

"I promise."

"Not to your boss, not to your wife, not to anyone."

Stallings was genuinely terrified. And if he was right about The Roundtable, Kevin had no trouble understanding why.

"I'll call you before tomorrow night," Stallings said. They exchanged business cards, and each wrote his home phone number on the back. "And Kevin, please wait five or ten minutes after I go before you start back."

"I'll be in touch."

Sir Gawaine took his briefcase and headed off toward the subway station. Kevin stood there, numb and unseeing, his mind unwilling to sort through what had just been shared with him, except to acknowledge that if the situation was as Stallings believed, the possibilities open to them were all unacceptable.

"Mister! Hey, mister!"

Kevin turned, startled. Two youths in shorts and Yankee caps stood on the sidewalk. They looked about ten—his son Nicky's age. Each wore a baseball glove.

"Yes, what is it?"

"Our ball, mister. It's right by your foot. Could you throw it to us?"

Kevin picked up the scuffed, grass-stained hardball and tossed it back. The taller of the two boys snagged it easily, in a way Kevin had watched Nicky catch a thousand of his throws.

"Thanks, mister," the youth called. "Nice arm. Nice arm."

CHAPTER 26

The night was warm and extremely muggy—the sort of night that invariably brought out the most vivid versions of the dream. He lay facedown on a sheet that was already drenched. His fists were tightly clenched and every muscle in his body was taut. At some level, he knew that it was all in his past, that he was only reliving the hideous experience in his mind.

But as always, he was powerless to wake himself.

". . . . Hyconidol almost matches, atom for atom, the pain fiber neurotransmitter chemical. That means I can fire those nerves off all at once and at will. Every single one of them. Think of it, Mr. Santana. No injury . . . no mess . . . no blood. Just pain. Pure pain. Except in the work I do, hyconidol has absolutely no clinical value. But if we ever do market it, I thought an appropriate name for it might be Agonyl. It's incredible stuff, if I do say so myself. A small injection? A little tingle. A larger one? Well, I'm sure you get the picture."

Ray's mouth becomes desert dry. The pounding within his chest is so forceful that he feels certain The Doctor can see it.

Please don't do this, he screams silently. *Please . . .*

Perchek's thumb tightens on the plunger.

"I think we'll start with something modest," he says, "equivalent, perhaps, to nothing more than a little cool breeze over the cavities in your teeth. Our interest is in the identities of the Mexican undercover agents, Mr. Santana. Mr. Orsino will write down any names you choose to give. And I should warn you. Some of the names we wish you to give us we already know. It would be most unpleasant for you should we catch you attempting any sort of stall or deception."

"Go fuck yourselves. How's that for a stall or deception?"

The Doctor merely smiles.

The last voice Ray hears before the injection is Joe Dash's.

There are three ways a man can choose to handle dying. . . .

The plunger of the syringe is depressed just a bit.

In less than half a minute, Ray experiences a mild vibration throughout his body, as if a low-grade electric current has been turned on. His scalp tightens. The muscles in his face twitch. He rubs his fingertips together, trying to rid them of an unpleasant numbness. Perchek, meanwhile, has taken a handheld stopwatch from his valise.

"I would expect that minuscule dose to last one minute and twenty seconds," he says. "Higher doses persist somewhat longer. Although in this business, for you, time will become quite relative. A few seconds will seem like an hour. A minute like a lifetime. Have you some names for us?"

"Cary Grant, Mick Jagger, Marilyn Monroe . . ."

Perchek shrugs and depresses the plunger once more. The sensation doubles in intensity and quadruples in unpleasantness. This time, the pain is more burning than electric. Hot knives cut into Ray's hands and feet, into his abdomen, groin, and lower back. Sweat bathes him with the suddenness of a summer thunderstorm, stinging his eyes, soaking his T-shirt.

"Just a slightly higher dose and we'll hold it at that level for a while," Perchek says, checking Ray's blood pressure and pulse. "We're in no particular hurry, are we, Mr. Orsino?"

From outside, above and just beyond the walls of the chamber, Ray can hear the revelry of the Fiesta de Nogales. The fireworks and the music. The noisy celebration will go on throughout the night. It is doubtful he will be alive by the time it ends.

The Doctor is right. For Santana, the hour that follows is an eternity. Twice he nearly passes out from the pain. Each time, Perchek uses a shot of some sort and an increase in the IV infusion to bring him around for the next series of injections. Ray becomes used to the sound of his own screaming. Somewhere along the way he wets himself. In between injections, his muscles now continue to spasm uncontrollably. Several times he groans out names. Perchek glances over at Orsino, who shakes his head. Ray's punishment for lying is an increase in the dosage. His response, more screaming.

. . . *Three ways a man can handle dying . . . three ways . . . three ways . . . three ways . . .*

His head lolls back. His vision blurs. Staring at the light from the bare bulb overhead no longer bothers his eyes. It is as if the hideous pain has dulled his sight. Sweat continues pouring from his body. His nervous system is shattered, his mind ready to snap. He has to give them a name they can verify—something, anything to stop Perchek's chemical onslaught, even for a little while. He has done his best to drag out Joe Dash's first two stages. Now, his resistance is gone. He has to give them something that will stop the pain.

"You bastard!" he screeches as the dose is increased once more. "You fucking bastard! Okay. Okay. No more. I'll—"

He is cut short by the tunnel door behind him scraping open. Through a dense haze, he hears a man's breathless voice.

"Anton, there are government troops outside!" the man exclaims in perfect English. "Dozens of them. I think they have Alacante. U.S. agents just raided the Arizona house, too. The tunnel entrance is still closed, but it's only a matter of time before they find it. They're after you, Anton. I don't know how they found out, but they know you're here."

The voice. Ray strains to pull together the floating fragments of his thoughts. He knows the voice.

"Orsino, is there another way out of here?" Perchek asks.

"Through that door, Doctor. There's a short tunnel to a house across the street. Alacante had it built."

"Listen," the voice says, "I've got to get back before they find the main tunnel and me in it."

"I am grateful for the warning, my friend."

"You know how to reach me if there's anything I can do."

The tunnel door scrapes shut. There are a few seconds of echoing footsteps, then silence. But in those moments, Ray's clouded mind locks in on the voice.

Sean Garvey!

"Garvey, you bastard! . . . You son of a bitch!" he shrieks, remembering the moment he and his boss had been hauled off by Alacante's men.

The signs that something was rotten with Garvey had been there a dozen times over, he thinks now. *How careless it had been not to have picked up on them. How stupid.*

"Mr. Santana, it appears our business must come to a premature closure," Perchek says.

From somewhere on the floor above them comes the sound of a door being smashed in. Then there is gunfire.

"Doctor, I think we should go," Orsino says.

"You are right, Mr. Orsino," Perchek replies. "But only up to a point."

His back turned, he reaches into his valise. When he turns back, he is holding a snub-nosed revolver. Before Orsino can react, he is shot through the bull's-eye that is his half mouth. His head snaps back. He spins full-circle in a graceless pirouette, then crumples to the dusty floor.

The shooting upstairs has stopped. The footsteps are closer now, and they can hear voices. The Doctor levels the automatic at the center of Santana's forehead. Ray clenches his teeth and forces his eyes to remain open for the last moment he will ever see anything. Then, with the smile Ray has come both to fear and loathe, Perchek lowers the revolver, steps forward, and empties the still nearly full syringe into the intravenous line.

"Don't worry," he says. "You should die from this dose long before it has its full effect."

He whirls, steps over Orsino's corpse, and hurries toward the escape tunnel.

"Garvey!" Santana screams, his final fury fixed not on the madman, but on the friend who has betrayed him. *"Garvey, you'll rot in hell for this!"*

A moment later his nervous system explodes in a volcano of pain. He shrieks again and again. He thrashes his head about. He bites through his lip and hurls himself sideways onto the floor. The agony, in every nerve, every fiber of his body, intensifies.

"Garveeeey!"

Soaked in sweat, Walter Concepcion sat bolt upright in bed. After more than seven years, he had almost become inured to the nightmare. But some journeys back to the basement sessions with The Doctor were still worse than others. And this one —his first in the weeks since arriving in Manhattan from his home in Tennessee—had been a motherfucker.

It was the pain that had brought on the flashback. It usually was. The electric nerve pain that had been part of his life for almost every moment of the seven years since The Doctor emptied the syringe into his body. Ray wiped off his forehead and face with the sheet and fumbled through the bedside table drawer for the Bible he had hollowed out to hold his Percodans. He could stand to have everything he owned in the rented room ripped off, even his gun. But not his Percodans. His doc at home understood. After years of neurologic consultations, psychotherapy, AA, NA, and hospitalizations, the man had given up trying for a cure, and now just wrote the scripts. The local pharmacist understood, too, and just filled them. To those men and the others who knew the whole story, Ray was a legend. The man who had captured Anton Perchek.

Santana had brought along enough pills to last a month, provided the chronic pain didn't get any worse than it had been. He had no desire to take to the streets for drugs, but he would if he had to. Anton Perchek was alive and plying his miserable trade in New York. And there was no way Ray was leaving the city until the man was dead.

He had heard from Harry about the successful session with the hypnotist. Next, Maura would be meeting with the criminologist her brother knew. Together, they would make computer renderings of her drawing in a variety of disguises. Those drawings would be put up in hospitals throughout the city. Santana's plan was simple. Keep jabbing at The Doctor. Irritate him enough, and sooner or later, he would do something rash. Sooner or later, he would make a mistake.

He tossed two Percodans into the back of his throat and washed them down with a glass of water. Then he set out clothes for his meeting with Page. He would wear his sports jacket so that he could conceal the shoulder holster and his .38. He didn't expect trouble, but he anticipated it. Since his betrayal and capture in Nogales, he always anticipated it.

He reached beneath the pillow, withdrew his pistol, and

unscrewed the silencer. It was bulky, and although it had worked just fine that evening in Central Park, it tended to cut down on accuracy. Besides, he thought, when he finally stood face-to-face with Anton Perchek, when he finally leveled the .38 at a spot between his eyes and pulled the trigger, he wanted The Doctor to hear the sound.

CHAPTER 27

"This hearing isn't going to be pleasant," Mel Wetstone said to Harry as they drove across town to the hospital. "But I promise you we are not going to take any bullshit from these people."

He had picked Harry up in the Mercedes Philip had sold him—the one that Phil claimed defined the man as an attorney. The four doors as well as the trunk had electronic closing mechanisms, and the rear couch—*seat* hardly did it justice—reclined. It was certainly reassuring to see that Wetstone was successful enough to afford such transportation. But today the Mercedes had tapped into Harry's midlife feelings of inadequacy. And block by smooth air-conditioned block, it was inflating them like a Thanksgiving Day float. Gratefully, there were just a few more blocks to go.

"Did Sam Rennick say what they were going for?" he asked.

"Sam plays things pretty close to the vest, but it was clear that he isn't willing to concede any of the points we've presented to him—not the sketch from Ms. Hughes, not the floor buffer theory, not the call to your office from the killer. They want you off the staff until the case is resolved."

"Can they do that?"

"Probably. There are a few spots in the hospital bylaws where the language about who can do what to whom is vague—purposely vague, we think. The bottom line is that if they vote you out—and believe me, we've got some cards to play before they do—we can try for an injunction. But we'd better get a damn sympathetic judge. A far better idea would be to beat them back right here and now. That's what I intend to do."

Harry stared out the sun-sensitive window at the passing scene. He had no desire to be booted from the MMC staff. For one thing, his patients were his emotional and financial life-blood; for another, being barred from practice in the hospital would make it that much harder to put the pressure on the killer. And they had made enough progress since connecting with Walter Concepcion to believe that before long, some sort of strategy for putting pressure on him might actually evolve.

Maura was on her way to meet with her brother's friend, Lonnie Sims. The Dweeb had access to the latest in the graphics software being used to assist witnesses in creating drawings of suspects. Together they would enhance Maura's sketch and add photographic quality, coloring, and detail. The result would be, essentially, a full-color mug shot, front and side views. They would then add and subtract, mix and match, until they had similar photos of the man with his appearance altered.

When Harry and his lawyer entered the executive conference room for the second time since Evie's death, the atmosphere was distinctly more formal—and more threatening. Recording microphones had been placed at several spots around the massive table. The players from the first drama were all there already, along with a number of notable newcomers including members of the hospital board of trustees, the department heads who made up the medical staff executive committee, the head nurses from Alexander 9 and Alexander 5, Caspar Sidonis, and a legal stenographer. There was also a man sitting beside the hospital attorney whom Harry did not know—a rough-hewn man in an ill-fitting blue suit.

Steve Josephson squeezed Harry's hand as he passed. Doug Atwater smiled uncomfortably and came over.

"Harry," he whispered, "I'm glad I got this chance to talk with you. I hope you understand that the other day I was only suggesting what I thought would be best for you. Obviously, I upset you, and I'm sorry for that. I wanted to be sure you know that I'm behind you a hundred percent in this thing."

Half a dozen snide responses sped through Harry's head. None of them made it to his mouth. Atwater didn't deserve it. Over the years he had been most supportive of Harry and his struggles to keep family practice a respected option. Suggesting that Harry take a voluntary leave from the hospital was the only way he could think of to avoid the hearing that was about to take place—a hearing in which Harry seemed destined to be humiliated and ultimately swept aside.

"I understand, Doug," he said. "But I haven't done anything wrong, so I just can't go down without a fight."

"In that case, give 'em hell, Harry." Atwater grinned.

Sam Rennick reviewed the ground rules that had been agreed upon by him and Mel Wetstone.

Witnesses would give a statement and answer questions from first Rennick, then Wetstone. Harry would be permitted to speak after each witness, but only to respond to questions from his lawyer, not to address any of the witnesses directly. When the hearing was concluded, the joint hospital and medical staff executive committees would vote by secret ballot whether to suspend Harry's admitting privileges or not.

"Before you begin, Mr. Rennick," Doug Atwater said, "I would like it to go on record that the Manhattan Health Cooperative will abide by the ruling of this hearing." He looked over at Harry. "Dr. Corbett's status as a physician provider for MHC will remain intact so long as he has admitting privileges at this hospital."

Considering that the health plan was bound only by its own laws in picking and removing physician providers, Atwater's statement amounted to an endorsement. His company could have made the results of this hearing essentially moot by simply cutting Harry from its rolls. It was a move Harry had feared they might make. He was doubly glad, now, that he had held his temper with Doug.

The head nurse from Alexander 9 started things off by reading affidavits from both of the nurses who had been on duty the night of Evie's death. There was no question in either of their minds that, except for Maura Hughes, Harry was the last one to see his wife before the lethal rupture of her aneurysm. Sue Jilson recounted in some detail Harry's request to leave the floor for a milk shake and then return. The hospital attorney used his questions to pin down the nurse about the security setup on the floor. Then he homed in on the clinical condition of Maura Hughes.

"She was about the most classic case of the DTs I've ever seen," the woman said. "She was restless and combative, sweating profusely, and disoriented most of the time. When she wasn't accusing the staff of ignoring her, she was swatting at insects that weren't there. She was medicated almost the entire time she was on our service, and despite that, she was still one of the most disruptive patients we've had in a long time."

Harry and Mel Wetstone exchanged glances. The hospital attorney knew Maura's sketch was about to be presented, and was effectively destroying its credibility by painting such an unappealing picture of her. It was the reason Harry had argued against having Maura attend the hearing to present her drawing herself. Mel had warned him what she might hear.

Wetstone cleared his throat, took a slow swallow of water, and favored the nurse with an icy smile.

"I'm sorry Ms. Hughes was so disruptive to your neurosurgical floor," he said.

"Thank you," the nurse replied, completely missing Wetstone's sarcasm.

"You don't have very warm feelings toward alcoholics, do you?"

"Does anyone?"

Wetstone allowed half a minute for the response to sink in around the room.

"As a matter of fact, yes. Some people do," he said softly. "The American Medical Association has formally classified alcoholism as a disease. The American Psychiatric Association has also. I hope you're not prejudiced against too many *other* diseases as well. I have no further questions of you."

The head nurse, beet red, folded her notes and stared off at a spot that would keep her from eye contact with anyone. If the impact of her testimony hadn't been neutralized entirely, it had certainly been diminished. Wetstone turned to Harry.

"Dr. Corbett, have you been in touch with Maura Hughes since her discharge?"

"I have."

"And how's she doing?"

"Quite well, actually. She hasn't had a drink since her surgery, and she's starting back on her painting."

The white lie was one they had agreed upon the previous day.

"Oh, yes, she's an accomplished and well-regarded artist, isn't she? You have a drawing of hers here with you?"

"A copy of it, yes. Miss Hughes had trouble recalling some of the details of the man's face, so we went to see a hypnotist."

"That would be Dr. Pavel Nemec?"

The murmur around the room suggested that The Hungarian was known to most of those present.

"I'm not sure he's a doctor," Harry said. "But yes. He had no trouble helping her reconnect with her memories. One session, about fifteen or twenty minutes, was all it took."

"Mr. Rennick," Wetstone said. "Here is a notarized affidavit from Pavel Nemec attesting to his certainty that the drawing you are about to see represents the face remembered by Maura Hughes—the man who came into room nine twenty-eight after Dr. Corbett left to get his wife a milk shake." He waited until everyone that mattered had a copy before he continued. "Dr. Corbett, have you ever seen the man depicted in Ms. Hughes's drawing?"

"I have. He was dressed as a hospital maintenance man, buffing the floors outside room nine twenty-eight when I arrived. When I left for the milk shakes, he was still there. When I came back with them he was gone."

"You're sure of this?"

"Positive. It's an extremely good likeness of him. Maura Hughes has an incredible eye for detail. She says she suspects that the tie was a clip-on because the knot was just too perfect."

Several people laughed out loud.

"This is ridiculous," Caspar Sidonis muttered, though loudly enough for everyone to hear.

"So what you're telling us, Dr. Corbett," Wetstone said, "is that this man—" He waved the drawing for emphasis. "This man waited for an opportune moment, put on a doctor's clinic coat taken from within the casing of his floor buffer, walked boldly into room nine twenty-eight, and injected your wife with a killing dose of Aramine."

"I believe that is exactly what he did."

Many of the faces around the room were expressionless. But Harry's unofficial visual poll said that the majority still had strong doubts about him.

Without comment, Wetstone motioned that he was done. Since the burden of proof was, in theory at least, on the hospital, Harry would not be cross-examined by the hospital attorney. It was one of several procedural points Wetstone had won.

Sam Rennick next introduced the man in the ill-fitting blue suit, Willard McDevitt, the head of maintenance for the hospital. McDevitt, in his fifties with a ruddy complexion and a nose that appeared to have been broken more than once or twice, spoke with the force of one convinced he was incapable of being wrong about anything. He reminded Harry of Bumpy Giannetti, the hulking bully who had stalked him after school and beaten him up with biologic regularity from grades seven through ten. He wondered in passing if Bumpy would respect him now that he was the chief suspect in two murders.

"Mr. McDevitt, is the man in that drawing anyone you recognize?" Rennick asked, after establishing the man's credentials.

"Absolutely not. I never saw him before in my life." He looked haughtily over at Harry.

"And what about that industrial floor buffer—the one Dr. Corbett claims the killer used that night?"

"Well, first of all let me say that if there was a buffer on Alexander Nine that night, it was one of mine. And if it was one of mine, one of my men was runnin' it."

"Could someone have brought one into the hospital?"

"Anything's possible. But those babies weigh close to a quarter ton and are bigger 'n a clothes dryer. It's hard to imagine someone sneakin' one into the hospital without being noticed."

"Could they have stolen one from your department?"

"Not unless it was at gunpoint. We have a sign-out system I designed myself to prevent any unauthorized person from usin' any of our equipment. Even a wrench has to be accounted for. I don't think we'd exactly misplace a five-hundred-pound buffer."

"Thank you, Mr. McDevitt."

Rennick nodded toward Wetstone without actually looking at him. Harry saw the gesture and reflected cynically on the foolishness of a profession in which sub-rosa byplay was an accepted, even rehearsed, part of the practice. Then he noticed Caspar Sidonis exchanging whispered comments with the trustee seated next to him, motioning toward Harry at the same time. The byplay in medicine might be more subtle than in law, but it was no less nasty.

"Mr. McDevitt," Mel began, "where are these floor buffers kept?"

"Locked in a room in the subbasement—double locked as a matter of fact. Only me an' Gus Gustavson, my head of floor maintenance, have the key. Every one of them buffers that's taken from that room has to be signed out by him or me."

"I understand. Mr. McDevitt, I'd like to ask you again whether you believe there is any way a man who was not in your employ could get at one of those buffers?"

"Absolutely none."

That look again. Harry met the man's gaze in a way he had never faced up to Bumpy Giannetti, held it, and even managed a weak smile. Had Mel Wetstone shared with him the next part of his strategy, his smile would have been much broader. Wetstone stood, walked to the door, opened it, and stepped back. A curious silence held for several seconds, then was shattered by a machinery hum. A tall blond man dressed in a tan MMC maintenance jumpsuit entered the room. He wore a standard hospital photo identification badge and was polishing the tile surrounding the plush Oriental rug with an industrial buffer. *PROPERTY OF MMC* was stenciled in red on the side.

"What in the hell?" Willard McDevitt exclaimed.

Wetstone nodded toward the buffer man and the machine was shut off.

"Mr. McDevitt, do you know this man?"

"I do not."

"Mr. Crawford, do you work for this hospital?"

"I do not."

"Mr. Crawford, where did you get that contraption?"

"From the room marked *Floor Maintenance* in the subbasement."

"And was it difficult for you to get?"

The blond man grinned.

"Piece of cake," he said. "I'll return it now if that's okay."

He spun the machine around and wheeled it out. Instantly, it seemed as if everyone was talking and gesturing at once. Harry noticed that several members of the medical staff were laughing. Willard McDevitt looked as if he was going to charge Mel Wetstone. Instead, he listened to some whispered words from the hospital attorney, shoved his chair back, and stalked out. For his part, Wetstone carefully avoided appearing smug, or even pleased. He sat placidly, allowing his theatrics to hold sway. For the first time, Harry felt that the emotion in the room might be turning in his favor. If Rennick and his witness could be so wrong about the floor buffer, people had to be thinking, maybe they could be wrong about other things as well.

"Now just a minute. Just one damn minute!"

Caspar Sidonis had clearly taken as much as he could. He stood and strode to the head of the table. Owen Erdman, the hospital president, moved his chair aside for him.

"This man is a huckster," Sidonis said, motioning toward Wetstone. "A snake oil salesman. He's using misdirection and tricks to keep you from focusing on the important points in this case. And Sam, I'm afraid all you've done is make it that much easier for him. This isn't a courtroom, it's a hospital. We're not here to debate fine points of law. We're here to see to it that our thousands and thousands of patients—patients who could take their business to any number of facilities—have the confidence in the Manhattan Medical Center to continue coming here. We're meeting here today to prevent our hospital from becoming the laughingstock of the city. We're here to ensure that the medical school graduates, with every hospital in the country to choose from, think enough of this place to apply for residency here."

The man was good, damn good, Harry acknowledged. This was revenge for Evie and payback for the humiliation of the amphitheater all rolled into one. And most important, his force and effectiveness sprang from his hatred of Harry and his consuming belief in Harry's guilt. Harry took another silent poll of the room. Already things didn't look as promising as they had. Mel Wetstone seemed on the point of rising to object to Sidonis's tirade, but he thought better of it and sank back in his chair. Trying to stop the powerful chief of cardiac surgery from expressing his opinion could only hurt them.

"I am not embarrassed to say that Evie DellaRosa and I were in love," Sidonis went on. "For years, she and Harry Corbett had had a marriage in name only. The night before she entered this hospital, the night before she was murdered, she told him about us. I know that for a fact. That gives him a motive. A two-hundred-and-fifty-thousand-dollar insurance policy gives him another. The nurses have already testified to his opportunity. And certainly the method chosen was one only a physician would know. Now, it's remotely possible that Dr. Corbett is as innocent as he claims. It's remotely possible that every crazy alternative explanation he has come up with actually happened. But even his innocence does not change the fact that two of our patients with strong connections to him are dead. The newspapers are having a field day at our hospital's expense. The public confidence we have worked so hard to build is plummeting.

"Harry Corbett owes this hospital the respect and consideration to remove himself from the staff until this whole matter is resolved one way or the other. Since he has refused to honor that responsibility, this group must take action. I promise you here and now, I will not continue to practice at an institution without the gumption to stand up for itself and do what is right for its staff and patients. Thank you."

Drained, or apparently so, Sidonis used the backs of chairs to help him return to his seat. Mel Wetstone inhaled deeply, then let out a sigh. Harry felt flushed and self-conscious. Sidonis had threatened the hospital and the board of trustees with a massive blow to their two most vulnerable areas: reputation and pocketbook. *World Famous Heart Surgeon Quits Hospital Over Handling of Doctor Doom*. Harry could just see the headlines in the *Daily News*. He leaned over to his lawyer.

There was a commotion outside the room. The doors burst open and Owen Erdman's staid secretary rushed in.

"I'm sorry, Dr. Erdman," she said breathlessly. "I tried to explain to them, but they wouldn't listen. Sandy's called security. They're on their way."

She stepped aside as a small mob marched into the room. Leading the way was Mary Tobin, and close behind her was Marv

Lorello. Next came all the other members of the family medicine department, along with a number of Harry's patients, some with their children in tow. *Two dozen people in all*, Harry guessed. *No, closer to three.* Among them he recognized Clayton Miller, the man whose severe pulmonary edema he and Steve Josephson had reversed by removing almost a unit of blood. The group crowded into one end of the conference room. Then several people moved aside and Harry's patient Mabel Espinoza stepped forward. Two of her grandchildren clung to her skirt.

"My name is Ms. Mabel Espinoza," she said. Her Latino accent was dense, but no one ever had trouble understanding her. She faced the hearing with the stout dignity that had always made her one of Harry's favorites. "I am eighty-one years old. Dr. Corbett has cared for me and my family for twenty years. I am alive today because he is such a wonderful doctor. Many others could say the same thing. When I am too sick, he comes to see me at my home. When someone cannot pay, he is patient. I have signed the petition. In less than one day, more than two hundred have signed. Thank you."

"This was your Mary's idea," Wetstone whispered to Harry. "I never thought she could pull anything like this, though."

Another woman stepped forward and introduced herself as Doris Cummings, an elementary-school teacher in a Harlem school. She read the petition, signed by 203 of Harry's patients, enumerating the reasons Harry was essential to their well-being and that of their families.

". . . If Dr. Corbett is removed from the staff of the Manhattan Medical Center without absolute just cause," the petition concluded, "we the undersigned intend to take our health care to another hospital. If leaving the Manhattan Health HMO is necessary and possible, we intend to do that as well. This man has been an important part of our lives. We do not want to lose him."

Marv Lorello whispered in Cummings's ear and motioned toward Owen Erdman. Cummings circled the table and set the petition in front of the hospital president. Across from Harry, a distinguished woman named Holden, who was a past president of the board of trustees, brushed aside a tear. Standing to her right, Mary Tobin was beaming like a mother at her child's graduation.

Next, Marv Lorello spoke on behalf of the department of family medicine, describing Harry as an invaluable friend and powerful example to those in the department, especially those newly in practice. He read a statement signed by every member of the department, in effect threatening to move their services to another facility if Harry should be removed from the hospital staff without absolute, legally binding proof of his misconduct. He set the document on top of the petition in front of Owen Erdman. Then the group trooped out of the hearing.

There was no further discussion. The vote was a formality, although two of the twelve submitting ballots did endorse Harry's removal from the staff. Caspar Sidonis left the room as soon as the result was read.

"Dr. Corbett," Erdman said coolly, "that was an impressive show of regard for you. It would be tragic to learn that such loyalty is not deserved. Have you anything further to say?"

"Only that I'm grateful for the vote. I *am* innocent, and I intend to prove that, and to find this man. I would hope to begin by posting this likeness around the hospital."

"Absolutely not!" Erdman snapped. "My staff will discreetly distribute that sketch to our department heads. But we will not lay ourselves open to the public suggestion that a murderer could just waltz into our hospital, disguise himself behind one of our floor polishers, and murder one of our patients. I demand your promise of cooperation in this regard."

Harry looked over at Mel Wetstone, who simply shrugged and nodded.

"You have my word," Harry said.

"In that case," Erdman concluded, "you have our blessing to continue with your work."

"Are you going home?" Wetstone asked as they headed out of the hospital.

"No, I'm headed to the office. I think Mary deserves a lunch."

"Dinner at the Ritz would be more like it."

CHAPTER 28

The thermometer, mounted on the wall just outside the Battery Park IRT station, was in direct sunlight. Still, ninety-four degrees was ninety-four degrees. As he entered the station, damp and uncomfortable, his briefcase in one hand and his suit coat scrunched in the other, James Stallings cursed his penchant for dark dress shirts. He loved the way they looked on him, and the statement that they made among his white-shirted colleagues. But on a day like today, wearing royal blue was simply dumb.

But then again, he had been doing a lot of dumb things lately.

The station was mobbed. Tourists from Ellis Island and the Statue of Liberty jostled with passengers off the Staten Island ferry and a crowd of kids in their early teens wearing Camp Cityside T-shirts. Almost everyone was talking about the heat. Stallings shuffled through the turnstile behind two Cityside girls, who were giggling about a boy being disallowed on their field trip. Caught up in their conversation, Stallings tried to piece together what it was the boy had done and where they were all headed. But before he could, the teens took up with a dozen other campers and moved like a jabbering phalanx down the broad stairs.

There was a train waiting at the platform. Battery Park was at the beginning of the run, so there were almost always seats, even at rush hour. Today, though, it was standing room only. From snatches of irritated conversation around him, Stallings discerned that there was a delay of some sort. And of course, while the cars themselves were air-conditioned, the platforms were not. Thick, steamy air billowed in with the passengers and overwhelmed what little cooling the system was generating. Beneath his arms, Stallings's shirt was soaked through. He glanced out the window at the crowd still pouring down the stairs and across the concrete platform. Loomis was supposed to wait ten minutes before heading back to Crown. It had probably been close to that already. Not that it really mattered if they ended up on the same train. Especially different cars. But Stallings, who had never been the nervous or paranoid type, was frightened—*irrationally frightened*, he kept trying to convince himself.

Sir Lionel had posed something of a threat to The Round-table, and he had died suddenly and mysteriously. A year or so later, Evelyn DellaRosa had been murdered in her hospital bed. She, too, had crossed paths with the society. The drug used to poison her *had* been discovered, but almost by accident. Were the two deaths coincidence? *Possible, but doubtful*, Stallings thought. Now, within twenty-four hours, he would either have to submit a list of hospitalized clients to be terminated, or become a potential threat to The Roundtable himself.

Meeting with Kevin Loomis was the right thing to have done, he decided. Loomis seemed like an up-front, decent enough guy. Even though he remained noncommittal and maybe even unconvinced, as soon as he had the chance to sort through everything, he would come around. And together they would figure out something. They simply had to. Stallings wiped perspiration from his forehead with his shirtsleeve. The car was nearly packed. The heat oppressive. It was only a matter of time before someone passed out.

"Hey, watch it!" one of the passengers snapped.

"Fuck you," came the quick retort.

A gnarled old woman with a pronounced hump and an overfilled shopping bag worked her way between him and the seats and stopped with one of her heels resting solidly on Stallings's toe. Stallings excused himself and pulled his foot free. The crone glared up at him with reddened eyes and muttered something that he was grateful he couldn't understand.

The doors glided shut and for a moment it seemed as if they had been condemned to a new brand of torture. But slowly, almost reluctantly, the train began to move. Stallings was taller than most of those standing in the car. Clutching his briefcase and his hopelessly wrinkled suit coat in his left hand, he was able to keep his balance in part by holding onto the bar over the old lady's head, and in part by the force of those pressing around him. He commuted to work from the Upper East Side on the IRT, and so was an inveterate and extremely tolerant rider. But this was about as bad as he could ever remember. To make matters even worse, the train was lurching mercilessly—perhaps responding to an effort by the driver to make up for lost time.

A minute out of the station, the old lady's heel again came down on his foot. This time Stallings nudged her away, earning another glare and another epithet. Moments later, a particularly vicious lurch threw a crush of people against him. He felt a sharp sting in his right flank, just above his belt. A bee? A spider? He reached down with his right hand and rubbed at the spot. The stinging sensation was already almost gone. His shirt was still tucked in all around. His hand was still off the bar when a tight curve pitched him against the passengers behind him.

"Hang on to something, for chrissake," someone cried as he was pushed back upright.

"Idiot," someone else added.

"Sorry," Stallings muttered, still trying to make sense of having been stung in such a way. He had been stung before, any number of times, by both bees and spiders. He wasn't allergic to either. But whatever had bitten him this time had done so right through his shirt.

The train slowed as they entered the City Hall station. The crush of passengers intensified as some tried to make their way to the doors.

"Excuse me," a woman said, trying to get past Stallings. "Sir?"

Stallings couldn't respond. His heart had started pumping wildly. His pulse was resonating in his ears like artillery fire. He felt a terrifying nausea and dizziness taking hold. Sweat cascaded down his face. The car lights blurred, then began spinning, faster and faster. His chest felt empty, as if his lungs and heart had been torn out. He needed desperately to lie down.

"Hey, what are you doing?" someone shouted.

His hand had slipped off the steel bar.

"Hey, buddy . . ."

Stallings felt his knees buckling. His head lolled back.

"Hey, back away, back away! He's passing out!"

Stallings knew he was on the floor, his arms and legs jerking uncontrollably. Feet hit against him as people tried to back away. He sensed himself bite through his lip, but felt no pain. A flood of words reached him as distant echoes through a long, metal tunnel.

"He's having a seizure" . . . "Get something in his mouth" . . . "Roll him over! Roll him over on his side!" . . . "I'm a paramedic. Move aside, everyone. Move aside" . . . "Somebody do something" . . . "I am, lady, just back off" . . . "Get a cop. . . ."

The words became more disconnected, more garbled. Stallings felt the people kneeling around him, touching him, but he was powerless to react. He knew he was losing consciousness. Blood flowed from his lip onto his royal blue shirt. He sensed his bladder give way. The blurred images faded to blackness. The voices and sounds died away. . . .

All but one of the tangle of people were focused on Stallings. This one, a nondescript man in a print sports shirt, reached between two would-be rescuers and grasped the handle of Stallings's briefcase. Then, ever so slowly, he slid it free of the crowd. He smiled inwardly at the image of Sir Gawaine utilizing one evasive tactic after another to avoid being followed to Battery Park, never realizing that the state-of-the-art bugs Galahad routinely placed in each knight's room had made tailing him quite unnecessary.

The car doors were open now, and people were pushing and jamming to get out onto the platform. The man with Stallings's briefcase moved calmly with the flow. The syringe in his pocket would be tossed into a sewer within a block. The cardiotoxin he had emptied into Stallings was one of his favorite weapons—a drug virtually unknown outside of the lower Amazon, so potent that the poison remaining along the barrel of the syringe would probably still be enough to kill. The thirty-gauge needle attached to the syringe was so fine it could pass through a pore, making the puncture wound essentially invisible. And even if the injection had produced a tiny droplet of blood, the man's dark blue shirt would have made it virtually impossible to notice. Just another statistic—another heat-related death. *Beautiful, just beautiful.*

Anton Perchek exited the station just as two policemen were rushing in.

"Take your time, gentlemen," he whispered. "Believe me, there is no need to rush."

CHAPTER 29

The mood in Harry's apartment was decidedly upbeat. Walter Concepcion and Maura arrived within a few minutes of each other, both with good news.

Harry needed it. After the hearing, as he was getting out of Mel Wetstone's Mercedes in front of his office, he had experienced another bout of chest pain—more sharp than dull or squeezing, moving from deep in his back through to the middle of his breastbone. The whole episode didn't last long—maybe three or four minutes. And it wasn't all that severe. But it was the worst pain he had had in a while. By the time he had given Mary Tobin a quick kiss of gratitude and hurried to the medication cabinet to try a nitroglycerine pill, the pain was subsiding. If it was angina, he told himself again, it certainly wasn't a textbook case.

Still, Maura was going to keep her part of their bargain by going to an AA meeting with Concepcion. The least he could do was schedule a stress test. He went back to his desk, dialed the office number of a cardiologist friend, and actually let the phone ring once before he hung up. He would keep the nitroglycerine in his pocket, he decided, and take it at the first sign of chest pain. If it worked, if the pain subsided, there was a fairly strong likelihood that the problem was his heart. Then he would call the cardiologist. Meanwhile, he told himself, the stress test could wait.

Harry gave Maura and Concepcion a vivid account of the hearing at the hospital—especially the nearly catastrophic speech by Caspar Sidonis, and the remarkable performances by Mel Wetstone and Mary Tobin.

"This Sidonis," Concepcion said when he had finished, "does he know about your wife—I mean, the research she was doing?"

"I don't think so. I haven't shared what I know about her other life with anyone except the police. Telling Sidonis seemed to serve no purpose. I doubt he would believe it anyway."

"He sounds like he could be a dangerous enemy. I would recommend you stay as far away from him as possible. Will he follow through on his threat to quit?"

"I doubt it, but you never know. He makes it sound like he could just walk out of MMC and hang up his shingle at another hospital. But he has a huge research lab, and when you're in the million-plus-a-year category, which I'm sure he is, things are seldom that simple. There's no hospital in the city without a chief of cardiac surgery. And I doubt any of them would be too pleased to have ol' Caspar decide to horn in on their territory."

Maura next told of how Lonnie Sims had helped her produce a series of photo-quality pictures of the man she had seen. There was the original, and three other front-and-side views— one with glasses and a beard, one with a mustache and blond hair, another with blue eyes and long dark hair. Sims had reduced them all in size and placed them on a single legal-size sheet along with an empty box for the addition of other information. He then printed out ten copies for her.

"Should have done one as a woman," Concepcion said, studying the images.

"What?"

"Nothing. Just blabbing. This guy seems like he can almost walk through walls in hospitals, so I was wondering what he'd look like as a nurse."

"Actually, Lonnie tried out a number of feminine wigs and makeup of various kinds. That opened up dozens of combinations and possibilities. The pictures would have been awfully small if we had tried to print too many. Plus, we felt it might be too confusing for anyone looking at a set of fifteen or twenty composites to focus in on one of them."

"Good point," Concepcion said. "We'll get a batch of color Xeroxes and put them up on every floor in the hospital. Maybe in other hospitals, too."

"We can't," Harry said.

He reviewed his clash with Owen Erdman and his agreement that Erdman alone would supervise distribution of the drawings, and then only privately to department heads.

"It won't work," Concepcion said, more agitated than Harry had ever seen him.

"What do you mean?"

"There's not much chance that someone's just going to look at these posters and say, 'Ah ha! That's our man right over there.' It happens that way sometimes, but not often. What we're really trying to do is annoy The Doctor, upset him to the point where he does something careless—jab and run, jab and run until he doesn't care about anything except getting even with you."

"You talk as if you know him," Harry said.

The tic at the corner of Concepcion's mouth fired off several times.

"I don't know *him* specifically, Harry," he said. "But I know psychos. Our tripping up that man is not nearly as likely as his stumbling over his own ego. But our best chance of having that happen is to find a way to rile him up."

"I'm sorry, but I can't do it, Walter. I gave the hospital president my word. My position's shaky enough around that place without pushing my luck with him. He's famous for his temper. In a week or so, we can try approaching him again. But not now."

"Whatever you say, Doc."

Concepcion studied one of the posters for a few seconds.

"Maura, this is really quite amazing," he said, slipping it into a battered leather portfolio.

She looked at him curiously.

"How do you know?"

"Hey, I may be a little rough around the edges," he responded cheerily, "but I know good artwork when I see it."

"Thanks," she said, shrugging off her momentary concern. "We'll know just how amazing a likeness that is when we see the guy looking out at us from behind a set of bars."

If he lives that long. For a moment, Concepcion was afraid he had said the words out loud.

It seemed to Maura as if a shadow had passed over Concepcion's face—as if he had quite suddenly drifted off to some faraway place. He took a long drink of the lemonade Harry had made for them. When he set his glass down, the shadow was gone. His grin was broad and engaging.

"So, then, *mis amigos*," he said, "it's my turn to tell you about Elegance, The Escort Service for Discerning Gentlemen. The woman who runs it is Page. She wouldn't tell me any more than that. I met her at this dark bar on the East Side that has no windows. Not one. It turns out that my suspicions were right. Desiree did a kind of freelance work for Elegance on and off for four or five months. Um . . . I'm sorry to say this, Harry, but apparently she was very much in demand."

"Swell."

"Hey, are you going to be okay with this?"

Harry shrugged. "Go ahead."

"Okay. Anyhow, this Page is very angry because some wealthy, powerful people pulled out of a contract with her when they found out Desiree was a reporter. What happened was Desiree tried interviewing some of the other girls and one of them ratted on her. Page thought that by firing Desiree she'd get rewarded. Instead, she and Elegance got canceled. She ended up losing a hell of a lot of money. She seemed angry enough to talk about the men involved, but she also seemed really frightened of them. Apparently two of them paid her a visit and gave her the third degree about Desiree. I couldn't get her to tell me anything at all about them at first. So I kept sweetening the pot until she did. . . . Harry, I'm . . . ah . . . I'm afraid the fifteen hundred's gone."

"All of it?"

"It was kind of a do-or-die situation. She'd had a few drinks, and was just on the edge. I figured that if I didn't nudge her over with a good offer, I might lose her for good."

"Well, five hundred of that's yours," Harry said.

"Harry!" Maura exclaimed.

"Sorry, sorry. Go on, Walter. I trust you. Really I do."

"She didn't know any of the men's names except someone named Lance. I guess that's his last name. He paid her in cash and let her know if a girl was unsatisfactory for whatever reason. The girls, seven of her very best, went to the Camelot Hotel twice a month and stayed the night. She didn't know for certain what the men were doing there, but from things her girls told her from time to time, she thought some of them might have been in the insurance business."

"Insurance?"

"That's all she said. It isn't that much, but it certainly got my attention. I was thinking I could approach some of the chambermaids at the Camelot. Chambermaids in hotels know everything, and in this city half of them are Latino. Maybe I can learn who some of the guys are, and we can go from there."

They meet every two weeks at the Camelot Hotel. . . .

"I don't think that's going to be necessary," Harry said, remembering one of the few lines of Desiree's writing he had gotten the chance to read. "I think Evie might have already named a couple of them for us."

He had copied the two names he found in Evie's address book and kept the copy in his wallet. The original was wedged into the toe of an old pair of sneakers in the hall closet. Now, he smoothed the names on the table, called information, and then dialed the New York Public Library. He was looking for a reference-room librarian named Stephanie Barnes. Barnes had been one of his first medical assistants, and one of the few who left the office to go back to school rather than to have babies or to make more money than he could afford to pay. Harry had given her a nice bonus to help with her first year. Now, happily married, with a master's degree in library science, she had both the babies *and* more money than he could afford to pay.

Over the years of their continuing friendship, she had taught Harry something that he had already long suspected— that a resourceful, imaginative reference-room librarian could find out almost anything.

"Stephanie, I have two names along with addresses and even Social Security numbers," he said, after accepting her condolences about Evie and assuring her that he had nothing to do with her death. "I think both men might be involved with the insurance business in some way. I want any information you can dig up on either of them, especially where they work and what they do. Tomorrow would be okay if you're too busy, but I was actually thinking more in the line of the next hour or so."

Stephanie told him not to expect anything, but it was just thirty minutes later when she called back.

"Bingo!" Harry said after he took down the information. "Walter, you've done it again. James Stallings, vice president of Interstate Health Care. Kevin Loomis, first vice president of Crown Health and Casualty. They both seem to be stars on the rise, too. Loomis had two years at a community college in New Jersey, and was just a sales agent until a couple of years ago. Now he's big stuff. I'm not sure what he's doing living in Queens with what he must be making. Stallings is private school all the way—St. Stephen's, Dartmouth, and Wharton business school. He's won a ton of awards for performance in the company and the industry."

"Do you want me to look up the company phone numbers?" Maura asked.

Harry tapped his page of notes.

"You obviously haven't had any experience with people like my friend Stephanie. Office and home numbers for both."

"Which one are you going to try first?"

Harry looked over at Concepcion.

"Why, the award-winning executive, of course," Walter said. "Is it worth talking through how you're going to approach him?"

"I think I might be better improvising," Harry said.

He dialed the number for the Manhattan office of Interstate Health Care and asked for James Stallings. In a few moments, Stallings's secretary came on the line.

"Mr. Stallings's office."

"Hi," Harry said. "I'm trying to reach Jim Stallings. My name's Collins, Harrison Collins. I was a classmate of Jim's at Dartmouth. I'm with the selection committee for next year's graduation. Jim's name has been submitted for a distinguished alumnus award, and I need to go over some details with him."

Harry got two thumbs up from his small audience. There was an unnaturally long pause before the secretary responded.

"I'm sorry, Mr. Collins," she said. "Mr. Stallings isn't able to take your call."

"Well, when should I call back?"

Again, there was an uncomfortably long pause.

"What was this about again?"

"An award. Dartmouth is giving Mr. Stallings an award."

"Mr. Collins, I'm afraid Mr. Stallings is ill. Quite ill. He . . . he's in the intensive care unit at Memorial Hospital."

"Oh, that's terrible. Will he, I mean, is he going to be all right?"

"I can't tell you any more than that without permission. I'm sorry."

Harry reviewed the conversation for Maura and Concepcion, and then used his title and knowledge of hospital procedure to get through to a nurse in the Memorial Hospital ICU. His conversation with the woman lasted only a minute. He slowly set the receiver down.

"Stallings had a cardiac arrest on the subway this afternoon," he said. "He's on a ventilator, essentially brain-dead. She couldn't tell me any more than that."

"How old was he?" Maura asked.

Harry glanced at his notes.

"Forty-two."

"Not exactly cardiac arrest age," Concepcion said.

"What do you think?"

"I don't like it. I don't like it at all. I think you should call that other one. What's his name?"

Harry was already dialing Crown Health and Casualty.

"Loomis," he said. "Kevin Loomis."

Harry modified the tale he told to Loomis's secretary. Harrison Collins was with the Executive of the Year committee of the American Insurance Association. Loomis was to be one of three nominees for this year's award. Harry knew the lie sounded good even as he said it. In a few seconds, Loomis was on the line.

"What can I do for you, Mr. Collins?" he said.

"Are you the only one on this line?" Harry asked.

"What?"

"Can you talk safely?"

"Of course I can. What's this all about?"

"Mr. Loomis, my name isn't Collins, it's Corbett. Dr. Harry Corbett. Do you know who I am?"

"I read the papers."

"This is about my wife, Mr. Loomis. My late wife Evelyn."

"Why are you calling me?"

"Mr. Loomis, in trying to clear myself of charges that I murdered my wife, I've been investigating her life. I've learned that she worked for the Elegance escort service. I know she saw you and James Stallings as clients at the Camelot Hotel."

"That's nonsense. I've never been to the Camelot Hotel, I don't know your wife, and I don't know anyone named Stallings. Now, I'm very busy and—"

"Your name, address, and Social Security number were on a note in my wife's possession when she died. So were Stallings's. It seemed to me she must have got them from your driver's licenses. Now, you can talk to me or talk to the police."

"Dr. Corbett, I don't like people threatening me. I don't know you and I don't know your wife. I'm going to hang up now. Don't call me again."

"Mr. Loomis, I just hung up from talking with a nurse in the Memorial Hospital ICU. James Stallings had some sort of cardiac arrest today. He's unconscious and on a respirator, but he's never going to wake up again. He's brain-dead. Irreversibly brain-dead."

The prolonged silence was a positive response.

"I don't know Stallings, and I have nothing more to say to you."

"My number is 870-3400 in Manhattan. Call me anytime, but make it soon. I have a feeling we need to talk."

Kevin Loomis hung up without responding.

"He's going to check on what I told him about Stallings," Harry told the others. "After that I think I'll be hearing from him."

"One way or the other," Maura responded warily. "For all we know, he may have been the one who hired Evie's killer."

CHAPTER 30

Each patient was allowed two visitors in the Memorial Hospital ICU. When Kevin Loomis arrived there at two-fifteen the following afternoon, James Stallings already had his quota. He was directed to a small family room with overstuffed furniture, a selection of religious and inspirational reading material, and a television that was turned to the cartoon channel.

Visiting hours were from noon until eight, but this was Kevin's first opportunity to get to the hospital since receiving the call from Harry Corbett. As soon as he had hung up on Corbett, Kevin had called Memorial. Patient information could tell him nothing more than that James Stallings was a patient in the ICU, and that his condition was critical. He dialed Stallings's office at Interstate Health, hoping to learn more, but hung up as soon as the secretary asked his name. Badly shaken, he managed to make it through an hour-long meeting at work—a meeting in which Burt Dreiser sat directly across the table, smiling at him benevolently.

Burt, you know Sir Gawaine, the tall, good-looking guy who came on board The Roundtable about six or seven months before I did? You wouldn't happen to know how he ended up in critical condition in the Memorial Hospital ICU, would you?

After the meeting, Kevin had barely had time to make it home for Julie's dance recital. He would have preferred to have been assigned to Nicky's Little League game, but his deal with Nancy was that they would alternate. Now, with little Brian scheduled to begin various lessons as soon as they were settled in Port Chester, the formula would have to be revamped.

By the time he caught up with Nancy, it was almost nine. The kids were finally all in their rooms. With Kevin having spent the previous night at the Garfield Suites, it had been a day and a half since he and Nancy had said more than a few words to one another. She had picked up on his uncharacteristic tenseness and asked about it. He made no attempt to disagree. Work had been unusually heavy, he said. When she asked how he had made out in his poker game, he chose the "won a few dollars" lie. Then she ran down two days' worth of family news, and began flirting with him, stroking the inside of his leg. It had been a couple of weeks since they had made love—since before the previous Roundtable meeting, in fact. But this just wasn't going to be the night. He begged off, citing a splitting headache, exhaustion, and a phone call he had to make to Burt. He forced himself not to look at her hurt and concern, and shuffled down to his basement office. There he called Memorial Hospital once again. *ICU, critical.*

"Excuse me."

"Huh?"

Kevin had been staring unseeing at a Bugs Bunny classic. A woman stood in the doorway of the family room. She was tall and slender with sandy hair cut short. Her narrow face was attractive, and might have been beautiful were it not for the dark circles under her eyes.

"You're here to see Jim Stallings?"

"I am, yes."

The woman stepped forward and extended her hand.

"I'm Vicky Stallings. Jim's wife."

Kevin stood.

"Kevin Loomis. I'm with Crown Health. I . . . I play cards with Jim."

"Oh, then you saw him just the night before . . . before this happened. Did he seem all right?"

"Perfectly normal."

"He was in the subway when he collapsed," she said, talking

as much to herself as to Kevin. "City Hall station. His secretary said he had some sort of appointment downtown, but she had no idea what. How did you say you knew Jim?"

"I . . . um . . . I play cards in the same game he does."

"Oh, yes. You just said that, didn't you. I can't seem to keep a thought in my head. I assume he lost again," she said, desperately distraught, but still trying for civility. "Jim never was very interested in card games, or very good at them from what I could tell. But he would never miss that game. I gather it was as much about business as about poker."

Kevin felt strange hearing the lie from someone else's wife.

"I'm really sorry about what's happened," he said. "I couldn't get any information from the hospital other than that his condition was critical. Is he . . . I mean, does he . . ."

Vicky Stallings shook her head and then suddenly and rapidly unraveled. Kevin stood by awkwardly until she had regained some control. Her sobbing let up. Embarrassed, she apologized. He told her there was nothing to apologize for.

"My sister just left," she managed. "Why don't you go on in there alone. I'll be by in just a bit. Jim hasn't mentioned you, but he kept that poker game pretty much to himself. It's very good of you to come."

"I'm sorry this has happened," Kevin said again.

For as long as he could remember, Kevin had had an intense aversion to hospitals. He disliked intensive care units even more. He checked in with the nurse at the desk and was directed to cubicle 3, a glass-enclosed box with drapes partially blocking the windows. The patient in the cubicle bore scant resemblance to the urbane executive who had sat across from him through nearly five months of Roundtable meetings. Tape across his puffy face held tubes in place through his nose and mouth. Beside the bed, a large respirator hissed and whirred, its display flashing like some obscene electronic game. Stallings's lips—what Kevin could see of them—were swollen, cracked, and bruised. His eyes were taped shut. Periodically, every muscle in his body seemed to go into spasm, with his rigid arms twisting inward until his palms faced away from his sides. Overhead, the monitor screen displayed a heart rhythm that was quite regular. Kevin knew the innocent pattern was deceiving.

Brain-dead. That's how Dr. Harry Corbett had put it. *Brain-dead.*

Kevin pictured Evelyn DellaRosa as shown in the newspapers and as he remembered her. Such a remarkable looking woman—so classically stunning. Was this how she ended up, too? Tubes coming out of every body orifice? Puffed and brain-dead on artificial ventilation, alive only until some doctor finally strolled in and simply pulled the plug? Was this what was in store for Kevin Loomis as well?

He moved closer to the bedside.

Was there any way Stallings's cardiac arrest on the IRT could have been a coincidence? The man was incredibly stressed over the situation with The Roundtable. It was a hundred degrees on the subway platform and not much better in the cars. And what if he was unlucky enough to get one of the old un-air-conditioned ones? Perhaps some preexisting condition caused his heart to just crap out. On the other hand, perhaps they were being watched all the time at Battery Park. Perhaps Stallings had recognized someone from The Roundtable in the subway. Perhaps they had done something to him.

Dammit, James, what in the hell happened? his mind screamed. *What am I supposed to do?*

"Thank you for being so patient, Mr. Loomis."

Vicky Stallings had washed her face and put on a bit of makeup.

"It's Kevin," he said. "This is so sad. Do his doctors have any idea what could have happened?"

"I'd be happy to talk with you, Kevin," she whispered. "But I would prefer doing it in the family room. It's doubtful Jim can hear, but there's always the chance."

"I understand."

They returned to the small room. Wile E. Coyote was lashing himself to a huge rocket just as the Road Runner was flashing past. Kevin reached up and flicked the set off.

"You don't have to talk about this with me if it's too painful," he said.

"There's not much to say, actually. The doctors have said there's no hope. They estimate his heart stopped for eight or nine minutes. People were doing CPR, but I guess it wasn't enough. The rescue squad finally got him going."

"Was he, I mean, did he have any heart problems before?" Kevin sensed how desperately he was hoping for a positive answer.

"Kevin, Jim ran last year's New York Marathon in three and a half hours. About six months ago, he took out a large insurance policy. They required a stress test. Jim said he did so well that the doctor who performed it eventually had to stop the test to go on to the next patient."

A *large insurance policy.* Reflexively, Kevin ran through his own coverage. As soon as he joined The Roundtable, he had beefed it up. *Two million five with an additional half a million for accidental death.*

"He always looked fit to me," he said.

"The doctors say that maybe it was his potassium dropping due to the heat and sweating. Apparently the heart is very sensitive to potassium. It depends on what he was doing for the hour or so before . . ."

Vicky Stallings's voice once more grew strained. Kevin could see that she was precariously close to coming apart again. In fact, he was rather close himself. Stallings's death was no coincidence, any more than Evelyn DellaRosa's or the knight named Sir Lionel's was a coincidence. Somehow, they had followed Stallings, or perhaps even Kevin, to Battery Park. Then somehow, they had gotten to him. Now, he was a vegetable. The unflappable Sir Gawaine. Kevin wondered if he, too, had gone out and bought a new house as soon as his appointment to The Roundtable was a fact.

Kevin wanted to scream. He made a pretense of glancing at his watch. Vicky Stallings saved him any embarrassment.

"I really appreciate your coming like this, Kevin," she said, again reaching out to shake his hand. "And who knows? It will take a miracle, but there have been miracles before. Many of them."

"I'll be praying for him," Kevin said, backing out of the room. He felt light-headed and desperately wanted a drink.

Kevin stopped in the first bar he passed, downed a couple of quick vodka tonics and then returned to Crown. Brenda Wallace had some letters for him to sign and a list of calls to return. He watched her move about her office, tanned and lithe and utterly sensual. Burt Dreiser had the corner office, the yacht, *and* Brenda Wallace. When had Burt decided he could handle whatever The Roundtable wanted of him? Had *he* been part of the planning that put the whole program together? And most important, why in the hell couldn't Kevin be like him?

He finished his work and sat for a time, staring out at the city. Then he picked up the phone and called George Illych, the underwriter at Crown who had handled all of his policies.

"George, Kevin Loomis here. How goes it?"

"Hey, fine, Kevin. What can I do for you?"

Kevin pictured George Illych leaning back in his chair, looking longingly at his beloved Winstons. A jovial, overweight billiard and golf hustler, Illych smoked two packs a day and was one of the poorest insurance risks Kevin knew.

"Nancy and I have just bought a house in Port Chester."

"Hey great, that's great. First the big promotion, then the big house."

"Then the big coverage. George, I've decided, with the new house and my income up near $300,000 counting bonuses, that I want a bit more coverage."

"Hey, no problem. What did we write for you recently?"

"A million. That was four months ago. My physical's still good, yes?"

"Up to six months. How much do you have total?"

"This million would make it three and a half." *Plus an additional $500,000 accidental,* he added, but didn't say.

"All to Nancy?"

"Yes."

"Hey, pal, no problem. I'll have the paperwork up to you within a couple of days."

"Perfect. Thanks, George."

"How about shooting a little pool after work sometime soon?"

"Pool against you? I couldn't afford it, George."

"Hey, wait a minute. You just became the three-and-a-half-million-dollar man."

"That's only if I'm dead, George."

"Oh, yeah. You've got a point there."

Half an hour later Brenda Wallace stopped by to say good night. Kevin quickly stacked the papers he had been working on and slid them inside his desk drawer. There was nothing further, he told Brenda. She gave him one of her most dazzling smiles before heading home.

Kevin opened his briefcase and took out a newspaper clipping about Evelyn DellaRosa. He was looking at her picture when he dialed Harry Corbett's line.

"Corbett, this is the man you called earlier," he said to Harry's answering machine. "I want to talk with you. Be home tomorrow morning at nine. I'll call."

He set the articles back in his briefcase and then tossed the drawings he had been making in on top of them. They were a series of diagrams and sketches of the basement of his house in Queens, most particularly emphasizing the position of the washing machine, dryer, bulkhead entryway, and especially the electrical power source.

CHAPTER 31

It was nearly midnight when Harry heard Maura's soft knock on his partially open bedroom door. He was lying on his back, wide awake, trying to will himself to sleep. But he was still far too keyed up. Things were continuing to break for them, as they had since the moment Maura convinced him to hire Walter Concepcion. Now the insurance executive Kevin Loomis had left a message on his answering machine. He wanted to talk. In the morning he was going to call. Bit by bit, the circle was closing. Step by minuscule step, they were drawing closer to Evie and Andy Barlow's killer.

"Come on in, I'm awake," he said.

"I just wanted to see if I could talk you into some tea, and maybe a little company."

Wearing loose cotton pants and a tank top, she stood in the doorway, framed by the light behind her. If her goal at that moment was to look alluring and incredibly sexy, she had succeeded admirably. Harry pushed himself up and motioned her to a spot on the bed a fairly safe distance away.

"No tea, thanks, but a little company would be fine."

A *little company*. Harry's attraction to the woman had begun within minutes of their meeting at her apartment, and had grown steadily since. It was dumb, he knew. Dumb and dangerous. Both of them were fragile and vulnerable. His wife had been dead just a few weeks. Maura had fallen off the wagon. And they had business to attend to—a madman who wanted both of them dead.

"Harry, I've decided to go home tomorrow," she said suddenly.

He tried to mask his surprise and hurt.

"You don't have to do that."

"I know. But sooner or later I do. It's not to get away from anything here. I hope you know that. It's just that all of a sudden, my head is full of the paintings I want to do. They're flashing through my brain like comets."

"That's terrific. But I don't think it's safe yet."

"Not from the killer, I agree. But that danger's here, too. It'll be everywhere I go until we nail him. What I am safe from now is the booze. That was the big worry for me—even more dangerous than the killer. The AA meeting tonight made me even more certain. I'm not taking anything for granted, and I'm going to keep going to the meetings, but I *know* I'm going to be all right. With all the terrible things that've happened, that's one good thing to come out of this mess." She smiled at him. "But now I feel like I ought to be alone, and I know you need some space."

She sat with her legs tucked underneath her. Her body was silhouetted by the hall light. Harry tried to remember the last time he had held Evie—the last time they had had sex. The last time he had really cared. He sensed the stirrings in his body. Over the past days he had managed to overcome them. *Now?* He reached out tentatively and took her hand.

"I don't need space, and I don't want you to go," he said.

She moved closer. He breathed in the scent of her and knew that whatever resistance he had been clinging to was gone.

"You don't know me, Harry," she said. "I'm tough. I've been known to eat nice, kind men like you for breakfast and spit out the seeds."

He backed away and peered at her.

"That sounds like something you heard in a movie."

"It is, actually. I think it might have been Garbo. But I've sort of always wanted to try the line out myself. Unfortunately, though, it's true. I can't remember the last lover I cared about as anything more than some sort of perverse validation that I was a worthwhile person."

"You *are* a worthwhile person," he said, "and incredibly sexy."

"Even with no hair?"

"You have plenty. Besides, that minimalist coif just lets me focus more on the rest of you."

He drew her toward him and gently cupped her breast. She made a soft, excited sound, pressed his hand in more tightly, and nestled her head against his chest.

"Harry, I've wanted you to want me since I first saw you walking up the stairs to my place. Now I really am frightened. We're both going through so much—we've had so much hurt."

"Maura, we don't have to make love. We can just lie here and hold one another."

She slid her hand down his shorts.

"Don't let me talk you out of this," she said.

Propped against the headboard, he kissed her lightly on her lips, on her neck, on her throat. She knelt astride him and pulled off his T-shirt. Then, with his lips just inches from her breasts, she swept off her tank top and threw it aside. Instantly, his mouth was on her, sucking her, caressing her nipple with his tongue.

"Making love sober is going to be a hell of an experience for me."

"We don't have to do it tonight."

"Shut up. . . . Harry, listen, though. I really don't feel right making love with you unless it's safe. It's been quite a while for me, I think. But you know how us blackout drinkers are."

"Don't worry. Evie was the condom queen. The latest box is in the drawer by the bed. It's been there for months. I don't think it's even been opened."

"Well, it's about to be."

They kissed, gently, longingly. He worked his hand inside her pants over her buttocks, farther and farther, until he could touch her new dampness. Instantly, she was wet. She let him stroke her that way for as long as she could stand. Then she slid down him, pulling his shorts free and running her lips and tongue over him again and again.

"Go slow, Maura," he begged. "I'm really out of practice and I want this to last."

"Where does it say you only get one try?" she murmured, moving up to his lips and helping him slide her pants down.

Completely nude, with wonderfully white skin and only the shortest, soft bristles of hair on her head, she was the sexiest woman he had ever been with. She lay stretched out on her belly now, toes pointed. He knelt beside her and ran his hand down her long, silky body, pausing to stroke her buttocks again and again. Then he rolled gently on top of her, kneading the muscles in her back, spreading her legs apart with his knees. He was so aroused, so large, he ached. He kissed the inside of her thighs and touched between her legs. She was ready, too—incredibly ready.

"Please, Harry," she moaned. "Not this way. I want to look at you this first time. I want to see your face. I want to see your wonderful face."

He kissed her behind the neck and helped her roll over. She drew her knees up and took him in her hand. For several magically suspended seconds they remained that way, their eyes fixed on one another.

"Keep looking at me," she whispered as she guided him inside her. "Baby, please, keep your eyes open. Just a little longer. Keep your eyes open and see how happy this makes me. See how much I love doing this with you."

The light of morning was filtering through the blinds when the phone began ringing. Harry couldn't remember when they had finally drifted off to sleep, but he knew it couldn't have been very long ago. They had made love, then rested, then made love, then showered and ate, and then made love again.

"If this is you at fifty," Maura had gasped at one point, "I'm sure glad I didn't meet you when you were twenty-five."

"You would have been eleven," he said.

"That's just the point."

An hour later, as she lay beside him, she gently touched the patchwork of scars covering his back. He had already told her about Nha-trang.

"Hey, you can tell me the real story now," she said. "I'll certainly understand. What was her name?"

The ringing persisted. He reached across her for the phone just as she was beginning to stir. The digital display on his clock radio read 7:50.

"Hello?"

"Harry?"

"Yes."

"Harry, it's Doug. Sorry to wake you."

"Hey, I've been up for hours."

Maura, now almost fully awake, reached playfully under the sheet to touch him. He pushed her hand aside, stifling a laugh.

"Harry, what in the hell is going on?" Atwater asked.

From the tension in Doug's voice, it was clear he was not referring to what was going on at that moment in Harry's bedroom.

"With what?" Harry asked.

"With those posters, dammit. Harry, please, we're friends. Don't play games with me."

Harry was wide awake now, sitting bolt upright. Maura, sensing trouble, was up, too.

"Doug, you have to believe me, I don't know what you're talking about."

"There are posters on every bulletin board in the hospital, and in at least two other hospitals we know of. Posters with eight versions of that drawing of the man you think killed your wife. Owen is furious, Harry."

Harry groaned and put his hand over the receiver.

"The posters are up all over the hospital, goddammit. It's got to be Concepcion." He returned to Atwater. "Doug, I swear, it was a guy I hired to help us out who did it. I told him not to, but apparently he did it anyway. Is it just the pictures? I mean, does the poster say anything?"

"Of course it does, Harry. Listen, I'm not an idiot. Don't treat me like—"

"Doug, please, what does it say?"

Harry could hear Atwater sigh, trying to compose himself.

"It says that this man is wanted for the murder of Evelyn

DellaRosa, and that anyone with information should contact you at the number I just dialed. There's a fifty-thousand-dollar reward for information leading to his arrest and conviction."

"How much?"

"Fifty thousand."

"Fifty thousand?"

"Harry, Owen is berserk about this."

"Tell him I'm sorry. I'll be calling to explain and I'll take every one of them down."

"It's more than just this hospital, Harry. University has called, and St. Bart's. I suspect there may be others."

"I'll take care of it, Doug. I'll take care of them all."

"Who's the guy who did this?"

"No one you know. Listen, thanks, Doug. Thanks for calling me." He set the receiver down. "No one *I* know either," he muttered. "Maura, can you get hold of your brother?"

"I think so."

"I want to know if there was ever a licensed detective in New York named Walter Concepcion."

The call from Kevin Loomis came precisely on time, at nine o'clock. By that time, three other calls had come in as well. One was from a maintenance worker at MMC, one from University Hospital, and one from Bellevue. Each of them reported seeing the man in the poster. Two of them wanted an advance on the reward before giving any information. Harry found a notebook in the study and began keeping a log. He also began letting his machine screen calls.

"Goddamn Concepcion," he said after each of the calls. "Goddamn Concepcion."

Loomis, calling from a pay phone, would say only that he was willing for the two of them to meet. He sounded tense, but not excessively so.

"Be at the southeast corner of the intersection of Third Avenue and Fifty-first at eleven o'clock tonight," he said. "Wear a baseball cap. I'll pick you up."

He hung up before Harry could ask any questions.

Over the next half an hour, there were two more calls with

tips and inquiries about the reward. Maura answered both. Neither seemed that promising.

"We're going to have to develop a system for evaluating these," she said. "I suppose we should say that if the caller can point the man out to us we're interested. Otherwise, thanks, but no thanks."

"Maura, I don't *have* fifty thousand dollars."

"Hey, first things first," she said. "Don't you remember hearing the speaker say that at the AA meeting last night?"

"God, I've created a monster."

The third call was from Tom Hughes. He would keep looking, but as far as he could tell, there had never been a licensed private eye in Manhattan or any city in New York State named Walter Concepcion. Harry slammed down the receiver, then snatched it up and called Concepcion's rooming house. Walter himself answered.

"Concepcion, I want to know who in the hell you are, and why you've stabbed me in the back like this."

For fifteen seconds, there was silence.

"Your place or mine," Concepcion said finally.

CHAPTER 32

". . . I couldn't see the man's face because of the way I was tied up, but even through the drugs and the pain, I recognized his voice. It was my boss, Sean Garvey. He was what we called a floater—sort of part CIA, part DEA, part above it all. It was his job to coordinate our side of the undercover operation in northern Mexico. But he sold me out and brought in his friend Perchek to work on me. . . ."

When the man Harry had known as Walter Concepcion arrived at the apartment, Harry immediately lost control. Without waiting for any explanation, he spun Concepcion against the hallway wall and was so close to striking him that Maura had to restrain him. Now, he and Maura sat together on the sofa in his living room, listening in stunned silence as Ray Santana took them through his three years as an undercover Drug Enforcement Agency operative in Mexico, then his capture, and his torture at the hands of Anton Perchek.

". . . After Garvey left the cellar, Orsino, one of the drug lord's lieutenants, told Perchek about an escape tunnel leading to a house across the street. With the festival going on in Nogales, and crowds of people all over the city, they would have a perfect chance to slip away from the Mexican police. Poor Orsino obviously didn't appreciate who he was dealing with. It wasn't by accident that no pictures or reliable descriptions of

The Doctor existed. Perchek pulled a pistol from his medical bag and just as calmly as you please, shot him through the mouth. Then he pointed the gun at me. But he was furious with me because I hadn't broken. It was the ultimate insult to him. He wanted me to die, but not a quick death. Instead of shooting me, he emptied the whole syringeful of hyconidol into me."

"Oh, God," Maura said.

Santana shuddered.

"It was horrible. Indescribably horrible. But it was also a mistake. I didn't die. . . ."

Fascinated, Harry studied the man as he continued. Santana's voice was animated enough, but there was a blankness in his eyes—a strange, detached distance. Outwardly, he was telling his story, but in his mind, Harry realized, he was living it.

". . . Ray . . . for God's sake, Ray. Come on."

A man's urgent voice pries into Santana's consciousness. Ray fights to stay within the darkness. Finally, though, he groans, opens his eyes a bit, and strains to focus on the face behind the words. His body feels as if it has been worked over with a baseball bat. He is on his back on the grimy cellar floor, a makeshift pillow beneath his head.

"Ray, it's me, Vargas. Ray, where is he? Where's Perchek? Come on, Ray. We've lost a lot of time."

The face comes into focus. Joaquin Vargas. One of Alacante's most trusted lieutenants. One of the men Ray was preparing to have arrested. Vargas—Mexican undercover all the time!

"Vargas . . . I never thought you—"

"Never mind that. Where's Perchek?"

With great effort, Ray pushes himself up. His head is clearing rapidly. Apparently, The Doctor does not know his revered pain drug as intimately as he thinks. Or maybe he just doesn't know Ray Santana.

"How long have you been here with me?" Santana asks.

"Half an hour. Maybe a little more. You've been out like a fish on ice. At first, we thought you were dead."

"He went out a tunnel somewhere over there. It goes to the house across the street."

"The tunnel," Vargas orders.

Immediately, three uniformed policemen race that way.

"They don't know what he looks like," Ray says. "I do. I need a gun."

"Ray, you're too—"

"I'm fine. Joaquin, you have no idea what that bastard did to me. Please. Give me your gun."

Reluctantly, Vargas hands over his revolver—a nine millimeter Smith & Wesson. Ray cradles the gun and pats the Mexican on the arm.

"You sure as hell had me fooled," he says.

Without waiting for a reply, Ray hurries up the stairs. If the streets are as Garvey has warned, crawling with police checking out any and all gringos, there is still a chance Perchek hasn't found a safe way out.

It is nearly six P.M. Long, late-afternoon shadows stretch down the main street, where a small parade is wending its way toward the plaza. The crowd along the sidewalks is modest— probably in a lull between the afternoon and evening festivities. But a number of those celebrating are wearing costumes . . . and masks. Chances are, Perchek is behind one of them, possibly in the midst of the parade. Or perhaps he is headed out of town by now. But policemen are everywhere, knocking on doors, checking alleys, and blocking the main exits from town. There is still a chance.

Ray is more wobbly from his ordeal than he wishes to admit. But each step feels more assured than the last. And he knows that when and if he does need the strength, it will be there. He starts to follow the parade. But after a few yards, one of Vargas's men calls to him. The policeman is approaching with a thin, agitated man who is gesticulating wildly and chattering nonstop. The man is naked save for a pair of red silk bikini briefs.

"Mr. Santana," the officer says, "we found this man bound and gagged with adhesive tape in an alley two blocks in that direction. He says that not ten minutes ago a gringo put a gun to his head, took his costume, and tied him up. We're looking for a clown with a red polka-dot suit, mask, and bright orange hair. From this fellow's description, I doubt he'll be hard to spot. Only ten minutes ago. There's no way he can escape us. We're closing in on the plaza."

Ray voices his approval, but he senses something is wrong. Anton Perchek had shot Orsino to death without a flicker of hesitation. An ally of his. *Why allow the man in the clown suit, who has also seen his face, to live?*

He slips the Smith & Wesson beneath his belt and heads away from the plaza toward the alley where the clown was found. A tangled ball of adhesive tape shows him the exact spot. The alley is deserted. With firecrackers going off every few minutes, there is no way a gunshot would have even been noticed. Yet the man is alive.

Not at all certain what he is searching for, Santana makes his way around the tawdry block. Then quickly around the next one. And the next. Litter from the fiesta is everywhere. A number of celebrants lie in doorways or between trash barrels in deep, alcohol-induced siesta. One of them, somewhat removed from any others, catches Santana's eye. It is a young woman with a rather pretty face, perhaps in her early twenties. She is sleeping on her side, her back pressed against a building, covered to the neck with a tattered Mexican blanket. Ray approaches. But five yards before he reaches her, he knows she is dead.

He pulls back the blanket. She is dressed only in a pair of white cotton panties, and she is pregnant—perhaps seven months, perhaps eight. A single bullet hole stares up at him obscenely from a spot just above her engorged left nipple. The blood that has oozed from it has already clotted. Santana bets that The Doctor had the woman's clothes hidden away even before he took the clown's.

Driven by a jet of adrenaline, his legs are suddenly responsive. He pulls the revolver free as he sprints toward the main street. A juggler in a skeleton's costume and mask is entertaining a crowd of fifty or so. Shielded by the corner of a building, Ray studies the crowd and then turns his attention to the street. Everyone seems to be involved in conversation, in commerce with one of the street vendors, or watching the juggler.

Then suddenly he sees her. Across the street and a block away. She is walking slowly, unobtrusively, away from the crowd —away from him. What strikes him, though, is her very unobtrusiveness. Her feet are bare, her head covered by a shawl. An unremarkable pedestrian in a very remarkable scene. *Unremarkable*. The Doctor's most valuable attribute.

Santana moves ahead, keeping the crowd between himself and the woman. If it is Perchek, taking him will not be easy. There are dozens of potential hostages around, and scores of potential victims should any sort of shooting erupt. *One move.* That is all he has. If he is wrong, there will be one shocked, bruised woman. But nearly fifteen years as a cop tell him he isn't wrong. *One move.*

He remains in the shadows of the building for as long as he can. Then he breaks across the street and dashes toward the woman from directly behind her. At the last possible moment, she senses movement and begins to turn around. But Ray, his gun drawn, is already airborne. His shoulder slams into her back, sending her sprawling onto the rutted dirt street. The moment he impacts with her—the instant he feels the bulk and the tightened muscles—Ray knows it is Perchek.

Shrieking in Russian, The Doctor spins to his back, struggling to free the gun in his right hand. But the loose maternity dress slows him, and Santana is ready for the move. He pins Perchek's wrist with his left hand, and simultaneously thrusts the Smith & Wesson up into the soft flesh beneath his chin.

"Drop it!" he barks. "Drop it now or it's your fucking head, Perchek. I mean it!"

The Doctor's ice blue eyes sear him. His mouth is twisted in a snarling rictus of hate. Then slowly, ever so slowly, Anton Perchek releases his weapon and lets it drop from his fingertip. . . .

Harry worked his neck around and realized he hadn't moved a muscle for some time. Across from him, Ray Santana sagged visibly, exhausted from recounting the ordeal that should have killed him. Without speaking, Maura went to the kitchen and returned with coffee. Nobody spoke until she had poured three cups.

"Can you tell us what happened after that?" Harry asked.

"Nothing good. Perchek's injection didn't kill me, but over the last seven years I often wish it had. Something irreversible happened to the pain fibers in my nervous system. They fire off with no cause. Sometimes a little. Sometimes absolute hell."

"I assume you've seen doctors."

"Without the chemical Perchek used, they didn't even know where to begin. Most of them thought I was crazy. You know how doctors are about things they didn't learn in some textbook. They thought I was just after drugs or a government pension. Finally, I took a medical discharge from the agency and got one hundred percent disability. I go to AA and NA periodically, but the pain always wins out. Fortunately, I have a doctor and pharmacist at home in Tennessee who understand. So getting Percodan prescriptions is no problem."

"And your family?" Maura asked.

Santana shrugged sadly.

"My wife—Eliza—tried to understand what had happened to me and what I was going through. But with no encouragement or insight from any of the doctors, she finally gave up. Last year she got married to a teacher from Knoxville."

"And your son?"

"He's at the university. From time to time, when he can, he calls. I haven't seen him in a while."

"This is very sad," Maura said.

"I was managing—at least until a few weeks ago I was. About a year after Perchek was locked up in the Mexican federal penitentiary just outside of Tampico, I got word that he was dead, killed in a helicopter crash during an escape attempt. I didn't trust the report. In Mexico, if you have enough money, you can make just about anything happen—or appear to happen. There had been an explosion over water, I was told. The chopper blew up, there were several reliable witnesses. What was fished out of the Atlantic was identified as Perchek through dental X rays."

"You sound as if you weren't convinced."

"Let's just say that what I wanted to believe and what I believed in my heart were not the same thing."

"But how did you end up here?" Harry asked.

"I got a call from an old friend in forensics at the bureau in D.C. That expert of yours, Mr. Sims, had sent down a number of prints for identification. One of them, a thumbprint, matched Perchek's with about a ninety-five percent certainty. I wasn't that surprised—especially when I learned it had been lifted from the room of a woman who had been murdered in a hospital. I came here and began making plans to get close to you. My friend in D.C. promised to give me a little time before identifying the print for Sims."

"But why didn't you tell us who you were?"

"Well, the truth is I wasn't sure what side you were on. I thought maybe you had hired Perchek to kill your wife. I wasn't even a hundred percent certain after that night in Central Park."

Harry groaned.

"That was you. You shot that man."

"You look upset."

"I am upset."

"I saved Maura's life. Maybe yours, too."

"If you had taken those men in instead of killing one, Andy Barlow might still be alive."

Now it was Santana who lashed out.

"Harry, don't be an ass. We're dealing with killers, here. Not college professors, not social workers—killers. Got that? These people don't stand around and let someone *escort* them to the police. They kill. It's too bad about Barlow. He shouldn't've died. But get it through your head—it wasn't my fault."

"You're dangerous, Santana," Harry snapped back. "A walking stick of dynamite with a short fuse. You don't really care who gets blown away as long as Anton Perchek goes along with them."

"You've got that right, brother."

"Well, I might get booted out of my hospital because of what you've done, *brother.*"

"Come on, Harry," Santana said. "You might get reprimanded, but you won't get kicked out. Your lawyer's too good. Listen, we'll go take the posters down. They've been up most of the night now, and that means they've already succeeded in rankling Perchek, which is pretty much what I wanted them to do."

"*Rankling Perchek.* You are really a piece of work," Harry said, not at all kindly. "Have you heard how many times the goddamn phone has rung since you got here? That's a growing percentage of all the nutcases in Manhattan, each one convinced I can be conned out of fifty thousand dollars. *Rankling*

Perchek. Santana, just get out of here. I'm having enough trouble with my enemies without getting blindsided by my so-called friends."

Maura had heard enough.

"Listen, you two," she snapped. "Sit down and shut up for a minute, both of you. I don't care how you feel about one another, but neither of you operating alone has much chance of getting this Perchek. Harry, you're a doctor, not a cop. And Ray, you can't get inside hospitals, and that's where your man is. You two need one another. Face it."

Harry glared at Santana. Maura stalked across the room and stood over him, hands on hips.

"Do you guys want me to make you shake hands like we used to do after fights in junior high school? Okay, then. We stick together, and we try to clear things with one another before we do them. Deal?"

"Deal," the two men grumbled.

"Well, come on, then," Maura cut in before they could get started again. "We've got some posters to take down."

★   ★   ★

A small crowd clustered around the bulletin board outside the MMC surgical suite. There were nurses, technicians, and physicians, including an anesthesiologist, an ENT specialist, and Caspar Sidonis. Everyone, it seemed, was talking at once about the posters that had appeared overnight throughout the hospital.

"You know," one of the nurses said, pointing to the rendering of Perchek with a beard, "I actually think I've seen this guy."

"Janine," another nurse said, "since you kicked Billy out last year you've seen most of the guys in the city."

"Not funny," Janine said.

"I agree, Janine," Sidonis said. "And neither is this . . . this latest humiliation for our hospital." At the first words from the cardiac surgical chief, all extraneous conversation stopped. "Everyone in the hospital knows that Harry Corbett killed his wife. He couldn't stand the thought of losing her and so he killed her. It's as simple as that. These drawings are just a smoke screen, a misdirection play. The man is absolutely certifiable, and so is the woman who drew these. They are the product of an alcoholic's distorted mind, and nothing more. You'll all see. I've had it up to here with Corbett and the way he's manipulating everyone in the place. Fifty-thousand-dollar reward, indeed."

Embarrassed by the surgeon's rambling outburst and the stories they all knew about his involvement with the murdered woman, the crowd quickly dispersed. As Sidonis turned to go, he nearly collided with a man in a full-length lab coat, whose photo badge identified him as Heinrich Hauser, a research professor from the department of endocrinology.

"I agree with you completely, Doctor," Hauser said in a dense German accent. "This Corbett makes trouble for everyone."

"Thank you, Doctor," Sidonis replied.

He glanced at the man, who was four or five inches shorter than he was, with gray-white, crew-cut hair, thick glasses, and yellowed teeth. The teeth disgusted Sidonis. Instinctively, he backed away, fearing a blast of bad breath. He had not seen the man before that he could remember, but he seldom took notice of anyone with whom he didn't have important business.

"Have a good day, now," Hauser said.

"Yes. You, too." Sidonis paused and looked at the man once more. "Have we met?"

The man's ocher smile prompted Sidonis to look away.

"I don't think so, Doctor," he said. "But perhaps we shall meet again sometime."

CHAPTER 33

By nightfall the three-day heat wave had yielded to a pleasant summer rain. Harry left the apartment at ten-thirty and took a cab to the East Side. As instructed, he was wearing a baseball-style cap—the only one he could find in the apartment. It was Evie's from her Washington days, navy blue with *U.S. Senate* in gold just above the brim. After reading the introduction to Desiree's book, *Between the Sheets,* he couldn't help but wonder if the cap was a trophy.

Harry had been loudly rebuked by Owen Erdman for breaking their agreement and putting up the posters. But as Santana had predicted, he did not appear to be in danger of losing his staff privileges so long as they were taken down promptly. Harry would do MMC. Santana and the man he had hired to help cover every hospital in the city would take care of the six others they had done so far.

When they had left Harry's apartment, there was still a good deal of tension lingering between the two of them. Harry felt he could no longer trust Ray Santana to act in anyone's interest but his own. To his credit, Santana did not dispute that point. But he maintained that any sacrifice, by anyone, that resulted in The Doctor's death would have been worth it.

They briefly considered bringing Albert Dickinson up to speed on the developments in the case. But neither of them were in favor of doing that. The chances of getting anything helpful from him were significantly lower than the chances of his causing more trouble for them. Perchek was arrogant and fearless, but he was not foolish. Dickinson would more than likely end up driving him underground—perhaps the worst thing that could happen. Since it was still not at all clear what The Doctor was doing in Manhattan or how he came to kill Evie, there was no way of predicting how long he would stick around.

While Harry and Santana were off to tear down posters, Maura stayed at the apartment to screen phone calls. There was a steady flow of them now at about two or three an hour. Most of the calls were clearly cranks. But some sounded interesting. Maura dutifully logged each one and promised to get back to the caller.

With fifteen minutes to go before he was to meet Kevin Loomis, Harry paid the cabby off at Park and Fifty-first and walked the remaining blocks. Although he wasn't particularly worried about being followed, he had not forgotten his experience in Desiree's apartment. He cut down to Forty-ninth and back, pausing in several doorways to survey the street. *Nothing.* It was a garbage collection night, and the light rain did little to wash away the stench from the mountains of plastic bags awaiting pickup. It had been a while since the last protracted garbage strike in Manhattan. On summer nights like this, he could understand why they seldom went unresolved for very long.

Traffic was light, and the intersection of Fifty-first and Third was nearly deserted. With Evie's U.S. Senate cap pulled low over his eyes, Harry leaned against a light post and waited. At exactly 11:05, a Yellow cab pulled up. The front passenger door swung open.

"Get in, Doctor," the driver said, his voice like number thirty-six sandpaper.

"You Loomis?" Harry asked as the cab pulled away and headed uptown.

"Nope." The driver said nothing more until they neared Fifth Avenue at Fifty-seventh. "As soon as I'm across Fifth, jump out and hurry up to the corner of Sixtieth. You'll be picked up there. I've already been paid, so just get out quickly and go."

He slowed until the light was just about to turn red, then

spurted across the intersection just ahead of the oncoming Fifth Avenue traffic. The maneuver drew an angry volley of horn blasts, but ensured that no car could make it through behind them. Harry hurried up Fifth to Sixtieth. As soon as he reached the corner, a black Lexus rolled up. The door opened and Harry jumped in while the car was still moving. The driver, a good-looking man about forty, swung onto Central Park South and accelerated.

"Kevin Loomis," he said. "Sorry for the cloak-and-dagger stuff. I'm not even sure it'll do any good. Stallings and I took every precaution we could think of when we went to meet at Battery Park, but somehow they still managed to follow one or both of us. Stallings was on the way back to his office from our meeting when he had his cardiac arrest."

"Who are *they?*" Harry asked.

"*They* are the people I think are responsible for killing your wife. That's why I decided to see you tonight. They're health insurance people. They call themselves The Roundtable."

"You mean like the Million Dollar Roundtable?"

"More like the Hundred Million Dollar Roundtable. . . . I'm part of it."

They turned onto the West Side Highway and headed uptown. Harry listened in near disbelief as Kevin Loomis described the secret society and his recent involvement with it. Harry liked the man immediately—the hard edge to his speech, the street-smart toughness underlying the newly acquired executive's manners. If The Roundtable was as elite and exclusive as Loomis depicted, it was a bit difficult to imagine him belonging.

As he listened, there were two things that struck Harry almost from the beginning. The first was the secrecy and mistrust —how little Loomis had been allowed to know about the other knights. It sounded more like a covert government operation than an old-boys club. The second was something about the man, himself. Clearly Loomis was saddened by what had happened—to Evie *and* to James Stallings. But while he certainly wasn't flip or glib, neither did he seem that distraught or desperate—or even frightened. He sounded much calmer tonight than when they first spoke on the phone. Calm and detached.

"As far as your wife goes," Loomis said, "I'm just guessing at what might have happened. I'm assuming you had nothing to do with her death."

"Our marriage was on the rocks, just like the newspapers said. But I would never have harmed her."

"The people on The Roundtable are terribly paranoid. They were worried that Desiree was investigating them."

"She wasn't," Harry said. "She was writing a book and preparing a tabloid TV report on the power of sex in business and politics." He reviewed the night he had spent in Desiree's apartment, omitting any mention of The Doctor. "Her involvement with your group was primarily research," he concluded. "She probably went through your wallets when she had the chance. She figured out you were in the insurance business, but that was all she knew. I don't think she had the faintest notion what you were meeting for."

"Well, apparently The Roundtable didn't buy that. I was there for the discussion, and there was not even a hint that they planned to track her down and kill her. But now I'm sure they did. I have no idea who actually injected her with that chemical. I would imagine it's the same guy who carries out the terminations of policyholders who cost our companies too much money. Hell, for all I know, there may even be more than one of them."

Harry decided to wait until he knew a bit more of Loomis and his motives before sharing the news of Anton Perchek. They entered the Bronx on the Henry Hudson Parkway and continued driving away from Manhattan, toward Van Cortland Park. Harry remained uneasy about Loomis's affect, and wondered if the man was lying or perhaps holding something back.

"Kevin," he said, "why have you decided to tell me all this? I mean, you're part of it. If The Roundtable is destroyed, there's a good chance you'll suffer, too."

"There are a few reasons, actually. I've read a lot about you, and I don't like what they're doing to you—they're destroying your life. You won a medal for getting shot up in Nam. I was too young to fight, but my older brother Michael lost a leg there. Also, the whole thing's getting to be too much for me. Now, don't get me wrong. I'm no angel. Far from it. I could do most of what The Roundtable wanted and not bat an eye. But I draw the line at killing people, no matter how sick they are or how much they're going to cost us. I intend to turn state's evidence and make some sort of deal with the DA's office—that is, if I ever get my hands on any evidence."

"What do you mean?"

"There's nothing on paper. Nothing at all. Stallings was the only one who might have backed me up. I'll go ahead anyway—tell the same story I just told you and name what names I can. But I suspect the lawyers for the other knights will cut me to shreds."

"Maybe not. You know, all along I've had a theory about why whoever killed Evie seemed to be going out of their way *not* to harm me. I figured it was because I was the perfect fall guy—why get rid of me? Now I realize I've probably been right. With every sign pointing to me, you and Stallings weren't likely to challenge The Roundtable."

"Exactly. You said your wife's killer has been trying to get you to kill yourself. That would have been the clincher. I don't know about Stallings, but I would have immediately stopped suspecting The Roundtable."

Harry turned to Loomis.

"What you're doing takes a lot of guts," he said. "When you do go to the authorities, I'll be right there with you, if that's any comfort."

"Thanks. But from what I've read in the papers, I'm not sure that would be a plus. The cops really hate you."

Harry smiled.

"Touché. Kevin, listen. I'm thinking about something pretty far-out that might help us. Could you go over the criteria you remember from that sheet Stallings gave you?"

"I can do better than that."

He handed over the printout of Merlin's program—the criteria that had cost Beth DeSenza her job. Then he looped onto the Mosholu Parkway, heading back toward the Major Deegan Expressway and the city.

"How many companies are involved?" Harry asked.

"Probably five—that's not counting my company or Stallings's. I know two of them for sure—Comprehensive Neighborhood Health and Northeast Life and Casualty. What companies the other three represent, I don't know yet, although I might be able to find out if I really work at it."

"Don't do anything to ruffle anyone's feathers. These guys

clearly don't have much patience with people who upset them."
Harry studied the criteria. "The lowest projected cost to qualify
for termination was—what again? Half a million?"

"Exactly."

Harry rolled up the printout and tapped it against his fist.
His idea was beginning to take shape.

"Kevin, I really appreciate that you've come to me before
going to the DA," he said. "Now I've got something to show
you."

He handed over a folded copy of the poster. Kevin glanced
at it, then pulled off into the breakdown lane and turned on the
interior light.

"Never saw him before," he said after half a minute.

"He's the man who killed Evie. We have proof. I saw him
outside her room just before the injection. Her roommate saw
him *in* the room. And he left a fingerprint that was identified by
the FBI lab. His name's Anton Perchek. He's a doctor, Kevin.
An M.D. He's known all over the world as a master of torture,
and for keeping victims alive and awake during torture. He was
supposed to have died in a helicopter accident escaping from
prison six years ago."

"And you think he's involved with The Roundtable?"

"I do. I think he's the one who carries out these . . . these
terminations."

Kevin handed back the poster and swung the car onto the
highway. For a time they rode in silence.

"You've got to nail that guy," Kevin said.

You've got to? Harry looked at him curiously, but didn't comment. Kevin's eyes remained fixed on the road.

"I have a thought," Harry said. "You said two of the companies involved were Comprehensive Neighborhood Health and
Northeast Life and Casualty. I don't have many patients with
Comprehensive, but I do have quite a few covered by Northeast
Life. Suppose I admitted one to my hospital and made up a
diagnosis that would qualify him for termination under this protocol?"

"Could you do that?"

"I think so. The real question is whether your knight from
Northeast Casualty would bite. What's his name?"

"Pat Harper. He's Lancelot, the one who made Stallings the offer to join the inner circle."

"So if anyone's actively involved in this thing, it would be him. That's good."

"But you're suggesting taking a patient and deliberately exposing him to this Anton Perchek? Who would do such a thing?"

"Actually," Harry said, "I have someone in mind who would be happy to. Only he's not exactly a patient of mine. Could you take me to my office? It's on 116th near Fifth."

"Sure. I knew it was right to contact you."

Once again, Loomis's words and the way he spoke them made Harry feel uneasy. Not once had he talked about the implications for him and his family of what he was doing. In fact, not once had he spoken of his family at all. He had chosen to contact Harry before going to the DA. Why? *You've got to nail that guy.* Why not *we?*

Suddenly Harry knew. What had been troubling him so about the man was that he sounded detached, as if the events he described had happened to someone else entirely. He had chosen to speak with Harry before seeking out the DA because he never had any intention of going to the authorities. In fact, he had no intention of seeing this thing through. All at once a good deal about this strange ride made sense. Loomis's calmness. His lack of fear. Loomis was an insurance executive. Harry suspected that his death would leave his family well provided for.

"You okay?" Harry asked as they approached the lights of the city.

"Huh? Oh, sure. I'm still worried about what's going to happen. But I feel much more hopeful after talking to you."

"Good. We *can* put an end to The Roundtable, you know."

"I know."

The sadness in his voice was unmistakable now.

"Kevin, you said you knew about me and the war."

"What I read in the papers."

"The platoon I was with was ambushed. We were caught in a vicious firefight, with mortar shells dropping on us from a nearby hill. Most of our kids were killed or hurt badly. I managed to drag three of them to the medevac chopper. That's what I got the decoration for—as if I even knew what I was doing at that point. Then a shell exploded right behind me. I think it hit a mine, because it seemed like half the jungle blew up. I have no idea who dragged me out of there. It was about a week before I woke up. They had taken what metal and other debris they could out of my back, along with part of one kidney. I spent months in a rehab hospital. The pain was wicked, and for a long time I thought I might not walk."

"But you did."

"That's sort of the point. About three months into my rehab, I decided I couldn't take it anymore. I snuck off in my wheelchair with a revolver tucked under the sheet. For half an hour—oh hell, I really don't even know how long—I sat in the woods with this gun in my mouth and my finger on the trigger."

"Why didn't you pull it?"

Harry shrugged.

"I guess I just decided it wasn't my job."

They had crossed the river into the city now, and were heading toward Harry's office.

"Good for you."

"Hopeless is a relative term, Kevin. James Stallings is pretty much hopeless. You aren't. Think about that, will you?"

For a moment it seemed Kevin was about to say something, but instead he just nodded and focused on the road. Harry felt he had gone as far as he could in counseling a man he did not know. At least he had made his point. They rode in silence until Loomis pulled up at Harry's office.

"Is there anything else I should know before I go about creating a worm for Sir Lancelot to bite on?"

"Just follow the protocol," Loomis said. "I wish you luck."

Harry stepped out onto the street. The rain had stopped, but the humidity was still close to 100 percent.

"I'd like about a week before you go to the DA," he said. "If we're going to pull this off, publicity would really hurt."

"No problem. I'll check with you first, anyway."

"Thanks. And Kevin?"

"Yes?"

"Do everyone a favor and see this one through."

Loomis looked at him without making eye contact. "Yeah, sure," he said. "Thanks."

It was the middle of the night before Harry found what he was looking for—a male patient, age thirty-five to fifty-five, whose insurance carrier was Northeast Life and Casualty. Max Garabedian, a forty-eight-year-old school custodian. Garabedian, who was compulsive about his work and his body, was something of a hypochondriac. But in the main, he was healthy. And that was what Harry needed to know. There was only one way his scheme could work, and countless ways in which it could go haywire. But barring a freak accident, having Max Garabedian show up in some hospital when he was already an inpatient at MMC would not be one of them.

Harry considered calling Garabedian to explain what he was about to do. But if the man agreed, he would be open to charges of insurance fraud. *No,* he decided. Max Garabedian would have to be hospitalized for treatment of his expensive, potentially fatal illness without his knowledge. Harry copied down all the pertinent data the hospital admitting office would need to know.

Now there were only two problems: coming up with an appropriately dire condition, and convincing Ray Santana to become the bait.

CHAPTER 34

Harry stepped off the elevator onto Grey 2 and headed directly for the chart rack next to the nurse's station. He was trying to be unobtrusive, but he knew that every nurse, aide, and secretary on the floor was aware of his arrival. He was also trying to appear nonchalant, although he felt more and more like he was on night patrol in the jungle. It was his third day of making rounds on the patient in room 218, the man registered as Max Garabedian. In order to clear his name from one felony, he was willfully committing another, probably *several* others. That their charade had survived even this long was a tribute to meticulous preparation and incredible luck. But the clock was ticking.

It had taken two days of intense work before Harry was set to admit Ray Santana to the Manhattan Medical Center. The diagnosis he had chosen for his creation was acute lymphocytic leukemia, complicated by a low white-blood-cell level and bacterial endocarditis—a serious, potentially lethal infection of the heart valves. To up the ante for Sir Lancelot's insurance company, he added a code and special note implying that Garabedian was being evaluated for total body radiation and a bone marrow transplant.

To test the case, Kevin Loomis had run the data through the computers of Crown Health and Casualty. The projected cost of treating Max Garabedian's illnesses over the 2.2 years he was projected to have left to live was $697,000. A bone marrow transplant would add $226,000 to the equation, partly by increasing his life expectancy 13.6 years. If Lancelot was using The Roundtable's selection program, Max Garabedian would light up on the Northeast Life computers like a flare.

Harry opened Garabedian's record and reviewed the notes and laboratory reports he had inserted there, including a dictation he had done using the name of the chief of hematology. He had signed the note himself and intercepted the copy as it was being placed in the hematologist's cubby. Such maneuvers were necessary to keep the nurses and chart reviewers from becoming suspicious. But each move carried with it the danger of discovery, and Harry was definitely feeling the strain. He had been sleeping only four or five hours a night, had absolutely no appetite, and had developed a nasty, dry cough that he felt certain was nothing more than nerves.

And to heighten the tension, there had been absolutely no sign that The Roundtable or The Doctor was nibbling at the bait.

Harry wrote a lengthy, problem-oriented progress note in the chart. As had been the case during the first two days of rounds, no one spoke to him unless he addressed them directly. It was just as well. The less anyone asked him, the less he would have to lie. And lying was something he had never done very smoothly.

To discourage hospital personnel from visiting Max's room, Harry also added "probable tuberculosis" to the mix—all in all, enough pathology to give even the most intrepid caregiver pause. Given Ray Santana's gaunt appearance, sallow complexion, and chronic five o'clock shadow, Harry knew that hospital personnel would have no trouble connecting him with his frightening inventory of diagnoses.

Felony.

Garabedian, whom Harry had labeled in his admission history "a successful commodities trader," was admitted to an isolation room. Throughout his hospitalization, he would be tended to by his own special-duty nurses. The night-shift "nurse" was a private detective named Paula Underhill. The day and evening shifts were being covered by Maura, wearing glasses and a brunette wig. As Garabedian would be on precautions, both "nurses" would be required to wear surgical masks and gowns. Of course, Anton Perchek would be masked and gowned as well. But both Maura and Santana felt they would still be able to pick him out. And Paula Underhill, a wiry, Brooklyn-born black belt in Kenpo karate, was more than willing to try.

Felony.

Having special-duty nurses also helped solve one of the thornier problems Harry had tackled: laboratory tests. He ordered blood work each day, but none of it included Ray's white-blood-cell count, which would have been normal. But with Garabedian having his own nurses, the nurses on the floor would almost certainly follow his laboratory tests less closely, if at all. The trick had been to create a patient requiring an insufferable amount of work, and then to provide the regular staff with the salvation of a private nurse. Harry did insert fabricated admission blood counts from his office into the inpatient chart and decided he could improvise and produce more lab work depending on what he was hearing from the staff. He was hearing nothing.

Most of the other details were simple to work out—at least in theory. The intravenous line would be taped to Ray's skin and wrapped in gauze. IV medications would be run into the gauze or into the sink. Oral medications would be discarded immediately or squirreled away beneath Ray's tongue until they could be. And of course, Percodan or Demerol would be ordered every three to four hours as needed for pain.

Felony.

The final hurdle was Ray's absolute insistence on having his gun close at hand. Both the private detective, who was carrying a gun of her own, and Maura, who was not, agreed to help him conceal the weapon if needed.

Felony. Felony. Felony.

Harry finished his note by indicating that Garabedian's condition was improving slightly, but that another ten to fourteen days of hospitalization were anticipated. His goal was to fabricate as many complications as possible. Northeast Life and Casualty, like most insurers in the brave new medical world, had a team of peer reviewers that checked the records of hospitalized patients, poised to terminate benefits if the database said it was time for "the diagnosis" to be treated at home.

Outside room 218 was a steel cart with the gloves, gowns, and masks required for infectious-disease isolation. Harry prepared himself and entered the room, closing the door tightly behind him. Maura was in a chair, sketching in an artist's pad. Ray was propped in bed watching *Regis and Kathie Lee*.

"Any problems?" Harry asked.

"He wants me to give him a bed bath," Maura said.

"Hey, I got one a couple of times a day from the nurses the last time I was in the hospital," Ray whined. "Just because I'm not sick is no reason I shouldn't get tender loving care."

"No bed baths," Harry said, "but I will write orders for three enemas a day instead."

"And to think, I was embarrassed even to ask for one."

"I assume there haven't been any sightings."

"Not even of a nurse. It's like they think the plague is in here."

"They do. Maura, anything I can do for you?"

"Just find a way to have you-know-who make an appearance."

Harry motioned to Ray's pillow.

"No problem keeping that concealed?"

"Not as long as my nurse, here, keeps volunteering to do things so the people out there don't have to. They've already thanked her so many times, I wouldn't be surprised if they took up a collection for her. Any progress in the outside world?"

"The calls have slowed down, but they're still coming in. One lab tech from Good Samaritan swears our man was a balding medical resident from Poland. A nurse from University Hospital is certain he's an orderly there, only with dark hair and an earring."

"He probably was both," Santana said. "If we could ever pinpoint what days he was spotted in those hospitals, I'd bet we'd find a death or two in patients insured by The Roundtable companies."

"Well, if what we're doing here doesn't work, I promise I'll help you put those posters back up. By that time, I'll have nothing to lose."

"True enough. But if something goes wrong here and we get caught, I'd be surprised if they'd even let you back in this hospital as a patient."

"But hey, amigo, we've got our system down pat," Harry said with comic bravado. "What on earth could possibly go wrong?"

All day Ray Santana had been having a more difficult time than usual with pain, primarily behind his eyes and in his fingertips. He had received a Percodan at ten in the morning and required a shot of Demerol five hours later. Finally, fifteen minutes after the shot, he drifted off into a fitful sleep. A powerful antibiotic, ordered to treat his heart-valve infection, was dripping from a plastic IV bottle into the thick gauze bandage wrapped around his arm.

Maura washed her face in preparation for her sixth eighthour shift in three days, and her second one in a row. She felt tired, but still keyed up. Their trap had been a long shot from the very beginning. But it hadn't collapsed around them yet.

Santana was beginning to breathe more deeply and regularly as Maura settled down in her chair with the latest *People*. Next to alcohol, the magazine remained the most addictive thing she had ever found. And like booze, it was perfectly easy to keep away from—as long as she didn't start. The door to the room was nearly closed. From out on the floor, she heard the footsteps and multiple conversations of a group of people approaching. Then there was a man's voice.

". . . The hospital has three rooms with the reverse ventilation necessary for proper infectious-disease isolation," he was saying. "The new wing will be connected through this floor, and will provide three more. That will make this hospital number one in the city in the event of an infectious epidemic. . . ."

Maura, her concentration split between the magazine and the lecture, did not realize that Santana was suddenly awake, up on one elbow, rubbing at his eyes.

"Maura," he rasped, "can you see him?"

"Can I see who?"

"The man, dammit! The man who's talking!"

His eyes were wild from the drug, his mouth cotton-dry.

". . . But you say the cost per day of these rooms is now more than double a standard room?" a second voice was asking.

"Yes, but compared with what's charged at medical centers comparable to this one, that's still a bargain. Now, if you ladies and gentlemen will follow me this way, I'll show you the latest in . . ."

Santana was sitting bolt upright now, the pillow on his lap shielding his gun. Panicked, Maura threw her magazine aside and moved toward him. Ray, perspiring profusely now, was clumsily trying to disengage himself from the bedclothes and IV line at the same time.

"Open the door!" he demanded in a gravelly whisper. "Open it now!"

"Please, tell me what's going on."

"Dammit, Maura, hurry! Open the fucking door!"

Santana was on his feet now, still shielding his pistol. Maura swung the door open. About ten yards down the hall, amidst the usual midday crowd of nurses, patients, and visitors, a group of ten or eleven well-dressed men and women were moving slowly away from them.

"Excuse me," Maura called out to them. "Excuse me, please."

The speaker stopped and the group turned in unison. For several frozen seconds, they stood there as Santana peered out at them from beside his bed. Maura scanned the group, too. But at that distance she was unable to determine which of them, if any, was Anton Perchek.

"You son of a bitch!" Santana suddenly yelled, raising his gun. "You fucking son of a bitch!"

Instantly, there was screaming and chaos in the hallway as the business people and perhaps a dozen others dove for cover or turned to run.

The IV line pulled away from the plastic bottle as Santana bolted toward the door. The portable pole on which it hung clattered to the floor. He stumbled over it and lurched against Maura, knocking her to one knee and momentarily losing his balance at the same time.

"You son of a bitch!" he hollered again.

The IV line dangling from beneath the bandage on his arm, he braced himself against the doorway, leveled his gun, and fired the length of the hallway. The shot reverberated like a cannon blast. Everyone who was still standing dove to the floor. The screaming intensified. Scrambling to her feet behind Santana, Maura saw the glass that was covering a large floral print at the very far end of the hallway shatter from the bullet. Several feet to the right of the picture, three of the businessmen jammed through the door to the stairway. Waving his gun wildly with his IV line snapping like a whip, Santana sprinted barefoot after the men, down a gauntlet of screaming, terrified visitors, staff, and patients.

"Call security!" someone shouted.

"Get him!" someone else yelled.

Several men had gotten to their feet and were running— though with some caution—after Ray, who had now reached the end of the corridor and exploded through the stairway door. Another gunshot echoed back through Grey 2, then another.

Maura stripped off her gown and mask. Her only thought was to get away before anyone remembered her and started asking her questions. She was wearing a store-bought nurse's uniform and a shoulder-length wig. While the action and attention were still fixed on the far end of the hallway, she moved quickly in the opposite direction, to the stairway past the elevators. Once on the stairs, she raced down to the first floor, then took a calming breath and stepped into the main corridor of the hospital. She had gone less than ten feet when two uniformed security men charged past her and up the stairs. Moments later, two NYPD officers, one of them shouting into a radio, ran past, heading for the far end of the hospital.

The response to the crisis was rapid and well coordinated. Maura felt certain that it would be only a few minutes before Ray Santana was captured . . . or worse. She found herself hoping that before he was taken or killed, he at least got a clean shot at The Doctor.

Battling to maintain her composure, she strolled through the crowded front lobby. There was a mounting electricity in the air, along with an urgent exodus through the main doors, as word spread of a crazed gunman loose in the hospital.

"Not another one," she heard someone say as she exited with the crush into bright late-afternoon sunlight. "It seems like every time you turn around some wacko is shooting up a post office or hospital."

With police sirens blaring, Maura walked away from the medical center. In less than a block, half a dozen cruisers had screamed past her. Loudspeakers were blaring, and a number of uniformed policemen were sprinting toward the streets circumscribing the medical center.

She was two blocks from the hospital when she finally felt safe stopping to call Harry. She phoned the office first. Mary Tobin was there, but Harry had had no further patients and had left for home half an hour before. He had told her he would be in the hospital at five, making evening rounds on his two inpatients.

"Mary, there's been some trouble at the hospital," Maura said. "I can't explain right now, but I suspect before too long you'll get some details if you turn on the news. I think you ought to close the office as soon as possible and go home."

Mary was too wise, and had been through too much in the past weeks, to ask for clarification.

"Whatever you say, child," she said.

"Thanks for understanding," Maura said. "Now, I've got to call Harry. Oh, by the way, the Max Garabedian you'll hear them talking about on the news is Ray Santana."

"Who?"

"Ray—I mean Walter Concepcion. We'll get back to you as soon as we can, Mary. Please go home. Get out of there now."

Maura fished out another quarter and called the apartment. The machine answered.

"Harry, please, it's me, Maura," she said. "Harry, if you're listening, please pick up. . . . Harry? . . ."

She was about to hang up when he came on the line.

"Maura, hi. Sorry to make you do that. I'm still screening calls. But listen, we've had a break. Maybe a big one. I'll be heading into the hospital in just a few minutes to tell you and Ray about it."

"Harry," she said, "I don't think I'd do that if I were you. . . ."

CHAPTER 35

By the time Maura reached the apartment, news bulletins of the crazed gunman at the Manhattan Medical Center were already blanketing the airways. Max J. Garabedian, a forty-eight-year-old stockbroker, had quite suddenly charged from his hospital room wildly firing a gun down the hallway. Details were sketchy, but as yet no injuries had been reported. And Garabedian, who was wearing blue pajamas and no shoes at the time, remained at large.

Furious at Santana, and as close to panic as Maura had ever seen him, Harry paced from one end of the apartment to the other, speaking as much to himself as to her.

"I shouldn't have trusted him. As soon as he put those damn posters up I should have brushed him off like—like . . . I hope he's okay. But right now I want to strangle him. I absolutely want to strangle him. . . . It must have been Perchek out there to upset him so. But why didn't *you* spot him? . . . The police could show up here any minute, Maura. Insurance fraud, attempted murder—who knows what else? . . . Dickinson will have a field day with this one, a jubilee. . . . What in the hell am I supposed to do now?"

The fiasco at the hospital wasn't the only serious development Harry had to deal with. He had only a short time left in which to make a decision that would cost him twenty-five thousand dollars—almost every bit of savings he had. Santana's meltdown had forced him into a corner. The police were certain to arrive at the apartment before long. If he was going to accept the deal offered by a stranger on the phone, he had to make preparations and leave before they came.

"Please sit, honey," she said. "Just for a couple of minutes. Sit and try to relax a little."

She turned back to Channel 11. The reports were varying widely from station to station, most of which were still rushing crews over to the hospital. But Channel 11 and one other station had already announced that Garabedian's physician was Dr. Harry Corbett, still the chief suspect in the bizarre murder of his wife, Evelyn DellaRosa, who had also been a patient at MMC.

Harry was concerned for what the real Max Garabedian was about to go through. He had tried calling the school custodian at home, but got no answer. Almost certainly, the man was still at his job, although Harry had no idea at which school. Maura tried calling the Department of Education, but got no response there either.

"Only four-thirty and no one's there," she said. "No wonder so many kids in this town can't read."

"I don't know what to do," Harry said, for perhaps the tenth time. "That guy is expecting me in New Jersey at nine. The bank closes in another hour and fifteen minutes." He started pacing again. "We've got to start moving and moving fast. The longer I wait, the more likely it is the people at the bank will have learned that I'm in the news again. As it is, I'm not sure how happy they're going to be about forking over twenty-five thousand in cash. No matter what we decide, I've got to go and get that money now. Then I don't think we can come back here."

The call that had upped the ante by twenty-five thousand dollars had come to the apartment around the same time Ray Santana was shooting up Grey 2. When Harry arrived home from the office there were two messages on his machine, neither of them any more promising than the several dozen others they had logged over the past four days. Thinking that this call might be the change-of-shift check-in from Maura, Harry preempted the machine.

"Hello?"

"Is this Dr. Harry Corbett?"

The voice was a man's, youngish to middle-aged, with an accent Harry couldn't place with certainty—possibly German or Swiss.

"It is," Harry said.

"I am calling about the man in your poster and the fifty-thousand-dollar reward."

Harry made a face and wished he had let the answering machine do its job. Instead, he opened the log notebook and wrote in the time of the call.

"Go ahead," he said. "What hospital are you with?"

"I am with no hospital," the man said. "I learned about the flyers and your reward from my employer."

"And who is that?"

"The man in the poster. His initials are A.P. I will not speak his name over the phone. But you may already know it."

Harry stiffened at the mention of The Doctor's initials and immediately wondered if the caller could be Perchek, himself. But the voice was just too different from The Doctor's. Harry tried desperately to think of any reason why he should deny knowing who Anton Perchek was. *Would he be giving anything away?*

"Who are you?" he finally said.

"I handle security at his mansion and work as one of his bodyguards when he needs me to do so. I am at a pay phone right now. If you know A.P. at all, you know that he would not hesitate to kill me on the spot for making this call."

Harry had opened the spiral-bound notebook and was writing down as much of what the man was saying as possible.

"Go on," he said.

"I wish to meet with you tonight and to make an exchange. My information for your money."

"How much money?"

"I do not intend to remain in this area or even in this country after we meet. The Doctor and I have had some problems between us. I have reason to believe he intends to kill me. I will settle for half of what you have offered. Twenty-five thousand in cash."

"I don't have it."

"Then get it. I will not negotiate any lower than that. Twenty-five thousand or no deal. In exchange, I will give you the location of The Doctor's mansion and a recent photo of him taken without his knowledge. I will also tell you what security he has at the mansion. There you will find proof of his role in the death of your wife, and other evidence against him as well. How you handle that evidence will be up to you."

"But—"

"Dr. Corbett, I have no time for this. I have preparations of my own to make. Nine o'clock tonight. If you know The Doctor, you know why I do not trust anyone. You must do exactly as I say or we will both lose out. Now, here is what you are to do . . ."

Harry's bank was open until six that night. He had a total of $29,350 in his savings account, plus another five thousand or so in checking. He also had no personal connection whatsoever with anyone at the bank. Cursing himself for not making more money, and for not having taken the Hollins/McCue job, and for not going into ophthalmology, and for ever trusting Ray Santana, Harry took his savings and checkbooks and, with Maura, slipped out the rear basement door. They hurried to his garage for the BMW, stopped briefly at a newsstand, and then drove to his bank. With no idea how much space twenty-five thousand dollars would take up, especially in bill sizes of one hundred dollars or less, as the caller demanded, Harry had dumped out a briefcase and brought it along.

He entered the bank half an hour before closing. It was a moderately large branch and was still servicing a line waiting to see the six tellers. Twenty-five thousand was more cash than he had ever handled at one time. Was it conceivable the bank wouldn't have that much on hand?

Outside, Maura sat behind the wheel of Harry's BMW, the driver of the getaway car. The ground rules Perchek's security chief had laid down were that Harry was to bring the money to a landfill on the New Jersey side of the Hudson, not far from the city of Fort Lee. He was to come alone and to arrive at exactly 9 P.M. The directions to the spot were minutely detailed. The landfill was a dump site at the end of a winding dirt and gravel road. Harry was to drive to the center of the clearing, flash his lights four times, and wait beside the driver's-side door. The caller insisted on knowing the make and plate number of his car. If any other vehicle approached the landfill, whether it had anything to do with Harry or not, the meeting would be off . . . forever.

"The money means a lot to me," the caller had said, "but not enough to die for."

"How do I know this isn't a trap?" Harry asked.

"What kind of trap? To what end? If my employer wanted to kill you, you would be dead. It is that simple. If you know him at all, surely you know that. You are much more important to him alive. Besides, he delights in inflicting pain. The permanence and peace of death are his enemy."

Harry fought off an involuntary chill.

"I'll have a gun."

"You would be foolish if you didn't. I can assure you I will."

"I want a chance to inspect what you have before I turn over the money."

"You will have five minutes. . . ."

The young teller studied Harry's withdrawal slip for fifteen seconds. Then she verified his balance and looked through her Plexiglas cage at him, smiling.

"How will you want this?" she asked.

This was New York City, Harry reminded himself, not some boondocks village. A twenty-five-thousand-dollar cash withdrawal was everything to him, but probably not so uncommon to any of these people.

"Hundreds or less," he said, knowing that there was no sense trying for an air of nonchalance when she had his bank balance on the screen right in front of her.

"Did you bring something to carry the money in?" she asked, "or would you like one of our bags?"

"I have a briefcase."

He held it up for her to see. Her expression made it clear that she knew he was not one of the do-this-all-the-time people.

"I'll need to get an authorization from Mr. Kinchley," she said.

She left her post and headed out from behind the cages to

the desks where the junior officers sat. Harry followed her with his eyes and saw her approach a nattily dressed man in his late thirties with a sailor's tan and a chiseled jaw.

Come on, Harry thought. *Just give me the goddamn money*. If the bank withdrawal fell through, he had decided to call his brother Phil, who lived in Short Hills, about forty-five minutes from Fort Lee. But if he had to go that route, everything would become immeasurably more complicated.

He risked a glance out the front window. Maura was parked directly across the street. She was wearing dark glasses and a white, floppy-brimmed hat, which was bobbing animatedly—probably to something on the radio. The sight of her that way brought Harry a smile in spite of the tenseness of his situation.

Their relationship was being forged in the intense heat of the events that had drawn them together. But in just a short time, they had become friends in a way he and Evie never had. And that friendship, in turn, had given their lovemaking an openness and mutual caring that had never existed in his marriage.

Now, reluctantly, he was testing that friendship. Despite the mysterious caller's quite credible story, and his use of Perchek's initials, neither Harry nor Maura was at all comfortable with what he was being asked to do. Still, as the caller had said, they could think of no reason Perchek would want to lure him into a trap. It couldn't be for the money. Surely, twenty-five thousand dollars was nothing more than petty cash to the man.

It seemed as if there was nothing he could do but follow the instructions to the letter and hope for the best. But when Maura noticed the phone Evie had installed in the BMW, she had the germ of an idea. And soon after that, they had a plan. There were three elements essential to their strategy, and Maura possessed them all: another car, a cellular phone, and the courage and willingness to put herself in harm's way. They had stopped by a newsstand and bought a detailed street map of the area surrounding Fort Lee. On it, the landfill was nothing more than a blank spot near the river, two blocks square, surrounded by suburban streets. As soon as possible, Maura would pick up her car and her phone. She would then drive someplace near the landfill and, without being seen, find her way to a spot where she could hide and watch the field. At eight-twenty, after he had left the garage, she would call him. She would check in once again after he had reached the New Jersey side. If there was no sign of a trap, he could proceed to the landfill with more confidence. If problems did develop, she would have the phone to call for help. They had a gun, the one Harry had taken from the killer in Central Park. After arguing for Harry to keep it, she finally agreed that it made more sense for her to have it.

"Sir, I'm sorry for the delay."

Harry spun around to the teller's cage and then realized that the young woman was standing next to him.

"Oh, yes. No problem."

He held his breath and clenched his fists to keep his hands from shaking. It was already nearing rush hour. If the bank came through, Maura would still have a tough enough time getting across the George Washington Bridge, finding a place to leave her car, and then locating a back way into the landfill. If they had to deal with Phil, whether or not he came through with the money, it would be nearly impossible for her to get there in time.

"If you'll come with me, sir, Mr. Kinchley will have your money."

"That would be fine," he said, smiling calmly, his pulse hammering in his ears.

★　★　★

Kevin Loomis sat alone in his basement office, photographs of his family and his life with Nancy spread out on his desk beneath a checklist he had drawn up. Every item on the list had been taken care of now. The insurance policies were absolutely airtight as long as there was no suspicion that his death was a suicide. Suicide would cost him—would cost *Nancy*—two million of the three and a half million he had in force, to say nothing of five hundred thousand dollars in double indemnity accidental-death benefits. But he had worked out every movement, every moment, in the most exhaustive detail. There would be no suspicion of suicide.

He had put careful thought into the guest list he had drawn up for the barbecue dinner party they were giving the following night. The guests, fourteen in all, included the most respected, successful, influential, and community-conscious people they knew. Their pastor and his wife, Nancy's boss and his wife, the lawyer who was head of the local Little League association, the president of the Rotary Club. Nancy thought it a bit strange that Kevin had chosen to invite only two of their more fun-loving, beer-drinking friends, but she accepted Kevin's explanation that he wanted to thank some people before the move to Port Chester.

In fact, he wanted guests who would most effectively and eloquently vouch for his cheerfulness and his hospitality right up until the moment of the accident, as well as to the fact that he had "had a few." Two of them would accompany him down to the basement. The two he planned to pick were men at whose homes he had done minor repair work in the past, a store manager and the pastor. They would be on the stairs, their flashlight beams fixed on the water gushing from the detached washing machine hose. They would attest to Kevin having the skills necessary to take care of the emergency and would report on his movements through the inches-deep water on the concrete floor. The moment Kevin's hand came down on the shorted wire of the dryer would remain forever fixed in their minds. But what the hell. They were friends who would do anything for Nancy. And he was paying a far greater price.

The children were accounted for as well. Nicky and Julie were going to spend the night with friends. Brian would be with Nancy's parents. It was strange to think that tomorrow afternoon, when he sent them off, he would be looking at each of them for the last time. They would have a tough time of it, but not nearly as tough as if their family became destitute and their father went to prison.

Perhaps there really is an afterlife, he thought now. *Perhaps I'll be able to look in on them every single day.*

He stacked the photos up and reviewed each one for a final time. Then he wrapped them with a rubber band and set them in a drawer. The lists he tore up and threw in a plastic bag full of trash, which he would put in the barrels in the garage. Finally, he went once more to the washer and dryer to check on his handiwork. The twine that ran from the loosened hose out the basement window was in place. One pull and the hose would come free. Cutting the twine off and discarding it would be his next to last act on earth. The last would be innocently setting his hand on the back of the dryer.

Kevin knew that Harry Corbett suspected what he was planning to do. There was nothing subtle about the Vietnam story he had told that night in the car. And in fact, he had thought a great deal about what Corbett was trying to tell him, that his situation wasn't hopeless. That was all well and good for Corbett to say. He didn't have three kids to provide for.

Kevin had spoken with him several times since then and had been careful to sound upbeat and positive. He did not believe Corbett intended to act on his concerns. What was there for him to do, anyway? A little more than twenty-four hours and it would all be over.

Kevin inspected the setup he had created around the washing machine and dryer. The police would come over and file some sort of report. But there was no way anyone could prove this wasn't an accident. Absolutely none.

He sighed the relief of a man who had just completed a job and done it well. Tonight he would have a wonderful dinner with his family. And later on, he would make love to Nancy as he had never made love before.

CHAPTER 36

The late summer heat wave that had been blamed for brownouts, accidents, and deaths throughout the city had finally broken. The early evening temperature was in the mid-sixties, with a decent breeze and the threat of rain. Harry dropped Maura at her car at exactly six and then returned to the parking-space condominium to await his eight-fifteen departure. The BMW's dashboard clock had been out of commission for years, and neither he nor Evie had ever bothered to get it fixed, so he was using his Casio to keep track of time. He was nearing the garage when Maura called to check in, test her cellular phone, and report that traffic from her apartment to the bridge was only moderate. Her next call would be the one at eight-twenty that they had prearranged.

"This is it, Harry," she said. "You'll see. By ten o'clock tonight we'll be ready to go to the police. They'll have to believe us this time. Just hang in there."

"*You* hang in there. And please be careful."

Harry parked in his spot and walked out of the garage. A police cruiser was moving slowly along, half a block away, perhaps looking for him, perhaps not. Thanks to Ray Santana, there was now absolutely no place where he could safely go. He returned to the BMW, flipped on the radio again, and waited.

WINS, the all-news station, was still broadcasting updates

every ten minutes or so on the bizarre developments surrounding the gunman at Manhattan Medical Center. The real Max Garabedian had been taken into police custody, questioned, and released. He had returned to his 103rd Street apartment and was refusing to speak to the press until advised to do so by his attorney. In a prepared statement, read by his lawyer, Garabedian denied knowing anything of the man admitted to Manhattan Medical Center under his name. He denied having any relationship with Harry other than patient/physician, but called Harry "an intelligent, dedicated doctor," and expressed his determination to hold off on any judgment until the truth came out.

Harry gave passing thought to trying to call Garabedian from his car phone. But this was no time for him to be doing anything at all except sitting and waiting until eight-fifteen.

There was more. Ray Santana had not been caught. Authorities were at a loss to explain how a gunman in pajamas with no shoes or socks could have made it out of the hospital with security police and dozens of NYPD officers ringing the place. The broadcaster, clearly losing a battle with self-restraint, opined that this was New York, after all. Maybe the oddly clad fugitive had simply stepped onto the streets of Manhattan and blended in.

At seven o'clock, MMC public-relations director Barbara Hinkle held a news conference, excerpted on WINS. The hospital, she said, was grateful no one had been hurt in the unfortunate incident. Hospital officials would have nothing further to say until a preliminary investigation into the near-calamity was completed. She did add that hospital authorities as yet had had no luck in reaching Dr. Harry Corbett, the physician who admitted the gunman to Grey 218.

"I am sure you all know," she said, "that Dr. Corbett has been under a great strain lately as the result of the tragic death of his wife. I have been told he has been under a physician's care for his grief reaction, as well as for some post-traumatic stress issues related to his heroic service in Vietnam. . . ."

Post-traumatic stress!

"Hospital Barbie speaks with forked tongue," Harry said aloud.

Clearly, MMC's spin doctors had already met and decided on their strategy for dealing with the collective disasters brought down on their house by Dr. Harry Corbett—post-traumatic stress. Harry wondered what name they would come up with if anyone ever demanded to know who his shrink was.

". . . We at the hospital are speculating that Dr. Corbett borrowed the name of Max Garabedian in order to hospitalize someone he cared about who was very ill but without health insurance," Hinkle went on, "possibly a fellow Vietnam veteran. The plan backfired when his patient went haywire."

"Nice," Harry said. "Not bad."

And not that far off, either, he thought.

The rest of Hinkle's press conference added nothing of substance except that nursing officials were looking into the identities and backgrounds of the special-duty nurses brought into the hospital by the gunman.

For forty minutes, nothing new was broadcast. Then, with just half an hour to go before Harry was to leave, one of the many mysteries connected with the case was reported solved. An electrician doing work on the heating system of the hospital had been found by a maintenance man, bound and gagged in the subbasement. He had been robbed at gunpoint by a man answering the fugitive's description. His clothes and shoes were taken, along with twenty-five dollars from his wallet. The wallet was then returned to him. Police were checking it for fingerprints, as well as the hospital room where the gunman was a patient for three days.

"He was nervous and scared, I think," the electrician said. "But he was decent enough to me. He gave me back my wallet because he said he knows what a hassle it is getting a new driver's license. He didn't hurt me. But I think maybe he would have if I didn't do as he asked. . . ."

Harry checked the time. Eight-ten. Outside the garage, dusk was gradually yielding to night. The lights of the city were on. He started the BMW and slowly, ever so slowly, rolled down the ramp to the exit. Finally, at exactly eight-fifteen, he shut off the radio and pulled out onto the street. The game was afoot.

Harry drove past one block, then another. He didn't feel all that nervous, but his hands were white on the wheel. He glanced at his watch. It was twenty past. *Where was she? Where was the call?* He checked the time again. *Okay,* he decided, *maybe it's only eight-eighteen.* Moments later, the phone buzzed. He snatched up the receiver.

"Yes," he said.

"Harry, I'm in a tree," Maura whispered with breathless excitement. "I'm up in a fucking tree in the woods next to a dump. Do you believe it? If I had known there was a man around like you who could get me to climb trees at garbage dumps at night in New Jersey with a gun in my fanny pack, I never would have bothered drinking."

"Well, I'm no place that exotic," Harry said, whispering although there was no need to. "Ninety-sixth, heading for the parkway. Is anyone there yet?"

"Not a soul. I found a great place to leave the car and a perfect place to hide."

"And you're sure no one saw you?"

"Positive. Are you being followed?"

"I can't tell yet."

"It doesn't make any difference whether they do or not. Listen, Harry, I think I see a car coming up the road. I'll call you again at ten of nine unless he's standing too close to this tree."

"You're doing great, Maura. Are you warm enough? I think it's going to rain soon."

"Hey, I'm fine. I told you. Tonight's the night."

With one eye on the road ahead and one on the rearview mirror, Harry swung onto the Henry Hudson Parkway. Several cars behind, he caught sight of a dark sedan, which he felt fairly certain had been with him from the beginning. Maura was right, though. It really didn't matter whether the caller had someone tailing him or not. He was going to follow instructions to the letter. Maura was their ace in the hole.

By the time he had crossed the George Washington Bridge, a misty rain had begun to fall. Harry found windshield wipers annoying and had always postponed turning them on until he absolutely had to. This time he switched them on at the first droplets. If things came unraveled tonight, it wasn't going to be because he did something pigheaded or stupid.

Once on the New Jersey side of the river, he consulted the directions. After two miles he swung off the main road into a densely built, working-class neighborhood. The streets were tree-lined, and the small yards of the clapboard houses were strewn with balls, Big Wheels, and the other trappings of new families. The sedan followed several blocks behind, its lights off. Harry felt certain he could see two people silhouetted inside. He easily located the corner where he had been instructed to stop and wait for one minute. He was pulling away when the phone buzzed. Maura was several minutes early. And Harry knew as he was reaching for the receiver that there was trouble.

"Yes?"

"Harry, stop right now!" she said in a panic-driven whisper. "This place is crawling with police. A dozen of them. Maybe more. Their cruisers are out of sight, and you wouldn't know a thing was wrong. But they're here."

His blood suddenly ice, Harry glanced in the mirror. The sedan was still there, about two or three blocks back. He shifted into gear and began slowly rolling down the street.

"Go on," he said.

"Harry, your friend Dickinson's here. At one point he was about ten feet from this tree. Now he's strolling around checking that everyone's in place."

"You're sure?"

"I'm sure. He's working with some lieutenant who seems to be from the local police. He's very excited about being here to nail you. From what I could hear, someone called and tipped off the police that you had demanded a meeting at this place, that you have a body with you, and will pay twenty-five thousand dollars for this guy to get it a thousand miles from here and bury it where it will never be dug up. The man said you were crazy. That you killed people for fun. He wanted nothing to do with you, except to have you in jail where you couldn't hurt him. You've got to get out of here, Harry."

His mind whirling, Harry began slowly to accelerate.

"Just stay out of sight until it's safe to go home," he said. "Then go to my apartment. I'll be in touch."

He heard her telling him to be careful as he set the receiver down. Then he glanced at the directions he had written down. In one more block, he would go left or straight instead of turning right as instructed. It would take the men in the sedan several seconds to realize he was diverging from the plan. Three or four seconds at the most. That was all he had. His best bet was to try and get back to the highway. He sped up to around forty.

Bury a body? How could Perchek ever expect such an out-landish story to get Harry into trouble? . . . Unless . . .

In the same instant Harry understood what was happening, he cut his lights, swung a sharp left, and hit the gas. He made a sliding right, then another left. The siren was on behind him now, and he could see the blue strobe through the trees. The streets, baked to bone-dry for almost two weeks, were slick with rain and oil. He skidded into another turn, onto a street that was a long straightaway to the main road. The speedometer was near-ing eighty. He had always been a laid-back driver and rarely drove this fast even on a turnpike. A couple backing out of their drive to go to the store, a kid on her bicycle—there were any number of possibilities for disaster now. Undoubtedly, the men in the unmarked cruiser had called for backup as well.

He tried desperately to think things through. The best he could do was to acknowledge that the situation was absolutely horrible. He was racing around rain-soaked streets in a neighbor-hood that was completely foreign to him, at night, in a seven-year-old car, almost certainly with a body in the trunk. *One minute.* That was about all he had left. One minute before they caught up with him or the backups cut him off.

He was closing fast on a main road. Assuming it was the one he had taken in, it was a four-laner with no divider. The sedan was on the straightaway now, no more than three blocks behind and gaining. Harry was about to brake so that he could turn into the northbound lane. But at the last moment, he saw a small gap in the traffic each way. He slammed down the acceler-ator and barreled across all four lanes. A tractor trailer was com-ing from each direction. In a cacophony of air brakes, screeching tires, and horns, they both swerved, skidding in a ponderous, grotesque pas de deux. The cruiser had no choice but to stop and back away from the potentially deadly dance. There was a street directly across from the one Harry had come up. He shot down it. Slowing a bit, he glanced behind him just as one of the trail-ers, in excruciating slow motion, toppled onto its side.

In the distance, he could hear sirens—many of them. He

swung into a side street, and then halfway up the driveway of a darkened house. The sirens were getting louder. He stepped quietly out of the car, expecting at any moment to have all the lights in the house go on at once, or else to be attacked by a rottweiler. He glanced about. He had no idea at all where he was, except that the river was somewhere in the direction the house was facing. Just past the garage, he could see woods beyond the backyard, to the west. With luck he could make it there. Then he would have to see. He snapped open the briefcase and stuffed what he thought was about seven thousand dollars into his pockets. He was wearing slacks and dress shoes—the perfect outfit for impressing the people at the bank, but not much good for running from the police. Unfortunately, at this moment, he would have to make do.

He took the key and inserted it in the trunk. Part of him wanted just to leave it closed and run. He dreaded confronting this part of the nightmare Perchek had conjured up for him. Later, wherever he was, he could find out from the news bulletins what was inside. A siren sounded from close by, and moments later a squad car raced down the street, its strobes flashing. Harry threw himself into the shadows. The net was closing. He had little time left. He turned the key, hesitated again, and then threw the trunk open.

Hot air, heavy with the stench of blood and death, immediately wafted up into his face. Below him, crammed into the smallish trunk, lay Caspar Sidonis. His perfect face was waxen, his hair matted with blood from entry and exit bullet holes just above his ears.

Bile washed up into Harry's throat. He hesitated, actually trying to think of something he should be doing. Then, swallowing back the burning acid, he quietly lowered the trunk.

"Poor bastard," he whispered.

A second cruiser, this one with no lights or siren, made its way past, checking every house and driveway on the other side of the street with a spotlight. Harry again ducked into the shadows. His side of the street would be next. With a final glance at the trunk, he moved quickly into the backyard and scaled a five-foot chain-link fence. As he leapt to the ground, he experienced a breath-catching pain in his chest, exploding from just beneath his sternum up into his jaws and ears. He stumbled, then fell to the rain-soaked, mossy ground. Instantly, he was drenched, both from the rain and from his own sudden perspiration.

The sirens seemed to be all around him now. He crawled deeper into the woods and then pulled himself upright on the trunk of a tree. The pain was leveling off. He battled back a wave of nausea without getting sick. Then he closed his eyes and took several calming breaths. Giving up was a very real possibility. Surely someone would believe he had been set up. Mel Wetstone had worked near-miracles already. Perhaps he could pull this one off as well.

No. The thought of being taken prisoner, of jail, of Albert Dickinson, was more than he could stand.

From a hundred yards behind him, he could hear voices. They had found the car. The pain was much less now. Almost gone. With the jungle survival training he had had in Vietnam and several thousand dollars in cash, at least he had a slim chance of escaping. He stuffed the money deeper in his pockets and pushed off from the tree. Then, keeping low and moving as quietly as possible, he began an awkward jog through the dense woods.

CHAPTER 37

High Hill, in elegant Short Hills, New Jersey, was an expansive fifteen-room colonial with a coach house and pool on three rolling acres. Built and christened by a liquor baron in 1920, it had kept its name through four subsequent masters. Phil Corbett, the latest in the line, had been living in the estate with his family for almost three years. He disliked the pretentiousness of house names and was constantly threatening to replace the *High Hill* placard on the fieldstone stele at the base of the driveway with one reading *High Upkeep*.

When the phone began ringing at ten-thirty on the night of August 30, Phil was eight hundred dollars up and studying a possible royal flush. The once-a-month, six-man game rotated from house to house, but the participants enjoyed playing at High Hill the most. Shortly after moving in, Phil had converted the music room into a soundproof, walnut-paneled, Wild West card room, complete with honky-tonk background music, sawdust on the floor, an overhead fan, Cuban cheroots, and brass spittoons. Stakes in the game were high enough to make it interesting. But there wasn't one of the players who couldn't comfortably absorb a five-thousand-dollar ding.

Earlier in the evening, several of the men had mentioned the latest news blitz involving Phil's older brother. Two of them,

Matt McCann and Ziggy White, both millionaires who had never finished college, had grown up with Phil in Montclair, and had known Harry fairly well.

"Talk about your big-time comedown," Matt said. "Remember how we all used to idolize Harry? He was the scholar who was going to go to college. We were the little shits who were going to go to jail."

"You *still* should idolize him," Phil replied. "He's a terrific guy. While we're all out trying to make an obscene amount of money, he's off helping people get well. Half the time, he doesn't even get paid."

"But what about all this nonsense at the hospital? This post-traumatic stress?"

"Harry has about as much post-traumatic stress as you do. Someone's out to get him. That's what he tells me, and that's what I believe."

"I hope you're right," Ziggy said. "I always liked Harry a lot. But you know, even Dillinger had a brother."

"He's not Dillinger, Ziggy. . . ."

The ringing persisted—five, six, seven times. Phil's agreement with Gail was that if she was in the house on poker night, she would answer all phone calls. But tonight, she had gone to the movies with friends. Phil studied his ten, jack, queen, king of diamonds, and then glared over at the phone, trying to will it to cease. Finally, he slapped his cards down.

"You gentlemen'll have to wait a minute for me to take your money," he said, rising. "But I'd advise you all to fold. I'm working on a straight flush."

"Yeah, sure," someone muttered.

"Hello?"

"Phil, it's me. Are you alone?"

Phil had no trouble picking up the urgency in his brother's voice.

"Ah, no. No, I'm not."

"Change phones, please."

Phil put the call on hold.

"I was lying about the straight flush," he said, burying his cards at the bottom of the deck. "You guys play on without me for a while."

In twenty minutes, Phil was back, his face heavy with concern.

"There's been some problems with my brother," he said. "I'm afraid we're going to have to call it a night."

"Anything we can do?" White asked.

"Actually, there is. I'd like it if you and Matt could stay behind. The rest of you just head home as quickly as possible. We'll settle up tomorrow. And if any of you want to, feel free to say a prayer for Harry. He's in it pretty deep right now and he's going to need all the help he can get."

"Phil, you be careful, now," one of the other three men said. "No one wants to believe somebody in their family could get into big-time trouble, but it happens."

"I know, Stan. Thanks. I'd like you to forget I got that call just now, but in the end, that's up to you."

The three men exchanged concerned glances. Then, without further question, they hurried for their cars. Ziggy White and Matt McCann remained behind. A few moments after the last car had left, a police cruiser, lights flashing, came up the drive.

"Matt, I'm going to need you to stay and watch the kids until Gail gets home," Phil said. "Maybe around eleven-thirty. Ziggy, I'm going to speak with these guys. Then I have to get out of here without being followed. Any ideas?"

During their school years, White had been a daredevil among daredevils—always diving in from the highest rock or shoplifting some unneeded item from the most theft-conscious store. He had gone on to make a small fortune as an options trader. Now, he mulled over the problem for just a few seconds.

"No sweat," he said, excitedly. "Matt'll hide while the cops are here. You make it clear your wife is out and you're babysitting. I'll walk them out and have a chat with them by the squad car. Meanwhile, you slip out the back. Take a flashlight, but only use it when you're certain it's safe. Go through your backyard and then across that little brook you have back there. If they're going to stake you out, they'll have to wait somewhere past the end of the driveway. I'll leave when they do and head out like I'm going home, but I'll turn off at Maitland. I'll meet you right by the Griffins' driveway. They're in England until after Labor Day. You know where that is, right? Okay. You can drop me off someplace near my house and keep the car as long as you need it."

★　★　★

Harry knelt in the dense undergrowth just beyond the soft shoulder of a rural two-lane road. The night wasn't that chilly, but he was soaked through and shivering. Thank God Phil had been home. Thank God he hadn't hesitated in agreeing to help. Now, if he would only show up. Accessory to murder was nothing he wanted to expose his brother to. But until he found Anton Perchek and a way to bring him down, staying free was the only realistic chance he had.

The biggest problem, since he didn't know exactly where he was calling Phil from, and Phil didn't know the Fort Lee area well at all, was finding a way to meet up. It was finally left to Harry to choose the right person to bribe into driving him to a spot they both knew—a little-traveled roadway that swung past a power substation not far from their childhood home in Montclair. It was the place where Harry first took his younger brother to introduce him to beer and cigarettes, only to find that Phil was already well acquainted with both.

The lucky man Harry selected was a motorcyclist on a Harley chopper. Harry watched from the woods beside a service station as the biker lumbered into the rest room and called him over as soon as he came out. The man was well tattooed and grizzly bear huge—as unlikely to be frightened off by Harry as he was to be tight with the police. The fare for the half-hour ride was agreed upon in seconds—a thousand dollars. Over his years in medicine, Harry had seen the ravages of bike accidents often enough to have developed a healthy fear of ever riding on what the ER docs cynically referred to as "donorcycles." But the biker, whose name was Claude, was worth the risk. Harry donned the spare Panzer Division helmet, hunched as low as the raised passenger seat would allow, clenched his teeth, and wrapped his arms around the bear.

"Hey, if you're gonna get that friendly, I want another hundred," the biker said, laughing.

"You don't speed and I won't get fresh," Harry replied.

Within the first mile or two, they had passed four police cars heading in the opposite direction.

"You must be some hot stuff," Claude called over his shoulder.

"Parking tickets," Harry yelled back.

During the half hour Harry had been crouched in the bushes by the substation, six cars had passed, one of them a Montclair police cruiser. Now, as he wiped a muddy hand across his forehead, he wondered what his next move should be. If there was any workable option available to him, any at all, his mind hadn't settled on it yet. On the plus side, he had miraculously made it through the trap Perchek had set for him in Fort Lee. Still, by the time the forty-minute ride was over, Harry's teeth were chattering mercilessly. He tipped the biker with a hundred-dollar bill as casually as if it were a one and accepted a death's-head pin in return. Now, as the fear that he and Phil had somehow miscommunicated took hold, he wished he had kept Claude around.

There were bends in the road about fifty yards in either direction from where Harry was concealed. The headlights of approaching cars reflected off the trees several seconds before they actually came into sight. Each time, as soon as he heard the engine noise or saw the reflected light, he flattened down in the shallow swale beside the road. And each time he got a bit filthier and, if possible, a bit more sodden.

Through the darkness and the persistent drizzle, he heard engine noise to his left. Moments later, reflected light shimmered high off the trees. A *truck*, he thought, burrowing back under cover. What it was instead was a mobile home, as large as a bus, moving along slowly, followed closely by a car. Harry froze as the two-vehicle caravan slowed even more and then stopped not ten feet away. Both drivers cut their engines and killed their headlights. Immediately, heavy darkness settled in again. The interior light on the massive RV flashed on and off as the door opened and closed. For several seconds there was dense silence. Then Phil called out.

"Harry? You out there?"

Before he could even reply, Harry had to work the immense tension from his muscles and his jaw. He worried in passing about the second car, but at this point he had to trust that Phil knew what he was doing.

"Right here, bro," he said.

He pushed himself to his feet and made an ineffectual stab at brushing some mud off. Phil met him at the front of the RV, which Harry could see now was a Winnebago.

"You okay?"

"Soaked, scared to death. Is that the same as okay?"

"Well, believe it or not, I have a warm-up suit inside that'll fit you."

"Who's in the car?"

"It's Ziggy White. Remember him?"

"The one who used to bet people he could drive a mile blindfolded?"

"I didn't want him to come with me, but he insisted. He can't get enough of living on the edge—you'd think being an options trader would do it. Besides, he says he'll never forget that you once kept Bumpy Giannetti from beating the snot out of him."

"Thank Ziggy for me," Harry said as Phil helped him up the step. "But tell him that if that's really the case, I probably just showed up at the right moment and presented Bumpy with a punching bag less likely to hit back."

The interior of the Winnebago was as grand as any hotel Harry had ever stayed in.

"This is incredible," he said, stripping off his shirt. "Is this yours?"

"For the time being, it's yours. The Luxor. Thirty-seven feet of everything you could ever ask for in a motor home. Two TVs with a dish on the roof, fax, phone, bar, ice maker, stereo system, washer/dryer, driver *and* passenger airbags, cherrywood cabinets. You told me you needed a car, but I got to thinking that you also needed a safe place to stay. Then I realized I had both all rolled up in one. We lease this baby from time to time to some people who need a hotel room, but don't want a hotel. It's registered to my corporation. The registration's in the glove compartment, along with a couple of sheets on where you can and can't take it and park it. My beeper number's there, too. You can reach me twenty-four hours a day."

"Phil, I . . . thanks. Thanks a lot. This is perfect. How much does it—"

"Hey," Phil said, stopping him with a raised hand. "If you have to ask, you really don't want to know."

Harry toweled off and pulled the stacks of soggy bills from his pockets.

"You neglected to mention the all-important microwave," he said.

"Just don't do them all at once." Phil tossed over the black Nike warm-up suit. "I don't think I could stand the thought of all that cash vaporizing in my RV. The fridge is pretty well stocked and there are some clothes in the closet that I think will fit you. Just be careful and don't stay in one place too long. Is there anything else you need?"

Harry thought for a moment, then took a pen and paper from the small mahogany writing desk and dashed off a note to Maura.

"The doorman at my co-op will take this up to her," he said. "Then I want you to back off and keep out of this. You've done way more than enough."

Phil slipped the letter into his pocket.

"We've had a funny life, Harry," he said. "I won't deny that over the years, especially after you won those medals in Vietnam, I pushed myself in business because I wanted to beat you out at something."

"Well, you did."

"So what? The point is it was always just something inside me. You never did or said anything to make me feel I had to top you. What difference does it make anyhow? It's not a contest. It never has been. It's our lives. You're my only brother, Harry. I don't want to lose you."

Harry stared at his brother through the dim light. It was the first time he had ever heard Phil talk this way. He leaned against the soft, leather headrest of the passenger seat.

"Remember that day in front of my office when you told me not to worry, that something would come along for me to push against? Well, something has, Phil. A monster. His name's Anton Perchek. He's an M.D. And I'm not going to stop pushing against him until he's finished or I am." He wrote the name down and passed it over. "If anything happens to me, this is the man who killed Evie. He also killed Caspar Sidonis, Andy Barlow, one of my favorite patients, and God only knows how many other people. The Feds know who he is, but they might not admit it. I think he did some torture work for the CIA. He's supposed to have died years ago, but they have a fingerprint of his taken from Evie's hospital room.

"I had stopped caring, Phil. I don't know why—maybe turning fifty, maybe Evie, maybe that goddamn family curse I've been so wrapped up in. But I care now, Phil. Thanks to that bastard, Perchek, things matter to me again. That woman, Maura, the one the note is for, she's very special. I want the chance to get to know her better. Maybe get married again someday—if not to her, then to someone like her. Maybe have a kid or two so *you* can be an uncle."

"I'll spoil the hell out of them. Do you know where you're going from here?"

"I do, but I don't want you to know. You're already going to have to lie to the police because of me."

"You know how to get hold of me."

"I do. Don't worry, Phil. I'm gonna win this one."

"I know. I know you are. Well . . . um . . . we'd better get going."

"Thank Ziggy for me. And give my love to Gail and the kids."

For a few seconds, the brothers stood in silence by the door. Then, for the first time since the death of their father, they embraced.

★   ★   ★

Rocky Martino, the night doorman at Harry's apartment building, had more than enough reason for having an extra nip or two. It had been the longest, most stressful night of his life. In the space of just a few hours, half of Manhattan seemed to have descended on him, everyone looking for Harry Corbett. The Manhattan police, the New Jersey police, even the FBI—something about moving a body across state lines. Crews from several TV stations and some radio people as well had come by and spoken with him. But all he could tell any of them was that he had no idea when Harry Corbett had left the building or when he would be back.

The one thing that he did not tell any of the news people, but he did tell the police, was that Maura Hughes had come back to the apartment at ten-thirty and was still there. Two officers had gone up and spoken to her for over an hour.

Early on, Rocky knew that he was in over his head and had the presence of mind to call down Shirley Bowditch, the president of the co-op association. She had handled everything. Now, at last, he was alone. He went to the maintenance closet just behind the door to the cellar. On the bottom shelf, in the base of a locked tool box, was his supply of nips. He selected an ounce of Absolut and downed it in a single gulp. The raspy burning brought warm, familiar tears to his eyes. When he returned to the lobby, a tall, broad-shouldered man in a sports coat was tapping on the glass, holding up a police badge. Rocky buzzed him in. The huge man introduced himself and the branch he was with, but whatever he said didn't register. Rocky told him his name.

"We need your help," the policeman said. "How long are you going to be on duty?"

"Noon," Rocky said. "I work midnight until noon. Armand Rojas, the other doorman and I decid—"

"Good. Good, Rocky. Now listen up. There's a woman up in Harry Corbett's apartment. Her name's Maura Hughes."

"So?"

"If she goes by cab to meet up with him, we want to be driving her." He guided Rocky to the street and pointed at a cab parked half a block away. "When you want a cab for her, just point at that one. We'll do the rest."

"O-Okay," Rocky said, intimidated by the man's size and brusqueness.

The giant fished out a bill from his wallet and handed it over. It was a fifty.

"Do this right, Rocky, and not a word to anyone, and there'll be another one of these in it for you."

Rocky took the bill and watched until the policeman had disappeared from sight. Then he headed back to the tool kit. He would do what the man asked because he was frightened of what would happen if he didn't, and because he wanted the other fifty. The guy who had gone upstairs an hour before with an envelope for Maura had only given him a twenty. He polished off another vodka. He liked Harry Corbett, and was sorry he was in such trouble. But hell, it wasn't Rocky Martino's fault.

He returned to the lobby. It was almost five in the morning. He had new money in his pocket and a glow in his gut as warm as sunrise. Outside, half a block away, the cab stood waiting. He licked his lips and thought about the sudden windfall, soon to be increased by another fifty bucks. No one could criticize him for cooperating with the police. No one at all.

CHAPTER 38

Four o'clock . . . five . . . five-thirty . . . The phone in Harry's apartment continued ringing almost incessantly. The bizarre events surrounding the gunman at Manhattan Medical Center, followed by the execution-style slaying of Caspar Sidonis, had thrust him into the center of the media spotlight. Maura sat alone in the den, watching the story evolve on local and national TV as she used the answering machine to screen calls. The Simpson and Tonya Harding cases had dominated the airwaves more, but not by that much. Stations were breaking for updates every five or ten minutes, and one was rehashing the events continuously. Footage of Sidonis's life and many accomplishments was beginning to appear.

Maura was emotionally and physically exhausted. But she was far too keyed up and worried about Harry to sleep. Tucked between the pillows of the sofa was the note that a man named White had delivered just a few hours before.

Maura—
   I'm okay. Meet me at 10 a.m. right in front of the place where we first met with Walter. If I don't show up, try again in three hours. I will do the same. Take several

*different cabs, then the subway, then walk. Be careful. You
will probably be followed.*
        Love,
           Harry

White would say nothing to her except that Harry was unharmed and safe. An hour later, Albert Dickinson had come up
to see her. Guns drawn, he and another policeman had searched
the apartment. Despite the other officer, Dickinson was as abra-
sive and disrespectful as he had been in the hospital. He had no
patience for hearing any stories from her about Harry Corbett's
innocence, Anton Perchek, or anyone else. All he wanted to
know was where he could find his man.

"Miss Hughes, do you know the penalties in this state for
aiding and abetting a fugitive wanted for murder?" he asked. "If
you know where Corbett is, and you don't tell us, I promise that
you will spend most of the rest of your life in prison."

"I can't imagine a prison that could be any more unpleasant
than this conversation," Maura said, smiling sweetly.

"Being a wiseass must be genetic. I'm pleased to tell you we
just gave that detective's job away to someone who was more of a
team player and less of a wiseass than your Yalie brother."

"Lieutenant, if you're going to smoke, you'll have to do it
outside."

Maura pointed to the sixth-story window rather than the
door. For a frozen moment, she thought Dickinson was going to
strike her. Finally, with a *fuck you*, he stormed out. She triple-
locked the door behind him, actually managing a smile at the
new definition of "police lock."

Now, she sat back and watched reruns of the interviews
with MMC officials, nurses, police, the electrician victimized by
the gunman, and Max Garabedian. The only new news was the
old news that the bogus Garabedian had been neither appre-
hended nor identified, but that fingerprints lifted from the hospital room were being analyzed.

Go Ray, she silently cheered.

She was pleased that at no time during the difficult, stressful
night had she felt the urge to drink. But she also knew that she
needed to sleep. She set the alarm for 8:30, turned off the ringer

on all the phones in the apartment, and positioned the answering machine not far from her head. If Harry did call with a change of plans, she at least wanted a chance to hear his message. Finally, she picked up one of the phones.

"You guys get some rest," she said. Then she slammed the receiver back down.

At eight A.M., a message from the producer of *Inside Edition* worked its way into her consciousness. He was promising Harry enough money to hire a first-class defense team in exchange for an exclusive on his story. She showered, made some coffee, and glanced out the window. Cloudy, but no rain. C.C.'s Cellar wasn't all that far from the co-op, but she wanted to allow an hour to get there. She would take a cab across town and down to somewhere near the UN. Then she would cut back by foot to a subway station. Then another cab and perhaps a trip through a store with multiple exits. And finally, a third cab to within a block or two of the club. It seemed to her that in a place as crowded as Manhattan, with subways and so many stores to duck into, it shouldn't be that hard to ensure that she wasn't being followed.

She dressed in jeans, sneakers, and a plaid button-down shirt, and then selected a deep cloth bag from a collection of them in Evie's closet. She dropped in her wallet, the dark wig she had worn in the hospital, and a white shirt in case she needed to change her look. Then, just in case, she threw in a shirt, jeans, and sneakers for Harry. It was doubtful he was going to be returning to the apartment in any hurry. The revolver she kept strapped in front of her in her leather fanny pack. The security of having it at hand felt greater than the fear of being arrested for carrying an unlicensed handgun.

She took the stairs down six flights, startling Rocky Martino when she came through the stairway door behind him. He bolted to his feet and stepped back, but not before Maura caught a strong whiff of alcohol. His eyes were bloodshot and his hands slightly tremulous, but he made a laudable stab at decorum.

"Miss Hughes, you gave me a bit of a fright," he said, moistening his lips with his tongue. "What can I do for you?"

Maura wondered how many times she had done as ineffectual a job at covering up her intoxication as Rocky was doing, all the while thinking, as he probably was, that she was pulling it off.

"Could you please get me a cab?" she said, fumbling through the bag for her wallet.

"Yes, ma'am," Martino said. "No problem. Any word from Dr. Corbett?"

"No, Rocky. Nothing."

"Well, my fingers are crossed that he's okay."

He stepped back from the desk. With exaggerated, broad-based steps, he shuffled outside and waved up the street. Moments later, a cab pulled up. Maura handed Rocky a one, hesitated, and then gave him a five as well.

"Take a break and have breakfast on me, Rocky," she said.

He jammed the bills in his pants.

"Oh, I will, ma'am. I will."

Something about his smile made Maura feel uneasy. She hurried past him into the cab.

"The UN," she ordered, immediately looking behind them as they pulled away. "I'll tell you how I want you to go. Don't worry if it's not the most direct way. I'll pay."

The cabby nodded.

If there was someone following them, they were damn good. Within a block, Maura was convinced that the street behind them was clear. It was possible that someone was driving in front of them with a radio, but she would take care of that soon enough. They passed a newsstand. She could see Harry's photo on every front page. *Hey, read all about it! Doctor Death Strikes Again!* There was nothing the least bit witty or romantic or adventurous about any of this anymore. For a time last night, perched in that tree by the landfill, thinking everything was about to work out for them, she had felt like Grace Kelly in *To Catch a Thief* or Audrey Hepburn in *Charade*. This morning she felt deflated, exhausted, and frightened. She tried to imagine how Harry had felt when he lifted up the trunk of his car.

They were on Broadway now, heading south. She counted off three more blocks.

"Turn right here," she ordered. The cab continued going straight. She rapped on the Plexiglas shield. "Hey, I said, turn right here."

The cab made a sharp left, heading for the park. Halfway

down the block, it began to slow. Maura stopped pounding on the Plexiglas. Desperately, she tried to figure out what was happening. She thought about the gun in the pack strapped around her waist, but she sensed that what she needed was just to get the hell out of this cab. She reached for the door just as the electronic locks snapped open. The cab was still rolling. Suddenly, her door was snatched open. A man jumped in almost on top of her. He was a giant, perhaps six-six, and broad across the shoulders. He shoved her aside with one hand as if she were a doll. Her head struck the window, just behind her healed incision. Without a word of instruction, the driver accelerated, cutting back west, toward the Hudson.

Maura recognized the behemoth immediately. He was Perchek's thug—the survivor from the park. Snarling, she leapt at him, pounding at his face with her right hand as she tried to unzip the fanny pack with her left. Her first blow, with her fist, caught him on the bone just above his eye. He cried out, pawing at it with one hand, lashing out at her with the other. She ducked under his blow and felt her hand inside the pack close on the grip of the revolver. In one motion, she pulled it out, jammed the muzzle into his ribs, and fired.

Nothing happened. Absolutely nothing. The one chance she might have had was gone. The killer snatched the gun away and slapped her viciously across the face. Her lip split and tore against her teeth. Her head snapped back against the window. Then she pitched face-forward almost onto his lap.

"Safety, safety," he teased, his voice surprisingly high-pitched. "We mustn't try to shoot our little gun until we release the safety."

He grabbed her by the neck and pulled her upright. She spit at him, spattering his shirt and face with blood. He wiped off his cheek with the back of his hand, slowly, furiously. And then he hit her again, as forcefully as the first time. Now, she was limp. He pushed her down to her knees and roughly pressed her face onto the seat.

"We're looking for your pal Corbett," he said.

"I don't know," Maura managed. Her face was throbbing and his grip on her neck was hurting as well. But she was determined not to give him the pleasure of making her cry. "I don't know where he is or even if he's alive."

The killer pulled Harry's shirt out of her bag. He jerked her
face up to show her.

"Sure you don't," he said.

"Even if I did know where he was, I'd never tell you."

He pressed her face back into the seat.

"The Doctor will be pleased to hear that," he said.

★   ★   ★

The most sought-after fugitive in New York carefully maneuvered the huge Winnebago Luxor through the streets of
Manhattan, trying not to attract any unnecessary attention. He
was sticking as much as possible to the broad, north-south ave-
nues, terrified of turning onto a crosstown street that was narrowed with trucks or construction. Spending most of his life in
the city, where his car often remained in the parking garage for
weeks at a time, his driving was rusty. Backing up the BMW
often presented a challenge. Backing the motor home out of a
narrow city street lined on both sides with cars would be potential disaster. His picture was all over the place. A fender bender,
a cop, an arrest. It would probably be that simple.

It was ten minutes of ten. Harry was easing his way down
Columbus Avenue, trying to time it so that he turned onto Fifty-
sixth at exactly ten. Once he had Maura, they could get out of
the city and find a place to stop and sort things out. There were
those who knew, or at least *believed*, he was innocent—Maura,
Tom Hughes, Mary Tobin, Kevin Loomis, Steve Josephson, Doug
Atwater, Julia Ransome, Phil, Gail. Harry glanced down at the
console-mounted clipboard and the pad on which he was writing
down the names, and added Ray Santana to the list. He had a
number of friends, work associates, and even patients who would
be hard-pressed ever to believe he was capable of *any* crime, let
alone murder. But the question was who among them would be
willing to take chances for him.

Together, he and Maura would be able to figure out something—especially if they were somehow able to locate Ray. Santana had contributed mightily to the mess he was in, but he
certainly hadn't caused it. Now, if he could be brought together
with Loomis, a breakthrough was quite possible. *If.* First Harry
had to reconnect with Maura; then he had to do what he could
to ensure that Kevin Loomis stayed alive; and finally, he had to

find Santana—and do it all while keeping himself out of jail. *First Things First*, he thought, recalling one of the blue and gold banners he had seen on the wall of the AA meeting. *First Things First*.

He turned onto Fifty-sixth Street. Gratefully, there were no delivery trucks, road crews, or double parkers. But there was also no Maura. The front of C.C.'s was deserted, and the place looked to be locked up. Harry slowed and considered stopping to check the door. But an insistent horn from behind saved him the trouble of making a decision. He drove up Amsterdam for a few blocks, then swung over to Columbus and made another pass. Nothing. He tried calling her apartment and his, but got answering machines in both places. There was no answer at C.C.'s. Finally, he paged Phil.

"Hey, Harry," Phil said. "Good to hear from you. I think I caught some little item about you on the news or someplace."

"Very funny. How are Gail and the kids holding up?"

"Let's just say we're all having to defend the family name a bit. How're you doing?"

"Thanks to you, I'm still on the loose. Phil, that note I gave you set up a meeting time with Maura. But so far she hasn't showed. Are you sure it was delivered?"

"Positive. I spoke to Ziggy this morning. He put it in her hand personally at about three A.M."

"Shit."

"Anything I can do?"

"Not for now. You've done more than enough already. Phil, thanks. I'll be in touch."

"Just take good care of my baby, there. I've been promising Gail a weekend away in her. Now that you've gotten first dibs, I'm going to have to deliver."

Harry cruised around his loop for almost an hour, careful to widen it or shorten it each time. No Maura. Something was definitely wrong. He got Kevin Loomis's home phone number from information and tried him there. Daddy was at the store getting ice for a party, a child informed him. Mommy was in the bathroom. Harry said he'd call back in an hour.

It was nearly eleven—almost two hours before the second scheduled try at connecting outside of C.C.'s. Harry would be there, but he felt almost certain that Maura would not. *Perchek?*

Dickinson? Booze? Of the three, only a fall off the wagon seemed unlikely. He checked the gas gauge and the rest of the jet plane dashboard panel. No problems . . . so far. He headed downtown.

The only option he had, it seemed, was to try and find Ray Santana. He had no desire to put Mary Tobin at risk, but he really had no choice. Besides, he thought smiling, in any match between the authorities and Mary, his sympathies would have to go out to the cops. He reached her at home. As he expected, she was anxious to do whatever she could to help him and had an enormous extended family who were willing to help out as well.

"My son-in-law, Darryl, is the only one who has bad-mouthed you," she said. "He'll be back home just as soon as they finish the X rays and the stitches. An' that's just from my daughter. He'll still have to deal with me."

It took almost forty-five minutes for her to get Walter Concepcion's address and number and make it back home. As soon as she entered the office, the two policemen who were staking out the place had barged in and questioned her.

"We're going to get him," one of them had said. "Just don't you be helping him when we do."

"I've got twenty-one grandchildren and seven great-grand-children, young man," Mary replied. "I'm sure you'll be a big hit with your family and fellow officers when you haul me off to jail."

At precisely noon, she called Harry with Concepcion's number and address and a report of her conversation with police. He called immediately and got no answer. Then, when he was a block away from the rooming house, he tried again. This time, Santana picked up. Three minutes later, he loped out of the house and jumped into the passenger seat. Harry knew the moment he saw the man that his anger was gone. He was merely grateful that where there had been one, now there were two. He swung onto the Harlem River Drive, heading north.

"Now this is my idea of a getaway car," Santana said.

Ray was well past needing a shave and looked as wasted and hyper as Harry had ever seen him.

"It's a loaner from my brother. I'm glad you got away. Are you all right? You don't look so hot."

"Just the usual, only more of it than usual. I screwed up at the hospital, Harry. I'm really sorry."

"Was it Perchek you saw?"

"No, not Perchek. It was Garvey, Harry. Sean Garvey, the bastard who served me up to Perchek. I was lying there half asleep when I heard his voice outside the door. It's been seven years, but I knew in two seconds that it was him. Our eyes met and he recognized me, too. I'm certain of it. He was with a bunch of people in suits. He's lightened his hair and had some sort of stuff done to his face, but it was him. By the time I reached the doorway of my room, he was pulling away from me. I . . . I lost my cool and fired at him. The rest I guess you know."

"Do you have any idea who Garvey is now? What he might be doing at a hospital in New York?"

"None. After Nogales, he disappeared, almost into thin air. He either had some powerful friends in high places, or he had the goods on them. I pulled every string I could to find him. Nothing. No records he ever worked for the government. No Social Security number. No tax returns. Nothing. Witness relocation times fifty. I called in every marker I could think of around the agency and the CIA. Zip. You have coffee in here?"

Harry motioned to the thermos. Santana poured himself a cup and then flipped on the nine-inch television bolted on a swivel atop the passenger-side dash. The reporter was updating developments in the dual manhunt for Dr. Harry Corbett and a man tentatively identified as Raymond Santana, a former DEA undercover agent, whose fingerprints were among those taken from Grey 218.

"So much for the element of surprise," Ray said. "It was only a matter of time. You think Maura's in trouble?"

"I *know* she is. Listen, I'm going to head back to the club soon. The note I sent her said we'd try again at one if either of us didn't show up."

"That body in your trunk sounds like Perchek's work. Do you suppose he's got her?"

Harry shook his head. "I don't want to think about it."

"First this Roundtable, then Perchek, and now goddamn Sean Garvey to boot. This is really the mother lode, Harry."

"Where do you think we should start? . . . Ray? . . ."

Santana, eyes narrowed, was peering at the screen from just a few inches away.

"Douglas Atwater, vice president of Manhattan Health. You know him, Harry?"

"I know him well. He's one of my few enduring supporters at the hospital."

"He's on this station live, right now, issuing a plea for you to give yourself up before anyone gets hurt."

"So?"

"Well," Santana said, "your enduring supporter at the hospital is also the man I tried to kill yesterday."

"Garvey?"

"In the flesh."

CHAPTER 39

It made no sense for them to remain in the city, and there were a number of good reasons not to. With Harry driving, he and Santana left Manhattan and headed north on Route 684 toward the New York–Connecticut border. Their mood was grim. Maura had not shown up at C.C.'s at one, and it seemed fairly certain now that Perchek, not the police, had her.

"You know," Harry said, "the more I think about Atwater, the stupider I feel."

"What do you mean?"

Santana, his feet up on the dash, had turned off the TV. He was gazing out the side window at an approaching bank of storm clouds.

"Getting an IV into Evie and injecting her with Aramine took some planning," Harry explained. "Whoever did it had to know that she was coming into the hospital that day. And I didn't know myself until twenty-four hours before. Doug was one of the few people besides me who was aware that her admission date had changed."

"When did he start working for your hospital?"

"He doesn't work for the hospital exactly, he works for the managed care outfit that has a contract with the hospital."

"*Managed care*. That's very creepy sounding if you ask me."

"It's a far cry from some ol' doc riding up in his buggy with his black bag, I'll tell you that much. Anyhow, Doug's been around for about five or six years, I think."

"Sounds right. Someone high up in the agency did a hell of a job of making him disappear—a new life, a new face, and no records that he ever existed. Garvey probably brought his pal Anton up to New York as soon as he was settled in his new position with the *managed care* company. There must be a hell of a lot of money in this Roundtable business for Perchek not to go back to his old globe-hopping ways."

"Maybe The Doctor just wanted to settle down."

"Sure, that's it. He's in semiretirement. Just five or six killings a week."

"Well, what do we do now?"

"I've been thinking that maybe we should give ol' Garves a call," Santana said. "Things are unraveling for him just about as fast as they're unraveling for us. Garvey knows I'm around now. And until I'm *not* around, he won't ever be able to stop looking over his shoulder. That shot I fired in the hospital may have missed, but it did send a clear message that I'm not in a negotiating frame of mind. Also, he must realize that you know about The Roundtable. Why else would you have set me up in the hospital?"

"But we have no proof of anything or we would have gone to the police. They must know that, too."

"I agree. That gives them a chance to stay in business, but only if you're in jail or dead and I'm successfully bought off or dead."

"What about Maura?"

Santana shook his head, his expression grave.

"Assuming they have her, she's a bargaining chip so long as we're around, and a loose end as soon as we're not."

"Let me call him," Harry said angrily. "I want to thank him for being such a devoted friend all these years."

"Just be cool."

He pulled into a rest area and dialed Atwater's office at MMC.

"Whom should I say is calling, please?" Atwater's secretary asked.

Harry hesitated for a moment, then said, "It's Dr. Mingus. Dr. Charles Mingus."

Mingus, one of Harry's idols, was acknowledged by many, including Atwater, to be the greatest jazz bass player ever. He had been dead for fifteen or twenty years. It took just a few seconds for Atwater to come on the line.

"Harry, is that you?" he said.

"Hi, Doug. Okay to talk?"

"Absolutely. Dr. Charles Mingus. Clever. Very clever. You are a trip, Harry."

"I saw you on the tube a little while ago. Thanks for worrying about me."

"Hey, I'm just glad to hear your voice, pal. I'm glad you're all right. Where in the heck are you anyway?"

"Oh, around. I'm trying to find Maura Hughes, Doug. I thought maybe you'd know where she was."

"That was some damn good drawing she did, wasn't it, Harry?"

"Does Perchek have her?"

"Perchek. Perchek. Now there's a name that doesn't ring any bells with me at all. Gee, I'm sorry about your friend Maura. I only met her that one time in the hospital, but I'll wager she's a beautiful woman when she's sober and not all banged up, and has a full head of hair. Not a looker like Evie was, mind you, but then again, who is?"

Harry put his hand over the mouthpiece. "He's got her," he whispered. He took his hand away. "What do you want for her, Doug?"

"Harry, aren't you paying attention? I said I only met her that one time at the hospital."

"I know where Ray Santana is, Doug. That's the trade. Santana for Maura."

"Now this is without a doubt the craziest conversation I've ever had. First someone named Perchek, whom I've never heard of, then someone named Santana, whom I've also never heard of."

"Doug, I really care about that woman. I don't want her hurt. Just tell me what you want."

"You know, ever since that fake patient of yours took a shot at me, I've been wondering why in the heck you went to such trouble to put him in the hospital in the first place?"

Again, Harry covered the mouthpiece.

"He's nibbling," he whispered. "Okay, Doug, listen. Let's not fuck around with each other. You deliver Maura Hughes to me unharmed, and I'll not only pinpoint Santana for you, I'll tell you all I know about The Roundtable, which of your knights are close to blowing the whistle on the whole operation, and exactly what they have on you."

This time there was no immediate response.

"Then what do you plan to do?" Atwater asked.

"I'm getting out. I've got it all set up—tickets, passport, money, safe destination. The works. But I'm not leaving without Maura."

"God, Harry. You've got it that bad, huh? Take it from me, none of them are worth it—except the next one."

"Without her, I don't care what happens to me, and I don't leave. That means you don't get Santana and The Roundtable collapses around your ears. If we *do* go, we've got to leave by dawn tomorrow. You and I do business tonight or it doesn't happen."

There was another prolonged pause.

"Where can I call you?"

"Not a chance, Doug. I'm frantic, but I'm not stupid."

"I should say you're not. Okay, pal, have you got something to write with?"

"I'm ready."

Atwater gave him a number in the 201 area—the northern New Jersey area that included Fort Lee.

"Call me tonight at nine," he said. "We'll talk."

"Nine it is. Now listen, Doug. I don't have much left to lose. If Perchek hurts Maura Hughes, I swear I'm going to kill you both."

"Hey, Harry, easy on the hot sauce, brother. We'll talk, and then we'll see what we can do."

"Nine o'clock." Harry hung up.

"Bravo. Bravo," Santana said, applauding. "That was one hell of a performance."

Harry's eyes were flint.

"It was even better than you think," he said. "I know exactly where she is."

·   ·   ·

It was raining steadily when they crossed the Tappan Zee Bridge heading for New Jersey. The digital clock on the Winnebago dashboard read 7:06 P.M. A small digital calendar mounted right next to it read *August 31*.

August 31—Corbett curse minus one.

Harry concentrated on the road ahead as Santana prepared himself. Harry knew he might drop dead on September 1st, as had his grandfather at seventy and his father, to all intents, at sixty. But the chances of his being killed tonight were far, far greater. Still, Santana was a professional, Harry had been under fire before in his life, and they were not going after Maura unprepared. Before crossing the bridge, they had left the highway and searched until they found an army-navy store. Ray spent half an hour inside and emerged with a rifle, two knapsacks full of equipment, and a receipt for $1123.37. The stock in the place was limited, but the big-ticket items—the rifle, telescopic sight, and binoculars—he pronounced as "adequate."

"Did you really kill a guy in the war like the papers said?" Santana asked, inspecting the rifle as they pulled away.

"It's nothing I'm proud of."

"That's okay. Killing a person is something that once you've done it, you know you can do it. That's all that matters to me."

"I'm filled with hate, Ray. It wouldn't be that hard for me to kill either of them."

"One less thing for me to worry about."

Harry had never been inside Doug Atwater's house, but he had seen it from the water and from the land. Three years before, Harry had rented a yacht for a surprise party for Evie's birthday. The boat was huge—large enough to hold the combo from the club and about forty guests, with room to spare. It was chartered for a circumnavigation of Manhattan Island, and was by far the most extravagant thing Harry had ever done. But their marriage was already crumbling over his conservative lifestyle, and he was desperate to make a statement. That evening was the last time he could remember Evie seeming truly happy.

Atwater had shown up for the affair with his usual gorgeous *blonde du jour*—an actress of some sort, Harry recalled. *Sandi? Patti?* She and Harry were standing alone by the rail at dusk, watching the Palisades of New Jersey glide by, when suddenly she began gesturing wildly at a spectacular modern house built on the very brink of one of them.

"That's Dougie's!" she exclaimed. "That's Dougie's house. See that deck? We had mimosas out there this morning. You wouldn't believe the view. Have you ever been there?"

In fact, until that moment Harry had known only that Atwater lived in an elegant penthouse on East Forty-ninth Street. They had met there several times when he and Evie had gone out with Atwater and his date. Curious about the house, he glanced back across at the New York side of the river and fixed a couple of landmarks in his mind. Later in the evening, the captain used his navigational charts to pinpoint the spot exactly. It was not very far from Fort Lee. Harry had considered mentioning the house to Atwater, but now he felt certain that he never had. He and Atwater were friendly, but obviously not that close, because Harry had never been invited over.

A month or two later, after visiting his mother in the nursing home, Harry had found himself just a few miles from where he thought the house to be. It was surprisingly easy to find—a sprawling, California-style mansion at the crest of a rising, tree-lined driveway at least a hundred yards long. The massive wrought-iron gate at the end of the drive was closed. A six-foot-high, fieldstone-in-cement wall stretched along the roadway in both directions, giving the impression that the entire property was enclosed. He did not consider dropping in.

But tonight, he and Santana would pay a call.

"Pull off at the next rest area," Santana said. "You need to get ready, and I need to check this sight out."

Despite his gaunt physical appearance and nervous tics, Ray had always seemed somewhat cocky and self-assured. But following Harry's conversation with Sean Garvey, he had become withdrawn and subdued. The tic at the corner of his mouth had diminished until it was just a faint suggestion, and his hands were rock steady. Harry bet that this was exactly the way Santana had looked as he crouched, aimed, and fired that night in Central Park.

He pulled off into a sparsely occupied rest stop. Santana

tossed him a black turtleneck, ammo vest, and watch cap, and a small jar of black greasepaint labeled *Nightstalker*.

"Don't forget the backs of your hands," he said as he left the camper cradling the rifle in a canvas wrap.

Outside, the rain had begun falling harder. To the east, in the distance, lightning glinted off the blackening sky.

Harry set the clothes beside his seat. *Evie, Andy Barlow, Sidonis. Maura?* He was ready to fight—ready for whatever. But there was one more piece of business he had to take care of before they headed into battle—a phone call.

* * *

Kevin Loomis glanced up at the clock and tried to imagine what the mounting flood in the basement was looking like. Rain had forced the barbecue indoors, but it really didn't matter. Everything was moving along as he had planned. It wouldn't be long now.

It had been about thirty minutes since he left the party through the back door, ostensibly to get a scorecard from his golf bag in the garage. He grabbed the card, which he had set by the garage door, then cut around to the side of the house to dislodge the washing machine hose. His setup worked even better than he expected. One tug on the heavy twine had pulled the hose free, and the twine had slipped off so that he was able to pull it through the basement window. Now, there were about ten minutes left before he would "discover" the disaster.

He made his way through the guests, trading stories, laughing at jokes, and doing a fairly effective job of getting drunk. It was strange knowing when the exact moment of one's death was going to occur. What if he had known from the very beginning? Would he have done anything differently? The question was rhetorical. He would always have joined The Roundtable as he understood it to be. And the moment he entered his first Roundtable meeting, he was one of them. From then on, nothing he did would change a thing.

He had said goodbye to each of the kids in his own way and had managed half-decent sex with Nancy before tension overwhelmed him. Now, he stood in the kitchen and glanced over at the drawer where he had placed the flashlights. Just a few more minutes. Suddenly, he realized the phone was ringing. His first thought was that something had happened to one of the kids. He snatched it up.

"Hello?"

"Kevin Loomis?"

"Yes."

"It's Harry. Harry Corbett. How're you doing?"

"Fine. We're having a party here, though. I really can't talk."

"That's okay. You can just listen. I won't take long. The murder they want me for, the surgeon . . . ?"

"Yes."

From the doorway, Nancy asked with body language if the call was anything for her to be concerned with. Kevin shook his head.

"It's Atwater, Kevin," Harry went on. "Doug Atwater from Manhattan Health. He's the knight behind the killings, behind that Dr. Perchek I told you about."

"I suspected as much. Atwater's Galahad, the knight in charge of security. I saw him earlier today on the news."

"The others in your group may have participated, but I believe he's the mastermind. We're going after him and Perchek right now."

"Good luck."

"Kevin, I'm calling to beg you to see this thing through. If we get them, we're going to need you to testify against them. If we fail, all those patients at risk are going to need you even more."

"I . . . I don't know what you're talking about," Kevin said. "Of course I'm going to see this through. I wish you luck tonight. I've got to go now."

"Kevin, please be strong. You have too much to lose. We all do."

Kevin set the receiver down without replying. *Damn Corbett. He didn't even have any kids.* He turned on the sink water, which was now little more than a trickle.

"Hey, Fred," he called to one of the two men he had selected, "we've got no water pressure all of a sudden. What do you think?"

The man shrugged.

"Guess we ought to check the basement," he said.

Kevin allowed him to open the basement door and try the light.

"Bulb's out," the man said. "Or else the power down there's dead."

From below, they could clearly hear the sound of gushing water. Kevin handed him a flashlight and then called over Reverend Pete Peterson and handed him one as well. His pulse was beginning to race.

"It looks like the great flood down there," he said. "Unfortunately, my waders are right in the middle of it. You guys hang on the stairway and follow me with your lights. I'll see what I can see."

It was about to happen, Kevin was thinking. It felt strange, so strange that his whole life had come down to these few moments.

He led the two men down to the basement and stepped into a foot and a half of water. "It's the washing machine hose," he called out from the blackness. "It's snapped off. Keep your lights on it."

All those things in life that had seemed so damn important at the time . . . all meaningless . . .

"Just be careful," Peterson said.

Kevin jammed the hose back onto its housing.

"See," he said, "no problem. No problem at all."

What I'm doing is right. Best for Nancy. Best for the kids. Best for everyone. God, forgive me. . . .

Sir Tristram, Knight of The Roundtable, took a single deep breath and then set his hand down on the back of the dryer. His body stiffened. Sparks shot from his legs at the waterline. His heart went into immediate standstill. The muscles in his hand, in a viselike spasm, tightened around the frayed wire. He had been dead for fifteen seconds by the time the weight of his body pulled him free of the wire and allowed him to drop into the water.

CHAPTER 40

"Green Dolphin Street."

They were still a ways from Atwater's mansion when Harry began hearing the tune in his head. He tapped out the rhythm on the steering wheel and bobbed his head to the bass line.

"What are you doing?" Santana asked.

"Listening to music. It's a tune that pops into my brain when I'm keyed up. Sometimes I don't even realize I'm tense until I hear it."

Santana studied him. From within the black greasepaint, his eyes were glowing discs of pearl.

"Keep listening," he said finally.

They drove toward the Hudson until they found the narrow, winding roadway that paralleled the Palisades. Harry cut the headlights and slowed down. There were no cars on either side, moving or parked. The houses, each overlooking the Hudson from a majestic height, were widely spaced and nestled in the woods a good distance from the road. Through the rain and the gloom, it was impossible to make out much more than lights from any of them.

"You still think you know where we are?" Santana asked.

"I'm not as certain as I was a little while ago," Harry said, peering through the Winnebago windshield, which was being squeegeed by wiper blades as big as hockey sticks. "Maybe that's why the damn tune in my head keeps getting louder."

"Maybe it's time to stop listening. How're you even going to know we're there?"

"I'm looking for that wall I told you about. That stone wall."

At almost the moment he said the word, they saw it—fieldstone set in cement, two feet thick, running along the road as far as they could see. To their right, a six-foot-high chain-link fence extended from the wall toward the cliffs. Harry pulled as far off the road as he could, cut the engine, and gestured toward the fence.

"I would guess there's another one like this on the other side, and then the cliffs in the back. So the place is completely enclosed."

"A big corral," Santana said. "What better place for a gunfight?"

Peering down the road, they could just make out the main gate, perhaps fifty yards away. Santana used a hooded flashlight and set out their equipment, which included a snub-nosed revolver and the silenced semiautomatic that Harry knew had killed the gunman in the park. In addition, there was rope, adhesive tape, switchblade knives, wire cutters, wire, Swiss Army knives, powerful flashlights, and several boxes of ammunition. Santana handed Harry the revolver and some bullets.

"The safety's here," he said. "Flip it off after you load it. Then just point and shoot."

"Just point and shoot," Harry echoed. "The ultimate Kodak moment."

"Load up your rucksack and be ready."

Santana took the binoculars and the rifle, switched off the interior lights of the RV, then opened the door and slipped out. Harry watched, impressed, as the former DEA undercover agent moved quickly and silently to the wall and scaled it in a heartbeat. He lay flattened on the top, scanning the property. Then, after a few minutes, he was back.

"The house is pretty well lit and not that far away. I can actually see into some of the windows. There's one guard in a little house by the gate. I didn't see anyone else."

"Any dogs?"

"Not that I could see."

"Shouldn't we have brought some big T-bone steaks just in case?"

"You mean like they do in the movies?"

"Exactly."

"Harry, any attack dog that's worth its salt knows the difference between the kind of meat that just lies there and the kind of fresh meat it gets to hunt down and kill. We see a dog, we shoot it. That's too simple for the movies, but it's damn efficient. Now, here's what I think we should do. I'm going back up on the wall, about halfway down. When I flash one time, call the house and demand to speak with Maura. That way we'll know for certain she's there. Hopefully I'll see her through one of the windows. If not, we'll just have to get close enough to figure out where she is. If I flash twice, come along. Three times, there's trouble of some kind. In that case, hop up on the wall right over here, and be ready to use that gun. Lock the doors and leave the key wedged under the right rear tire. Questions?"

"None."

"You ready?"

"I am. Ray, I guess there is one thing."

"Go ahead."

"Please don't take this wrong. I've got a score to settle with these people too. A big score. I just want to remind you to . . . to keep your cool."

Santana's response was not what Harry expected. He glared at him in an unsettling, frightening way. The tic by his eye and at the corner of his mouth intensified.

"Okay, you asked, now you listen," he snapped. "I've lived in pain every second of every minute of every hour of every fucking day since that bastard shot that stuff into my body. *Seven years.* The only peace I ever got during that time was when I was able to imagine what it was like for him in that filthy Mexican prison. Now he's up there in that mansion along with the bastard who set me up to be tortured. Don't you tell me to keep my cool."

Harry felt himself recoil from the man's fury. It took some time for him to regain his composure. Finally, he reached out and rested his hand on Santana's arm.

"Sorry, Ray," he said. "We'll get them. I promise you we will."

Santana left and quickly flattened himself against the wall. The rain had let up considerably, and the gate was easier to see. Harry peered at it for a second or two. When he looked back, Santana was again atop the wall. A moment later, his light flashed once. Harry checked the time, 9:08, and dialed the number Atwater had given him. Atwater answered on the second ring.

"Dr. Mingus?" Atwater said.

"It is."

"Tell me again what you have for me."

"I want proof that Maura's okay."

"Tell me what you have."

"Santana is staying at a rooming house in Spanish Harlem. I'll tell you the address and the name he's using when you let Maura leave."

"How did he find me up here?"

"Perchek left a thumbprint in Evie's room. Someone at the bureau told Santana. He's pledged the guy to secrecy. No one else knows about it except him and me—not even the crime guy who lifted the print in the first place."

"How'll I prove you're telling me the truth?"

"Doug, I don't give a shit about you, what you prove or don't prove. Every cop in New York is looking for me. Once I have Maura, I'm out of here. That's all I care about. Now, where is she?"

"Who have you been in touch with on The Roundtable?"

"Two men. Jim Stallings is one. Now he's dead. The other one I'll name as soon as I speak to Maura. He's told me all the other names."

"Give me one."

"Someone named Loomis. I can't remember his first name, but I have it written down."

"He's not the other one you've spoken to?"

"No. Now, no more delay. I can't stay here that long."

"Call this number back in exactly five minutes."

Harry hung up and waited in the dark. Up ahead, he could barely make out the shadow that was Santana, pressed on the top of the wall. The rain had all but stopped now. The country air wafting through the open passenger-side door was scrubbed and sweet. The songs of peepers and crickets filled the heavy silence. Harry ran his fingers over the greasepaint coating the backs of his hands.

9:13. Harry picked up the receiver and hit *redial.*

"All right," Atwater said as soon as he heard Harry's voice. "You have thirty seconds. I'm standing right next to her, listening on a portable phone. Don't upset me."

"Hello?"

"Maura, it's me. Are you okay?"

"Harry. I've been so worried about you. I'm all right. They . . . they made me drink bourbon. I fought it, but they made me. Then they gave that up and shot me with some drug to make me tell them where you were. But I couldn't tell them what I didn't know."

Her voice sounded strained, but strong.

"Maura, just be tough. I have everything we need to get us out of the country."

There was the briefest hesitation, then she quickly covered up her confusion.

"I didn't think you could pull it all together so quickly," she said. "I'm ready."

Her extension clicked off.

"Okay, Harry. Call this number again in five more minutes and we deal."

"Make it half an hour. I can't stay where I am any longer."

"Who's the other man on The Roundtable you've spoken to?"

"Harper. Pat Harper. Northeast Life and Casualty."

Kevin Loomis had said the man's name just once, but it had been easy for Harry to remember. A girl named Pat Harper had been his first crush in junior high. Dropping Harper's name now was perfect. If Harry didn't make it through this night, at least Loomis would be safe from reprisal.

"Okay. Thirty minutes," Atwater said.

Harry listened to the dial tone and tried to imagine what was transpiring behind the wall. For two minutes, there was only blackness up ahead. Then Santana's light flashed twice. It was time.

Harry slipped on the rucksack and snapped the revolver into a holster on his belt. Keeping low, he flattened himself against the wall and moved along it until he reached Santana, who was standing on the road side.

"They're not keeping her in the house," he whispered. "Someone, I think it was Garvey, left by a side door and walked north. In a minute or so, he came back with her. Then they went back again and Garvey returned alone. Now, he's back in the house."

"Where to first?"

"The guard by the gate. If there's going to be any shooting, try and let me do it. My gun doesn't make any noise."

"I remember."

Santana set the rifle by the wall.

"It looks like it's all going to be close-in work," he said. "Maybe I can get a refund for this."

The fieldstones offered easy purchase for scaling the wall. Together, they reached the top, lowered themselves halfway down the other side, and dropped to the sodden ground. Harry found himself anticipating pain in his chest before he hit. In fact, he did experience a brief jab, though not nearly as bad as when he jumped the backyard fence in Fort Lee. If this was as bad as it got tonight, he could handle it easily.

Guns drawn, they inched up on the small gatehouse. There was a dark, four-door sedan parked beside it. Through the small side window of the house, they could see the guard talking on the phone.

"If this is a check-in call, we're in luck," Santana whispered. "One less thing to go wrong. Have some two-inch adhesive tape ready."

He motioned Harry to the far side of the gatehouse door, then tapped lightly on it once and flattened himself against the wall. The door opened cautiously. Gun drawn, the guard stepped out. Harry hadn't time to fully appreciate Santana's moves before it was over. Ray brought his pistol down sharply on the man's wrist. The guard's hand went limp and the gun dropped as if it had suddenly become electrified. Before he could even cry out, Ray was on him, a hand tightly across his mouth, his leg around the back of his calf. The takedown was quick and silent. Ray came down straddling the man's chest with the muzzle of his silenced revolver jammed between his teeth.

"Not a sound!" Ray growled. "Understand?"

The man nodded. Keeping the silencer in his mouth, Ray rolled him onto his side and motioned Harry to tie his hands behind him. Then he again rolled him to his back. He pulled his gun out and pressed it under the guard's jaw.

"Okay, where's the girl?"

The man stared up at Ray's blackened face. Harry could see him assessing the benefits and dangers of trying to lie. The internal debate lasted only seconds.

"Guest house . . . down a path to the left . . ."

"Is Perchek with her?"

The mention of The Doctor's name brought a flash of fear to the guard's eyes. He hesitated, then nodded.

"How many men?" Ray waited for a response, and then set the silencer muzzle squarely on the man's left eye. "How many?"

"One with P-Perchek in the cottage," he stammered. "Two in the house."

"Plus Garvey?"

"Who?"

"Atwater."

"Yes. Two plus him."

"Put a bandana in his mouth and tape it in tightly," Santana whispered to Harry. "Wrap the tape all the way around his head twice. Then tie his ankles."

Harry did so efficiently, and together they dragged the man ten yards to a tree and tied him there. Santana checked inside the gatehouse.

"The gate release is right inside the door," he said. "The door beside the gate is unlocked." He glanced at his watch. "We've got about twenty minutes. Let's go get her."

They stayed close to the wall, which met the chain-link fence on the far side of the property in a copse of low shrubs. Up the hill and to their right was the main house, with lights shining through every window and spots illuminating the front walk. Fifty yards or more to the left of the main house, shining through a small woods, were more lights.

"There," Harry whispered, pointing.

Ray nodded and led the way. They reached the trees and moved through them carefully, keeping low. The guest house, a miniature version of the mansion, was itself spectacular. It was almost all glass, built on steel girders that thrust up from the cliff so that its deck was cantilevered out perhaps a hundred feet above the Hudson. Harry peered over the precipice. There was a shoreline of boulders extending out ten or fifteen feet from the base of the cliff. And directly across the still, black river, glittering like the Milky Way, was Manhattan.

Against the cliff, beneath the main floor, was a set of rooms not visible from the front of the guest house. Through one window, which was barred, they could see Maura alternately sitting on the edge of a bed and pacing. She appeared worn and tired, but reasonably steady. Santana put a finger to his lips and pointed toward the house. Moving closer, they peered in through a massive picture window. The expansive space—living room, dining room, and kitchen—was tent-shaped, gleaming hardwood and glass with a cedar ceiling and a center pole fifteen feet high. French doors opened onto the deck, and half a dozen large windows offered stunning views of the city. A guard, his weapon in a shoulder holster, was pouring coffee. Behind him, reading at a table, sat The Doctor.

At the sight of him, an unnatural, guttural noise emerged from Santana's throat—the sound of hatred. He picked up a shot-put-size rock and motioned with his gun for Harry to follow him. They stopped just outside the glass door.

"Me first," he whispered.

Before Harry could respond, Santana hefted the rock and hurled it face-high through the door. The thick glass exploded inward. Ray was inside at almost the instant the rock hit the floor.

"Don't!" he barked as the gunman reached for his weapon.

Harry stepped through the empty door frame and took the man's gun. Anton Perchek, who had not even lowered his book, looked up first at him, then at Santana. His smile was one of bemusement. The irises of his eyes were so pale as to appear almost white. His pupils were wide, black holes in the snow. There was not a hint of fear in the man that Harry could see—or of any emotion at all, for that matter.

"Down on your face!" Santana ordered the gunman.

When the man hesitated, Ray dropped him with a pistol butt behind the ear, all the while keeping his attention fixed on Perchek. The gunman was moaning but awake as Harry bound him with the technique he had perfected on the gatekeeper. Santana pulled a chair away from the table. With his silenced revolver still aimed at Perchek, he helped Harry lift the semiconscious man into the chair. Harry tied him there. Then he stepped back, closer to Santana.

The Doctor eyed the two of them curiously. He was certainly the man Harry had seen outside of Evie's room, the man Maura had drawn. But in some ways he wasn't. He looked like all of the computer renderings, but none of them. He would have fit in perfectly behind the counter of a convenience store or beside an operating table, sweeping streets or piloting a jet. He was nobody and everybody. When he spoke, his voice was mellow, hypnotic, and totally devoid of emotion.

"Well, Ray. It's been a while, hasn't it," he said.

Santana pushed the table away from Perchek with his foot. Even through the black greasepaint, Harry could see the tension in his face. Clearly, Perchek sensed it, too.

"You don't look so good, Ray," he said, as Santana was taping his wrists to the wrought-iron arms of the chair. "The muscle wasting in those hands. That twitch by your eye. What is it—drugs? Some sort of disease?"

Harry noticed that The Doctor's arms, especially his forearms, were thickly muscled. His biceps stretched the sleeves of his sky blue polo shirt. Santana checked him for a weapon, but found none.

"The key to Maura's room," Ray demanded.

Perchek shrugged as if the business was too mundane for him to bother with.

"No key," he said. "Just a dead bolt on this side."

Santana motioned Harry down the short flight of stairs. In half a minute he was back with her. She was hollow-eyed from strain and her lip was swollen and crusted with blood, but otherwise she seemed unharmed.

"The big guy hit her when they kidnapped her," Harry explained.

"Anything else?" Santana asked.

"Except for forcing the booze down me, they haven't really hurt me. I managed to spit a lot of it out, and after they left me alone I made myself throw up. I was drunk for a while, but I'm sober now. They thought I'd start begging them for more, but I hated the feeling and even the taste."

Harry put his arm around her and held her tightly.

Santana glared down at Perchek.

"Who in the agency helped Garvey disappear so cleanly?" he asked.

Perchek continued smiling at him benignly.

"Ray, you look terrible. Absolutely terrible." His speech was as sterile as his eyes. "You know, I keep thinking that back in Nogales I never had the chance to give you the antidote for my hyconidol. That's what's wrong with you, isn't it. My Lord, Ray, what an oversight. I am so sorry. So truly sorry."

"Shut up and tell me who sent Garvey out with a new identity."

"There is an antidote, you know. And a damn effective one it is, too. The biochemical process is quite simple, actually. It's called competitive inhibition. The antidote just floods the bloodstream and replaces those nasty little molecules that have been locked onto those nerve endings of yours all these years, and *Bingo,* you're cured. No more pain, Ray. Think of it. Why . . . why, just look at your eyes. You're addicted, too, aren't you. Oh, Ray. I can just imagine what you've been through all these years. Why, it's a wonder you haven't done yourself in before now. . . ."

Santana listened as if transfixed. Perchek was soothing, seductive, hypnotic—and totally believable. Harry wanted to say something, anything to break spell of The Doctor's rhetoric. Instead, he too stood motionless. It was Santana's pain.

". . . Well, now you don't have to hurt anymore, Ray. Those horrible pain flashes you keep having? I can make them go away for good. I promise you. No more need for narcotics. You'll feel the difference in only a few minutes, Ray. Just think of it. No more pain ever again. Guaranteed. You can keep me tied up while you try it. Then you can leave. I promise no one will touch you. All I want is him." He nodded toward Harry. "In exchange for the antidote, all I want is half an hour with him."

Perchek looked over at Harry and for the first time, Harry

could see emotion in the man's eyes—a consuming, contemptuous loathing, focused directly and completely on him. Harry glanced back at Santana and saw a flicker of uncertainty. Perchek saw it, too, and was again smiling benignly.

Santana set his pistol on the table. Then he whirled and stretched two-inch-wide adhesive tape tightly across The Doctor's mouth. Next he pulled out a contraption from his pocket—an arcane metal frame with five finger rests and pointed screws over each. Perchek stiffened momentarily, but made no move to resist as Ray locked the fingers and thumb of his right hand in place.

"I don't have a pain drug," he said, "but I do have this thing I've been hanging on to for years. A friend brought it back from China. I'll bet you've used something like it yourself from time to time. First nail, then flesh, then bone, then through the other side. Eight fingers, two thumbs, millimeter by millimeter. I've been saving it, and I didn't even know why . . . until now."

He tightened the screws down so that each nail blanched. Perchek reacted not at all.

"Ray, don't let him make you into *him*," Harry begged. "There's no antidote for that drug. And even if there were, you know he'd never give it to you. I need him, Ray. They want me for murders he committed. Let's just take him in and get him locked up. Don't sink to his level."

"You don't understand, Harry," Santana said icily. "*Siempre estaba yo a su nivel.* I was always at his level. Now get out!" He snapped the words like a whip.

Harry started to protest, but he knew it would serve no purpose. He took Maura by the arm.

"We'll be right outside," he said. "We only have about ten minutes before Garvey starts wondering why I haven't called."

They left as Santana was tightening the first screw.

"Who did Garvey own at the agency?" he asked. "Who's protecting him now?"

Perchek smiled beneath the tape. Santana tightened the screw through the nail. Blood spurted out around the metal. Perchek stared ahead.

"Pain or answers," Santana said. "You've got a choice to make."

"No, Ray. It's you who have the choice. . . ."

Sean Garvey spoke to him from just outside the front door. He held a gun to Harry's head. They stepped into the room. The huge thug followed, roughly dragging Maura by the arm, then shoving her to the floor. His gun was leveled directly at Ray.

". . . And you don't have a lot of time."

CHAPTER 41

"Raymond, you were careless seven years ago," Garvey said. "And you were careless tonight." Still holding his revolver to Harry's temple, he shuffled sideways away from the front door, until his back was to the river. "My man Big Jerry, here, called the gatehouse to set up a golf game with his pal. And what do you know? No answer. Now then, get that thing off Dr. Perchek's hand."

Santana didn't move. "You son of a bitch," he said. "How many of our guys did you get killed? How did you get paid? By the scalp?"

Ray glanced toward the door. It was only the slightest movement, but Harry caught it. So did Garvey.

"Don't try to pull that shit with me," he said. "There's no one out there, and you know it. Face it, Raymond. You tried, you lost. Now take that off Anton's hand."

Santana again glanced toward the door—just a flick of his eyes. Then he reached over and loosened the screw. Perchek flexed his fingers and the device clattered to the oak floor.

"A lot of the guys you sold out had families," Ray said. "Kids that had to grow up without a father. We worked for shit pay and took crazy risks because we believed in what we were doing. We all trusted you. And you just handed us over one by one. I can understand him." He gestured toward The Doctor.

"He works for the highest bidder, whoever it happens to be. He's a machine. But you . . . you're something worse. You're scum—a soulless, gutless traitor."

"The tape," Garvey snapped. "Take it off his mouth." Santana complied, though not at all gently. "You should have stayed back in Kentucky, or wherever the hell you were, Raymond. Everyone would have been much better off. Now we've got to run some sort of damage control in order to keep my pet project up and rolling."

"Is that why you broke Perchek out of prison? To work for The Roundtable?"

"Let's just say that as soon as I got the hang of my new career in the health insurance business, I appreciated the possibilities. Now, however, I need to find out who among my knights needs to be taught a lesson in loyalty. Fortunately for us, I believe our friend Dr. Corbett can come up with that information. And coincidentally, we have just the man here who can help him do it. You will help, won't you Anton?"

Perchek smiled. "It will be a pleasure."

"So move aside there, Raymond. Big Jerry will untie The Doctor. Harry, would you be so kind as to crawl over and take Dr. Perchek's place in that chair?"

Garvey placed his gun barrel at the base of Harry's skull and forced him down to his hands and knees. Slowly, Harry moved across to Maura, still on the floor. His eyes were fixed on Santana, who remained crouched beside Perchek.

For the third time, Ray glanced minutely, almost inadvertently, toward the front door. Harry found himself beginning to believe there actually *was* someone out there. Sean Garvey clearly felt the same way.

"Jerry, I'm sure our friend Raymond is running a scam, but just take a quick look outside, will you? Then untie the good doctor."

Harry heard the motion behind him as Jerry moved to the front door.

Then suddenly, snarling with rage and hatred, Santana sprang from his crouch and charged his onetime boss. Garvey shot him from point-blank range—once, then again. Jerry whirled quickly and twice fired into him from behind. But Santana's unearthly cry only grew louder. He collided chest high with Garvey, driving him backward through the screen door and out onto the deck. Jerry lunged toward them, but Harry could see he was too late. Santana, silent now, had his nemesis in a death grip. His legs were churning like a halfback's even though life had already left his body. Garvey hit the top of the waist-high guardrail just as Ray pushed off, and the two men flipped over the railing like toys. Garvey's scream filled the night. Then it stopped with the suddenness of a guillotine.

Jerry was staring at the spot where the two men had vanished when Perchek cried out his name. He spun around just as Harry dove from his knees for the corner of the table where Santana had placed his gun. Harry grasped the butt of the pistol at the moment the killer fired. The edge of the table shattered. Harry rolled, then rolled again as a shot slammed into the floor behind him. There was pain in his chest, but he was far beyond reacting to it. Then suddenly, he was on his belly, sighting down the barrel of his gun at the chest of a man who was preparing to kill him. It was his recurring Nha-trang dream. This time, though, there was no youthful Asian face, no loud report echoing in his ears—only a soft spitting sound and a flash of flame. The front of the behemoth's neck blew apart, just above his jersey. He flew backward, exploding through the plate glass window and onto the deck.

Harry scrambled to his feet, prepared to fire again. But there was no need. The man lay motionless, blood spurting from his severed carotid artery. In just a few seconds, the spurting became a trickle. Maura raced to Harry's side. He slipped off his rucksack and took out the powerful flashlight. Together, they peered over the railing of the deck. Santana and Garvey, their bodies shattered, lay on the rocks a hundred feet below.

"Oh, Ray," Harry murmured.

Maura quickly turned away.

"At least Ray's pain is finally over," she said, stepping clear of the huge corpse, stretched out on a bier of broken glass just a few feet away. "He told me in the hospital that he didn't think he could go on much longer. When he got the call about Perchek's fingerprint, he'd been thinking more and more about suicide."

Out of Maura's line of sight, Harry braced himself on the railing until the boring pain beneath his breastbone began to subside.

Damn. Not now.

"Perchek injected him with that hyconidol," he said finally. "Ray hated him. But Garvey was the one he really wanted. Garvey was the one who handed him and the other undercover agents over. Listen, we ought to get out of here before the other guys at the main house come over. We can call the police from my RV." He left the railing and followed Maura back inside. "Okay, Perchek, let's go. Mess with me in any way, and I swear I'll kill you."

"I can see that you are very good at that," The Doctor said.

Harry replaced the adhesive tape gag, cut the rope binding him to the chair, and forced him facedown on the floor. Once again he noted that Perchek was powerfully built, especially through the shoulders and arms. And even with his revolver pressed against the man's spine, Harry still felt at risk.

"Tightly," he said as Maura tied Perchek's hands behind him. "Make sure his hands are relaxed. I don't want even a little slack. Then take that gun on the floor over there. Be sure the safety is—"

"I know. I know."

Harry pulled Perchek to his feet and forced him through the door. Across the room, bound and gagged, the guard watched them go.

"Down this way, along the fence," Harry ordered in a whisper. "Maura, keep your eyes out for the other two guys."

They moved carefully through rain-soaked bushes and shrubs. Ten yards. Twenty. The fieldstone wall was easy to see now.

"There!" Maura whispered urgently.

She pointed at a figure moving stealthily toward them across the lawn, gun drawn. Harry pulled the adhesive tape from Perchek's mouth.

"Tell him to stop right there," he said.

Perchek said nothing. Harry jammed the muzzle into the base of his neck.

"Dammit, do as I say, or I swear I'll kill you right now!"

"It's me, Perchek. Don't come any closer. The good doctor has a gun in my back."

"Where's Doug?" the guard called back.

"Dead. Now just stay where you are."

"No, back away!" Harry yelled. "Back away now! But stay on the grass where I can see you. Maura, we're going to head for the gate. There's one more of them somewhere, so keep looking."

They crossed the lawn. Harry held the rope binding Perchek's wrists in one hand and Santana's silenced pistol in the other. Maura kept her revolver poised to fire.

"You'd best kill me," Perchek said.

"Shut up."

"Santana didn't take advantage of the opportunity when he had it, and look how he ended up."

They had reached the gate. Harry checked inside the guard house. No one.

"Keep close," he whispered. "Is that guy still out on the lawn?"

"Still there," she said.

"Okay."

He held his breath, pulled Perchek closer, and guided him through the ornate wrought-iron pedestrian gate, adjacent to the massive main gate. The Winnebago was right where they had left it, fifty yards down the road.

"Maura, that mobile home is ours. The key is under the right rear tire. You drive, I'll stay with him. It looks imposing, but there's no trick to driving it. Just turn it on and go. Until we get there, keep your eye behind us. Shoot anything that moves."

"Last chance," Perchek said.

Harry did not bother responding. His attention was fixed on the huge mobile home, now no more than thirty feet away.

"Everything still okay back there?"

"No problem," Maura said.

"We're almost there."

They were at the corner of the wall now, less than ten feet from the RV. It appeared undisturbed.

"Okay. You go for the key. I'll cover you."

Harry pressed back against the side of the Winnebago.

Maura ducked past him, ran to the rear tire, and swept her hand beneath it. Again, Harry held his breath.

Be there, he prayed.

"Got it," she said.

She hurried back to the door on the passenger side, opened it, and clambered across into the driver's seat. Harry guided The Doctor over to the step.

"Okay, Perchek. Step up and get onto that couch over there," he said.

At that moment, a gunshot cracked from somewhere atop the wall near the gate and a bullet slammed into the metal by Harry's face. Before he could react, a second shot tore through his upper arm. He cried out and reeled back against the side of the RV clutching the wound. The gun dropped from his hand. It took only a second for Perchek, his hands still tightly bound behind him, to sprint off toward the gate. Another bullet snapped into the side of the Winnebago. Maura jumped to the ground, but Perchek was already diving to safety through the pedestrian gate. She fired three times toward the wall, but the shadow on top of it had disappeared.

"I'm okay," Harry said. "Get up there and start this thing. I can make it."

He followed her into the Winnebago and slammed the door behind him. Seconds later, Maura pulled away. He tore away the sleeve of his turtleneck. The bullet had hit the meat part of his deltoid and exited only an inch or so lateral to where it went in. Blood was oozing steadily from the wounds, but it was venous bleeding, not arterial. He could move his fingers and his elbow, although there was a good deal of pain—enough to think the shaft of the humerus might have been hit as well. He wrapped the sleeve around the wounds and used his teeth and free hand to tie it as tightly as he could stand. As Maura sped past the massive gate, the headlights of the sedan that had been parked there flicked on. Harry cursed himself for not thinking to shoot out a tire as they walked past it.

"They're coming after us," he said.

"Where should I go?"

"The river's off to the right. Stay on this road and look for a left you can make."

"Harry, this thing is huge."

"Just take it up to as fast as you can handle it and then go a little faster." He snatched up the phone and dialed 911. "This is Dr. Harry Corbett! I'm wanted by the police. Right now we're driving along the Palisades in a Winnebago motor home, being chased by men who want to kill us. We're—"

The window beside Maura exploded inward, showering her with glass. Reflexively, she ducked, then poked her head up and accelerated through forty.

"You all right?"

"Cut on my arm and my face, but I'm okay."

Tires and brakes screeched as she snapped the wheel to the left. They skidded on the wet pavement, then felt a bump and heard the crunch of metal against metal. The lurch sent cabinets flying open. The fax machine snapped off its stand and shattered against the wall. Pots, pans, and canned goods clattered out onto the carpet and bounced off the teak dining table.

"Can you put your seat belt on?"

"I can't let go of the wheel!"

Harry dropped the phone, picked up Maura's gun, and raced to the driver's-side window in the lounge.

"I don't see them!" he cried. "Maybe you knocked them off the—"

The window behind him shattered. He whirled and fired three shots just as Maura pulled the wheel sharply to the right. He lost his balance and cried out as his wounded arm struck a counter. The collision with the sedan was louder and more forceful this time. The heavy sedan was much faster, but hardly a match for the Luxor in close-in battle.

"Harry?"

"I'm okay. There are three of them, I think! Perchek's in the back seat! I'm sure of that!"

He had to holler now to be heard over the rush of wind and the roar of the two engines. They were heading down a fairly steep hill.

"Harry, I can barely stay on the road!"

"Is there any way you can make a left onto a side street?"

"I'm going fifty-five! I'd have to slow to ten! I just hope this road doesn't turn too sharply, or we're going to tip over!"

"Hang in there! You're doing great!"

The sedan pulled alongside them again. This time, the center window on the driver's side was shot in. Harry braced himself and pulled the trigger of his revolver, but got only an impotent click. The pursuers inched forward.

"Watch it, Maura!" he cried.

A shot came up through the vacant window beside her and spiderwebbed half the windshield. She whipped the wheel to the left. Only the pressure from the sedan kept them from flipping. Harry scrambled into the passenger seat, fumbled for the seat belt with his wounded arm, and then gave up trying. If she didn't have one on, he didn't want one either.

"Harry, they're in front of us, trying to cut us off!" she yelled. "I can hardly see through this windshield! Harry, watch out! The road's gone! They're in front of us!"

The sedan had spun against the grille of the Winnebago, beneath the massive windshield. It was being pushed sideways, plowing through a forest of saplings and low bushes at fifty miles an hour. Trees snapped like firecrackers as the Winnebago barreled forward, brakes screeching. Several larger trees flashed past, their branches whipping through the empty windows. Again and again, the wheel spun out of Maura's grasp. Each time she managed to steady it. Then suddenly, the dense young woods fell away. A ten-yard stretch of wild grass ended in blackness. Ahead of them were the lights of Manhattan. Well below them was the Hudson.

"Harry! Harry!" Maura cried, bracing herself. "We're going over!"

The sedan and motor home hurled off the edge of the precipice together. Harry grabbed the edge of his seat, stiffened his legs, and watched through the cracked windshield in numb horror as the car tumbled away from them and hit the water just beneath them. The Winnebago nosed slightly downward as it passed over the spot where the sedan had splashed down. It hammered into the ebony water with dizzying force, striking it first with the front bumper. Instantly, the windshield collapsed inward, and the massive dual airbags filled. Chilly water flooded the cabin.

Harry snapped forward and collided with the dash at the

instant the airbag drove him back into the seat. The pain in his chest, which had never fully abated, exploded through him once again.

"Maura!" he cried.

The river poured in with force, filling the Winnebago in seconds. Still tilted forward, the huge RV glided downward, beneath the surface. Harry, battling the rushing water, the airbag, and the pain in his arm and chest, inhaled deeply and clawed his way toward the driver's seat, expecting at any moment to connect with Maura's body. The murky river pushed him backward toward the sitting area. He kicked off his sneakers and struggled to calm and orient himself. The blackness was total. *Where were the windows?* Below him? Above? Were they still sinking? His breath was going. He kicked and battled to find a way out. Nothing. Water was entering his nose and mouth. Soon, any second now, he would have to take a breath. He felt the consuming panic of being trapped in water—panic unlike any he had ever known.

His movements grew weaker, more futile. The pain in his chest grew worse. Water seeped down his throat.

Breathe, his mind cried. *You must take a breath.*

Darkness closed in.

Reluctantly, Harry surrendered to it. His arms grew heavy. The dreadful ache beneath his breastbone began to fade. Then, at the instant his consciousness vanished, he felt a hand take hold of the back of his shirt.

CHAPTER 42

Harry's first awareness was the smell—the unmistakable amalgam of cleaning solutions, antiseptic, laundry starch, and human illness. It was an aroma as familiar to him as his own room. He was in a hospital, cranked up in bed at a forty-five-degree angle.

Piece by piece, image by image, the nightmare began returning to him. He was dead. Had to be. The god-awful sensation of muddy river water filling his mouth and lungs—it had to have been fatal. *Is this Heaven? No, it's Iowa. . . .* He was dead, and it really wasn't all that bad. He would open his eyes now and there would be clouds billowing about his feet. James Mason would be ushering new recruits to the celestial escalator that would take them to the next level.

"Dr. Corbett? Dr. Corbett, open your eyes."

A woman's voice. Harry did not respond immediately, although he sensed that he could. Instead, he tested his limbs. First his legs, then his left arm, and finally his right. There was no movement there. *The arm was gone!* The bullet had severed an artery and the arm was gone. He opened his eyes a slit and peered down at his chest. His arm and hand were there, resting in a loose cloth sling, working exactly as they were supposed to.

"Maura . . ."

He murmured the word, then said it again, louder.

"Who's Maura?" the woman asked.

Harry opened his eyes fully and turned to the voice. A young woman with short, sandy hair and an attractive, intelligent face looked down at him. She had on a white clinic coat with a blue name tag that read *Carole Zane, M.D. Cardiology.*

"Maura Hughes is the woman who was with me," Harry said, his senses clearing rapidly.

"There *was* a woman survivor from the accident, but I don't know her name. From what I heard, you were in worse shape than she was. I think she was taken to a hospital in Newark."

Thank God she's alive, was all he could think.

"Do you know anything else about the accident?" he asked.

"Nothing at all except that you were in a camper and you flew off a thirty-foot cliff into the Hudson."

"Some camper," Harry said. "Where am I now?"

"You're in the coronary care unit of University Hospital in Manhattan. I'm Dr. Zane, one of the cardiac fellows. You were brought here by chopper last night. Apparently we were the closest facility to the accident with an available cardiac bed."

"What day is it?"

"Saturday."

"The first?"

"The first of September. Yes."

September first. The end for Gramps. The beginning of the end for Dad. Now it's Harry's turn. . . .

"Have I had a coronary?"

"Maybe. We don't know for sure. I understand you are a physician?"

"A GP, yes."

"Okay, then. You've been shot through your upper arm. The humerus has been chipped, but it's intact. They wanted to explore the wound last night, but they couldn't because your EKG is abnormal. It's showing ST segment changes suggesting acute posterior wall injury. Your cardiac enzymes are slightly elevated as well, so there definitely has been some minor cardiac muscle damage already."

"So I've had a coronary?"

"Not *had.* The EKG patterns keep changing. Whatever is going on is still evolving. That means we have a chance to fix it."

"With a balloon?"

"Or a bypass."

"Damn."

Harry quickly reviewed his family history and his months of intermittent symptoms. The physician took notes, stopping him from time to time to clarify a point. She was quite obviously bright, but more important to Harry, she was also kind, attentive, and careful not to show him how rushed she was.

"Are you having any pain now?" she asked.

"No. I never have had pain when I'm at rest. Mostly I tend to get it when I run hard or jump."

"Well, we've decided against blood thinners and clot dissolvers because of the gunshot wound and the possibility of internal injuries we don't know about yet. You *are* on a nitroglycerine drip."

She motioned to the plastic bags draining into his left hand. The nitro drip was running piggyback through a long, slender needle inserted through the rubber infusion port of the primary line—sugar water, which was keeping the vein open.

"No problem," Harry said, wondering how he might best go about finding out where Maura was and how she was doing.

"We'd like to do a cardiac catheterization on you as soon as possible," Zane said.

"Do whatever you have to."

She handed him a clipboard—the operative permit.

"There are a number of potential problems with this procedure listed on page two. I am required to inform you of them one at a time."

"Don't bother," Harry said, signing. "I've already been dead once, and it didn't feel all that bad. Do you think I could make a phone call or two?"

"First let me listen to your heart and lungs. Then there's someone here to see you."

Curious, Harry let himself be examined. Then Carole Zane promised to meet him in the cardiac cath lab as soon as possible and turned toward the door. Harry followed her with his eyes. Only then did he notice the uniformed policeman seated just across from his glass-enclosed cubicle, facing him.

"Dr. Zane?"

She turned back.

"Yes?"

"What's the policeman doing here?"

She smiled at him patiently.

"Well, from what I've been told, you are under arrest. I'll see you downstairs."

Harry electronically cranked himself up another few degrees and searched about for a phone. If he was under arrest, then Phil had to be in trouble as well. Undoubtedly the police had already traced the Winnebago to him.

"One call, Corbett. Just like you were in jail."

Albert Dickinson walked into the room and stopped at the foot of the bed. He was wearing his usual suit and smelled as if he had just smoked an entire pack of cigarettes at once. Harry felt a mix of anger and disgust at the sight of him.

"Have you gotten people out to Doug Atwater's house?" he asked.

"The New Jersey police are working on it."

"Maybe you should all just wait until someone burns the place down. Do you know anything about Maura?"

"She's not in the DTs yet, if that's what you mean."

"You snide bastard. Isn't there any kindness inside you at all?"

"Not toward murderers or drunks. No, not much."

"You're going to feel very dumb when the truth comes out. Now what about Maura?"

"She's in Newark City Hospital. Hurt, but not badly. From what I hear, she's the one who saved you. Apparently she went up to the surface, couldn't find you, and then dived back down. The docs tell me you were on your way out when she pulled you to shore. Apparently you were having a coronary."

"So they say. What about the sedan that went over with us?"

"They're hauling that up right now."

"Any survivors?"

Dickinson shook his head.

"None."

"How many were in there?"

"Dunno. I'll be looking into that and into who they were

later today. I'm going to wait until after you're taken care of to get a statement from you, so you'll have some time to put together a real doozy. Your file in the office is already three inches thick with fairy tales. I ought to tell you that we know where that monster mobile home came from. The Jersey police will be paying your brother a visit as soon as our DA tells them we want to press aiding and abetting charges, which we do."

Harry adjusted the oxygen prongs in his nose and wondered if the detective was trying to provoke him on purpose just to see what a full-blown coronary looked like.

A nurse came in with a syringe.

"What's that?" Harry asked.

"Just some Demerol to keep you relaxed during your catheterization. The cath lab people will be up for you in a minute."

"No medicine, please," Harry said. "I'll be calm. I promise."

"Okay," the nurse replied. "But I'll have to notify Dr. Zane."

"This man is under arrest, Miss," Dickinson said. "If he goes anywhere, an officer must go with him."

The nurse's expression suggested that she was not nearly as taken with Dickinson's importance as he would have liked. Harry asked her for a phone.

"One call," Dickinson reminded him.

Harry swallowed back a dozen or so comments on the policeman and his ancestry. Then he called his brother collect. Phil had just heard about the accident and was getting set to drive to the hospital. As Harry would have predicted, he made light of the loss of the elegant mobile home.

"Hey, that was going to be your fiftieth-birthday present anyway, Harry. I was just waiting to have it wrapped."

He was, however, concerned about Harry's cardiac situation.

"Sounds like you just worried about that curse and worried about it until it came true," he said.

"Maybe so."

Phil promised to find out what he could about Maura and to see Harry in a couple of hours. Moments later, a gurney was wheeled in by a stoop-shouldered man with horn-rimmed glasses and a graying moustache. He was wearing surgical scrubs beneath a loose surgical gown. He transferred Harry's IV bags to a pole on the gurney and then grabbed the sheet beneath Harry's head. Two nurses on opposite sides of the bed grasped the same sheet at hip level.

"Hey, don't just stand there," one of them said to Dickinson. "Grab this sheet beneath his feet and help us lift him."

Dickinson complied, but looked revolted.

"Okay," the other nurse said. "One, two, three."

The four of them swung Harry to the gurney as if he were weightless. The landing caused a twinge in his upper arm and perhaps something, real or imagined, in his chest.

"How long is this going to take?" Dickinson asked.

The nurse shrugged.

"One to two hours," she said, setting a portable cardiac monitor/defibrillator between Harry's feet. "Depends on what they find and what they do. He may end up in the OR for a bypass."

The nurses hooked a small oxygen tank to Harry's prongs and floated a sheet onto him. Then Dickinson followed the stretcher and one of the nurses out of the room.

"Take a break," he said to the uniformed policeman. "I'll go down with him. I'll call you up here in half an hour and tell you what's what."

With the nurse on one side of the gurney and Dickinson on the other, Harry was wheeled to the elevator. The monitor between his feet silently charted out his heartbeats. Facing cardiac surgery, he felt detached, surreal, and very mortal. But in truth, he had felt that way most of the time since the night he walked back onto Alexander 9 with a milk shake for Evie. The gurney was pushed onto the elevator by the man from the cath lab. Dickinson and the nurse squeezed in alongside it. There was a second set of doors beyond Harry's feet, opposite the one through which they had entered. Harry heard the doors behind him glide closed. He heard a key being inserted in the control panel so that their trip could be made with no stops.

"Hey," the nurse said, "what are you doing? The cath lab's on the eighth floor, not the subbasement."

At that moment, her expression turned to terror. Dickinson, looking with wide-eyed surprise at the old man from the cath lab, was fumbling inside his coat for his gun when Harry heard the soft spit of a silenced revolver from just beside his ear. The nurse spun 180 degrees, slammed into the metal door, and dropped. Dickinson, clearly beaten, lowered his hand in a gesture of surrender. The silenced revolver spit again and created an instant hole in the white shirt over his left breast. For two horrible seconds he stared at the wound. A halo of crimson appeared around the hole. He looked up at Harry, his expression a mix of astonishment and utter dismay. Then his eyes rolled up and without a word, he crumpled to the floor.

Harry was too shocked and horrified to speak. The heart rate on the screen between his feet was one seventy. He expected any moment to see the beating stop entirely.

"I told you you should have killed me when you had the chance," Anton Perchek said dispassionately. "Now, you must get ready for your great escape."

The elevator stopped at the subbasement, but Perchek kept the doors from opening.

"You'll never make it," Harry said.

"I made it this far, didn't I?" Perchek boasted. "A brief stop for some things at my Manhattan apartment, and I arrived here to begin preparation just a few hours after you did. They couldn't have chosen a better hospital for my purposes. I have several different excellent ID badges from here. And having handled a number of cases here for The Roundtable, I know my way around the place pretty well."

"You're insane."

"So, then, Doctor. We must get a move on. I have a laundry hamper waiting just outside the door. It's Saturday so the laundry is almost deserted. A little IV Pentothal for you and we should be able to roll right past the pressing machines and out of this place."

"Why don't you just kill me?" Harry asked.

The Doctor circled around the gurney so that Harry could see the loathing in his eyes . . . and the glee.

"Oh, Harry, the idea is not to *kill* you," he said. "The idea is to have you *beg* me to kill you."

Harry cast about for something, anything, he could use as a weapon. There was not going to be any abduction and torture. It was going to end for them right here, right now. He fixed on the *Door Open* button near his right foot. The laundry was through the door behind him. Something, possibly an equipment supply room or the power plant, had to be on the other side of this one. If he could just get there, he had a chance. At the very least, Perchek would have to decide whether to pursue him or flee.

The sling was loose enough to allow some movement. Shielded by the sheet, he slid his right hand across his body. The pain in his shoulder grew more intense with every millimeter, but he ignored it. Finally, his fingers closed on the only weapon he could think of—the one-and-a-half-inch needle in his IV hookup. Carefully, he eased it free from the infusion port and shifted it to his left hand.

Perchek released the door behind Harry's head.

"There's our hamper, right where I left it," he said, setting the silenced revolver down as he pulled the gurney out far enough to drop the side rail. "Now, just the right amount of Pentothal and—"

At that moment, the nurse crumpled on the floor moaned loudly. Perchek turned.

Now! Harry screamed to himself.

He gripped the needle tightly and drove it to the hilt in the soft spot just below The Doctor's right ear. Perchek bellowed with pain and surprise, and reeled backward, pawing the spot. Harry pushed himself off the stretcher and swung backhand as hard as he could, connecting with Perchek's left cheek and sending him sprawling to the concrete floor next to the hamper. Then he whirled and hit *Door Open* on the panel just above where Albert Dickinson lay. He could sense Perchek stumbling to his feet as the other set of elevator doors glided open. Head down, Harry raced across a small, enclosed waiting area, burst through a set of swinging doors, and charged straight into hell.

He was on a long cement walk in the cavernous hospital power plant. The temperature was over one hundred, and the noise level was deafening—machinery whirring and rumbling above the constant churning of circulating water. Harry pulled off his sling and threw it aside as he ran awkwardly away from the elevator, expecting at any moment to be shot in the back. To his right was a safety railing, and fifteen feet below that was the massive turbine—a gray monolith, rising out of a concrete slab. The pulsating, high-energy drone it emitted bludgeoned Harry's chest like a heavyweight's fist.

To his left, reaching seventy feet toward a grimy, glass-paneled ceiling, were the boilers—foreboding giants, radiating heat and energy. Thirty yards straight ahead and up a short staircase was the glass-enclosed control booth. Inside, his back to Harry, a large man in a tan jumpsuit and yellow hard hat was watching TV.

"Help!" Harry screamed. "Help me!"

His cry was swallowed by the noise. He stumbled on, sweat already cascading down his face and stinging his eyes. The unremitting pulsations from the turbine were making him intensely nauseous. He glanced back just as a bullet ricocheted off the steel column by his ear. Perchek had crawled over the gurney and now knelt at the head of the corridor, taking aim once more. Harry dove onto his belly, sending pain screaming from his shoulder and throughout his chest. The bullet missed by inches, stinging his cheek with concrete spray. Fifty feet ahead of him were the stairs to the control room, which he now realized had to be soundproof. *Fifty feet.* He could even make out the McDonald's bag on the counter by the television. But unless the engineer in the hard hat turned around and spotted him, the booth might as well have been on the moon. There was no way he could reach it before Perchek reached him.

Then, to his right, just a dozen or so feet away, he noticed the stairway down to the turbine floor. He scrambled forward on his left hand and knees. His right arm would bear no weight at all. The heat was intense, the air heavy and stagnant. The pain in his chest was unremitting. He half tumbled down the steel steps, scrambled across the concrete, and took cover behind the massive turbine. Ground zero. The droning vibration cut through his body like a chain saw.

Fifteen feet above him, on the corridor from the elevator, Perchek leaned over the metal railing, searching. Staying on to kill him was a foolish choice, but clearly The Doctor's pride and hatred had triumphed over logic.

Crouching behind the turbine, Harry circled, trying to keep out of Perchek's line of sight. Behind him was another safety railing, and beyond that another drop-off to a lower level. The entire windowless, three-tiered power plant was as vast as a cathedral. He could hear water flowing below—probably being pumped in from the river to cool the steam from the boilers after it had passed through the turbine. Harry wondered if the conduit returning water to the river was large enough to carry a man out.

Perchek had already moved over to cover the stairs up to the corridor. The stairs down to the lowest level were virtually a continuation of those. There was no chance Harry could make it either way. He continued inching to his left, trying to keep the hideous turbine between him and The Doctor. But at that moment, Perchek spotted him. Harry fell back as the revolver again spit flame. A piece of pipe directly over his head split open. With a freight train roar, steam under immense pressure spewed out, instantly flooding the whole area and billowing thirty feet upward to the ceiling. The temperature rose rapidly. The hot, wet air was painful to breathe. Hell.

Harry knew he was cut off from either staircase. But now, the swirling cloud of steam had completely engulfed the turbine. He pushed through the dense mist on his belly and slipped beneath the safety rail. The twelve- or thirteen-foot drop to the lowest level looked like a hundred. But there was no choice. Painfully, clinging to the rail with his one good hand, he lowered himself over the edge. He hung there for a moment, then dropped to the concrete floor, rolling gracelessly as he hit. Pain shot up from his feet through his chest, taking his breath away. It was several frightening seconds before he realized that he could still move.

He was at the very bottom of the hospital now. Beneath the concrete floor were the water tunnels, crawl space, and earth. The massive pedestal supporting the turbine extended upward from the ground, through the floor of the level Harry had just left. Ahead of him, flush with the concrete, was a steel grate. Harry crawled over and inspected it. It was four feet by three, placed to allow access into a concrete tunnel, which was about eight feet across. At the base of the tunnel, five feet below where Harry knelt, a stream flowed rapidly, discharging spent coolant water from the power plant to the river. Beside him, a control post with four buttons permitted the water to be stopped to service the system in either direction: *Open Inflow, Close Inflow, Open Outflow,* and *Close Outflow.* The prospect of trying to escape through the tunnel to the river was not appealing, but it was rapidly becoming his only option. With the drill-like pain in his chest getting even worse, it was possible he couldn't make it anyway.

On the turbine floor above him, steam continued hissing out. Perchek was up there somewhere, undoubtedly guarding the stairway, Harry's only way out. But now, he realized, The Doctor had another problem. Soon, dropping steam pressure had to set off an alarm. The engineer in the control room would have to look down and see what was going on. Any sane man would flee right now.

But Anton Perchek was hardly sane.

Harry tried the grate. It was heavy, but movable. With two good arms, it would have been rather easy. He kept glancing up at the stairs, expecting any moment to see Perchek step down from the cloud. The dreadful ache beneath his breastbone shot up into his jaws and ears. Inch by agonizing inch, he slid the grate aside. He estimated the rushing water below to be three feet deep. Not much cushion. He was weak, dizzy, and drenched with sweat—probably having a full-blown coronary. There was little chance he could survive dropping into the pitch-black tunnel to follow the outflow to the river. It would be better to try and hide behind the turbine pedestal. Any minute, someone had to come down.

He crawled over to the concrete base of the pedestal just as Perchek stepped out of the billowing steam and down the stairs. Harry crouched low, out of sight at least for the moment. Beside him was a rolling metal cart, loaded with tools. He tried hefting a hammer with his left hand. It was a worthy weapon, but he doubted he would be able to use it effectively. Still, it was something. Perchek scanned the area and peered into the tunnel. The open grate was a giveaway that Harry had been there. But it was also a source of confusion for Perchek. He had to make a decision.

Harry gripped the hammer and watched as The Doctor crouched by the opening, debating whether or not to jump in. The pain in Harry's chest was making it hard to breathe and even harder to concentrate. Then Perchek stood and turned away from the grate, again searching the room. Harry cursed softly. He had to do something—maybe attack, maybe try to sneak back up the stairs. Again, Perchek knelt and peered into the tunnel.

Suddenly, before he fully realized what he was doing, Harry was on his feet, charging toward The Doctor with every ounce of strength he had left, leaning on the tool cart as he pushed it ahead of him. The hissing steam and machinery rumble covered the sound of the wheels. Perchek sensed something and turned, but too late. The cart slammed into his shoulder, sending him over the edge and splashing into the water below. Harry collapsed to the concrete, gasping and perilously close to unconsciousness. Below him, he could see The Doctor on his hands and knees, groping in the black water for his gun.

Harry forced himself to move. He knelt beside the grate and, with agonizing slowness, pushed it back in position. Perchek looked up as the grate clanged into place. For the first time, Harry thought he could see panic on the man's face. Then he remembered the control panel. If he could close the outflow, the water would deepen and the gun would be harder to find. Anything that would buy even a little time was worth trying. With great effort he rolled over, reached up, and pushed the button. From somewhere beneath him came the vibration of gears engaging. He slumped facedown to the concrete floor, unable to move, barely able to breathe. The lights dimmed. The intense noise began to fade.

Time passed. A minute? An hour?

Then suddenly, the grate by Harry's face began to move. He opened his eyes and through a gray haze saw Perchek's fingers wrapped around the metal, thrusting upward in short bursts again and again. With the outflow closed, the rising water had floated him upward. His leverage was poor, but he was easily powerful enough to move the grate aside. In just a few seconds he would be out. Battling the darkness and the pain, Harry forced himself to one elbow. Then, with agonizing slowness, he toppled over onto his back, across the grate. Unable to move, he lay there, arms spread, as Perchek's fingers tore frantically at his scalp and his neck, and pulled at his shirt.

"Corbett, get off! Get off!"

"Go . . . to . . . hell. . . ."

"Corbett. . . ."

The Doctor's panicked words were cut off. His movements grew more feeble.

Harry felt the soothing coolness of water welling up around him, flowing out over the floor. The fingers clutching the metal beneath his head slipped away. Minutes passed. The water continued rising around him, now touching his neck, now his ears.

All at once, the cacophony of machines and steam stopped.

Dead, Harry thought. *At last, I'm dead. . . . But so is Perchek, Ray. . . . So is The Doctor. . . .*

A hand gently shook his shoulder. He peered up through the haze. The engineer knelt beside him—yellow hard hat, kind brown eyes behind protective glasses. . . .

"Are you crazy being down here like this, fella?" he said. "Why, it's a wonder you didn't get yourself killed."

EPILOGUE

The block print on the single day calendar directly opposite his bed was the first thing Harry saw when he opened his eyes. *September 2nd. Corbett Curse Plus One.* He had been awake sometime earlier and remembered being spoken to by nurses and doctors just before they took him off the ventilator. But he recalled little else except that he had had surgery. He was going to be a cardiac patient for the rest of his life, perhaps even a cardiac cripple. But at least he *had* a rest of his life.

He was back in an ICU room, though not the one he had been in before. He had on an oxygen mask and was hooked up with the usual array of lines, wires, and tubes. But he felt remarkably well. Dr. Carole Zane was standing at his bedside.

"Take a deep breath, Dr. Corbett," she said. "You must take deep breaths."

Harry had cared for enough of his patients after their coronary bypass surgeries to know that for two or three days, the pain from the sternum being split and wired back together was intense. Still, deep lung-clearing breaths were essential. He did as his doctor asked. There was a sharp jab in his left side, but no discomfort in his sternum. None at all. He moved his legs. There was no pain in either of them. One of them had to have been operated on to remove the vein for his bypass. He ran his hand over the inside of his thighs. No bandages. Then he touched his chest. The skin over his sternum was shaved, but intact.

"What's going on?" he asked.

"What do you mean?"

"The bypass—how did you do it without an incision here?"

She looked at him curiously, then understood.

"Dr. Corbett, I'm afraid we might have gone a little too heavy on the anesthesia and pain meds. I've told you what happened several times. You didn't have a bypass. And if your coronary arteriograms are any indication, you never will. Don't you remember seeing them?"

Harry shook his head. Carole Zane smiled her patient smile and turned to someone else in the room. Suddenly Maura appeared beside her. She had a blackened left eye and small bandages by her brow and on her cheek. But she still looked radiant.

"Hi, Doc," she said. "Remember me?"

"Hey, I think so. The one who saved my life in the Winnebago, right? I'm glad you're okay."

"Discharged early this morning. Ten stitches, but not much else. Harry, you didn't have a bypass operation. There's nothing wrong with your heart. Nothing at all."

He stared up at her, confused.

"I don't understand. The pain, the EKG—"

She held up a clear plastic baggie. Inside was a reddish brown spike, four inches long.

"They took this out of you, Harry," she said. "It's bamboo, so it never showed up on any X rays. It's been deep in your back since the war, gradually working its way forward. The point was right up against the back side of your heart."

"Once we saw the perfectly normal arteriograms we did a CT scan," Carole Zane explained. "And there it was. Taking it out was relatively easy."

"So much for the curse," Maura said.

"Except that being terminally dumb is a curse, too. So I still have one to worry about."

"I spoke with your brother and with mine, too. Tom's at

Atwater's place right now, and so is your lawyer. Tom says they've found a whole roomful of stuff from The Roundtable, including tapes and financial records."

"Perchek has a place in Manhattan somewhere," Harry said. "I think that's where he keeps the disguises and ID badges, and the poisons he used. If we can find that place, maybe we'll turn up the Aramine he used on Evie."

"Is this Perchek the man who killed the policeman in the elevator?" Dr. Zane asked.

"And the nurse."

"No. Not the nurse. She spent most of the night in surgery, but she's doing fairly well right now. I hear she's going to be okay."

"God, that's good news."

"They found a man floating directly beneath you in the power plant," Zane said. "Was that him?"

Harry nodded and smiled beneath his oxygen mask. He was thinking about Ray Santana.

"I think we'd better let him rest for a while," Zane said.

She squeezed his hand reassuringly, adjusted his monitor leads, and then left the room.

Maura lifted up the mask and kissed him on the lips.

"Bamboo," he said.

"Bamboo," she echoed. She stroked his forehead and kissed him again. "Hey," she exclaimed. "Anybody ever tell you that you look like Gene Hackman?"

ABOUT THE AUTHOR

MICHAEL PALMER, M.D., is the author of *Natural Causes*, *Extreme Measures*, *Flashback*, *Side Effects*, and *The Sisterhood*. His books have been translated into twenty languages. He trained in internal medicine at Boston City and Massachusetts General hospitals, spent twenty years as a full-time practitioner of internal and emergency medicine, and is now involved in the treatment of alcoholism and chemical dependence. He lives in Massachusetts.